RAGE TURNED TO ECSTACY

Picking up a cushion, Téoline flung it across the room and sent a vase crashing to the floor. The sound of the glass breaking added to the tempest in her head. She leaped to her feet and with one sweep of her arm sent the contents of the table hurtling to the ground. By now she was completely beside herself.

"Téoline!" Cameron spoke her name softly. Turning she sprang at him. Swiftly he encircled her in his arms. She writhed to free herself but all she could do was beat impotently against his chest with her fists. Cameron bent down and sought to stifle her screams with a kiss. Her rage turned to a savage ecstacy and she returned it, pressing her mouth against his. The world spun out and time ceased to exist. . . .

D0725644

The Touch of Fire

Nella Benson

AVON
PUBLISHERS OF BARD, CAMELOT, DISCUS AND FLARE BOOKS

THE TOUCH OF FIRE is an original publication of Avon Books. This work has never before appeared in book form.

AVON BOOKS
A division of
The Hearst Corporation
959 Eighth Avenue
New York, New York 10019

Copyright © 1982 by Nella Benson
Published by arrangement with the author
Library of Congress Catalog Card Number: 81-66483
ISBN: 0-380-77065-2

First Avon Printing, March, 1982

AVON TRADEMARK REG. U. S. PAT. OFF. AND IN
OTHER COUNTRIES, MARCA REGISTRADA, HECHO EN
U.S.A.

Printed in the U. S. A.

WFH 10 9 8 7 6 5 4 3 2 1

In memory of my son, Jonathan Noël

The Time-Piece

Oh for a lodge in some vast wilderness,
Some boundless contiguity of shade,
Where rumour of oppression and deceit,
Of unsuccessful or successful war,
Might never reach me more. My ear is pain'd,
My soul is sick, with ev'ry day's report
Of wrong and outrage with which earth is fill'd.
There is no flesh in man's obdurate heart,
It does not feel for man; the nat'ral bond
Of brotherhood is sever'd as the flax
That falls asunder at the touch of fire.
He finds his fellow guilty of a skin
Not colour'd like his own; and, having pow'r
T' enforce the wrong, for such a worthy cause
Dooms and devotes him as his lawful prey.
Lands intersected by a narrow frith
Abhor each other. Mountains interpos'd
Make enemies of nations, who had else,
Like kindred drops, been mingled into one.
Thus man devotes his brother, and destroys;
And, worse than all, and most to be deplor'd,
As human nature's broadest, foulest blot,
Chains him, and tasks him, and exacts his sweat
With stripes, that mercy, with a bleeding heart,
Weeps when she sees inflicted on a beast.
Then what is man? And what man, seeing this,
And having human feelings, does not blush
And hang his head, to think himself a man?

— William Cowper, 1731–1800;
excerpt from *The Task*, Book II

PARIS, 1789

Chapter One

"Forgive me, m'sieur, I'm afraid I do not recollect your name."
Mademoiselle Téoline de Pavigné smiled at the handsome olive-
skinned stranger who had just kissed her hand so passionately.
She was well aware, of course, that they had not been formally
introduced. Téo strongly suspected this had been a deliberate
omission on the part of her sister, Louise Duval. Nevertheless,
she had no intention of giving this audacious young man the satisfaction of asking his identity outright.

Fluttering her eyelashes demurely, Téoline sank into a deep
curtsy, far lower than either rank or custom demanded. As she
did so a faint blush spread over her fair skin, because, as she was
also well aware, when she leaned forward the bodice of her satin
gown fell away from her breasts in a most revealing fashion.

For some time she had been watching *les élégantes* preening,
powdered and painted, in their satins and lace. She had been
fascinated by the different wiles they used to focus attention
upon themselves. The flutter of a fan, a dropped kerchief, a pro-
vocative sigh in a moment of silence, would quickly bring a bevy
of gallants to their side. One of them had even feigned to swoon,
only to make a remarkable recovery the second the desired result was achieved. Téo considered that was carrying the art of
the coquette a little too far, but for the rest, she was prepared to
experiment.

The fashionable *beau monde* of Paris was dazzlingly new and
exciting to her. For the past eight of her sixteen years she had
been shut away in a convent at Caen. For the first time, Téoline
was discovering the power of her beauty and charm. That afternoon she had entranced the assembly at her sister's salon with
her quick wit; her convent education had given her a knowledge
of history and philosophy that had on one occasion outreached
that of the great Mirabeau himself. Her head was spinning; she
was intoxicated by the flattery. The young man holding her
hand had scarcely taken his eyes away from her since he entered
the salon. Only one man appeared not to have succumbed to her
charms . . . but she was sure he was of no account.

Téoline glanced up under her eyelashes to make sure he was
still watching her, for, although he had not fallen under her

spell, he had not been entirely indifferent. She had seen the corners of his mouth twitch with amusement when she scored her point over Mirabeau. She saw he was still watching her. He was still sitting in the corner where he had been all afternoon. His chin rested on his hands which clasped the silver knob of his malacca cane. She was annoyed that he caught her eye, for he stood up, bowed, and promptly sat down again. Impossible creature. Téoline smiled up provocatively at her companion.

Mademoiselle Téoline de Pavigné was far too young to appreciate what was really happening that afternoon in the Duvals' salon. But Andrew Cameron recognized that her translucent innocence was far more seductive than any of the wiles she attempted, not always successfully, to employ. Such pristine purity had a potent appeal for men whose appetites had become jaded by overindulgence. She was like a young fawn tantalizing its predators, so sure it could escape when the time came. The chase was all part of the game, and a few years ago he would have led the field. Now he found himself sorry for the prey.

Whatever Andrew Cameron might be thinking, on this occasion Téoline's efforts were more than rewarded. The hand holding hers tightened its grip as the man's eyes fell on the smooth contours of her young body. From the moment he had caught sight of her he had wanted to possess her. She had been sitting near the window, and a shaft of September sunlight had burnished her hair to the color of ripe corn. Her delicate oval face glowed with a country freshness, while the blue-green eyes reflected the changing moods of the sea. She was so different from the proud French beauties surrounding her; so unlike the dark-haired, olive-skinned girls one found in the West Indies. Any of those were his for the taking, but his heart desired Téoline de Pavigné. She was a goddess who would have to be wooed and won. For all that he was an accomplished gambler, for the first time in his life he wondered if the stakes were too high even for him.

"My name is Stefan Cambenet, ma'mselle," he said, raising her reluctantly to her feet. He smiled down at her, but there was an unmistakable passion smoldering in the depths of his large dark eyes. "You may rest assured that neither destiny nor I shall let you forget it a second time."

Téoline found his boldness disconcerting. She lowered her head and shyly turned aside. "I do not set much store in destiny, m'sieur. I put my faith in God."

Raising her hand to his lips yet again, Cambenet murmured,

"Call it what you will, Mademoiselle de Pavigné. My *loa* tells me that from this moment our destinies are forever entwined."

She wondered what *loa* meant, but only briefly. Something about the way he looked at her and his tone of voice sent a slight shiver down her spine. It was not altogether unpleasant, but very disturbing. His touch was magnetic; it was as if a magical flux had passed between them. Cambenet bowed again and stood back to let her pass. As she did so, Téoline noticed the other man was still watching her. He grinned and inclined his body slightly in the mockery of a bow. She tossed her head and swept out of the room.

"Téoline . . . a moment! I must speak with you." Louise Duval broke away from her guests and followed her sister through the vestibule to the front door of the apartment. She put a restraining hand upon her younger sister's arm.

"Téo, I beg you to be more discreet." Téoline responded to the rebuke with an icy stare. She was still glowing from all the acclaim she had received and was in no mood for criticism. "I know you appear to have captured everyone's heart this afternoon, but if you wish to retain a position in Parisian society you must be careful on whom you bestow your favors."

Téoline pursed her lips and studiously examined a marble plinth with a bust of Julius Caesar. She was exceedingly fond of her sister, but, at thirty-six, Louise was quite out of touch with the world. It was the same with most of the ladies present. They were not acquainted with the works of the ancients, nor could they discuss the works of Voltaire or Rousseau in any depth.

"Listen to me, Téoline! I mean what I say. I am more knowledgeable than you about what is happening in Paris at this moment." Louise had always loved her stepsister, though they had seen little of each other in recent years. Nevertheless, her tone was sharpened slightly by envy. She had been made to appear foolish and ill-informed by a girl half her age. It wasn't her fault that she had been educated by a governess, while Téoline had studied under a woman renowned for her superior intellect. The Mother Abbess at the Abbaye-aux-Dames was noted throughout France for her scholarship.

"I'll grant your knowledge of philosophy is quite remarkable, but it is unwise to speak too openly of your opinions on liberty and equality, whether they concern the rights of women or the state."

"Mirabeau, Lafayette, and Baroness de Staël all agreed with me," Téo responded, as though mention of such names should put an end to the subject.

11

"Possibly! What you don't realize is that each one of them sets their own value on such words. You still have to learn that there is a vast difference between what people may say and the meaning behind the words they use."

"I have said nothing of which I am ashamed, and Mirabeau . . ."

"Mirabeau!" Louise repeated with a wry smile. That Téo was so impressed by the Comte de Mirabeau's flattery only proved her inexperience. It was true that for the moment he was probably the most important man in France. Everyone hung on his words, because he appeared to hold the balance of power between the Court and a restless bourgeoisie. But he was a noted lecher, and anyone could see what was behind the attention he bestowed on Téoline.

"I'm not concerned with Mirabeau just now. I was referring to the abandoned way you were flirting with young Cambenet. You must not encourage his attentions." Madame Duval could see that her words were having little or no effect. However, as the wife of a wealthy banker, she knew the undercurrents at work in France at that moment and she was genuinely concerned for Téoline.

"I'll grant you he is handsome enough to set any woman's heart aflutter regardless of her age. I doubt that there is a woman in Paris who has not had or would not welcome an affair with him . . .!" She was trying to find a way to smooth Téo's ruffled plumage.

"I'm not impressed by physical appearances," Téo replied acidly. "When he spoke he was extremely intelligent and well informed." She would not admit that she had found his body equally as attractive as his mind. The shadow of the convent hovered over her, and she felt guilty of harboring evil thoughts.

"But that is where the greatest danger lies. Cambenet was educated in France, and that, together with his appearance and his money, most of which he wins at the gambling tables, has opened doors that under other circumstances would have been closed to him."

"I don't understand," Téoline said petulantly, tossing her head. Louise's lecture was tedious and she was already late.

"I mean that he knows too much for his own good. It is not wise for you to associate with him. I shall make a point of letting him see he will not be welcomed here again." It was Madame's turn to be peevish. Cambenet was popular and would be a great loss to her salons. Her other guests were capable of more discre-

12

tion, and it annoyed her to think she would have to change her plans.

"That's most unfair of you, Louise. Neither of us is guilty of conduct you could condemn. As for being too well informed . . . it is the case of others being ignorant. Charlotte Corday—"

"For pity's sake—do not quote that wretched girl again. She has filled your head with a lot of nonsense. Now you listen to me, Téo!" Madame Duval's voice took on a new note of authority. "It was all very well for you and Charlotte to spend your days at the convent debating on how to set the world to right. Here, in Paris, things are very different. The place is a tinderbox. It only needs a spark for all of us to be engulfed in flames."

Louise softened her tone a little and placed her arm about Téo's shoulder. "You know you are the only member of the family for whom I have any affection. Please believe me, Téoline, what I'm saying is only meant for your good. Stefan Cambenet is not just another wealthy Creole, although there are enough of them in France. He is a mulatto and has the jungle in his blood—"

"Since when is that a crime?" Téo rounded on her sister angrily. "Didn't you hear Mirabeau arguing for the abolition of slavery just now?"

"And if you had not been so enamored, you would have noticed that Stefan Cambenet did not speak to that point. He is not black; his blood is mixed with white."

"Through no fault of his!"

"That is not the thing that concerns me. He is an active member of the *Société des Amis des Noirs*. They don't care about freeing the slaves. All they want are civil rights for the people of color in the French colonies."

"There's nothing wrong in that. I refuse to let the color of a man's skin prevent me calling him my friend."

"In the name of Heaven!" Louise put a hand to her head in a gesture of despair. "What can I do with the child? Why do the young always see things as black or white . . . right or wrong?"

"Because that is the way things are, and I refuse to compromise." Téo's tone was so self-righteous that Louise was forced to laugh; her sister had the grace to blush.

"My poor little one!" Louise shook her head. "I can only pray that life will not hurt you too much." She slipped her arm through Téoline's and walked with her to the top of the broad staircase. "Tell me, haven't you heard Monsieur speak of the Club Massiac?"

13

"Yes. He gave a dinner for some of the members only last week. I was called down to be introduced to them afterwards."

"But have you any idea who they are?" Téoline shook her head. "They are either Creole planters home on leave or powerful Frenchmen with financial interests in the West Indies. They are intent on preventing the mulattoes from gaining their civil rights, and in this they have the ear of the King. And . . ." Louise paused to give her next words greater effect. "Their voice in this matter is the Duc de Pavigné!"

Téoline turned pale at the mention of their father's name, and Louise knew she had found her mark. "Come, Téo, I have no desire to spoil your fun. Heaven knows, having to live in the same house as Monsieur is punishment enough for anyone. Have an affair with any man in Paris, if you wish . . . providing you are discreet. But avoid Stefan Cambenet and his friends unless you wish to bring Monsieur's wrath down upon your head." She gave Téo's cheek an affectionate kiss.

"I don't have to try very hard to do that," Téo murmured ruefully. "I'm forever incurring his displeasure. One would think that I alone was responsible for the *sans-culottes* burning the convent, just to have an excuse to return home."

"I believe him capable of almost anything, but I do not think that."

Louise had little reason to love her father. At his behest she had married Charles Duval, a wealthy bourgeois; and for the most part it had been a happy marriage. But no sooner was she married to a man of lesser rank than she found herself excluded from the elegant circle at Versailles, to which by birth she was accustomed. Like both Louis and his Queen, Marie Antoinette, her father and the other courtiers were not above borrowing from the bankers or using their knowledge of world finance; however, they had no intention of accepting them as equals. Louise was constantly being reminded that she was now a member of the Third Estate, and she could never forgive her father for putting her in such a position. She rarely visited the Hôtel de Pavigné in the fashionable Faubourg Saint-Honoré.

Téoline only partially understood the reasons for the hostility between them, but she was fond of Louise. She returned her sister's kiss and turned to go. It was then that she saw the man who had been sitting in the corner watching her. He was leaning in the doorway of the salon and his interest in her had not abated.

He was so unlike the men who milled about him that it was impossible not to notice him. While they were dressed in silks

14

and satins, he wore a dark-blue broadcloth coat with a high black velvet collar. His clothes spoke of quality and he carried them with elegance. Though he was well above average height, his broad shoulders made him appear shorter. He was not handsome in the accepted sense. The deep-chestnut-colored hair fell in an unruly mass of curls and waves until it was caught at the nape of the neck in a plain black bow. It framed a face with features that were not unattractive, but Téoline could only think of his eyes. At the moment they were half hidden under heavy lids, but she recalled that they were dark gray, like the embers of a fire, ready to flare to life when provoked by anger or laughter.

"Who is he?" she whispered to Louise.

Madame Duval followed the line of her sister's gaze. "I'm not acquainted with him. He came with Mirabeau." She shrugged. "I believe his name is Cameron. He's an American . . . , an old friend of Lafayette's. He was hoping to meet him, but Gil had already left before he arrived."

A church clock chimed half past five and reminded Téo she should already be on her way. She ran down the stairs and waited while a powdered flunky called her chair. Settling back into the shadowy depths of the sedan, Téoline prayed that the men could get her home by six. She promised them a handsome gratuity if they could, but it was most unlikely. The traffic in the narrow streets of the city was heavy and the deep mud from recent rains made the going hard. She sighed; she would undoubtedly be late for her appointment with Monsieur and must prepare herself for yet another battle.

However, it was quite impossible for Téo to dwell on her many sins at that moment. Try as she would to feel suitably contrite, her heart was pounding with excitement, and the memory of all that had happened that afternoon prevented her. Mademoiselle Téoline de Pavigné was rather like a moth that suddenly discovers it was meant to be a beautiful butterfly. Scarcely more than a month ago, she had left the Abbaye to go to a smaller convent on the outskirts of Caen where she was to begin her novitiate. A little reluctantly, she had come to accept the fact that she was destined to spend the rest of her life behind the walls of a convent. Then fate, in the guise of a marauding band of rebels, had set the place ablaze and made it necessary for her to return to her father's *hôtel* in Paris.

The Duc de Pavigné had not been pleased. Téoline had thought it was because he did not want her at home. In actual fact he was disturbed because far too many such incidents were happening throughout France every day. Ever since the storming of the Bastille in July, the embers of revolt had been smoldering throughout the country. Gangs of peasants, inflamed by the pangs of hunger and incited by *sans-culottes*, as the rebels from the cities were called, roamed the land. They burned and pillaged the property of the Church and nobility and murdered anyone who stood in their way. If the truth were known, Monsieur regarded his daughter as property and had no intention of allowing any harm to come to her; he was therefore quite content to have her at home.

Téoline had not been out and about in the world long enough to appreciate any of this. She only knew that the endless restrictions and tedious duties had gone forever. She had thrown off the drab dark gowns and along with them an eternal penitence for sins not yet committed. The nuns had taught her that she was born with the stain of original sin on her soul, and she accepted that she was guilty of much of the wickedness inherent in man. Eve had tempted Adam—but exactly how, or what it all meant, Téoline only half understood.

Was it lust that sent shivers up and down her spine when men looked at her in a certain way? She recalled the expression she had caught lurking in the depths of the American's eyes. Was she guilty of fornication when she held her hand to her cheek and tried to recapture the feel of Cambenet's lips? Was this what the Mother Abbess had meant when she had warned her young charges against the evils of the flesh? If it was, Téoline resolved to confess her guilt that night and tell an extra rosary for penance. But, for now, she gave herself up to savoring to its full all the joys of mortal sin.

Chapter Two

The ormolu clock on the marble mantelpiece of the *petit salon* in the Hôtel de Pavigné chimed the hour. The gilt shepherdess and her lute-playing swain decorating the top of it remained frozen in an eternal flirtation, oblivious of the passage of time. But Jean-Louis, the tenth Duc de Pavigné, stopped pacing to and fro on the blue Persian carpet and glowered at the offending timepiece. He regarded it as a personal insult that the hour should have presumed to present itself without his prior consent.

Reaching into the pocket of his long embroidered waistcoat, he brought out a watch and held it up toward the light. The gold and diamonds sparkled, but his frown deepened as he saw that both clock and watch conspired against him; it was indeed six o'clock. This only confirmed his suspicions that conspiracy was everywhere, even in the very air he breathed.

He walked over to the long windows and looked out onto the garden that fronted the *hôtel*. The green lawns were bathed in the gold of a dying day. The rays from the setting sun shimmered on the dancing waters of the fountain and bathed the white marble goddess in a falsé glory. Along either side of the carriageway the tall poplar trees cast their shadows like thin fingers towards the house.

The picture reflected in the gilt-framed mirror on the wall of the *petit salon* was just as peaceful. The white plaster cherubs on the ceiling smiled down serenely, content with the order of things. And Madame Hélène Beaulieu, sitting in a dainty Louis Quinze chair near the window, was as still as the porcelain figures on the table at her side. The powdered white curls of her wig cascaded down over smooth shoulders. The lace on the blue satin bodice of her gown scarcely rose with her breath, and her tiny feet in their satin slippers were quite still beneath the full folds of her skirt. She too appeared frozen in time, but a careful observer would have detected the tension in her pose and noted the anxiety in her china-blue eyes as she watched her patron.

However, the Duc de Pavigné was not in the least interested in what his mistress might be thinking. In fact, his interest in her had been waning for some time. If he had not had so many other things on his mind, she would more than likely have been replaced by now. Under the circumstances it was just as well, for her thoughts were centered 'on Téoline. Had the duke suspected her sympathies were directed towards his wayward daughter, it would not have gone well for Madame.

He turned away from the window and stared fixedly at Hélène, making her tremble at the thought of what he might say. She need not have worried, for he did not even see her. He was concerned with his own conscience. He despised men like Lafayette and Mirabeau. De Pavigné considered them traitors to their own class. They pandered to the people and conversed with the *petite bourgeoisie*. Yet was he not planning a similar act of betrayal? He brushed the thought aside. There was a difference. Téoline was a woman; caste was not so important to a woman. It was strange, it had not upset him half so much with Louise; but then, his first marriage had been one of convenience. De Pavigné's jaw tightened and he struck the seat of a nearby chair with his riding crop. Why did he keep thinking of his late duchesse? Why was Téoline so like her mother? Was that the reason he had sent her away as a child? He did not want a man, especially one like de Beben, to despoil her, yet what else could he do? He had to think of Julien. He had to protect the name and honor of the de Pavignés, and for that he needed money.

Téoline shrank back into the shadows as the men pushed their way through the crowded streets. A peddler pressed his face against the glass and tried to see inside. She held her breath until he had gone, and then she peeped out at the motley throng. There were porters from Les Halles balancing baskets of fruit and vegetables on their heads; fishwives screaming their wares; workmen pushing their way to and from the slums of Saint-Eustache and Saint-Antoine. Their faces were grim and their bellies empty. There was no point in their going home. There was more fun to be had harassing the elite. From time to time they would get on either side of the sedan chair and shake it until it creaked and the carriers nearly lost their grip. Téoline breathed a sigh of relief as they reached the broader boulevards of the more modern Faubourg Saint-Honoré. She knew what it was like to be poor. She had helped the nuns succor the peasants at Caen. Her heart went out to these people in their poverty. It never dawned on Téoline they might hold her responsible for their plight.

As soon as the men set the chair down in front of the mansion,

Téo made a mad dash up the steps. She sent Le Beau, her father's steward, to pay the men and flung her cloak to Nina, Madame Beaulieu's maid, before running across the wide marble-tiled vestibule. If she had not sinned too greatly, the angels would be on her side and Monsieur would not have noticed she was a full five minutes late. But God or the fates were against her. The Duc de Pavigné was standing in front of the fireplace, legs apart, tapping his fine leather riding boots with the silver handle of his crop.

"I am more than sorry, m'sieur," Téoline gasped, as she sank to the floor in a full obeisance.

Curling his lip, her father glanced down at her before turning his back. Hélène Beaulieu got up out of her chair and hurried across. Holding out her hand, she helped Téo to rise. Madame's gentle face was full of misery. She paused for a moment, ostensibly to straighten the lace at the neck of Téoline's gown and shake out the fair curls.

"Softly, my little one . . . !" she whispered. Her blue eyes gave a warning glance in the direction of the duke. "I shall be waiting for you."

Téoline squeezed her hand. She did not dare risk speaking to Hélène. It might involve Madame in a family argument, and Téo had been quick to realize her father's mistress was no longer welcome in the house. She waited quietly until she heard the footman close the door behind Hélène, bracing herself for the storm to come.

The duke did not move. His back was to her but she could see the reflection of his face in the mirror. His features were as cold and hard as the marble statues that adorned the salon. "I thought I told you to remain here this afternoon," he said curtly, without turning round.

"No, m'sieur. You told me to wait upon you at six o'clock. It was a little over five minutes after the hour when I arrived, and for that I apologize." Téoline spoke quite softly, but the duke recognized the thin steel thread running through her tone. Her mother had defied and tantalized him in just such a way.

De Pavigné shifted uneasily and moved toward the window. "Don't be impertinent," he said, staring out into the darkening sky.

"Surely the truth can never be counted impertinent, m'sieur?"

He turned round very slowly and looked at her. In repose, her eyes reflected the tranquility of water on a summer day, soft and inviting. But now they were like storm clouds lit with flashes of lightning. If only she were not so like her mother. If only he could know what was in her mind. The duke was not good at reading other people's thoughts.

"I had a visitor whom I particularly wished you to meet . . . . He had to leave early . . . . He had to meet with some members of the Assembly . . . ." The duke flushed angrily; he was bumbling and she was no doubt laughing at him. She was standing there watching him with such an air of demure innocence — no woman could be that innocent!

"That is most unfortunate, m'sieur. But under the circumstances, even had I been here on time, we would still not have met." Téoline had an uneasy feeling that they were talking at cross purposes and was unsure how to placate him. "I did not realize how long it would take me to come from Louise's apartment at this time of day."

"Don't ply me with excuses." He glowered at her. "I don't think you fully realize your position in my household. If I order it so, then you have no right to leave this *hôtel* without my permission."

Téoline clenched her hands until her knuckles were white. Thank God the life in the convent had taught her to accept punishment with an apparent meekness even though she boiled with anger inside. "I am well aware of my rights, m'sieur." She was struggling to keep her tone even. "Without your permission, I have discovered that I have very few."

Again the duke's handsome face turned purple with rage, and he slashed wildly at the nearest object, which happened to be the small table with the porcelain figures. They shattered into pieces at his feet. How dare they break? . . . How dare this chit of a girl remain so calm? Louise would have been groveling at his feet by now; but then, she did not have the Gascon blood. The nuns should have been more diligent and taught his younger daughter the virtues of humility and obedience. "It is as well you remember your duty!"

"Yes, m'sieur!" Téoline curtsied to acknowledge his authority. She felt she was trembling on the brink of a precipice. There was something more to come—she was certain of that—and she prayed he would get on with it. Her father did not speak, but with studied venom ground the little pieces of porcelain into the carpet with the heel of his boot.

"Both the Comte de Mirabeau and General Lafayette asked me to tender to you their respects. They hope they will soon be honored by your company." Etiquette obliged the duke to give a slight bow of acknowledgement.

Damn Mirabeau! He had seen how the wretch ogled Téoline when they were at Versailles. As for that simple Caesar, Lafayette . . . . He had difficulty in not speaking his thoughts aloud. He was vaguely conscious that the momentum of the argument was slipping away from him. It was like the opening moments of a duel, when the protagonists prowled about each other trying to assess the other's play before making their move.

"I'm indebted to them for remembering me," he said icily. "Nevertheless, in future I forbid you to attend your sister's salons. The riffraff of Paris assembles there. Do you understand?"

"Yes, m'sieur!" Another deferential curtsy whilst Téo planned her next move. "I may not go to my sister's, but may I take it that you will not object to my attending the Baroness de Stael's salon next week?"

"Damnation!" the duke exploded. "How dare you mention that woman's name in this house? Most certainly. . ."

"Then I will write immediately to the Comte de Mirabeau and tell him you will not allow me to attend," Téoline cut in hastily. "He, especially, will be upset as he wished to hear what I had to say about the plight of the peasants around Caen."

Whether she knew it or not, Téoline had thwarted him. He would not dare risk offending Mirabeau. His eyes narrowed into slits and he gave a light laugh to cloak his irritation. "Very well, go if you wish. I'm sure the great Mirabeau is waiting with bated breath to catch the pearls of wisdom falling from your lips."

The pressure was too much and his temper flared. Advancing on her, he took her arm and shook her like a dog. "Do you really think he cares what a young fool like you has to say . . .?" He felt her flesh soft and warm beneath his touch, and it stirred memories of a passion he thought he had overcome. For a second he clasped her to his breast, satisfying a lonely yearning he had nursed throughout the years. Then he remembered she was the daughter and not the mother. He flung her away so that she stumbled over a chair.

"There is no greater libertine in the whole of France than Mirabeau. He is using flattery to turn your head and lead him to your bed . . .!" He broke off, ashamed of what he was saying; ashamed of his own longing. He shrugged and turned away; he could not bear the expression in her eyes.

Téoline's cheeks burned as the blood rushed to her head. She had suffered his anger many times, but there was something more to this. She was embarrassed to hear her father speak of sex. She started to play with the small fan hanging from her wrist. "I will make some other excuse," she said.

"Do what you will. I have more urgent matters to discuss with you. This afternoon I signed a marriage contract on your behalf!"

Téoline felt as if she turned to ice. Her father saw her blanch, but it gave him little satisfaction to know he was crushing the de Pavigné pride.

"Marriage . . . ?" she echoed.

"Yes, to Albert de Beben. You were presented to him the other evening when the Club Massiac came here to dine. He had hoped to meet you again today . . . but it is of no consequence." Seeing her glazed expression, the duke continued. "It is of no matter that you cannot recall him. You will know him well enough before long. He asked for your hand and I have given my consent." His thin aristocratic face almost cracked into a smile of relief. He had told her; the deed was done.

"But *I* have not consented," Téoline said with youthful belligerence. She was so stunned by the news she let down her guard and forgot even the semblance of respect. "I can't . . . I won't marry a man I do not know and for whom I have no regard . . ."

"Do you dare to defy me, mademoiselle?"

"In this, m'sieur. A woman must surely have some rights. Germaine de Staël says—" Téoline had not finished when she felt the lash of the riding crop bite into her arm, tearing the lace from her shoulder and drawing blood.

"Damn de Staël . . . and damn Necker for allowing his daughter the freedom to voice her thoughts. You are my chattel! You will do as I say!"

Téoline edged away, instinctively trying to ward off the blows that rained down relentlessly across her back. All the pent-up rage and frustration de Pavigné had been feeling for months was now unleashed. He lashed out wildly, his eyes blazing with a fear he mistakenly took for pride.

Chapter Three

"Zounds!" Andrew Cameron swore softly to himself and tugged at the neckpiece he was endeavoring to fold tastefully about his rather thick neck. His interest in clothes was spurred by the value others placed on them rather than his own desire to be a leader of fashion. Experience had taught him that to appear successful was more than halfway to succeeding; consequently his clothes and jewels were always of the finest cut and quality.

"I always have to fight this damned thing!" he explained jokingly to the man who was watching him in the mirror. Cameron was standing before a cheval glass in his apartment on the Boulevard Saint-Germain.

"In God's name, run it through and put me out of my misery," Lafayette responded. "I wouldn't be seen dead in such . . . such . . .!" Words failed him and he flapped his smooth white hands in a gesture of despair.

"These darker colors and simple lines are fast becoming all the rage in England. I've no doubt you will adopt them in time. They are far more serviceable than all your frills and fripperies," Cameron replied with a laugh. Gil shrugged and smoothed an imaginary crease from the full skirt of his pale-green satin coat.

"I fear your taste has not improved with the years, André. In your youth you were such a gay dog."

"That was when my mother's French blood was uppermost. I've become a hardheaded Yankee since then." Cameron rang the bell for his servant and ordered another log for the fire and some fresh wine to be brought. "You have not changed, Gil. You are as beautiful as ever." He cast his eye over the immaculately powdered hair and the silver lace and diamonds that adorned his friend's garb.

The wine arrived. He poured two glasses and passed one to Lafayette before raising his in a toast. "To General Lafayette, Commander of the National Guard and, next to Mirabeau, probably the most important man in France!" Gil bowed in acknowledgment. In spite of what Cameron had said, he had changed; underneath his suave composure, Lafayette was tense and ill-at-ease. Cameron could understand now why he was regarded as unreliable. The general's loyalties were said to change with the wind.

"From all reports, you are prospering, André!"

"I have no cause to complain. I own a fleet of vessels that ply betwixt the Indies, Canada, and the States. And I am expanding my enterprise to the oceangoing trade, which explains the purpose of my visit here."

"Ah! You intend to profit from the middle passage, no doubt. In spite of all the cries for abolition, the trade in slaves grows more prosperous by the hour."

"You should know me better than that, Gil," Cameron flared. "I'll trade in many things but not in human lives. From what I've seen in France, I'd judge it more profitable to carry arms. You will soon need them for defense."

Lafayette stirred uncomfortably in his chair. So Cameron still believed in the cause that had taken them to the New World as young men. He still thought there could be liberty and equality for all men. "I thought that perhaps you were homesick after all these years. France, after all, was the place of your birth." The general had never fully understood why Cameron had chosen to remain in the States.

"America has given me what I have today. It has a right to my loyalty as a matter of principle."

"But not of love, there is a difference," Lafayette smiled triumphantly. "No, André, you are a Frenchman before all else."

"I am a mongrel, a half-breed with no roots. My heart, if I still have one, belongs to no one but myself."

"Knowing you of old, I cannot believe that, while there is still a pretty woman around. But tell me, what does your father think of all this?" The elder Cameron had followed his son across the Atlantic after the War of Independence, and the general had last heard that they were in business together. "Is he still bitter about the Stuarts losing their cause?"

"I can't imagine so. It would be unprofitable and self-destructive to harbor a grudge for so long. The Stuart cause died at Culloden in '49. That was why he came to France." Cameron's tone made it evident that it was not a subject he wished to pursue. His relationship with his father was something he had no wish to dwell upon.

Having replenished his guest's glass along with his own, he returned his attention to his cravat, and this time succeeded in settling it to his satisfaction. He was anxious to look his best tonight.

"I wish I had known you would be free." Cameron signaled to his man to fetch his jacket. It was of dark-red velvet and looked well over his pale nankeen breeches that fitted his muscular thighs like a second skin. "Unfortunately I have already committed myself to supper with young Chantal or we could have gone to the Ruggieri Gardens. It would have been like old times." There was a certain lack of enthusiasm in Cameron's voice. His business interests were tied in with Lafayette, but for once, he discovered his personal preference did not incline that way. "Why don't you join us? I'm sure young Julien would not object."

Lafayette shook his head. "I've no objection to Julien, although I would have thought you would find him a trifle wet behind the ears. But I have no great love for the Duc de Pavigné or his clan."

"Surely that does not include his younger daughter Téoline?"

"Ah, the beautiful virgin! So you have met her, then?"

"I noticed her in passing this afternoon, at her sister's salon."

"Who could help but notice her? I doubt there is a man in Paris who does not desire to be the first to bed her."

"That was patently obvious this afternoon from the way they all fawned over her." Cameron was as surprised as his friend to discover a note of bitterness in his voice.

"Yes, it is a pity, but I'm afraid she will not remain immaculate for very long." Lafayette sighed. Then he added impishly, "Now I understand the reason for your visit. You are hoping to be that man, yes?"

"What nonsense!" Cameron settled his jacket over his deep-blue satin waistcoat and slipped a thin gold fob watch into the small embroidered pocket on the vest. "I am almost twice her age and far too many women down the road. And I've no doubt she is a spoiled brat like the rest of her class, although I'll grant she has more brains than most. No, I merely accepted Julien's invitation for old time's sake. The boy reminds me of his elder brother, Philippe, in many ways."

"Of course, I had forgotten, Julien is de Pavigné's second son. Philippe was killed in a riding accident, was he not?"

"Yes. Shortly after we left for the States, although I did not hear of his death for some time after that." Cameron's face became suddenly grim. This was not proving a good evening. Too many memories were flooding back. Scars he had thought long healed were beginning to smart.

"Maybe that is what helped to sour de Pavigné? It is not easy for a man to cope with the loss of a son."

25

"I doubt it. De Pavigné is of his kind. They think the rest of mankind were born to be their slaves."

Lafayette shrugged. It was a question with which he, himself, had to struggle. "One can hardly blame them. It is what they have been told from birth."

"They should learn to listen to the other voices being carried on the wind . . . . You did. Anyway, I gather from your tone that you have no great love for him?"

"He is not a man it is easy to love. Marie Antoinette is the exception; he is quite a favorite of hers."

"That is not to be wondered at. They share the same attitude toward the rank and file," Cameron replied.

"I must admit I am not happy to see him wield so much influence with the Queen. She controls the King, and that makes de Pavigné a power behind the throne." Gil gave a nervous laugh.

"There are always men behind the throne. We have them in the States."

"But you have no king!" Gil looked amazed. "That is what we fought for—to put an end to Farmer George."

It was Cameron's turn to shrug. "It matters little whether you call him King or President. There is a constant struggle to decide how much power he takes to himself and how much the people are willing to invest in him."

"And how does your friend Hamilton feel about that?" The general's tone had cooled. Cameron sensed he was treading on dangerous ground.

"Alex is a businessman. Given the chance, he will put America on the map financially."

"He has no love for France," was the sharp reply.

"I can tell you have been listening to that dreamer Jefferson whilst he was over here. It's merely that, for the moment, Hamilton takes a realistic stand. He regards England as the better trading risk. You must admit, Gil, that France is trembling on the brink of civil war."

"There'll be no war. Changes have to be made . . . but there'll be no war." Lafayette spoke as if to reassure himself. Then, looking at Cameron, he said, "If there were, whose interest would you favor?"

"My own," Cameron said curtly. "I've lost faith in causes. For that matter, I've lost faith in most things. I find I'm no longer capable of caring for anything other than remaining a success." After that there was an awkward pause while the servant looked to the fire and brought more candles to lighten the gathering gloom. When the man had left the room, Lafayette, forgetful of what had gone before, returned to a subject that interested him.

"You said little of your father, André. I hope he is well? I had a great liking for him."

"He is aging, like all of us, but I believe he is well. It is some years since I last saw him. He lives in Nova Scotia now."

"What, under the British flag?" The general found it hard to believe his ears.

"What matters the color of a flag, so long as a man is happy there? Anyway, there are as many Yankees in Nova Scotia as there are those claiming British birth." Cameron tried to disguise his irritation.

"You surprise me, André. The last I heard, he was living in Boston with you. I understood he was highly respected and had been appointed a magistrate."

"Aye, but the respect only lasted until he insisted on standing by what he had said. You know as well as I, people only want a semblance of justice and not the reality, if it runs contrary to their own ideas." This time there was no mistaking the bitterness Cameron felt.

"I'm sorry. I hope no ill befell him?" The general was shaken. He could feel Cameron's suppressed anger, and saw the torment on his face. "I should like to know what happened," he said after a moment's pause. Cameron walked across to the window and looked down upon the wet cobbles in the Boulevard Saint-Germain. When he spoke, it was in a staccato voice as if he were tearing bandages off old wounds one by one.

"He tried to protect Tory sympathizers who stayed behind after the war. The rabble turned on him, accusing him of Royalist sympathies. When principles become more important than people, men cease to be men and become mobs . . . unthinking, unfeeling mobs. Ready to be swayed to violence by anyone with a golden tongue who uses them for their own ends."

Lafayette sighed. He had seen that happening in France in recent months. "Are you saying that your father was attacked by people he thought his friends?"

"They tarred and feathered him . . . . And my sister Fiona . . ." Cameron's voice cracked. "You are a man, I don't need to tell you the rest. Then they ran them out of town."

"*Mon Dieu!* Is this what we went all that way to fight for?"

"Will it be any different here?" Cameron turned and thrust out his jaw pugnaciously. "If men . . . or women for that matter . . . have any love for their fellows, then I have yet to find it. It is the same wherever you go. That is why I chose not to leave when my father did. I saw no reason to turn my back on all we had built together. What happened could happen again anywhere, while men are as they are." His voice dropped and Lafayette murmured his sympathy. He thought Cameron was overcome by emotion, but in truth he was ashamed.

"And this caused a breach between you? I am deeply distressed."

"I do not take humiliation easily. My father chose to retreat with dignity, but I stayed and I worked. I worked hard until I had sufficient money and power to destroy everyone responsible for the outrage. But my father cannot understand that. He prefers to live in poverty and nurse his pride."

"As a Frenchman, I can understand his pride," Gil said quietly, hoping to calm his friend.

"Can you? Then pride does not mean the same to you as it does to me. If a man humiliates me, I'll see him grovel at my feet."

Lafayette had always known Cameron was quick to respond to a real or imaginary affront. He had judged it to be the rash hot blood of youth. Now, for a moment, he glimpsed a man with torment in his soul. He shook his head sadly. "That is not pride, my friend; that is revenge. Be careful or it may destroy you in the end."

Cameron had regained his composure and he smiled cynically. "Not if I keep my head."

"But you have a heart as well!"

"Not me! But come, we are growing far too serious. Have supper with me tomorrow night and I will show you how to put the world to right." Laughingly, Cameron slapped the Marquis de Lafayette on the back, making him wince and ruffling his dignity.

"Not only do you now speak French with an atrocious colonial accent, one can tell from your manners you have become an American!" The general rose from his chair and shook out the delicate lace frills of his jabot. "The trouble is, you are still basically British, and they lack . . ." He finished with a disdainful shrug.

"You mean we lack your sense of the dramatic." Cameron mimicked the mincing manners of a gallant, waving his hands about in the air and bowing flamboyantly. His size alone forced Lafayette to laugh at his antics.

"You know, Gil, although I spent my youth here, it is only since my return that I have begun to understand you French. You may play the romantic with great finesse, but your hearts are made of steel. You never once allow them to rule your heads. While the Americans ... or British, if you prefer to think of them as such ... appear cold-blooded but are incurable romantics at heart."

His guest gave a wry smile. "I'll take that as a compliment, André, although I doubt it was meant to be. But if it is true, take heed which rules, your head or your heart!"

"I am a Scot," Cameron replied laconically and grinned. His servant came forward with their hats and cloaks. "Do you see, Gil, in deference to your views, I'm wearing the red, white, and blue cockade on my hat?"

"That is as well, my friend. . . . It could well add years to your life. Make sure none of the de Pavignés persuade you to change it for Marie Antoinette's white one. The color wouldn't suit a Yankee!" Lafayette smiled and swept out of the room.

"You forget, white was the Stuart emblem. . . ." Cameron called down the stairs. "Let's hope your Queen doesn't share their fate, or you may find yourself becoming a Yankee yet!"

Cameron called for his horse to be brought round as soon as the general's carriage had left. Allowing the animal to set its own pace, he crossed the Pont de la Concorde, picking his way carefully among the stones from the Bastille which were being used to repair it. He was early for his appointment with the Comte de Chantal and in no mood to hurry.

A night mist had drifted over the river. In the distance he could see the dark windmills at Petit-Gentilly and Merveilles. Across the bridge his way led past the Tuileries, and his path was lit by the flares guiding the coaches and chair carriers on their way. He loved Paris at any time, but especially by night. Cameron questioned his reasons for staying away so long.

After Culloden, his father, like many Scots, had fled to France where the Jacobites were welcome. He married a Frenchwoman and settled down on a small estate near Chartres. Like most exiles they did not have much money, but Andrew looked back on the early days of his youth in a golden haze.

Their modest estate bordered one of the Duc de Pavigné's. It was there he had met Philippe, and he recalled how they had roamed the countryside. The forests and streams had provided a happy hunting ground for two boys in their teens. It had never worried either of them that the Camerons were considered petty

29

nobility. Angus Cameron had never mentioned to his son that he felt slighted at not being invited to the de Pavigné chateau. Then, unwittingly, Philippe committed an unpardonable mistake. With the enthusiasm of youth he invited Andrew to join a hunting party the duke had arranged. The elder Cameron tried to dissuade his son, but Andrew was in no mood to be stopped. He was young and sure of himself. A fine horseman for his age, he wanted to show his skill before the nobility of France.

Cameron's hand tightened on the rein. He could feel his blood rising as he recalled that day more than fifteen years ago. It was bright and clear; the air so crisp that every word of de Pavigné's tirade was carried to the assembled company. Before the cream of the French court, he had ordered his huntsmen to throw the boy off his land.

"Take this peasant away!" De Pavigné's words were etched in fire on his heart. "Cameron should know better than to presume his boy would be allowed to ride in such exalted company. Take him away! . . . And whip him if he sets foot on my land again!" Cameron could still feel the shame as he was hustled away. Philippe had tried to protest, but he had been sent back to the chateau in disgrace.

His shame that day had been the spur that drove Cameron on. Never again would any man have such power over him. Relentlessly he had climbed the ladder to success, allowing nothing to stand in his way. His father could not understand that he too had his pride. Running away from Boston would have been like de Pavigné ordering him off his land. As soon as he could, he had bought up the land of those who had injured his family and then had seen them struggling in poverty. Now men were afraid of him. He squared his shoulders and sat his horse jauntily. Only one thought still troubled him. Was Lafayette right? Was he confusing pride with revenge?

Chapter Four

Blind with rage and pain, Téoline raced up the wide marble staircase. Madame Beaulieu and their two maids were waiting anxiously at the top, but she rushed by them and down the broad corridor to the sanctuary of her apartment. Once inside her boudoir, Téoline flung herself down on the daybed and beat the cushions with her fists. Madame ordered the girls to fetch hot water, soft cloths, and liniment before hurrying after Téoline.

"My poor pet . . . !" she murmured softly, leaning over Téo and stroking her head. "Poor little one . . ."

"Don't dare pity me or I shall cry!" Téoline jumped to her feet. "I don't want pity from anyone!" Her eyes were stinging from the tears she was holding back, but she refused to let them fall. Hélène, on the other hand, was weeping enough for both.

Madame tried to ease the fragments of torn silk away from the wounds as gently as she could. Angrily, Téo grabbed at the bodice of her gown and ripped it away defiantly, easing her fury by adding pain.

"Look at it! Look what he did!" She looked over her shoulder at the reflection of her back in the mirror. Little beads of blood were oozing from the welts. Hélène was attempting to loosen the laces of the heavily boned corset Téo had been wearing, to see the full extent of the damage. "He is a fiend!" In a sudden burst of passion she rounded on Madame. "How can you pretend to love such a man . . . how can you stay with him?"

Hélène pressed a tiny lace handkerchief to her lips in a futile attempt to stem her tears. She was too shaken by what she saw, and Téo's unwarranted attack, to reply, but she continued with her task although Téo had begun to pace up and down the room.

"I wouldn't stay in this house another second if, like you, I were free to go!"

"The only freedom I have is to return to the gutters of Paris from which I came," Hélène managed to protest.

"Then I would do that. I would beg for my bread and sleep under the bridges of the Seine rather than stay here at his mercy."

"You do not know what you're saying, my dear!" Hélène

31

sobbed. "You have no idea what that means, or you could not suggest it!"

"Then find yourself a man and marry him if you cannot fend for yourself!" Téoline spat the words at her contemptuously. Hélène could see that the girl was beside herself, and she attempted to laugh off the attack.

"Marry? Who would marry me . . . a bastard? My mother was a *grisette*, a shop assistant, and little better than a whore . . . my father a porter from Les Halles as far as she could tell!" The recollection of her doubtful parentage sent Madame into a fresh flood of tears. The struggle with the corset was over and, as the pressure was released, Téo began to relax. The garment had taken the brunt of the blows; apart from the nasty cut on her shoulder, her back was only bruised. Seeing Hélène's distress, Téo suddenly realized what she had been saying, and for the first time her own eyes filled with tears.

"Oh, madame, forgive me?" She flung her arms about Hélène. "There are many men who would be joyed to marry you."

Madame Beaulieu collapsed in a dismal heap in the nearest chair and shook her head. "Not as I was then. A ragged urchin fit only to be a peasant's slave. And now . . ." She shrugged and laughed bitterly.

"Oh, Hélène, how could I be so cruel!" Téoline's grief was genuine and deeply felt. Madame had been the only person to show her any affection since her return home. She sank down at Hélène's side and put her head on Madame's lap. The duke's mistress smiled wanly and gently ran her fingers through Téo's hair. The child might have been her daughter under other circumstances.

"Neither Julie Saint-Laurent nor I would lead the life we do from choice. We were both too young to know at first . . . and then it was too late. Once you become a courtesan there is no turning back."

"Julie?" Téo recalled meeting the dark-haried, softly spoken young woman who appeared to be Hélène's only friend. She would never have guessed that she was merely the mistress of the Marquis de Permangle.

"Yes, didn't you realize that? Before Permangle became her patron, it was the Baron Fortisson. That's why he is suing the marquis. He claims Julie was stolen from him and his pride has been hurt. I'm afraid most men only regard us as their property."

"It isn't fair!" Téo retorted indignantly. "We aren't chattels and we should be allowed our rights." She got up and once again started to pace around the room. Her head was throbbing and her back was very sore.

"Women have no rights under the law, my dear, and there is nothing we can do." Hélène was beginning to regain her composure.

Nina and Lisette came in just then and signaled that there was someone in the corridor. Very little was said while they bathed Téoline's back. Everyone was aware the duke had his spies among the household staff. They applied some soothing balm to the angry welts before helping Téo into a soft white negligee. When they were ready to leave, Hélène followed them to the door and made sure the passage outside was clear. Then she closed the door and returned to Téoline, who was standing near the fire.

"Drink this!" she said, pouring some wine into a glass. Before handing it to Téo she added some white fluid from a phial she carried in her pompadour bag. "This will sooth your nerves, my sweet, and help you to sleep."

"I doubt if I will ever sleep again," Téo said, though she sipped the concoction obediently. "Did you know Monsieur was planning this marriage for me?"

"Not until today. He rarely speaks to me . . ." Hélène had been about to say "except in bed," but she was fairly certain Téo was too innocent to fully comprehend that side of their relationship. The little she knew of sex was in the abstract. "He wishes me to help you prepare your trousseau."

"There will be no need. I have no intention of marrying."

"But you can't refuse!"

"I have, and I mean to stand by it. What is the worst Monsieur can do to me? Send me back to a convent. I was prepared for that, and I'd sooner take the veil than live my life with a man I do not love." Téoline's blue-green eyes flashed defiantly.

"Oh, my dear," Hélène fluttered her limp white hands. "You are so very naïve if you think that is all the power he has. Have you never heard of *les lettres de cachet*?"

"Of course!" Everyone knew about the notorious system by which a letter from the King carried with it the authority to throw people in prison without trial or recourse to law. Mirabeau himself had suffered under it. His own father had the King imprison him in the Bastille. "But the use of such letters has been forbidden and the Bastille no longer exists." Téo laughed somewhat nervously.

"The people demanded they should be abolished, but the King and Queen still do as they please, and who's to know? As to the Bastille—there are other and worse prisons, asylums for the insane. You could be shut away in one of those and forgotten, if Monsieur were to ask the Queen." Madame held out her hand imploringly. "Téoline, I beg you, do not defy your father over this. I know he will not be easily thwarted."

Téoline stopped her pacing and looked around the room as if seeking some means of escape. Madame sat down on the daybed and patted the seat beside her. "Come sit down by me and let us make some plans. It will not be all bad, you see." She spoke encouragingly.

"The plans have all been made. I am to marry Albert de Beben!" Téoline spat back.

"He is very wealthy, I understand, and has large estates in the Indies," Hélène countered cheerfully. "Believe me, little one, this marriage could give you the independence you crave."

"I'll merely be exchanging one master for another." Téoline refused to be comforted.

"But no, dear heart! As a wife you have certain privileges . . . a certain hold over a man."

"You do not appear to have much success with Monsieur," Téo retorted with a touch of irony.

"I am not his wife." Madame sighed. "And I have neither your youth, your beauty, nor your rank. Monsieur de Beben is wealthy but he lacks position in society. Marrying you will give him this, therefore it is only right he should pay in other ways."

"He will have the right to bed me." Téoline's face expressed the disgust she felt at the idea, and Hélène found it hard not to laugh; the girl was so very young and inexperienced. "I only wish to do that with a man I love," Téo continued. "I can't understand how you can endure a man touching you when you have no feeling toward him."

"It becomes a way of life, and I suppose a kind of love results." Madame shrugged ruefully. "But it will not always be like that for you. De Beben is old and his demands are likely to be few. His main desire is for an heir and to have you as mistress of his household."

"I could not bear the child of a man I did not love." Téoline shuddered at the thought.

"You could love the child." Madame smiled indulgently. She was thinking how much she had come to care for Téoline and how much a child of her own blood would have meant to her.

"This means I shall never know love. I can never look at another man, for I shall be bound to my husband in the eyes of God." Hélène did not hear the last words, for Téo had almost whispered them.

"Believe me, my dear," Hélène continued happily—she was determined to make Téo see the best of things— "one day you will find someone whose glance will make your heart skip a beat. Whose touch will thrill you and whose kisses will set the world aflame. He will teach you the real meaning of romance . . . . This marriage will be no more than a tedious duty." Madame paused for a moment before adding wistfully, "A woman often has to close her eyes and imagine it is her lover's mouth against her lips . . . her lover's hand at her breast . . . no matter who the man that holds her in his arms . . ." She sighed and a tear rolled down her cheek. "I've had to learn to do that through the years. It was the only way I could survive."

Before Téo could reply, there was a knock at the door and Nina entered bearing a note addressed to Madame.

"It's from Rose Bertin, the couturière," Hélène said, looking up from reading it. "I requested she should attend us here so that we might discuss your trousseau. She has the effrontery to say she is too busy and suggests we visit her boutique and speak with one of her midinettes!" Madame pursed her lips to display her disapproval. "Really, Bertin is becoming insufferable. She has ideas above her station."

"Why should she care?" Nina sniffed. Madame's maid was a pert little girl from the back streets of Paris and she had few qualms about speaking her mind; especially as she regarded Hélène as little better than herself and Téoline as a child. "Bertin has only to crook her little finger and the Queen will rush to do her bidding," she finished waspishly.

"Well, she should think again before she insults the Duc de Pavigné's daughter. Monsieur also has the Queen's ear." Hélène scowled at her maid to silence her. Nina was a gossip and altogether too disrespectful. However, the girl was not willing to give way so easily.

"Do you know what happened when Picot met her the other day?" Her remark was addressed to Téo, but then she turned to Madame. "You remember Picot! She was the *premiere* assistant at 'The Grand Mogul' before she left to set up on her own." She did not wait for Hélène to reply before continuing. "Bertin was furious with Picot for leaving, and when they came face to face in the gardens of the Palais-Royal, she spat on her . . . right there . . . in front of everyone!" She paused to allow the enormity of the insult to take its full effect.

"Picot was furious and took the old bag to court. The judge found Bertin guilty and ordered her to pay damages. But did Picot get them? . . . of course not! The Queen had the order set aside!" The maid folded her arms and glowered belligerently. "I tell you, if the Queen is your friend you can get away with murder!"

Madame Beaulieu gestured impatiently to try again to silence the girl, but Téo wasn't paying attention to either of them. She was remembering how, on a recent visit to Versailles to watch the royal family dine, the Queen had so warmly welcomed Monsieur. If he should apply for a *lettre de cachet*, there was little doubt he would obtain one. Marie Antoinette would be more than willing to grant him a favor that would cost her nothing. There would be no public outcry because the Duc de Pavigné chose to imprison his own daughter.

"I wouldn't go to Bertin now if she were the last dressmaker in Paris," Téo burst out angrily. Nina's story only served to confirm what Hélène had said. All was lost. Life in a convent was one thing, but a prison—or worse, an asylum for the insane—was more than she could face.

"Oh, but she has such style," Hélène wailed. "Monsieur said we have *carte blanche*. I have been planning such a beautiful trousseau for you, my dear."

"I wouldn't count on that. After what happened today, I doubt if he'll even allow me to take the rags you pulled from my back."

"That's impossible! His pride would not allow him to do that. Anyway, it is the least he can do for you under the circumstances."

Téoline twirled around with a smile of pleasure at the sound of her brother's voice. They were the only two of the duke's children to share the same mother, and although they had seen little of each other since childhood, it gave them a deeper bond. The Comte de Chantal, elegant as always, was propped languidly against the gilt-framed doorway of the boudoir. He had obviously been listening to their conversation. At seventeen, he adored the fashions and foibles of the day as much as any woman and happily shared all the follies of the age.

"Why don't you send for Monsieur Beaulard? The Princesse de Lambelle speaks highly of him," he said, gliding forward and kissing his sister on the cheek. "It would annoy Bertin no end if

36

you were to patronize yet another of her rivals." He laughed boyishly, as the idea amused him.

"I may," Téo replied. "*If* I consent to go through with this marriage," she added with an air of bravado.

"So, Monsieur has told you about it at last." Julien picked at the grapes in a Sèvres dish on an ormolu table. "I wondered how long it would be before he got round to it."

"You mean you have known about this for some time, yet you said nothing to me?" Téoline eyed her brother reproachfully.

"It was more than I dare do. You should know that." Julien popped a grape into Nina's mouth and patted her rump. She responded by slapping his hand and giggling saucily, while Madame scowled at both of them.

"Look what he did when I refused." Téo slipped the negligee off her shoulders and showed the red welts across her back.

"What a bastard! But you know what he's like if you cross him."

Despite Téoline's agitation, Julien continued to flirt with Nina, and Hélène sensed that Téo was ready to explode. Hélène moved toward the door. "We'll leave you to discuss your private affairs . . . in private," she said, looking pointedly at the maid. "Come Nina, I'll write a note for you to take to Monsieur Beaulard."

"I knew you wouldn't like the idea of this marriage," Julien said a trifle sulkily after they had gone. He lolled back in an armchair beside the fire and contemplated the rings on his fingers. "I must admit, it is beyond me how Monsieur came to agree to this match. The man's a colonial . . . an upstart! Though I must admit it will make life easier for me."

"What do you mean?" Téo asked, coming to stand opposite him.

"Isn't it obvious? We need de Beben's money to manure our estate!" He shrugged, impatient at her lack of understanding.

At last the events of the afternoon began to fall into place. "Manuring one's estates" was the current phrase used by the impoverished nobility when they married off their daughters for money to men of lesser rank. This had been done in Louise's case, but Téoline had not even been born then.

"I did not know Monsieur was in need of funds," she said lamely.

"Why do you think he has not bought me a commission in the guards? Where do you think the money would come from to equip my regiment? I must say, de Beben has made a very generous settlement and given us a continuing interest in his plantations. Of course, he has other reasons for doing that. Monsieur will look after his interest through the Club Massiac. All the same, I wish we could have found a man of noble birth. Money isn't everything, and we shall have to live with de Beben as a member of the family."

"You mean *I'll* have to live with him," Téo replied somewhat peevishly. So de Beben had agreed to marry her without a dowry. She was to be the sacrificial lamb that saved the de Pavigné family. It explained her father's insistence on the match. As one born to the *noblesse de l'épée,* Téoline knew their ancient family name must be protected at all costs, but it irritated her to see Julien taking it all so casually.

"Why does it have to be me? Why couldn't you marry a wealthy woman?" She poked her brother with the sharp end of an ivory backscratcher.

"Because I have to be careful whom I choose. The bloodline must be pure, because they'll be de Pavignés. Your children won't count. It doesn't matter what color blood runs in their veins," her brother responded pompously. He had taken out a jeweled snuffbox and was helping himself to a pinch. He had not acquired the habit of doing it gracefully, and when Téo poked him again, he first sneezed and then dissolved into a fit of coughing.

Téoline giggled and pounded him hard on the back. "That serves you right, for not telling me all this before." She stopped abruptly as her efforts started her own wounds throbbing again. "But tell me, is this de Beben of mixed blood?"

Julien was busy trying to brush the remains of the snuff from his pastel satin suit. "I don't know . . . I've only seen him once, and that at a distance. He's a Creole, born in Saint-Domingue. Monsieur said he showed letters patent that are supposed to prove he has no colored blood, but Vincent Ogé is a mulatto. He says that means nothing. Many of the coloreds with pale skins will spend a fortune bribing officials to give them such letters."

At the mention of the French colony in the Caribbean, a sudden thought struck Téoline. "Julien, will this mean I shall have to leave France?" There was a catch in her voice, and for once her brother was quick to respond.

"I don't know. I hadn't thought of that." He sounded as surprised as she had been. "De Beben came to Paris hoping to be selected as a colonial delegate for the National Assembly; but he wasn't chosen. I suppose he'll go back to look after his estates."

"I can't go all that way away from you . . . I can't leave France!"

For once Julien was at a loss for words. "Perhaps it will not be such a bad thing for you to be out of France at the moment, Téo," he said, after a pause during which he got up and put his arm about her. "Things aren't very happy. Cameron is sure we are on the brink of revolution, and he should know. He's seen it happen before in the States."

"Cameron?" The name struck a chord in her memory. Wasn't that the name Louise had mentioned that afternoon? The man who had been staring at her so impertinently. Of course, it could be another of that name.

"Yes. Permangle introduced us last week in the Palais-Royal. I say, that's an idea. I've asked him to take supper with me. Father is dining at Versailles, so he will be out of the way. Cameron is as rich as Croesus, so I'm hoping to win at cards with him. But he knows the West Indies well. Join us and hear what he has to say."

"I may do that," Téo replied. But she was prompted by curiosity about Cameron rather than any wish to hear about Saint-Domingue.

The fire needed logs, and Lisette hadn't yet been in to light the candles. The room had darkened without their becoming aware of it. A sudden chill breeze blew open the window leading onto the small iron balcony in front of the *hôtel*. Slipping her hand into Julien's, Téoline led him across the room. Together they stood looking out over the city under the gathering dusk. A shiver ran through them and they clung together like two children bound by a sudden fear neither of them could fully comprehend.

Chapter Five

Téoline dismissed her maid and slid into the ornate gilded bath-tub that had been set up in front of the fire. The concoction Hé-lène had given her had helped her to sleep, and in spite of her physical discomfort she was feeling much better. The warm wa-ter was soothing and Téo lay back in it, watching the flames send delicate shadows over the white-and-gold wallpaper. The sweet odor of perfume filled the air, mingling with the woody smell of burning logs. The aura of elegance was comforting and seductive, but, for the first time in her life, Téoline was counting the cost. It was a pity everyone couldn't live in such luxury. She found herself sympathizing with Hélène. Given a choice be-tween this and a garret in Saint-Antoine, she could hardly be blamed for choosing to become a courtesan.

What would it be like to have dozens of different men make love to you? Was it possible to love that many, Téo wondered as she contemplated the gold cupids around the mirror. Before to-day she had assumed that love and marriage were one and the same thing. She reached out and turned the key of the little music box on the table at her side. It tinkled away and the two young lovers danced dreamily around a golden bower sparkling with jewels. Téo was sure that was how it was meant to be—aman and woman entwined in perfect harmony.

Getting out of the bath, she rang for Lisette to help her dress. Together they decided upon a gown of soft ivory silk. The wide lace decollatage was full enough to hide the cut on her shoulder left by the whip. The effect was as fragile and delicate as her mood. Lisette suggested she should color her cheeks. Although she was feeling rested, Téo looked pale and drawn. But she re-fused the rouge. Let Julien and this wretch Cameron see the anguish and suffering that was part of a woman's lot.

Téoline sat in front of the mirror while Lisette arranged her hair so that a cascade of gold ringlets fell over one shoulder. With the candlelight playing upon her face, Téo could see she was beginning to look her age. She had often wondered what it would be like to grow old, never thinking it would happen to her. Now she knew; she was no longer a child. Lisette stood back to admire her handiwork, and Téoline viewed herself in a full-length mirror. She wondered whether the American would notice that she was no longer the innocent young girl he had seen that afternoon; she was an experienced, weary woman of the world. Téo sighed, picked up a small ivory fan, and swept out of the room and down the grand staircase with the dignity of a duchess.

Andrew Cameron and the Comte de Chantal were playing cards at a table that had been set up in an alcove at one end of the music salon. Téo stood in the doorway watching them for a second or two before making her presence known. He was undoubtedly the man she had seen earlier, but he was much older than she had thought; he must be thirty at least. He sat back in his chair with one of his long legs stretched out in front of him. It was obvious he was thoroughly conceited and arrogant. He studied his cards with an air of detachment, as though it mattered little whether he won or lost, while Julien fussed over him anxiously. She must tell her brother not to be so gauche.

Hearing the soft *frou-frou* of her gown, the two men looked up. Julien came forward to greet her and Cameron stood waiting to be introduced. This afternoon he had thought of her as a pretty child and had been amused by her gullibility. This evening the sight of her made him catch his breath. She looked so fragile . . . so very vulnerable standing there in the candleglow. It was a crime to let such innocence loose in the world. She would be a target for all the evil of which the human race was capable.

"André, this is Téoline," Julien said with an informality his sister felt was out of place. "I have explained to André that you have only recently come from a convent and know very little of the ways of the world; so you can relax, Téo. Anyway, Yankees are much less formal than we are, so you don't have to play the lady with him."

Cameron had a job not to laugh as he saw Téo's jaw tighten and a pained expression come into her eyes. She could have killed her brother at that moment, of that Cameron was sure. "I am enchanted, Mademoiselle," he said, bowing over her hand.

"I think we should instruct her in the art of gambling, don't you, André?" Julien was intrigued by his guest's casual manner and was doing his best to ape it. If Cameron hadn't been so much taller, the count would have slapped him on the back.

"It would give me the greatest pleasure in the world to tutor you, ma'mselle." Cameron's gray eyes twinkled mischievously.

"Thank you, m'sieur!" Téoline drew herself up to her full

41

height and stared at the middle button on his waistcoat. "I'm afraid I'm not in the mood for such frivolities this evening." Glancing up, hoping to see him properly deflated, she saw the corners of his mouth twitching uncontrollably. Arching her neck like a swan and lifting her head, Téoline de Pavigné proudly sailed down to the other end of the room.

"That being the case, Julien, I suggest we close our accounts and turn our energies to amusing Téoline. Obviously in her present mood she needs entertaining!" Téo stopped short, her back to him, and fluttered her fan. His tone irritated her. Cameron was humoring her as he might a fractious child.

"I've no wish to take you from your game, m'sieur . . . if that is what amuses you?" she said pointedly. She might not be able to play cards, but she had other talents. She would show him. Téo went across to the piano and, while the two men were busy settling their debts, she let her hands stray into the graceful melody of a Mozart sonata. Her intention was to impress the upstart colonial, but slowly she succumbed to the music and it soothed away some of her frustrations. She became lost in it and was unaware that Cameron had come over and was standing at her side.

"That was magnificent, mademoiselle," he said with genuine admiration in his voice as the last notes died away. "Your interpretation shows great maturity . . .!" He had been about to say "for one so young," but sensed it might offend her. It did, because Téo read his thoughts.

"It is not always wise to assess a person's talents from appearance, m'sieur."

"Were I to have done that, ma'mselle, your beauty might have caused me to endow you with more than you perhaps possess. Won't you play something more?" Téoline was certain now that he was mocking her, although his manner could not have been more courteous.

"No!" she said curtly. "The mood has passed." She got up from the piano stool and went across to the fire. She would not add that the muscles in her back and arms were aching from the exertion and she had found it difficult to complete the piece.

Listening to the music and watching the rapt expression on her face, Cameron had been prepared to think that she had more depth than he had guessed. Now he changed his mind. She was as superficial as the rest of her kind. Ignoring her, he went over and sat at a small table next to Julien. The count poured his guest some wine and the two sat conversing quietly.

An enraged Téoline stood near the fire watching them. How dare he dismiss her from the conversation like a small child who has misbehaved? Since he would not give her the deference that was her due, she decided to take the lead herself. "My brother tells me that you are not happy about the conditions in France, m'sieur?"

"Are you?" Cameron said, setting down his glass. "The land has been ravaged by a bad harvest; the peasants are starving and the wealthy are keeping back the grain for greater profit. The country is seething with unrest." He was about to add that she was unlikely to be able to understand what that could mean, but once again he was caught by surprise. Standing there in the firelight with the candles in the wall sconces shedding a soft light on her hair, Téoline looked like a young madonna. Cameron found himself strangely disturbed. He had regarded her as a child, but in truth she was trembling on the brink of womanhood.

"I do not need to be told that, m'sieur. I am as well informed as you . . . possibly better. At Caen, it was a part of my duties to look to the needs of the poor. You see, over here we do not use slaves to do our dirty work!"

"A man can be a slave without having a black skin. By that reckoning you have plenty of them here in France," Cameron snapped back.

"It was the Americans who professed to be fighting a war for liberty and equality," Téo countered. She had captured his attention and was determined to make the most of it. "And according to your Thomas Jefferson, who spent much time in Paris, you still have many problems to solve. Perhaps you should set your own house in order before you trouble yourself about ours."

Téo snapped her fan shut with a click and turned her back on him.

Julien refilled Cameron's glass and grinned ruefully. Though he was accustomed to such verbal sparring with Téoline, he felt things were rapidly going beyond the bounds of courtesy. "Don't be disturbed by Téo's outspoken views, André. A wretched girl at the convent has filled her head with all kinds of revolutionary ideas; she'll grow out of it."

"Charlotte Corday is not a revolutionary." Téo rushed to her friend's defense. "She has no time for Marat and his seditious lies. I am not a revolutionary, m'sieur—" She turned to Cameron.

43

"I did not think so, ma'mselle. In your position, you have no need," Cameron broke in.

"There you are wrong, m'sjeur. As a woman I have every need. I am nothing but a chattel in my father's house . . ." Téoline's voice suddenly trembled. She was tired and her back was beginning to ache abominably. She was also fighting a verbal battle she was afraid she couldn't win. Turning away, she put up her arm to rest her hand on the mantelpiece lest he see the tears that had come into her eyes. The gesture caused her gown to slip, leaving the angry welt exposed. Cameron's eyes narrowed as he recognized there was only one weapon that would leave such a mark.

"When we are young we are all idealists, ma'mselle. We hope to put the world to rights," he said, trying to defuse the tension with generalities. "Unfortunately, experience teaches us that there is a vast difference between the idea and the reality . . . between men's words and their deeds."

"We must mean what we say or our words will lose all their value and we will be unable to communicate," Téo replied softly. Suddenly her anger was spent. She felt tired and drained of any will to spar with him. Had she not been afraid she had appeared discourteous, she would have excused herself to go to bed.

Cameron was too angry and disturbed by what he had just seen to carry the conversation any further. He knew enough of the ways of Frenchmen to know that only the duke would have dared to raise his hand against his daughter in that way. And, knowing the man of old, Cameron could well envision his doing it. Téoline became conscious of his scrutiny. Raising her head, she turned and looked at him, a stray tear sparkling like dew upon her cheek. Cameron felt beholden to break the silence. He was also curious to see the response to his next question.

"Your brother mentioned something about your being married before long, mademoiselle?"

"So I have been told." Things began to fall into place and Cameron understood what had been going on in the de Pavigné household.

"May I offer you my felicitations. I only hope your betrothed realizes how fortunate he is." Cameron's words were not meant as idle flattery. It took courage to behave as this girl had done. Another of her age would have had screaming hysteria and taken to her bed. He even managed a wry smile as he remembered how she had stood up to him in the arguments.

"I wouldn't know, m'sieur," Téo replied, settling herself on the settee. "I haven't met him yet."

"He's a lucky scoundrel, if you ask me . . . damned lucky," Julien chimed in. He had been drinking steadily all evening and he couldn't hold his wine. "You know the West Indies, André. Tell Téo what they're like." His speech was slurred but that didn't stop him from refilling his glass again.

"Does he come from the colonies, then?"

"Saint-Domingue," Julien supplied. "Albert de Beben from Saint-Domingue. Do you know him?"

"Who doesn't? . . . But not as a friend," Cameron added hastily. Suddenly the air around them had turned to ice. The other two looked at him, sensing there was something wrong. Cameron knew he must try and set things right. "Everyone with business in the Caribbean knows his name. He's one of the wealthiest landowners in Le Cap . . . Cap Français, that is." He had to find a way of extricating himself from a topic he did not wish to puruse. "They claim Le Cap is the Paris of the New World," he said to change the subject.

Téoline was about to ask him more details concerning the colony when they were disturbed by the sound of a fracas outside. A moment later Le Beau, the duke's steward, burst into the salon. He looked wild and disheveled. He had lost his wig and his coat was torn and caked with mud.

"In God's name, Le Beau! What is the meaning of this . . .?" exclaimed Julien. Both Julien and his guest rose from their chairs. Le Beau was plainly scared to death.

"M'sieur . . . le duc . . ." he gasped, and pointed towards the noise outside, which was gaining in intensity. "Sans-culottes! They are all over his carriage . . .! They'll not let it through the gates . . .!"

Cameron was the first out of the room, with Julien hard on his heels. The vestibule was crowded with footmen and porters, armed with a motley assortment of weapons. "Quickly, my sword!" Cameron shouted, and Lisette ran to fetch it for him. Julien followed suit and, as soon as they were armed, the two men led the small army towards the iron gates of the hôtel. It was with difficulty that Nina and Lisette prevented Téoline from following them.

"You will only get in the way, ma'mselle," Lisette wailed. Coming to her senses, Téo knew the girl spoke the truth. She sent the women scurrying to gather bandages and liniment before going to the window of the petit salon to watch.

"Do not show yourself, mademoiselle," Nina said, coming and standing at her side. "I know their like. The sight of you in your silks and satins will only madden them." Glancing at Madame's maid, Téo had the distinct feeling she was rather enjoying the fray. Setting aside the candle she had been holding, she peered into the darkness. The noise was deafening. The angry shouts of the mob mingled with screams of fright and pain and the neighing of horses terrified by the flames. Torches had been thrown into the shrubs inside the railings and there was danger that a spark blown on the wind could set the trees—perhaps even the house—ablaze. But it was impossible to see what was happening to any of the men. Some minutes passed until she heard the gates clang and the crunch of carriage wheels on the gravel drive. In the light from a torch, Téoline caught sight of Julien fighting a rear-guard action with some of the rabble left inside. His pale silk coat glistened in the light of the flare and she guessed that the tall, broad figure at his side must be Cameron.

Téoline raced out and called for the front doors to be unbarred, and the wounded were helped inside. Fortunately the sight of blood did not make her swoon. She had too often helped the nuns look to the sick and wounded around Caen. Because some of the wounds were severe, Téo sent a messenger to find a doctor. Having examined the others, she gave the servants instructions as to their treatment.

It was strange. This afternoon she felt she could have willingly killed her father. Now she found herself praying that nothing had happened to him.

Her brother and Cameron were the last to return. They came in, half carrying the duke between them. His face was ashen and his clothes were in shreds, but otherwise he appeared unharmed; like others of his kind he had been trained as swordsman from an early age. Cameron gave orders for the doors to be locked and barred once more, before assisting the duke into the *petit salon*.

"I'm relieved to see you well, m'sieur," Téoline said as she ran to help him into a chair. He was suddenly an old man and she could see fear written on his face. Julien handed him a glass of brandy, and for some minutes he sat sipping it. Slowly some life began to return to his veins and he looked up at Cameron, who was busy wiping his sword.

"I am much obliged to you, m'sieur." The duke raised his glass to him. "Your sword was of inestimable value. I could tell it was in an experienced hand."

"I have had plenty of practice, m'sieur. Lafayette and I spent many years helping the Yankees in their fight," Cameron replied courteously. For the first time Téoline noticed a nasty gash on the back of his hand and rushed to attend to it.

"It is only a scratch, Mademoiselle Téoline," he said softly; but he made no attempt to stop her holding his hand as she bathed away the grime.

"It was most fortunate that you were here," the duke said, watching them. "May I ask to whom I am indebted?"

Julien rushed forward, eager to claim his share of the credit. "M'sieur, this gentleman was my supper guest. May I present Colonel Andrew Cameron!"

The smile on the Duc de Pavigné's face froze. "Cameron?" He repeated the name slowly as though he were testing wine for bitterness. "Did your family have an estate near Chartres?"

Téoline felt Cameron's hand become tense. Cameron turned from her. Picking up his sword, he replaced it in his scabbard. "The same, m'sieur," he said, answering the implied question. "Though, as you can see, a few years older than when we last met." There was an unmistakable challenge in his voice which Téoline and her brother were at a loss to understand.

The duke's face was like marble and he made no attempt to speak. Reaching for his cane, he struggled to his feet and walked slowly to the door. Opening it, he signaled a lackey to come forward.

"Show this man to the door," he said. "Tell him I will be sending a servant to his lodgings tomorrow to recompense him for his pains, if he cares to leave his address." Without another word he limped across the vestibule and started up the stairs.

"M'sieur!" Téoline gasped and put out her hand towards Cameron's arm. Julien swore volubly under his breath. But Cameron stormed across to the door. Without a backward glance, he called for his horse and went out into the night.

Chapter Six

"Honoré Gabriel Riquetti . . . Comte de Mirabeau!" The name rang through the grand salon of the Hôtel de Pavigné.

On hearing it, everyone waiting in the receiving line drew back to give him precedence. Albert de Beben left his position at the head of the line and slithered forward to greet the new arrival, bowing profusely. Mirabeau stopped still in the middle of the floor and watched him with a look of disgust on his face. He waited for de Beben to arrive at his side, then, shaking back his long mane of black hair, inclined his head and strode past him to greet Téoline, who had been left standing alone.

"Mademoiselle . . . Téoline . . ." he murmured passionately. Raising her hand to his lips, he kissed her fingers . . . her wrist . . . her arm, in an outburst of emotion spawned by his Latin blood. "How can you do this to me?"

Téoline blushed deep crimson, knowing all eyes were focused on them. "I beg your pardon, monsieur," the baffled girl said pleadingly.

"Honoré!" he gasped, pressing her hand against his pock-marked face. Mirabeau was possibly one of the ugliest men in all France, yet such was his fascination, few people could resist him. His brilliant intellect and powers of oratory were only excelled by his determination, and he was determined to have Téoline.

"M'sieur . . . Honoré . . . I beg you!" Téo implored. "M'sieur de Beben . . . everyone . . . is staring at us!"

Mirabeau shrugged as if it mattered little to him, but stepped back and examined the diamond bracelet that matched a necklace about her slender throat. "Was this a gift from him?"

"Yes!" Although not intentionally, Téo's voice was singularly lacking in enthusiasm. "Aren't they magnificent?"

"A cheap price to pay for such a pearl. Allow me, and I will give you jewels that would ransom a king, my love?"

"I am deeply honored, m'sieur. Unfortunately you are in no position to give me a wedding ring."

Le Beau, who had been standing near them and was in charge of the proceedings, went across and spoke to the Duc de Pavigné. What he had to say obviously offended the duke's ears.

48

He glowered, then moved across and spoke to Mirabeau. His manner was gracious enough, and he tactfully drew the count away to join a small group from the Club Massiac.

Téoline was relieved to see him go. Her first meeting with Albert de Beben, as far as she could recall, had taken place only a few minutes before the reception to mark their betrothal was to begin. Of the two men she much preferred Mirabeau, but it was with de Beben that she would have to contend. However, she need not have worried, as he returned to her side smiling with delight. He was impressed to find her on such intimate terms with the great man.

"You are tired, my dear," he said anxiously, noticing how pale she looked. "The excitement is too much. Shall I call for a stool?" Téoline thanked him but refused, pointing out that they had nearly come to the end. De Beben was remiss in suggesting such a thing. Surely he was aware of the strict rules of etiquette governing the *tabaret*. There had been more than one duel fought over the right to sit down in the presence of certain ranks of society. Téo was nervous. Her fiancé had embarrassed her all evening with his repeated *faux pas*. If he wasn't fawning over people he believed to be important, he was turning his back on those he thought not. He had offended Téo mortally by the curt manner with which he treated Madame Beaulieu. Apparently he knew of her position in the household, and he had looked past her without so much as a nod.

Albert de Beben viewed his latest acquisition with grave concern before turning away to receive the next guest. Mademoiselle de Pavigné was likely to prove the most valuable property he had ever bought in his entire life. He smiled as he thought how the elite circle in Saint-Domingue would cringe before one of her rank. All those who had gone out of their way to ignore him would be forced to pay homage at her feet. She was a prize indeed, and for the moment he would have promised her anything. Unfortunately de Beben was not noted as a man to keep his promises.

Finally Téoline greeted the last of her guests. As they moved along to speak to de Beben, she was able to relax and observe him more closely than she had done before. He was much older than her father. Lisette had said that his black slave, Davide, had told them he was over seventy; but Samson, the mulatto dwarf who served as de Beben's valet, held that his master was no more than sixty. It was obvious that whatever he lacked in youth he more than made up for in wealth. His *toilette* outshone almost everybody else in the room.

At first glance, he had not appeared unattractive, and Téoline decided he had probably been quite handsome when he was young. However, on closer examination she was not impressed by what she saw. His best feature was a thick crop of immaculately dressed white hair. This was unusual because most men of his age wore wigs. His hair framed a broad face; his jawline had remained firm, but the flesh around his dark eyes sagged. And when, as now, he was hot, little rivulets of perspiration ran down the creases, turning the heavy makeup he was wearing into a sticky paste. His build was much heavier than her father's, and although de Beben was not fat, a general slackening of the muscles made him slightly paunchy in spite of his corsetting.

As soon as de Beben was free, Téoline excused herself. She said she needed to wash her hands, which had become clammy with so much fondling. Her fiancé was quite content to join the group surrounding Mirabeau and the Duc de Pavigné. Actually, Téo was anxious to seek out Louise, who was paying one of her rare visits to Saint-Honoré. She discovered her sister in the *petit salon* and insisted they go upstairs to the privacy of her apartment.

"Have you seen Julien?" Téo blurted out the question the moment the door was closed.

Louise looked surprised. "No. Surely he is here? It is difficult to tell amidst this crowd."

Briefly, Téoline told her what had happened the night Cameron was there.

"You say he left the house?"

"He stormed out, vowing he would never return. He said Monsieur had insulted his guest and he would never be able to show his face in society. It is almost a week ago and I have heard nothing from him."

"I shouldn't worry. He'll soon get over it." Louise was not overly fond of her half-brother, and she was not upset by what she regarded as his tantrums. She was far more disturbed about Téoline, because she had heard reports about de Beben that worried her. "Tell me," she said, "how did Julien react to news of your marriage?"

"He wished it were to someone other than de Beben," Téo replied.

Louise, who was normally very calm and self-contained, turned and looked into her young sister's face. Her own expression was troubled, as if she had something to say but was not sure if she should.

"He told me about the marriage settlement," Téo said. "I was very angry at first, but I'm beginning to understand why it is necessary."

"To protect the precious name of de Pavigné." Louise shrugged impatiently. "Neither he nor Monsieur have given a thought to the risks you may run in marrying this man."

Téo looked puzzled. "Risks?" she said. "I don't understand. The only risk I can see is that I shall be left a widow before long. And, as Hélène has said, that may not be such a terrible thing."

"Pray God you are, if this marriage should go ahead!"

Téo looked across at her sister, who was sitting on the *lit de repos*. There was something frightening in Louise's tone. "Louise, do you know something about Albert de Beben? Something I don't know? If so, it is your duty to tell me."

Louise walked over to the window, where she stood tapping the glass with her fan. Téoline tapped her foot and waited. She knew how stubborn her sister could be. Nothing would make her speak unless she wished.

"I discussed it with Charles," she said after a moment's pause. "He said I should leave matters alone. Arrangements for the marriage have gone too far. That is just like a man," she sighed. "He buries his head and hopes the nastiness will go away before he has to make a stand."

"But you are going to tell me?"

"I must," Louise replied without looking at her. "You are too young to go into this marriage without at least the protection of knowing the truth."

"And the truth is . . .?"

"Albert de Beben is given to bouts of madness!"

The silence in the room was almost tangible, and it was some time before Téoline spoke.

"How can you be sure of this? Surely Monsieur would not have agreed had this been true?"

"I have no love for him, but in this I think he was ignorant. I heard some idle gossip from my maid; her cousin is a whore. Charles has many contacts, and I got him to speak with a doctor he knows. De Beben will go to any lengths to prevent it becoming common knowledge, but he has frequent periods of near insanity. Since coming to France he has spent several weeks in a convent that looks after such people discreetly."

Téoline sank down into a chair and played with the diamond bracelet, twirling it around her slender wrist. "Can nothing be done to help him?"

"It passes, but it returns from time to time. I'm afraid he is reaping the reward of a misspent youth." Louise was watching Téoline. She did not know whether her sister would understand, but she had come too far to turn back now. "He suffers incurably from *lues venera* . . . that is . . ."

'There is no need for you to translate," Téoline flashed angrily. "Although they neglected to teach us many things at Caen, Latin was not one of them. For some time I did not understand the cause, but I have seen the sisters trying to treat the ravages of syphilis many times. I thought at first it was only something children had. I bathed their poor little bodies, covered with sores, and wept because so many of them were blind. I raged against God for allowing it to happen to so many of them. Then one day Sister Superior called me to one side and said God was not to blame; that it was the sins of the fathers being visited upon them, but even then I did not fully understand." Her voice was full of bitterness.

"But you do now?" Louise could see she was trembling, but wasn't sure whether it was from misery or rage.

"Oh, yes," Téoline laughed harshly. "Since then I've heard Nina and Lisette laughing over men who have caught the pox. They were only too willing to explain. I've learned a great deal listening to them."

"This is something you should never have had to learn. At least as far as your own husband was concerned."

"He is not my husband yet, and will never be if I can think of a way to avoid it." She asked Louise to leave her and sent a note down to de Beben saying she was feeling fatigued and would not be coming down again.

Téoline rose early the next day and went to Mass alone, save for Lisette, who always accompanied her. She did not want to talk to anyone, not even Hélène. She had spent a restless night and now a troubled time in church searching her soul, but to no avail. The priest preached eternal love, but all she could feel was hate. As they drove back to Saint-Honoré in the open carriage she noticed how the chestnut trees glowed in the October sun. She had always regarded the dancing leaves as gold; now their russet hues reminded her of flames. This was heightened by an unmistakable tension in the air.

Téoline was too preoccupied with her own worries to notice, but Lisette remarked upon the number of people standing about in little knots. Their heads bowed together gossiping as if there

52

was an item of some import. Téo paid scant attention until they arrived back at the *hôtel*. They had just entered the gates when she saw her father rush out of the front doors and jump upon his horse. He galloped past them down the drive and turned in the direction of Versailles.

She went upstairs and was greeted by Madame, who was weeping copiously over a copy of the *Courrier de Versailles.*

"What ever is the matter, Hélène?" Téoline was not in the mood to display sympathy toward anyone. She needed all she had for herself. The sight of Madame in tears was more than she could contend with, and her manner was abrupt. Madame thrust the journal towards her.

"Read it," she said. "And for the love of God keep out of Monsieur's way, for he is in an evil mood!"

Téoline could have remarked that that was not an unusual thing, but she was anxious to find out what all the fuss was about. She took the paper from Madame and went over to sit down near the open window leading onto the balcony. The air was fresh and the light was good.

On the front page of the popular journal she read a report of a banquet held recently at Versailles. It had been given by the officers of the garrison for their majesties. The writer gave explicit details of the food consumed and remarked on the excesses whilst the common people of Paris were crying out for a crust of bread. There was no doubt he intended it to be inflammatory, for he used words like "orgy" and "privilege." But the sting was in the tail. He reported how the guests had refused to drink to the health of the nation. And how, when the officers tore the tricolors from their hats and trampled them underfoot, Marie Antoinette had laughed.

As she put the paper down, Louise's words came back to haunt her: "Paris is like a tinderbox. It only needs a spark for all of us to be engulfed in flames!"

It was obvious from Hélène's state that Monsieur had vented his temper on her before he left. But there was nothing Téoline could do or say, and this news only made her own problems loom large. Leaving Nina and Lisette to try and calm Madame, she went to her own apartment and remained there all day, refusing to see anyone. Albert de Beben called, but she sent word down that she was indisposed. She had to decide what action to take before she could see the man again. Fortune was on her side, as he left a note to explain he had to go to Marseilles on business and looked forward to their marriage on his return.

She could only think of Louise and wonder whether his excuse was genuine. She watched his carriage drive away with his black coachman at the reins and Samson, the dwarf, beside him. De Beben obviously made a confidant of the man. Téoline could only pray that de Beben would never return.

She spent the day wondering about Julien and pondering how she could get out of the tangle she was in. What if her father did not know? If she told him, would he agree to stop the wedding? What would happen to Julien and the estates? Underneath it all was the fear that the very foundations of France were crumbling.

She was thoroughly dejected by the time she was ready to prepare for bed, but then a thought occurred to her. She would seek out Andrew Cameron and see if he had news of Julien. Téo had little hope he would, but perhaps he was not the kind of man to nurse a grudge. She would take that chance, because Andrew Cameron appeared to be her only chance of discovering Julien.

Lisette came in answer to the bell, but there was a smile on her face. *"Voilà, ma'mselle!* This letter has just been delivered for you. I think it must be from your brother. The messenger was so careful it should not fall into other hands."

Téo snatched it from her and eagerly tore the seal. It was from Julien, she recognized the hand.

"I am in dire need of help," it read. *"For the love of God, meet me tomorrow in the Lady Chapel of the Notre-Dame at ten o'clock. Till the morning . . . Your brother, Julien. P.S.— Bring what money you can."*

Téoline gave a sigh of relief. It was most certainly from Julien, there was no doubt about that. She quickly fell asleep, for she was tired after such a day, but she was awakened several times during the night by the tocsin. She was too drowsy to take in its meaning, but the people of Paris knew.

Chapter Seven

"Mademoiselle, I do not think your father would approve of you venturing into the streets today," Lisette protested. Téoline had just ordered a carriage to be brought round.

"My father is not here, and we shall be back before he returns," Téo said impatiently. She was well aware of the tension in the air. It was written on the faces of everyone in the *hôtel*. "I have to meet my brother at the Notre-Dame. If you are too scared to come, I shall go alone."

"But no, ma'mselle. I wouldn't let you do that." Lisette hurried away to fetch her cloak, muttering under her breath.

Téoline pulled a face as she counted out the few gold louis she had in her pompadour bag. Then suddenly an idea struck her. She opened the velvet case containing the diamonds de Beben had given her. Wrapping them in a lace kerchief, she slid them down the bodice of her gown.

The coachman added his doubts to those of Lisette, but, seeing it was of no avail, he turned the horses in the direction of the city. On either side, the narrow streets leading into the rue Saint-Honoré were packed with people apparently heading towards the Île de la Cité.

Téoline suppressed a shiver as she looked out on the sea of faces that surrounded the coach. A man stared in through the window of the coach, and there was no mistaking the hostility in his eyes. Téo was thankful that at the last minute she had decided to wear a plain woolen redigote over her blue silk gown; however, she wished she had chosen something less conspicuous than her high-crowned bonnet with its plumes. The effect was quite charming, but somehow she did not feel they would create the right impression today.

The coach clattered over the cobbles and turned into the rue de Rivoli, but as the crowds continued to thicken, its passage was slowed until they were almost standing still. Téoline exchanged anxious glances with her maid as they heard a distant roar. It rose and fell like a storm tide, and all the time, underlying it was the slow relentless throbbing of a drum. Lisette stuck her head out of the window and held a short but animated conversation with their driver.

"What is it? What's happening?" Téoline asked fearfully as the coach was rocked to and fro by the weight of bodies pressing around it.

"He cannot go any farther. There is a procession of some kind coming towards us. He says it looks like a lot of young girls all dressed in white. They're led by a child with a drum."

"It's probably a church festival," Téo said hopefully, as Lisette's head disappeared out of the window to make a further check. Then she began to make sense of some of the words shouted over the general roar.

"To Versailles! . . . To Versailles! . . . Cut the jade's throat! . . . To the devil with the Austrian whore!"

"My God!" Téo crossed herself. "They are going to Versailles to kill the Queen!"

By now the road was a seething mass and she noted with surprise that they all appeared to be women. They carried a wild assortment of weapons and were brandishing brooms and kitchen knives above their heads.

"Holy Mother of God!" Lisette exclaimed. Téoline rushed to look out of the opposite window. "See! They have taken the cannon from the front of the Hôtel de Ville."

The two girls hastily retreated into the shadow of the interior and closed the windows. Téo's heart was pounding. The cries of the mob became more and more demanding as their numbers rapidly increased.

"Bread . . . Give us bread! *To Versailles to fetch the baker and the baker's wife!"*

On the other side of the road they could see what only a moment before had been an elegant coach emblazoned with the owner's coat of arms. The windows were broken and the door hung from its hinge. There were women climbing all over it while others were busy dragging a terrified woman out by her hair. Her coachman tried in vain to beat off the attackers with his whip. Within seconds it had been snatched from his hand and turned against him. The woman disappeared in a flurry of silk and feathers, sucked down into the swirling mass amid cries of triumph.

Instinctively Téoline looked down at her own rich apparel. Lisette was quick to read her thoughts. "Quick, ma'mselle! Take off your coat and bonnet and hide your jewels in the coach. It could mean your life!" Téoline obeyed. She did not need to be told her life was at stake. Meanwhile Lisette had snatched off her own muslin cap and rammed it down over Téoline's curls. Her careful coiffure would surely give away her status.

"Here," she said wrapping her gray woolen cloak around Téo's shoulders. "This will hide your gown. Now come with me. You'll be safer out of this coach." Téoline hesitated—by now she was almost paralyzed with fear—but Lisette tugged at her arm. "Come with me, ma'mselle. I know the back streets of Paris. I was raised in the gutters!"

There was no time to think; Téo had to trust Lisette. They slid out of the door on the far side of the coach, where the crowd was thinner, and within seconds they had become a part of it. Blindly clinging to the hand of her maid, Téo was shoved and pushed along, quite powerless to change her course.

"To Versailles . . . To Versailles . . .!"

The screams were reaching fever pitch. At every junction a fresh wave flowed forward into the main stream. It had begun to drizzle and the cobbles beneath their feet were already slimy with mud. Téoline stumbled as a heavy wooden sabot crushed her dainty satin-slippered foot. The old harridan wearing it grabbed her to prevent her falling and gave a wide toothless grin.

"Up you get, dearie! We've got to go and give the Austrian bitch her deserts!"

Fortunately Téo did not have to reply. A fresh surge came and swept the old woman away. She put her hand up to straighten her cap, then remembered she must keep her gown hidden and grabbed at Lisette's cloak. The cap slipped off and within seconds her hair was matted with rain, which had started to fall quite heavily.

"Try to work your way backwards against the stream," Lisette whispered. They were being carried away from Saint-Honoré. "If we can get into one of the side streets, we may be able to get back to the *hôtel*."

Téo was afraid to speak and nodded to show she understood. An officer from the National Guard was pushing his horse into the edges of the crowd in an attempt to keep it in check. A voice next to her yelled across at him:

"Go to Versailles and tell Her Majesty that we're coming to cut her throat!"

Turning quickly, Téo found herself looking up into the bearded face of a man. His head was covered by a black shawl and he wore a striped skirt over his long pantalettes. It was then that she realized that a number of those she had supposed to be

57

women were men in disguise. Even in her panic, Téo was quick to realize that this uprising had been planned.

Téo stumbled again, and Lisette clung to her to prevent her being trampled underfoot. A second later there was another surge, and before Téo could stop her, Lisette was forced to let go. She was swept away in the crowd, and Téoline realized she was on her own.

Desperately she strove to control her increasing hysteria. She must not draw attention to herself; her life could depend on it. She eased first this way and then that, trying to edge herself towards the fringe of the crowd. But she was hemmed in on all sides by filthy, wet, sweating bodies. The faces were contorted and evil; the men brandished pikes and pitchforks and called out obscenities to each other as they went.

Téoline realized she had never really known terror until that moment. Her body was sore and aching from the constant jostling it had received. That did not prevent her jumping sharply as a cold metal blade pierced her sleeve through the cloak. She looked at her neighbor and again it was a man's face in a woman's guise.

He laughed coarsely as he saw her look of surprise. "I make a pretty wench, don't I? But not half as pretty as you." He caught her about the waist with his free hand and planted a kiss full on her lips. His breath was heavy with sour wine and onions. It almost suffocated her, and Téoline was afraid she was going to faint. Fortunately he was carried away from her by another sudden press of bodies.

Téo felt herself becoming dazed by all that was happening around her. She found herself losing all sense of identity, and for a time she became one with the crowd. How long she was carried on the tide of the crazed mass she had no idea. Suddenly she came to her senses and found she was chanting "To Versailles . . . To Versailles . . .!" with the rest of them. The shock brought her back to reality. She must retain her reason if she was to escape from this whirlpool. The wretched poor of Paris had suddenly become howling animals thirsting for blood.

They had reached the Champ-de-Mars, and on the far side a small group of National Guard officers were once more trying to restore some kind of order. If only she could reach them, Téoline thought there might be some hope of freeing herself from the rest of the mob.

Cautiously she began to weave her way crabwise across the steady flow. By now she was soaked to the skin. Her hair was no longer a problem. It straggled over her face and little rivulets of water cut through the dirt on her face and ran down between her breasts. She had only another foot or so to go when a sudden onrush sent a small child sprawling into the mud in front of her. Without a pause the wave swept over him, drowning his pathetic cries with their din. With an unexpected savagery, Téoline began fighting to free him from under the tramping feet. Slipping and slithering in the mud, she grabbed a staff from one of the women and started to flail them with it while the child managed to scramble to his feet.

This unexpected attack from in their midst caused them to pause and fall back, and Téo was suddenly alone in the midst of a small circle. A glancing blow from the staff had caught one of the *sans-culottes* on the shoulder. Enraged, he clutched at her cloak. As it came away in his hand, fury flamed in his eyes at the sight of her satin gown.

"Merde!" he spat at her. "Look at her! She's not one of us! She's one of the Queen's spies . . .!"

A murderous howl went up from the crowd as they closed in on her. "Death to the spy! To the gallows with the harlot!"

Téo fought like a tiger. If she was to die, then she would die like a de Pavigné. She hit out in all directions until the stave was wrenched from her grasp. Blows rained down on her from every side until, mercifully, she swirled down into the black depths of unconsciousness.

"Good God!" Lafayette struggled to rein in his big white charger as the animal reared onto its hind legs, terrified by the tumult around the Hôtel de Ville. His guardsmen were trying to prevent the mob from hauling away the cannon from outside the city hall.

"André, what in the name of God am I going to do? See for yourself, many of my men are refusing to obey my commands. They say they will not attack defenseless women."

"I'd hardly call them defenseless," Cameron replied grimly. They must have stripped the arsenal of every firearm in the place." What had started out to be a pleasant morning's ride with Gil was rapidly turning into a hideous nightmare. "Look out! That group over there has some torches!"

"Oh, no! If we don't find some means of stopping them, Paris will go up in flames."

A young officer ran up to them, and after coming smartly to attention pointed to a consumptive-looking man who had just climbed onto one of the cannon.

"It is Maillard, General! He's telling them to fetch their friends and meet him at the Place Louis. From there they will march on Versailles to deal with the King and Queen."

"Damned rabble-rouser!" Lafayette gave orders for a messenger to be sent to warn the King. Then he turned to his friend. "Well, André, the match has been struck! Where will all this end?"

"You think this worse than the storming of the Bastille?"

"See for yourself. There must be more than a thousand here, and others on the way. And my men are on the verge of mutiny. They're little better than a citizen army. Many of these women are likely to be their wives or sweethearts. I cannot blame them for not wanting to take arms against them. What am I to do?"

"In the long run you must find the ringleaders and silence them. Then the crowd might listen to reason. This way, they'll win nothing and destroy what little they have. For now, I suggest you join them. They respect you. Ride alongside them. You may be able to cool their passions before they reach Versailles; it will take them the better part of a day."

Lafayette nodded his assent. Cameron had served under him and he knew he was an excellent strategist. More than that, he had experience as a secret agent. Cameron guessed what his former commander was thinking.

"In the meantime, if you let me have a dozen or so of your most trusted men, I'll take them into the crowd and we'll do our best to calm them from inside. If a few hotheads can incite a mob, we'll try and make it work the other way. If nothing else, we can find out who some of the leaders are."

"Would you do that, André?" A look of intense relief came over the general's face.

"For old times' sake! Have you ever known me to miss a good scrap?" Cameron grinned. "Mind you, I can't promise how effective we'll be, but we'll do our best. Tell your men to meet me by the main entrance to the Tuileries in half an hour. Tell them to change out of uniform so they'll look like part of the mob . . . Oh, and send someone I know with them or they might start by arresting me." Cameron gave an abrupt nod and headed back towards the Notre-Dame.

The crowd had begun to thin out as the main body made its way towards the Place Louis. Cameron was making for the Pont Neuf and the Left Bank. He had already begun to spur his horse across the bridge when he heard a familiar voice calling his name. Before he could turn round, the disheveled figure of the young Comte de Chantal was clutching at his reins.

60

"My God!" Julien gasped. "Thank Heaven, I have found a friend!" He leaned against the horse breathless and white with fear.

"What in Heaven's name are you doing here? Get as far away as you can unless you want to be torn to shreds." Cameron was sorry for the boy. Nothing in his life would have prepared him for the rough handling to which he had obviously been subjected. All things considered, he appeared to have got off lightly, as he was physically unharmed.

"I can't . . . ." Julien shook his head and pointed towards the cathedral. "Téoline . . .!"

"Your sister's in this mob?" Cameron sat bolt upright in his saddle and started searching the crowd for any sign of Téoline.

"I don't know." Julien had regained his breath and was able to speak with some clarity. "The other night . . . after you left . . . I quarreled with my father. I left his house and vowed never to return. But I haven't any money. I sent a message to Téoline to meet me here this morning . . . . She'll be on her way."

"Not if she has any sense. Only a fool would risk her neck by coming out in this," Cameron snapped back. If he had judged Téoline de Pavigné correctly, she was no fool, but neither was she a coward. Which was more than he was beginning to think about her brother.

"I said I had to see her. I needed help," Julien whined. He sensed Cameron's contempt. "She'll come. I know Téoline. Even as a child she refused to let anything frighten her, however much she might really be terrified. She'll come if she thinks I need help."

Cameron scanned the crowds again, but he had little hope of finding anyone from that distance. "Come," he said. "Get up behind me. It isn't safe for you here. I have to fetch my pistols from my rooms in Saint-Germain. Then we'll go to the reassembly point."

When Cameron emerged from his apartment some fifteen minutes later, Julien could scarcely recognize him. He had exchanged his riding coat and breeches for some workman's clothes belonging to his landlady's son. He had on a pair of loose *pantelettes* and a tattered shirt, over which he wore an old waistcoat with the buttons missing. On his feet were the wooden sabots familiar to the *sans-culottes*. His hair was loose and hung about his shoulders under a red woolen cap. His face had been blackened with soot and so had his hands, in one of which he carried a bare-bladed small sword. A pistol was stuck into a

61

tricolor sash about his waist. He handed a second weapon to Julien, along with a tricolor cockade like the one in his own cap.

"Put this on, and for the love of Heaven look as though you enjoy wearing it." Julien started to protest, but Cameron cut him short. "This is no time for useless heroics." He mounted his chestnut mare and signaled for the count to get up behind him.

"What are we going to do now?" Julien asked a little fearfully. Cameron was someone to be reckoned with in his present mood.

"You're going to the Place Louis, when we get over the bridge. You can take my horse. Find General Lafayette and tell him you fear Téoline may be in the crowd. He'll instruct his men to be on the lookout for a lady of quality. You ride along with him and pray fortune is on your side."

"And you? . . . Where will you be?" Julien felt safer with Cameron at his side.

"I have arranged to meet some of Lafayette's men. We were going to mingle in the crowd. Now I shall have to give them their instructions and then try to make my way to the Hôtel de Pavigné in the hope Téoline may have had the good sense to stay there."

"But what if she has already left?"

"There's not much I can do except move about in the crowd and hope that by some coincidence I come across her." Cameron's face was grim and he set his horse at a pace that paid scant heed to the people who scrambled to get out of his way.

As soon as they reached the other side of the river he dismounted. "Here," he said, handing over the reins to Julien. "Now find the general as quickly as you can." He gave the mare a sharp tap on the rump and within seconds he was lost to view.

Chapter Eight

"Here you are, ma'mselle!" Téoline sipped gratefully at the hot coffee that was being held to her lips. "That will bring the roses back to your cheeks. I've bathed you well, and there are plenty of bruises but no bones broken, thank the good Lord." The speaker was a plump, wrinkled old woman with a cheerful smile and a soothing voice.

Téoline was too exhausted to speak. When she had drunk all she could, she lay back and tried to make out where she was. The light outside the window was already fading and the candles had been lit. Téo saw that it was a large comfortably furnished bedroom. She was propped against a pile of pillows in a bed with handsome drapes and crisp white sheets. Sensing she was safe, at least for the moment, Téoline relaxed and breathed a sigh of relief. Her hostess looked up from her task of collecting together the bowls and cloths she had been using.

"You may well sigh. It is truly a wicked world, little one! But rest there in peace. I'll away and get you some supper. You'll feel better when your belly is full."

"That goes for both of us, Madame Perrot. And while you're about it, tell Henri to bring another bottle of wine." Andrew Cameron was standing in the doorway; his hair was tousled and his shirt open and hanging loosely over his breeches. The old woman gave a little curtsy and left the room. Cameron ambled toward the bed, carrying a bottle and two glasses in his hand.

"Drink this glass of Malaga," he ordered. "It will do you more good than coffee in your present state."

Téo looked up at him with wide, wondering eyes and pulled the silk coverlet up to her chin. She could smell the sweet wine on his breath. He laughed amiably and set the glass down on the table by the bed.

"Don't worry, Téoline. My own bruises hurt too much to contemplate a further assault." Cameron stood looking down at her, then turned and abruptly left the room, leaving the door open behind him.

As soon as he had gone, Téoline slipped out of bed and pulled the silk bedcover about her slim body. She trailed after him into the other room. Hearing the soft rustle of the silk on the carpet,

Cameron looked up from where he was sitting at a desk. The warm glow from the fire encircled her, turning her hair to a halo of soft gold. He found the picture more than a little disturbing.

"Come on in and sit down," he said sharply. "I'm not going to harm you. I have other things to do." He turned his attention to the papers on his desk. Téo shuffled across to the window and saw that she was in a house on the Boulevard Saint-Germain.

"How did I get here?"

"I didn't abduct you, if that's what you think." Cameron laughed harshly. She was near enough for him to catch the occasional waft of perfume as she moved, and he found it more heady than any wine. My God! It had been a difficult day . . . a terrifying day. Probably one of the worst he had ever lived through.

For a moment, standing there with her in his arms, surrounded by a hostile, howling mob, he had thought they were both about to die. It was something he would never forget. Some said that if you saved a life a bond was forged that could only be severed by death. Was that why he was taken with an intense desire to hold her in his arms again? Getting up, he went over to the wine cabinet and poured himself another glass.

"Will you join me?"

Téoline shook her head and pulled the silk cover closer. She was uncomfortably aware that under the silk, she wore only the flimsiest cotton shift. When he did look at her, the intensity of his gaze was unnerving. Other than her father or Julien, she had never been alone with a man, apart from the priests, who didn't count.

"What happened to my clothes?"

"I imagine that what was left of them have already been consigned to the flames. They were in a worse state than mine, and you can see what is left of those." He pointed toward a pile of bloodstained rags that had been tossed into a corner prior to being taken away. Téoline went across and looked down at them. He saw her start to tremble and quickly turned away, pretending to study visions in the fire.

Téoline was slowly beginning to piece together the details of what had happened to her that day. Finally she recalled with horror the venomous faces of the crowd and had to clutch the back of a chair to prevent herself from swooning with the returning flood of fear that came with the memory.

"So it was you who rescued me? I did not see you there." She was still dazed by the events.

"That's hardly to be wondered at. We were not alone out there. It was fortunate I happened to be amongst the crowd. I heard a commotion and went to see what was happening."

"Thank you m'sieur," she said, moving over toward him near the fire. "You undoubtedly saved my life. I'm sorry I caused you such . . . such inconvenience." Téo searched his face as she fumbled for the right words. He was such a strange man; after the other night, she was not sure what position she held in his esteem.

"Inconvenience! I'd hardly describe what happened today as inconvenient. Do you realize we were only a hair's breadth away from having our heads carried on pikes to Versailles? If Lafayette and some of his men hadn't appeared at that moment, I dread to think what might have happened. I held them at bay as long as I could, but until the guards came it was a losing fight!"

Cameron's tone was brusque as he gazed down on her slender figure. Her skin was translucent in the shaft of moonlight and her thick dark lashes caressed her cheeks like butterfly wings. Irritably he turned away and walked swiftly to the window. Téoline thought she must have angered him and that he found her thanks inadequate.

"I must express my gratitude to the general when next we meet," she said, while trying to think of something that might appease Cameron. "I would like to find some form of recompense for your part, m'sieur . . ." Before she could finish, Cameron was across the room, his eyes blazing.

"It appears the de Pavignés make a habit of insulting their rescuers by offering largesse. What will you do now? Call a lackey and have him show me the door?"

Téoline put a hand to her mouth to stifle a cry. Too late, she realized what she had said. She had echoed her father's words, but with a totally different intent. In her anxiety she had allowed the coverlet to slip from her grasp, and she stood in the simple white shift, her body silhouetted against the flames. All the pent-up fury Cameron had felt against the mob . . . against the de Pavignés . . . against his own inadequacies . . . were suddenly directed against Téoline.

"You're right, mademoiselle. A laborer is worthy of his hire." Gathering her up into his arms, he carried her through to the other room and tossed her on the bed like a bundle of rags. "It's time I collected from a de Pavigné," he said. Ripping his shirt over his head, he flung himself down and rolled on top of her.

He pressed his mouth over hers so fiercely she could scarcely breathe, and under his weight it was impossible for her to move. He tore away the shift and she felt his hard warm chest against her naked flesh. "Damn de Pavigné!" he muttered, before kissing her again. His fingers explored the circle of her breast and traced the smooth firm lines of her thighs. She gasped for air as he moved his head to follow the line with his lips. Her perfume mixed with the Malaga in his brain and stirred him to a demon fury. After all these years this was a sweet revenge. As he kissed her mouth again, his lips tasted the salt of her tears.

For a second he remained quite still, feeling the trembling of her limbs beneath his own. She did not attempt to move and he knew she was his for the taking. Propping himself up, he looked down at her pale young face. Her eyes were closed but fresh tears sparkled on the lashes. In a startling flash, Cameron saw not Téoline, so limp and white, but his sister, Fiona Cameron. Such a brutish act as this had left her the merest shadow of a woman. For years she had drifted through life like flotsam after a storm. No revenge was worth that price. He rolled off the bed and without a backward glance went across to a stool. Picking up a silk dressing gown, he flung it across her naked form on the bed.

"Put that on and come to supper. I'll call Madame Perrot and have her find you some clothes. When we've eaten, I'll see if it is possible to take you home." He strode out of the room, slamming the door behind him.

For some time Téoline lay quite still, gazing at the shadows on the wall. Her mind was completely numb. All she could recall was Cameron's order to come to supper. Then slowly, mechanically, she dragged herself off the bed and slid into the gown. It was far too big, and she took time to adjust it with delicate precision, moving as though it were the most important task in the world.

When she had finished, she went over to the washstand and poured some water into the bowl. It was cold and refreshing. She moved trancelike to the dresser and, taking up a silver-backed brush, carefully arranged her hair. She could hear Sister Superior admonishing her to always be clean and tidy before going to supper. Perhaps, if she were obedient, she would never have to think or feel anything again.

There was a tap on the door and Madame Perrot came in. "Supper is served, ma'mselle. While you are eating it, I'll put out some clothes belonging to my daughter. She's married now and lives in Lyon, but I think I still have some of her things packed away." She curtsied and waited for Téoline to precede her into the front room.

A small table had been set up in front of the fire. On it there was a steaming tureen of soup, and from a basket came the sweet smell of fresh bread hot from the oven. The aroma of food reminded Téoline that she had not eaten since the previous day.

Cameron was standing in front of the fire smoking a long churchwarden pipe. He was fully clothed and wore black leather riding boots. "Sit down and get on with it," he said without looking at her. She might have been a child he was giving orders to. "I've sent my man to see if the streets are safe. When they are, I'll see you safely back to Saint-Honoré"

Madame Perrot had served two bowls of soup before leaving the room, but Téo made no attempt to touch the food. "Eat it!" Cameron said roughly as he took his place at the table opposite her. "After all you've been through, you need to build up your strength. There's no telling what further trouble may lie ahead." He glowered at her. Why didn't she say something? Cameron could have coped with her anger, even her contempt; but her silence disturbed him.

"Haven't you anything to say to me?" He slammed down his spoon. If only he could provoke some form of response.

"I think the soup is very good. It is very kind of Madame Perrot."

" . . . It's very kind of Madame Perrot . . .!" Cameron mimicked her with a savage cruelty. "My God! Haven't you the slightest idea what prompted me to behave so disgustingly just now?" He turned his contempt against himself.

Téoline stared back at him solemnly and spoke in a quiet voice. "You wanted revenge. I can understand. You thought I wanted to insult you as my father had done. But truly, nothing was farther from my mind."

The simplicity of her statement shattered him. He wished to Heaven it wasn't regarded as unmanly to cry. He felt that only tears could wash away his shame. Instead, he took the only recourse open to him.

"You're a child, Téoline; you must learn to grow up." His voice was tense as he tried to hold back a mounting desire to take her in his arms again. "Your innocence provokes men and the sin is yours. It is in such a way that Adam was tempted by Eve. You have only read of life in books. You speak knowingly of liberty and the value we place on words"—his voice rose an-

67

grily—"but you know nothing of the meaning of love. Grow up, Téoline!"

When he first began speaking, Téo's lip had started to tremble like a child's. But as his tempo quickened and the words found their mark, her pride surfaced along with all the pent-up terror of the day and moved her to rage.

"I hate you, André Cameron. I hate all men. They take what they want and leave women to pay," she screamed.

"Stop that! You're becoming hysterical." He went to put a hand on her shoulder, recognizing that in his own distress he had gone too far. She pushed him away.

"Get away," she screamed, flinging herself on the settee and beating it with her fists as she had done the day her father had taken his whip to her. "I hate you . . . I hate them . . .!" She was thinking of her father and de Beben. "Holy Mother of God! What is left for me?" A fresh flood of tears engulfed her.

Cameron stood helpless. He had never been faced with such anguish before. The girl was shaken to the very depths of her soul by all she had been through, and he had been the cause of her breaking down.

Picking up a cushion, Téoline flung it across the room and sent a vase crashing to the floor. The sound of the glass breaking added to the tempest in her head. She leaped to her feet and with one sweep of her arm sent the contents of the table hurtling to the ground. By now she was completely beside herself.

"Téoline!" Cameron spoke her name softly.

Turning, she sprang at him. Swiftly he encircled her in his arms. She writhed to free herself, but all she could do was beat impotently against his chest with her fists. Cameron bent down and sought to stifle her screams with a kiss. Her rage turned to a savage ecstasy and she returned it, pressing her mouth against his. The world spun out and time ceased to exist as they gazed into each other's eyes and saw their own unspoken desire reflected there. She slid her arm around his neck. He gathered her into his arms, and this time her body was soft and yielding to his touch. What had begun as a gesture of pity had become a passion he could no longer resist.

For a fleeting second, Cameron tried to reason against his own will, but the battle was already lost. Téo would inflame other men with this desire. They would savage and brutalize her with their lust. Better that she should learn from him. He swung her up into his arms and, carrying her into the other room, placed her gently on the bed.

Once or twice during the night, Téoline stirred in her sleep, disturbed by the torrential rains beating against the windows. Finding herself cradled in Cameron's arms, she snuggled closer and drifted back into the dream world their lovemaking had created. How long they had lain together entwined in each other's arms neither of them knew, but their sleep was suddenly shattered by a rude knocking on the door below.

Cameron was out of bed in a moment and struggling into his clothes. The moon had long since been hidden behind the clouds, and it was pitch black outside. He cursed loudly as he fumbled for a flint to light the candle; the fire had died and the embers afforded no glow.

"Quick," he said as the room sprang to life with the light. "Put on those clothes, but don't show yourself until I call."

He handed her a bundle Madame Perrot had left in the other room. Downstairs, the bolts on the front door were being drawn. Cameron went to see what it was all about.

Hastily Téoline obeyed; the times were too dangerous to delay. The voluminous cotton gown engulfed her, but she ripped the tape from a petticoat and tied it up about her waist. Setting a frilled white cap over her hair, she flung a gray woolen shawl about her shoulders. A quick glance in the mirror contented her that she could pass for a serving wench. She stole quietly over to the bedroom door and stood behind it, trying to hear what was being said in the hall below. The voices were agitated but too low for her to make sense of the words.

A few more seconds passed, and then she heard footsteps on the stairs. She drew back into the depth of the room and waited. "It's all right, Téoline. It's safe for you to come out." Cameron's voice was reassuring. Cautiously she edged her way into the front room. Their visitor was a frightened, wet, bedraggled boy.

"Julien!" She ran to her brother and flung her arms about him. "Oh, Julien, thank God you're safe." Tears of relief filled both pairs of eyes and the count clung to her pathetically.

"I was so afraid—" he started to say, but a warning glance from Cameron silenced him. A servant had just entered and was busy relighting the fire. As soon as he was done, Cameron sent the man to fetch a hot drink.

"What happened?" he inquired, once the man was safely out of hearing. He was standing by the window, having pulled back the drapes. Outside, the first gray fingers of dawn streaked the night sky. The rain had ceased. For the moment the city was still, but the very quiet seemed foreboding. "I thought their anger might have evaporated a little by the time the mob reached Versailles." He poured three glasses of Malaga and handed them around. This time Téoline did not refuse.

"It took more than six hours by the time they had stopped at all the taverns along the way. By then, most were so drunk or tired they only wanted to sleep," Julien began. "But there were always the few noisy ones ready to goad them on. Nevertheless, all seemed to go well at first. Mirabeau took some of them into the Assembly while Lafayette persuaded the King to speak with two of the women."

"That was a miracle in itself," Cameron commented.

"When they returned, they had the King's personal assurance their grievances would all be set right. There were loud chants of 'Long live the King,' and everyone thought the danger had passed. The members of the Assembly went home and took some of the younger women with them. Lafayette arranged for me to quarter with some of his officers . . . I was still hoping to get some word of you, Téo. Thank God you found her, André. I dread to think what might have happened to her in the midst of that mob."

Téoline opened her mouth to tell him her side of the story, but Julien did not wait for her to speak.

"Most of the people just camped around bonfires in the streets. The rain had stopped for a time, but then it began again, heavier than before. They were cold and hungry and they started to quarrel amongst themselves. The ringleaders were not content with the King's promises. I wasn't there, but I heard about it when a guard came to warn us they were on the march again. Rumor had spread that Paris had been kept without any bread for the past week on the express orders of the King and Queen. Their Majesties thought it would help quell the riots and keep the people quiet."

Cameron gave a wry laugh. "It's true the shortage was deliberate. But the orders for it came from the Duc de'Orléans. He and his coterie at the Palais-Royal obviously staged this. What quicker route to the throne of France than to have the people rise up and kill the King? But what happened then?"

"The mob went mad again. They stormed the palace and killed two of the Swiss Guard who tried to bar their way to the royal suite." Julien's voice broke and he covered his face with his hands. It was a moment or so before he could go on. "It was terrible. I was there when a big fellow with a beard hacked off their heads with a butcher's knife. He tossed them to the crowds, who were howling for blood like a pack of wild animals. They stuck the two heads onto pikes and carried them before them like trophies. At one point they dragged a barber from his bed and forced him to dress and powder the hair, which was matted with blood."

Téoline shuddered as she recalled the faces of the men in the crowd and wondered if the man who kissed her had done the deed.

"What happened to the King and Queen?" Cameron's face was grim. The details were bad enough but the portents could be worse. The rest of France might well follow the Paris mob.

"They were screaming for him and the head of 'the Austrian jade.' Lafayette and his men could do nothing against such odds. He managed to get them to agree to return to Paris—but only if the King and Queen accompanied them. They are bringing them back to reside in the Tuileries." Julien started, thinking he heard a noise. "That's probably them now. I left them more than an hour ago." Cameron went back to the window, and this time he left it open a little way. "It was so lucky I still had your horse, André, or I might never have been able to get away. But as soon as I got the chance I cut off across the fields."

"Shouldn't you have gone for help?" Téoline felt that something more should have been done, though exactly what, she was not sure.

Julien looked a little shamefaced and shook his head. "I could only think of getting away. Besides, I don't know who to trust."

"Julien was quite right," Cameron cut in. "In a situation such as this, expediency is best and self-preservation the only thing. There are too many men in Paris who are ready to sell France to the highest bidder."

Téoline looked from one to the other in bewilderment. "I cannot believe that," she said. "A man would always put his country before his personal greed. I, for one, would die for France."

"You may have to, but let's hope it won't come to that," Cameron said brusquely. "But this is no time for heroics, and it would be less wasteful if you were to *live* for it." His mind was already calculating what the cost would be for him and how all this might affect world trade. Not only did he have his own interests to look after but he felt a certain responsibility to these two children. "Forget the grand gestures, Téoline. No one would even notice if you went out there and offered yourself up as a sacrifice. Martyrs may have their place, but not at a time like this."

71

Téoline looked at him with a blank expression on her face. She couldn't believe this was the same man who had made sweet and passionate love to her only a few hours ago.

"Téoline, you'll find some dry clothes suitable for Julien in the armoire in there." Cameron nodded towards the bedroom. "Sort them out for him . . . and you, Julien, go in there and change. When you're ready, we'll discuss what is best to do." He was already busy sorting through the papers on his desk. In a few moments Téoline was back at his side.

"You don't need to worry," he said with his mind on other things. "I told Julien I brought you here for safety. He met Madame Perrot downstairs; your reputation is intact."

"I wasn't thinking of that, André. I was thinking about us. What is to happen now?" She kissed the top of his head as he bent low over the desk. He got up and went across to burn some documents in the fire. She followed him and put an arm about his waist.

He raised his hand and, gently pushing back the curls from her brow, kissed it; at the same time he removed her arm and stepped away. Then he gave a warning glance toward the bedroom door. "We'll talk about it as soon as Julien comes back." He returned to the desk. Sorting through the drawers, he produced some maps and laid them out upon the table. He appeared to be checking routes and distances; some of his vessels were due in French ports.

"But André . . ." The tears brimmed in Téoline's eyes. "I thought that after last night . . .?"

"Think of that as a wonderful dream. A precious moment in time that neither of us will quickly forget." The silence was so acute it forced him to look up and at the desolate Téoline.

"I shall never forget. I shall love you throughout eternity, André."

He laughed and pulled her hair playfully. "No, my love, love does not last as long as that. I sometimes doubt if there is such a thing."

"But last night . . . wasn't that love?"

"You may think of it like that if you wish. Some would call it lust. I think a more attractive word is desire." He took her hand and lifted it to his lips.

"I wouldn't know. It is the first time such a thing has happened to me. But I felt we had become one . . . that you were a part of me. I cannot let you go . . . André." She looked up at him pleadingly.

"I'm afraid you must, my dear. We both have things to do and different lives to lead." He turned back to his charts.

"But what do I do now?"

"Go home!" he said over his shoulder.

"And marry de Beben?"

"God forbid! Surely you have more pride than that!" He drew a line linking two ports and started to check the tides from an almanac. "You wait, Téoline. One day the right man will come along, you'll see."

"How little you know my father, if you think he would agree to that." At last his indifference was beginning to register on her.

"After what has happened here today, even the Duc de Pavigné might have second thoughts. If not, then leave him . . . leave his house." He raised his head and saw the look of blank amazement on her face. "If money is the problem, I'll set you up in an apartment—make you completely independent of him."

Memories of Julie Saint-Laurent and Hélène Beaulieu filtered into her mind. Was this how it had begun for them? Was she destined to become a courtesan, the mistress of any man willing to pay the price? She shuddered at the thought. Whatever André might say, she was sure she loved him; it would never be the same again.

"I'm not a common whore," she said, summoning what remained of her pride to her aid.

"Of course not! I never suggested you were," Cameron retorted angrily. "You don't think I was contemplating your becoming my mistress? If so, you may put the idea out of your head. I shall be at the other end of the world in a few weeks. But when I return to Paris, I will always call on you, if I may. In the meantime I will arrange with my bankers for a regular allowance to be paid in your name."

"Thank you, m'sieur. But that will not be necessary." She could bear no more. Her only protection was to let her love turn to hate. "I do not take such favors from a man I do not know."

She intended her words to sting, and they did. She walked over to the window and looked down into the street. He stopped what he was doing and stood still, watching her. A desperate sense of loss came over him. Téoline was not like the other women he had known. This night would be imprinted on his mind, if not his heart.

"Very well, Téoline. But I should not wish to see harm come to you." His voice was gruff to hide the emotion he dared not show.

"I absolve you from any guilt, m'sieur. We will consider this . . . incident . . . as the repayment of a debt."

She walked across to greet the returning Julien, leaving Cameron wondering who was the recipient. Did she mean that he had taken his revenge or that she no longer owed him for her life?

Julien was as distressed as she. "I don't know what to do. I cannot go home again, and I have no means of support."

"I've been thinking about that," Cameron said abruptly. He knew the duke was unlikely to be in a hurry to forgive his son, and he remembered how Philippe had died. It was a quarrel over him that had led the elder son to go on a wild ride to cool his rage. He had fallen and broken his neck. It had been Angus Cameron, his father, who found the body and took the news to the duke. He didn't want such a thing to happen again.

"You had best come with me. I'll be leaving for England as soon as I have attended to some matters here. I can give you letters of introduction and see you safely settled. There are already a number of émigrés over there. You can find work as they have done." He laughed at the expression of horror on the young count's face. "It won't kill you. Oh, and Téoline, you had better have these. Madame Perrot gave them to me. She found them tucked in the bodice of your gown." Cameron picked up the kerchief with de Beben's diamonds.

"Take them as payment for services rendered, m'sieur. If it is in excess after you have taken for Julien's passage, you may give the rest to him." Before Cameron could reply, she had gone to her brother and flung her arms around him.

"God keep you, Julien, and pray it will not be long before we meet again. Now, m'sieur, if you will instruct your man to see me home?"

"I'll take you myself," Cameron spat back. He was stung to the quick by her last remarks.

"That is not necessary, m'sieur. Dressed as I am, I'm not likely to be mistaken for a lady, and I would prefer not to be in your debt a second time."

Chapter Nine

"You are sure?"

"Yes, mademoiselle . . . madame." The doctor hastily corrected himself, although he was pretty certain his young patient wasn't married. Her attitude was far too naïve. "If all goes well, and there is no reason to suspect it shouldn't, your baby will be born in the late spring or early summer of next year." He was sorry for her. Most of his living came from attending ladies of questionable virtue; it was a pity she had started so young. Of course, it was not unusual, but this one seemed particularly pure and innocent. Unfortunately, that was life! The old man sighed and started to pack his instruments away. He guessed Madame Saint-Laurent would want him out of the house before too many people saw him. The gossips would soon be onto it anyway; he had no intention of helping them along.

He looked at his patient, who was sitting quietly in what appeared to be a state of shock. "Perhaps the gentleman concerned . . .?"

"He doesn't know, and I haven't the least intention of telling him!" The upsurge of hostility she felt toward Andrew Cameron brought Téoline to her senses. She reached into her little pompadour bag and took out a handful of gold louis. "I am obliged to you, m'sieur. I trust this will compensate you for your trouble?"

"But madame . . . ma'mselle! Half this will suffice." He was getting old and preferred to be able to sleep at night. He couldn't take advantage of such a child. But Téoline pressed the money into his hand; kind as he was, she wanted to be rid of him.

As soon as he had gone, she finished straightening her dress and went into the other room, where Julie Saint-Laurent and Hélène were waiting. It was obvious from the expression on their faces that they knew what the doctor's verdict was. Hélène had suspected it for some weeks, and after Monsieur Beaulard complained that he couldn't complete Mademoiselle de Pavigné's trousseau if she kept putting on weight, she suggested the visit that had just taken place. Julie had very sweetly offered to arrange it so that neither the duke nor his servants would be aware of the visit.

"Won't you tell us who is responsible?" Julie pleaded.

"Did it happen during that awful day when the women marched on Versailles? You know no other men apart from de Beben, and he is away. It was a rape, wasn't it?" Hélène had been racking her brains thinking of every possibility. She knew that was the only time it could have occurred, because her young charge was never alone long enough with a man.

Téoline shook her head. She knew they meant well, but she would not be drawn. "There was no rape . . . not of my body, anyway!" For almost two months now she had lain awake at night wondering what was happening to her body. She knew what had happened to her heart—it had turned to stone. Her only blessing, she thought bitterly, was that she was being allowed to suffer her torment alone.

De Beben was still away in Marseilles. Whether on business or undergoing treatment, Téo neither knew nor cared. As for her father, he was preoccupied with events in the capital and elsewhere in France. The royal family were lodged in the palace of the Tuileries, virtually prisoners of the people, although Louis was still acknowledged as their King. With municipal revolutions taking place in cities throughout the country, everyone was worried how long even this semblance of power would last. But for the moment, Mirabeau and Lafayette were managing to keep matters reasonably under control.

"What will you tell Monsieur and Albert de Beben?" Hélène asked anxiously. They were back in Téoline's apartment at Saint-Honoré. "You cannot go to Saint-Domingue without telling de Beben. It would be better that he rejected you and the child here in France. Out there, you will be so alone." Hélène was meaning to find some solution to the problem, but her words sent a shiver down Téo's spine. "Of course it is possible he may accept the child as his. It would not be the first time it has been done. But Monsieur . . .?"

"Monsieur would not hesitate. He would send me away to a convent, and when the baby was born it would be sent to an orphanage. I would never see it again."

"Do you want this child, Téoline?"

"More than anything in the world." Téoline could not have explained how much it meant to her. This child would be all she had to remind her of André. Although she told herself she hated the man who had led her to this, in her heart she knew she would never be able to free herself of his memory.

Madame Beaulieu fluttered around the boudoir like an agitated bird trying to escape a cage. She knew the duke's rage would be boundless if he learned his daughter had been seduced. Undoubtedly he would hold her to blame. Suddenly she stopped and looked at Téoline, who was resting on a chair.

"A patron, Téo, you must take a patron! Heaven knows it will be easy enough for you. You can take the pick of the crop. Why, Mirabeau himself would be overjoyed. Think of it, little one, no one would dare so much as whisper about you, if you were to give yourself to Mirabeau!" Hélène was delighted to think she had found such a perfect solution. Her words offered Téoline a glimmer of hope but she had already begun to formulate another plan.

The following day Albert de Beben returned. He said he was enchanted to see her and plied her with gifts; however, over supper that night he paid her scant attention. Téoline was more than happy, and knowing all that she did both about his health and her own condition, she preferred not to be forced into conversation. It sounded, from all he had to say to her father, that his visit to the south of France had indeed been for business.

"I am gravely concerned," he said over dessert. "This revolutionary fervor is spreading like the plague. It has reached the ports, and the sailors are proudly sporting the tricolor and calling for a republic. You know what this means, m'sieur? At any moment we can expect the infection to be spread throughout the colonies."

"Haven't the *grands blancs* in Saint-Domingue sufficient power to quell the first signs of it? It must be stamped out at once," the duke said sternly. "The germ must not be allowed to breed."

"I agree with you wholeheartedly, m'sieur. If I had my way, anyone who talked of granting the people of color their civil rights or freeing the slaves would be hanged. But I fear there are some, even amongst the white aristocracy, who tend to favor the mulattoes' cause. The slaves are less of a problem; they are scarcely better than animals and lack the intelligence to become organized."

"These terms concerning the people, Albert," Téoline said as she interrupted, "could you explain what they mean?" Though she had no desire to participate in this distasteful conversation, she wanted to know what might be awaiting her if she went to the colony.

"Most certainly, my dear, although you do not need to trouble your pretty head. But you will need to know the position or you may find yourself embarrassed by people who, in my opinion, should not even be allowed to live. The *grands blancs* are people of rank, like ourselves," he said, proud at being able to number himself with the de Pavignés. "Then there are the *petits blancs*—lawyers, doctors and such. Mark you, there are many who aspire to that estate although they are little better than scum. I have little truck with them; their loyalty to us is very fragile at the best of times. The *affranchis*, that is, the free coloreds, have in many cases accumulated considerable wealth, and the *petits blancs* are just as likely to be serving them. They tend to go where the money is."

"And the *gens de couleur*?" Téoline asked. The name of Stefan Cambenet had suddenly come into her mind although there was no reason to suspect he came from Saint-Domingue. However, the social divisions were likely to be the same whether there or in Martinique or other colonies in the Indies.

"They give us more trouble than anyone. Their colors range from black to almost white; it is hard to tell them apart by their skin. Most unfortunately, many of them have been highly educated, and for that the *grands blancs* must answer. In the past it was often the practice for the white colonists to send the children they had by their slaves to be educated in France. It salved their consciences and saved them the embarrassment of having to acknowledge them. Now many of them are coming home to plague us."

"Vincent Ogé is such a one, I presume?" the Duc de Pavigné inquired.

"Exactly! His mother is an *affranchie* with large estates near some of mine. He is a troublemaker bent on seeing the coloreds gain their rights. I dread to think what might happen if he were to return to Saint-Domingue."

"Then he must be prevented at all cost. Leave that to me, m'sieur. You have powerful friends in the Club Massiac, and—for the moment at least—we have the ear of Mirabeau," the duke replied. Téoline smiled quietly to herself.

A few months ago she would have counted it a grievous sin to even think of what she planned to do. But Téoline's initiation into the ways of the world had been a harsh one. She now accepted that to lie and cheat were not accounted sins; to do so was only to bow to expediency, not to do so made you look a fool. Honesty, loyalty, and truth were best left to books, and in any case, meant different things to different people. She had found that the men and women about her believed in equality and liberty for themselves and no one else. What distressed her most in all this was to discover that, if the occasion demanded, she too could turn her back on God and yet sleep.

De Beben became more and more worried about what might be happening back in Saint-Domingue, and the duke agreed it would be best if he were to return home. Under these circumstances the marriage date was set. It was to be a quiet ceremony, after which the bride and groom would leave immediately for the West Indies. In deference to de Beben's generous settlement and his own pride, the duke insisted on a grand reception the night before the wedding.

On learning these plans, Téoline penned her note to Mirabeau.

Albert de Beben viewed his future bride as though she were his own creation. He had not failed to notice that her figure was rounder and her beauty growing riper by the day. She had been no more than a pretty child when he first saw her. She was a woman now, and he chuckled with pride as he imagined how many heads she would turn in Saint-Domingue. She was wearing a blue satin gown, the lace at her bosom held by a diamond pin. He had given her the pin and many other gifts to replace the diamonds stolen from her coach during that terrible business at Versailles. It had pained him to hear how she was robbed, but the jewels were insured, so he did not feel the loss where it would have hurt most. He had no doubt at all that his investment was going to pay handsome dividends.

Téoline was thankful that she was less sick now than she had been in the early days of her pregnancy, but the heat and noise in the *grand salon* was making her feel dizzy. What if Mirabeau failed to come? She pushed such thoughts from her mind, as she remembered his admiring glances.

"Mademoiselle Téoline . . . sweetest . . . I was heartbroken when I received your letter of farewell. I cannot conceive of Paris without you." Mirabeau grasped her hand and smothered it with kisses. He also noticed how much softer and more seductive her figure was; it made his desire burn anew. "I must speak with you alone," he whispered, his tone filled with urgency. De Beben came forward, hoping to be included in the tête-à-tête.

"You are a lucky man, m'sieur." Mirabeau made no attempt to hide his distaste. "Take good care of her. I'll not dissemble, I would give anything to be in your place."

De Beben beamed; never had the great man troubled to speak to him before.

"Come, my little one. I have things I must say to you." Mirabeau drew Téoline's arm through his, and for once she did not mind that all eyes were upon her. She allowed him to lead her away into the seclusion of the *petit salon*.

"I cannot believe I shall never see you again, *ma chérie*." He drew her down beside him on the settee. Téoline fought to stifle a smile. All was not lost. Mirabeau still had hopes he might win her, if only for a night.

"You must know how you have tantalized me all these weeks . . . I will not be cheated, ma'mselle," he breathed in her ear. "I cannot live without you, my little flower." His ugly face was flushed and the hands that clasped hers to his heart were damp.

Téoline broke away and moved behind a small table. It was part of her design to be with Mirabeau alone for a time, but she had no wish for him to be so ardent in his protestations of undying love. She looked at him and thought of Andrew Cameron. What if he were right and there was only lust? She did not want to believe it was so.

"See . . .!" Mirabeau fumbled in the pocket of his velvet coat. "I commissioned this for you when I received your note saying you were going away." He held out a small miniature of himself painted on ivory and framed with diamonds.

Téoline took it and cooed with appropriate delight. He lies, she thought. There had not been time; he probably keeps a stock of these.

"Love me, *chérie*, and I will give you the world." He pursued her across the floor.

"I am honored, m'sieur," she said, stepping aside. "But we must let honor itself come before our own desires. I am committed to Albert de Beben as you . . ." She sought frantically to think of some means of distracting him. He was breathing heavily and she was afraid she would not be able to hold him at bay much longer. "As you, Honoré, are committed to France." Her words made him pause, and she was able to put a small distance between them.

"Let our regard for each other remain pure and unsullied . . . let it bind us in a troth that transcends mortality!" she said. Téoline had an uneasy feeling that she had read those words somewhere before, but she could find none of her own. "You can and must be the savior of France," she continued. This time her words were quite sincere. Rogue and libertine that he was,

Mirabeau had that power. The passionate sweetness of her appeal touched Mirabeau's romantic heart.

"Téoline,"—he dropped to his knees before her and clutched at her skirt—"you have understood me as no other woman has ever done. You see more than the pitiful beast in me . . ." The tears ran down his pudgy face.

"M'sieur . . . Honoré . . . you must not kneel to me!" She looked about her, seeking to find some means of comforting the morose creature weeping at her feet. It was then that her eyes fell on Albert de Beben, watching them from the doorway of the *petit salon.*

"I will kneel to you, Téoline . . . I shall see to it that all France kneels to you . . .!"

"Honoré," she said, bending down and murmuring softly in his ear, "France is waiting, and so is Monsieur de Beben!"

With great difficulty, Mirabeau struggled to his feet and once again pressed her hand to his lips. Téoline knew that he was too sophisticated to go against the tide of fortune. He bowed and walked toward the door with tremendous dignity. He was a fool where women were concerned, but he had a lion's heart. He stopped and looked at de Beben then said, in a voice ringing with emotion. "M'sieur, be warned! Allow any harm to come to Mademoiselle de Pavigné and you will answer not only to me . . . but to the whole of France!" The orator had spoken. He bowed again and stalked off like an overweight Caesar.

The tension of the past few minutes had been too much for Téoline, and she collapsed into a chair, laughing and crying hysterically. She was not sure whether she had the courage to go through with what she had so carefully planned. De Beben hurried to her side in a state of utter confusion. He was dazzled by the fact that Mirabeau had spoken to him again and charged him personally with Téoline's care.

"I cannot marry you, Albert!" She said after a few moment's silence.

"But no!" de Beben gasped with surprise. "I cannot believe my ears! Did you not hear? Mirabeau, himself, has charged me to watch over you."

"He has his own reasons, m'sieur, and I have mine. This marriage cannot take place. I cannot deceive you, I am carrying another man's child!"

Albert de Beben staggered as though he had been shot. Fearing he would collapse, Téoline got up quickly and assisted him into her chair. Opening the fan that hung from her wrist, she fluttered it across his face. "You must be careful, m'sieur. I understand you have been sick." Her concern was genuine. She had not intended to add salt to his wound.

"You have been listening to lies," he said, clasping her hand. "People have been telling you lies about me. I am not a young man, mademoiselle, but there is nothing wrong with me, I swear." The sweat rolled down the creases in his face.

"I believe you, m'sieur, as I expect you to believe me when I say I am sorry this marriage cannot take place."

"You intend to marry this other man, whoever he is?" he asked in a quavering voice.

"No, m'sieur. That is not possible. I have renounced him, and I doubt if we shall ever meet again."

"You will not tell me who he is?"

"I cannot. The secret is not mine alone; it might jeopardize the future of his child." De Beben's face twitched as conflicting emotions swept over him. His eyes fell on the little miniature. "Mirabeau gave you this?" he said picking it up.

"Yes . . .!" Téoline swallowed hard. Her plan was succeeding better than she could have ever hoped. "A keepsake that I shall one day pass on to my son." It was not a lie, she told herself, but a distortion of the truth. It was obvious from the expression in de Beben's eyes that she had directed him to see it as she wished him to.

"The child is Mirabeau's." He whispered the words. "That would explain everything." He looked up at her and said with a fierce glee, "Mirabeau cannot marry you, so he charges me to act as father to his child. Would you deny me this honor, mademoiselle?" He clasped her hand. "Believe me, Téoline, I swear it shall be as my own flesh and blood. It is true that I hoped to father an heir, but what better heir could a man have than the son of Mirabeau?"

"I would not want anyone to know," Téoline said gravely.

"The secret will be ours, *ma chérie*." De Beben's eyes glittered with delight. To be cuckolded before his wedding day was a small price to pay for such a prize. Mirabeau and all the power he commanded could be made to serve him. He offered Téoline his arm, and together they returned to the assembly.

Téoline was thankful to see that Mirabeau had already left. If God would forgive her, then no great harm had been done and her son's future was assured. It would be a boy; that she knew. It was a man's world, and she did not wish him to suffer as a woman would. He would look like André, but he would be hers and hers alone.

HISPANIOLA, 1790

Chapter Ten

Téoline gazed out over Cap Français to the line where the sea
and sky met at the edge of the world. She was standing on the
decorative iron balcony of de Beben's house in a cobbled square
of the city. She could see the terraced streets of Le Cap de-
scending to the palm-fringed shore of the bay. The last fingers
of light laced the darkening water with shadows from the masts
of the tall ships in the harbor.

As she watched, there was a sudden flash and the sun vanished behind the purple mountains that ringed the northern capital, leaving them drained of color. Their jagged peaks were
stark and forboding against the sky. It was no wonder the na-
tives called Hispaniola "the Magic Isle."

Evening had brought a cooling breeze after the oppressive
heat of the day. Téoline shivered, whether from the cold or the
utter loneliness of her situation she neither knew nor cared. Was
it six months ago or only yesterday that she had stood on a similar balcony outside the Hôtel de Pavigné with Julien at her side
and looked out over Paris? She sighed as she wondered if she
would ever see France again. So much had happened to her
since then; it seemed a lifetime ago.

Time was playing tricks. She was unaware of how long she
had been standing there; it might have been hours or minutes.
The present and the past, time and space, were dissolving into a
nightmare of unreality. Her world was fragmenting like the
glass in a kaleidoscope. The patterns were constantly changing,
yet the individual pieces remained the same. There was always
enough of the original design left to tempt her into a sense of se-
curity, yet her heart told her that world no longer existed.
Téoline was training herself to expect the unexpected.

A liveried footman came out of a house on the opposite side of
the square and took down a lantern from an iron hook in the
wall beside the front doors. It was a familiar task; she had seen
it performed many times by her father's servants in Paris. The
light from the candle flickered on his powdered wig and the gold
braid of his uniform, but there were no white stockings beneath
his satin breeches—his feet and legs were bare. The spell was
broken again. He turned round, and she saw his face was a deep

mahogany. There had been black servants in France, of course, but this man was a slave. The color of a person's skin had never worried her before, but then she had been living in a white world. Now, like the night, blackness was closing in on her.

The bell in the steeple of a nearby church began to toll the hour of the Angelus. Subconsciously, Téoline's lips moved in silent prayer, but the words were beginning to lose their potency. She wondered what Charlotte and the other novices were doing. Would they be wending their way to chapel for Benediction? . . . She wasn't sure. Again it was a question of time.

When she had finished, Téoline crossed herself and went into her boudoir, closing the shutters behind her. It added to the stifling heat inside the room, but it shut out the sight and some of the sounds of the city. Unfortunately the stench from the gutters filtered through the slats, mingling with the heavy perfume of jasmine and the cloying odors of sugar and spice.

The room was large, with a high ceiling elaborately decorated with white plaster cherubs garlanded with flowers. The furnishings, like most things on the island, including the stones for the house, had been imported from France or other parts of the civilized world. They were heavy, ornate, and very expensive, but they lacked a sense of taste. Téoline smiled to herself as she thought how Hélène Beaulieu would have reacted to such a crass display. "*Mon Dieu!*" she could hear Madame say. "It is a veritable mausoleum, is it not?" How she missed Hélène and the cool elegance of her apartment in Saint-Honoré.

Her baggage had been unpacked, and thankfully she changed into a loose gown. With tight corseting it was still impossible to diagnose her condition with any certainty. She had some difficulty in releasing the laces, but for the moment she didn't want to call a slave. She would have to find a new lady's maid. Nina had agreed to come with her, but the wretched girl had deserted her when the ship reached Martinique. She had taken a trunk full of Téo's new clothes and some of her jewelry. Albert had been furious and had sworn out a warrant for her arrest, but the governor of the island had warned them there was little chance of the girl's being caught. There were too many nearby islands and a pretty woman always had the means to buy passage anywhere she pleased.

What a journey it had been. A few days out of Le Havre, Albert had succumbed to an attack. Samson, the mulatto dwarf, had said it was no more than a fever, but he refused to let Téoline near the cabin, saying it could be contagious and that her husband would prefer she stayed away. The little man was almost excessively polite, but she mistrusted the glint in his sharp eyes. She was sure he resented her. He refused to discuss Albert's affairs with her, saying he must wait for the master's permission. It had made matters very difficult, especially as she had no knowledge of what awaited her in Saint-Domingue. Fortunately Albert had recovered by the time they reached the other island colonies. He had been anxious to show off his bride to the governors and local nobility. It had been very foolish of him because he was far too weak, and as a consequence he had had a relapse. By the time they docked at Le Cap he was unconscious.

Téoline had felt so helpless; she was entirely dependent upon Samson, and he refused to discuss anything with her. The ship's captain came to her rescue and said it would be wiser if a doctor were called before Albert was moved. Téo had insisted this should be done, and Samson had been forced to send Davide for Dr. Chevrier.

While she was waiting, Téo stood out on deck and watched the crowds thronging the quays. There were men and women of every nationality and color, but she noticed that for every white skin there were at least a dozen darker ones. There were hundreds of slaves laboring under the burning sun to unload the ships. She was appalled by the conditions under which they worked and shuddered at their cries when the overseers drove them on with whips.

Le Cap was one of the most prosperous ports in the world and a center for both merchants and visitors. It was interesting to see the variety of people but heartbreaking that they seemed totally indifferent to the plight of the slaves. Samson was quick to notice her discomfort. He appeared to be very amused by it and called out insults to the slaves who were carrying the baggage ashore. Téoline was a stranger in an alien land, so there was little she could do, but she vowed that when she knew a little more about conditions in Saint-Domingue, she would curb his power. A smile came to her face as she recalled the mulatto's consternation when Davide returned with a man he did not know.

"You stupid fool!" Samson had raged. "I sent you for Dr. Chevrier!'

"And that is where he went," the man accompanying the slave replied curtly. The sight of him made Téoline catch her breath; at first glance he bore a resemblance to Andrew Cameron. On closer examination she saw that he was older by some years; his dark hair was streaked with gray. He was also of a much slighter build. It was possibly wishful thinking on her part that made her think there was a likeness. She had never felt such a sense of loneliness in all her young life.

The doctor looked up from where he was standing on the quay and saw her watching him anxiously. "I am Peter Robillard. And you, I imagine, are Madame de Beben? Would you like me to come aboard?"

Before Téoline could reply, Samson broke in arrogantly. "My master will see no one but Dr. Chevrier."

"Then I'm afraid he will have to wait a very long time, and if he is as sick as I've been told, he may not appreciate that. Dr. Chevrier has retired. He is at present away in one of the other islands and it is doubtful that he will return." The doctor addressed his remarks to Téoline, ignoring the dwarf.

"In that case, I shall be most grateful for your advice, Dr. Robillard. Samson, show Dr. Robillard to your master's cabin at once."

Reluctantly the dwarf had given way, and Téo felt the first round of the battle had been won, thanks to Robillard. However, she was worried about her relationship with the other slaves. Samson had called them together to introduce their new mistress. They had shambled into a line and stared at her with large solemn eyes. There had been too many to remember their names, although Joseph, the little gray-haired butler, had mentioned some of them.

There was a timid knock at the door of the boudoir, and Téo called for whoever it was to enter. A young black girl came in carrying a lighted taper. Shyly she edged her way around the room, lighting the candles on the table and the sconces on the walls. She kept her eyes averted as though by doing so her presence would be less obvious. When she had finished she stood by the door, and Téoline wondered what she was waiting for. A few minutes went by and Téoline was not sure what she should do. At home Nina or Lisette would have lit the candles and left the room unless she requested them to stay, but this girl just stood there with fear in her eyes. Téoline thought: If only she knew, I am just as nervous of her as she is of me. However, someone had to break the silence.

"What is your name?" Téoline said gently. She also spoke very slowly, because she had heard the slaves speaking a strange dialect and assumed the girl might not be able to understand French.

"I am called Sonata, mistress," the slave replied shyly.

Téoline's face lit up with delight. "Tell me, Sonata, how is it you speak French so perfectly? I have not been able to understand the other servants." Téoline resolutely refused to call them slaves.

"Few of them speak French, mistress. They speak Creole or their own dialect."

"Then where did you learn French?" Téoline was amazed at the response her question provoked. Sonata started to tremble and her large dark eyes filled with tears. Téo repeated the question and, when the girl failed to reply, said, "Surely it is not a crime?" The slave nodded her head. Téoline thought she had made a mistake.

"Sonata, why should I be upset because you can speak to me in my own tongue?"

The girl buried her head down on her shoulder and whispered almost inaudibly: "Because a master does not like his slaves to be educated. If the master were to find out, he would sell me or turn me out to work with the brutes in the fields."

Téoline was shocked to hear Sonata speak of the other blacks so disparagingly, but for the moment she was more concerned with the rest of what the girl had said. "I find that hard to believe, but if it is so, it does not apply to me. I am very pleased. But where did you learn? Who has been teaching you?"

"Father François! He has taught me to read and write while the master has been away," Sonata said with a little more clarity.

"That is admirable. I hope I can persuade him to do the same for the others." The girl hung her head and stared at her bare feet. "Tell me, Sonata, have you had any training in the duties of a lady's maid?" The girl looked up with a happy smile on her face.

"Oh, yes, *maîtresse*. I have looked after the master's ladies since I was a small girl." Téoline found the reply a little disconcerting although she realized, knowing Albert's problems, that she should have been ready for it.

"I am not one of M'sieur's ladies, Sonata. I am his wife, and mistress of this house." There was a new note of authority in Téo's voice. It was obvious that she was going to have to establish her position with the household staff. "I should like you to be my personal maid. Would you like that?"

Sonata beamed, but she was plainly puzzled at being asked her opinion.

"Very well, that's settled, then. You understand, you will answer to me and no one else. And at all times you will speak to me in French." The fear returned to the slave's eyes. "For the moment Monsieur is ill, so it will be some weeks before he is likely to notice that your knowledge of the language has improved. When he does, he will assume you have learned it from me. And I do not wish you to call me mistress; 'madame' will do perfectly. Do you understand?" The girl nodded her head, completely dumbfounded by what Téoline had just said. "Very well, you may go."

The girl did not wait but dashed out of the room as though the devil himself were after her. Poor child, Téoline thought, and made a mental note to get the slave something else to wear, other than the torn white blouse and striped skirt. She had noticed how shabby they all looked and supposed it was because Albert had been away for so long.

Téoline opened the door and left it ajar so she could hear when the doctor left Albert's room down the corridor. A gallery ran round the second floor, encircling the vestibule below on three sides. As she mused over her conversation with Sonata and the events of the afternoon, she became conscious of women's voices wafting up from the hall below. She listened for a moment as the sound grew louder and more animated. Once again she found herself faced with the familiar and the unfamiliar.

They were speaking Creole, and Téo recognized some of the words, which had come down from the Norman French of the buccaneers. But these were mixed with a variety of words from other languages overlaid with snatches of African dialects. The result gave their conversation a strange gibberish quality that almost made sense to her, but left an eerie feeling of uncertainty.

She went out into the gallery and stood in the shadow of one of the large mahogany pillars. From the light of the crystal chandelier she could see Sonata speaking to another woman Téo had not seen before. She was much older than Sonata, who appeared to be about Téo's age. She was forty, maybe less; it was difficult to tell because a heavy coating of rice powder she had applied to make her skin appear paler gave her face a masklike quality.

She wore a red-and-gold silk turban drawn tightly around her head with the ends flared out into a fan. Heavy gold loops dangled from her ears and several chains cascaded over a fine white silk blouse. The silk fell carelessly over her slim coffee-colored shoulders and barely covered her breasts. She moved with a quick sensuous grace, expertly flicking a frilled green satin skirt as she walked. Her hand rested on the ivory knob of a tall green silk parasol. But the woman's most striking feature was her eyes. They were large and lustrous and flashed with a strange brilliance under her long dark lashes.

Téoline was so busy watching her, intrigued by the strange sight, that she had forgotten to listen to what they were saying. Suddenly the woman shrieked and started to belabor Sonata with her parasol. Angrily, Téo moved towards the stairs, determined to stop this violence, but the sound had already brought Robillard hurrying from Albert's room.

"Permit me, madame," he said, gently easing Téoline to one side. "I think I can better deal with this." He ran down the stairs, letting loose a tirade in Creole and pointing fiercely towards the door. The woman stopped screaming and looked up at him, then shifted her gaze to Téoline at the top of the stairs. After a moment, she started to move menacingly towards them; the expression in her eyes made Téoline's blood turn to ice. But Robillard barred her way and again gestured towards the door. Snapping her fingers under the doctor's nose, the woman turned and made for the front doors. She stood framed there and glowered at each person in turn, then with a final toss of her head, which sent the fan on her turban shivering wildly, she swept down the steps to a waiting carriage.

Peter Robillard held out his hand to Téoline. "You may come down now, madame. I doubt that she will trouble you again." Téo crept cautiously down the stairs as if afraid some new peril would pounce on her from the shadows.

"Who was she?" she whispered to Robillard as he met her halfway down the broad staircase.

"Madame Babette," he replied curtly. "Allow me." He offered Téoline his arm and escorted her to the main salon. It was quite apparent that he did not wish to divulge any further information about their visitor.

Téoline had scarcely had time to take in the details of the house; all her attention had been on de Beben and his problems. She suddenly realized that she was really seeing her new home for the first time. The main salon was a long narrow room; at one end, away from the street, wide doors led out into a large garden where tall palm trees stood like sentinels in the moonlight. Téo could hear a fountain splashing amidst the shrubbery.

89

Although the doors were open, a gauze screen kept out insects. Robillard placed a chair for her in a spot where she could feel the cool evening breeze blowing down from the mountains. As it reached her, Téo gave a sigh of relief.

"You're looking very pale and tired, madame," the doctor said. "If you don't rest, I fear I shall have another patient on my hands." Sonata had followed them into the room, and Robillard gave her instructions to fetch a bottle of wine. "No doubt you're also suffering from lack of food as well as strain. I know how poor the provisions can be on a long voyage."

At the mention of food, Téoline thought she was going to be sick, and the doctor raised his eyebrows inquiringly. He was in a very difficult position. Experience told him that young Madame de Beben was more than likely with child, yet he had just finished examining Monsieur de Beben, and he doubted very much that the man was capable of fathering anything.

"Thank you for your concern, m'sieur. I am just a little fatigued."

"And a little homesick too?" He smiled.

"Yes, I suppose that is true. You are very observant, Dr. Robillard."

"It goes with my profession."

"Then perhaps you will spare the time to console me. I should be glad of your company." Téoline felt in need of a friend just then; the thought of being left alone in the big old house with Albert upstairs sick and only the slaves for company was more than she could contend with.

"If that is all this patient needs, I shall be happy to oblige, in this instance," the doctor said laughingly as he drew up a chair and sat down opposite her.

"That sounds as though you do not often favor such treatment, *m'sieur le docteur?*" Téoline cheered up at the thought of having some company, if only for a while.

"With some ladies of my acquaintance, it might create a dangerous precedent. Being bored and having little to do with their time, they are always ready to encourage me to waste mine. However, in your case, it is what I would have prescribed, had I not been afraid you might think it presumptuous of me to do so on such a short acquaintance."

"I would never regard an act of kindness a presumption, m'sieur."

At that moment Joseph came in to announce that dinner was served. He waited for Téo to dismiss him, just as Sonata had done.

Robillard was watching her closely, and when the slave had gone he said, "No. I can see that you wouldn't. I can also see from the way you treat the slaves that you are not like most of the ladies out here."

"I hope I treat all God's creatures with the same courtesy that I would like them to use towards me," Téoline responded, a little uncomfortably. She wasn't sure whether he was being critical of her conduct with Joseph.

"Those are most unusual sentiments, madame, but ones with which I heartily agree. It is a pity that more people do not share them. They too often treat their slaves like animals."

Téoline confessed that she was nervous of them and not sure of what they expected her to do. She mentioned their habit of waiting to be told when they should come and go.

"You must remember, madame, a false move on their part could well cost any one of them his life."

"Surely you exaggerate, m'sieur?"

"I only wish I did. Do you know, only a few weeks ago, one of the ladies of whom I spoke just now had her cook thrown in the fire for burning a batch of cakes."

"I find that hard to believe, but if you say it is, then I must hold it true. And do these same people make claim to being Christians?"

"Most certainly. In fact, they consider themselves pillars of society."

"I thought conditions in France were bad enough, but this . . .?" Téoline looked dismayed.

"I'm afraid the country does not make the difference. The problems are with men themselves."

"I know. I've experienced what can happen when men become drunk with power and mobs run mad."

Téoline was beginning to feel much more in control of her life. For a while that afternoon she had seemed to be blown hither and thither by a malevolent fate. Talking with Peter Robillard was helping to restore her sense of identity. He reminded her in many ways of Andrew Cameron. Physically he was not so commanding and he lacked Cameron's self-confidence; but there was an inner strength about him that she found comforting. In Cameron this manifested itself in a kind of arrogance; he used it to mold the world to his way. With Robillard, Téo gained the impression that life had forced him into a mold which he accepted with quiet endurance. Cameron was the type of man who would always lead, whereas Robillard would doggedly remain in the fray to the bitter end. Feeling better, Téoline also discovered she did indeed have an appetite.

"Doctor Robillard, since you wish me to eat, I will obey; however, I insist you join me and take some of your own medicine." Robillard stood up and for a moment he seemed at a loss as to what to say. Then he gave her a quizzical smile and offered his arm.

"I think, under the circumstances, you might be allowed to get away with it this once. However, I would warn you, madame, it would be unwise to suggest such a thing again. I think you would find that neither your husband nor society would approve." He led her in to dinner before she could ask what he meant.

The quality and quantity of silver and porcelain set out on the long mahogany table made Téo catch her breath. In fact, the meal itself would have done credit to the tables at Versailles. But she found it a little disconcerting to have so many slaves, six at each place, eager to anticipate every desire. Their presence made conversation difficult; she wanted to know more about society in Le Cap, but her questions were silenced by a warning glance from her guest. The same thing happened when she started to tell him of the revolutionary fervor that was engulfing France.

Téoline chose to partake of a little cold ham and turkey, but the menu included fricasseed iguana, land crabs, and many other dishes. To follow this she was offered fruit from an enormous silver basket piled with pineapples, oranges, bananas, and more exotic fare she did not recognize.

Robillard applied himself to a wide variety of dishes with an enthusiasm that suggested he might not have eaten for days. Téo noticed for the first time that his clothes were worn and he carried not an ounce of spare flesh. He looked up and caught her watching and gave a sheepish grin.

"You must forgive me, madame. I rarely have the opportunity to sit down to such a feast." Téoline signaled a slave to replenish the doctor's plate.

"I gather your duties do not allow much time for a social life?" she said.

"That is one reason," he replied, but again he made no attempt to explain what he meant.

"Robillard . . . ? The name has a French ring. Yet from your accent . . . ?"

"I am a French Canadian, madame. My grandfather was a

Huguenot who settled in New France, or, as the English now call it, Canada."

"Does that make you an Englishman?" Téoline laughed.

"A mongrel, madame. War does that to men. The flags are changed and we lose our identity." He sighed. "But if we were honest, we would admit that we are all mongrels under the skin. My father and grandfather fought the British at the Heights of Abraham. Then, a few years later, I fought with the British against the Americans. That is the stupidity of war. Our lives and loyalties are always governed by expediency."

"But not our love. . . . Surely our hearts remain free?" Even as she said it, Téoline knew it was not true. Much as she tried to hate Cameron for the way he had cast her adrift, something told her that her heart was committed to him till the day she died . . . perhaps beyond, throughout eternity. She did not know if that was love. It was obvious the doctor did not agree.

"Unfortunately, madame, we appear to have little control over our hearts. If I were not a doctor, I would hesitate to agree we even had such a thing. . . . No, a heart is a very wayward thing."

When they had finished the meal, Robillard went up to take a final look at his patient. "He is sleeping peacefully," he said on his return. "I will look in on him tomorrow. In the meantime I will look up the notes on his case which Dr. Chevrier left with me."

Having thanked him, Téo said, "I'm afraid I have encroached upon your time, but you may charge it to my account. Your company has healed my spirits quicker than any medication could have done."

"Then I am more than recompensed," he said, taking her hand. "And in the circumstances, I know my wife will understand why I am late."

"Your wife . . . ?" His words took Téo by surprise. Somehow she had not thought of him as a married man.

"Yes, madame. Perhaps one day it will be possible for you to meet my Marie. . . . When conditions permit," he added hesitantly.

"I am sorry, is she indisposed?"

"No, madame, that is not the reason. Marie is of mixed blood. Her grandmother was an African slave and her mother the child of a French aristocrat. He granted his mistress her freedom, and their child, Marie, was sent to France to be educated." His tone was almost apologetic.

93

"Then I'd be delighted to meet her. We will probably have much in common. She may even know some of my friends in Paris. As soon as my husband recovers, you must certainly bring her here to dine."

The doctor flushed with embarrassment. "That is very kind of you, Madame de Beben, but I'm afraid there are many things about this colony that you do not as yet understand."

"Then you had better tell me, m'sieur. It would be safer were I to know when I am treading on unhallowed ground," Téo responded sharply. She was not certain whether his words were intended as a rebuff.

"The laws here forbid anyone with colored blood to sit at the same table with a person with a white skin." Robillard's face was grim and he was plainly distressed by what he said.

"That isn't possible. No one could be ignorant of the Code Noir—it goes back to the time of Louis the Fourteenth. It gave all freed slaves the full rights of a French citizen." Téo's eyes were flashing angrily.

"That may be so in France, madame. Out here the *grands blancs* make their own laws despite the fact this is a French colony. An *affranchi* is not permitted to carry arms, and many trades and professions are forbidden to them. They may not become goldsmiths lest they gain control of too much wealth; the practice of the law is also forbidden lest they gain influence . . . and . . ." He paused and gave a wry smile. "They may not become apothecaries in case they should rebel and poison the whites. That is why many look askance upon me because, as a doctor, I have access to drugs."

"Merely because your wife has colored blood?" Téoline was incredulous.

"When a man marries, his wife's shadow falls across everything he does. That is why I shall be forced to refuse should you invite me to dine with you again. I will not go where my wife cannot be received. And you, madame, will obviously have to abide by the rules your husband sets."

"If custom prevents you dining with me, I shall expect to receive your invitation. That way the onus for defying such wicked laws can rest on me." Téoline tossed her head defiantly.

Robillard raised her hand to his lips. "I admire your courage, madame. And I pray it may never desert you." Then he left.

Chapter Eleven

True to his word, Peter Robillard was a frequent visitor during the ensuing days. Ostensibly he came to see how his patient was progressing, but in truth he enjoyed conversing with Téoline. It was obvious from what he said that he was devoted to his wife although she was not interested in the deeper things of life. It delighted him to talk with Téoline, and they had many long conversations touching on the old philosophers. Gradually, through Robillard's eyes, Téoline came to understand some of the problems confronting the colony.

Albert de Beben began to recover; he was very anxious to take Téoline about and show off his latest piece of property. But he resented the warm friendship that had sprung up between his wife and the doctor. He complained that the younger man lacked Chevrier's experience and said he would be glad to see the back of him.

"I am planning to call upon Madame Robillard," Téo told her husband one day when he was beginning to sit out of bed.

"Never!" de Beben exploded. "I forbid it!" Téoline's eyes flashed more green than blue. Her husband was beginning to read this as a warning sign. He had seen it happen in several encounters she had had with Samson. He added hastily, "I mean, I do not think it wise for reasons you, as yet, cannot understand, my pet."

"I believe I do, m'sieur. You have a *petit bourgeois* society out here, which apes the manners of Paris but is not nearly so liberal in its views."

De Beben frowned. He was beginning to wonder whether he would be able to handle his young wife. An ordinary woman he could soon have put in her place, but Téoline was a de Pavigné and had that family's fierce pride; more important, he could not risk offending her for fear she would write to Mirabeau. He had a sneaking suspicion that she was often laughing at him; however, he had to admit that she was quickly learning to run his household with surprising efficiency. The strict training Téo had received at the convent had taught her how a large household should be organized. This had done nothing to endear her to Samson, who saw his power slipping away.

De Beben was also irritated by the way she was spending his money like water, although to his face she was as sweet as wine. This was not hypocrisy on Téoline's part. She had made a bargain for her child's future happiness and she was determined to do her part in keeping it, as she explained to her husband when he gently remonstrated with her over some bills.

"You have a position to keep up, m'sieur. People will think you are without means if they see your slaves so badly dressed. Civilized people will also consider us ignorant if they see your servants ill-abused," she added as a rider.

De Beben had to admit he had very little of which to complain. When they were able to go out, Téoline played her part like a queen, and society in Le Cap was suitably impressed. However, for the most part Téoline found Robillard's assessment of them to be right. There were one or two old families with an impressive ancestry, but for the most part the new nobility were descendants of buccaneers and villains who had escaped from the gutters and prisons of Europe to build themselves fortunes in the New World. They lacked the control of either honor or pride. They were, as she remarked to Robillard one day, "beggars on horseback," and as such ran their steeds to death.

As the days went by, Téoline's condition was becoming more evident; it was fortunate that de Beben was flattered to be thought capable of fathering a child. He was beginning to think about leaving Le Cap. His wife was growing weary of the exhausting round of assemblies and balls, and he was becoming jealous of the attention she received from both the young and old men in the colony. Consequently, Téo was not surprised when he said as much to Bayon de Libertat one day when they were all seated in the garden.

Téoline always welcomed a visit from Bayon and Madame de Libertat. She felt they were among the few genuine people in the colony. Unfortunately they would soon be leaving for Bréda, a plantation in the north which Bayon managed for a distant relation of his. On this particular afternoon she was sitting with Madame de Libertat on the edge of the fountain, her face shaded by a wide straw hat to keep off the sun's blistering rays. Robillard had warned against her being out in it too much, with her fair skin. This had further annoyed Albert. Being a Creole by birth, he was used to it and basked in the heat, but it gave Téo the excuse she needed to avoid spending more time than she had to with him. She sat listening to the two men while trailing her hand in the cool water of the pond and sipping a glass of lime juice.

"Tell me, Libertat," de Beben questioned his guest. "What has been happening here while I've been away?"

"I'm afraid that tensions have heightened a great deal. There was a slave uprising a few weeks ago."

"I hope they hanged the dogs," de Beben growled.

"They had their fun with them as usual." De Libertat curled his lip. "Some they burned, while others were hanged, and drawn and quartered. I cannot help feeling there is a more civilized way of keeping order."

"Nonsense! They must be made to know who their masters are," de Beben snapped. Unlike his host, de Libertat was not an argumentative man, so he tried to steer the conversation away, without much success.

"I think *Les Amis des Noirs* are gaining support. I feel that they are a force which we in the Colonial Assembly must be prepared to reckon with."

"Nonsense, I say again. We'll not parley with the children of ex-slaves. I suppose Vincent Ogé has been sending them reports of his schemes in Paris. But I can tell you he'll get no satisfaction there. The Club Massiac is too powerful, and besides . . ." He paused and smiled ingratiatingly at Téoline. "I can personally guarantee that we have Mirabeau's support."

Téo blushed and turned away. She still had some guilty qualms about deceiving de Beben, although as each day passed she became less concerned. The honor she was bringing to his name and the success she was making as a hostess could be reckoned a fair exchange.

"Paris is too far away," de Libertat said. "By the time we receive any directives from them, the crisis is already past. We must make our own decisions on what is best to be done, and I for one think we should listen to them sympathetically. Toussaint tells me that the news of the revolution in France is already common gossip amongst the slaves. Sailors coming ashore give them tricolor cockades and tell them they are the equal of any man. He is very worried at their growing discontent and says that unless conditions improve we shall have trouble before long."

"I've told you before, Toussaint is an old fool. I'd have hanged him years ago. I tell you, de Libertat, you put too much credence in that old slave. He's a mischief-maker, nothing more nor less."

"I'll not agree with that. And I'd as soon raise my hand against my own family. Toussaint has been a faithful friend. I sometimes think he has inherited the wisdom of the ages. He has more brains in his head than many of the whites, whatever their rank," de Libertat said indignantly.

"Because you've lent him the books and encouraged him. Whoever heard of a slave learning Latin and French and reading the philosophers? I tell you, you've been making a rod for your own back."

Seeing that her husband was growing very annoyed, Madame de Libertat decided it was time she cut in. "Tell me, Monsieur de Beben, when are you bringing your charming wife to stay at Cambenet? We shall of course expect you to dine at Bréda when you do."

"It will be a pleasure, madame, and one we will take advantage of before too long. The malarial season will be upon us soon, and I think my wife will fare better in the mountain air. And I, of course, wish to supervise the harvest."

De Beben turned back to her husband and got caught up in a discussion of sugar prices. Madame turned to Téoline.

"Why, my poor child, you've become quite pale. Are you feeling unwell?" She had been viewing the girl with a motherly eye and was certain her diagnosis was right despite Téoline's reticence about admitting her condition.

"It is nothing, madame. I am merely feeling the heat. I will go inside. But tell me first, did you say 'Cambenet'?"

"Why, yes! Has your husband not mentioned his plantation next to ours in the north?"

At that moment de Libertat got up to leave. Téoline and de Beben accompanied their guests to the door. As their carriage drew up outside, Téoline caught her first glimpse of Toussaint. After hearing her husband's remarks about him, she was very interested in the old man.

"Toussaint!" de Beben spat the name out with disgust. "De Libertat will be sorry he sets such store by him, you'll see." He cackled maliciously and hobbled away on his cane. Téoline waited behind to observe the quaint little man.

Toussaint presented a slightly grotesque figure in his gold-braided livery with a yellow madras kerchief tied over his graying hair. His face was very black and his long pointed chin emphasized a broad uptilted nose. He was lean and wiry for his age, which Téo guessed to be about fifty years. It was his great sense of dignity, however, that caught her attention. He helped his master and mistress into their carriage with grave courtesy; the careful dignity with which he tucked a dust sheet about their legs gave stature to that menial task. As he prepared to remount the box, he looked up and saw Téoline watching him. He returned her stare with a gentle smile, then bowed. After seating himself, he whipped up the horses and was gone. Téoline stared after him. Though it was only for a brief second that their eyes had met, her heart had been touched; she had seen a depth of understanding in his large dark eyes that went beyond words. Without knowing how or why, Téoline was left with the feeling that she had seen one of the great men of the world.

Téoline was more than happy to leave Le Cap, as she was quickly tiring of the endless round of visits; also she was curious to see Cambenet. Doctor Robillard, however, was not so pleased. Apart from any personal sense of loss he might have, she had told him of her condition and he was anxious about her health. He had approached de Beben on the subject, but without any success; in fact quite the reverse. De Beben had made it quite plain he did not wish the doctor to attend to Téoline, nor would Robillard be permitted to visit Cambenet. When the young doctor asked how Téoline would manage, her husband replied that it was quite usual for a black midwife to attend to such matters. Robillard had persisted, remarking that this child would be Téoline's first and that she was young; but his pleas were to no avail. The more he remonstrated, the more de Beben was convinced that the younger man had an ulterior motive for wanting to see Téoline.

Téoline was already tired when they set out from Cap Français. They departed in the early hours of the morning to avoid the heat of the day; the journey would have been quicker and more comfortable on horseback, but neither Téoline's condition nor Albert's health would allow that. Instead, they traveled in one of de Beben's older carriages, which had springs that left a great deal to be desired.

De Beben made little attempt to conceal his bad temper, which he vented on Davide, who was in the driver's box. He kept belaboring the poor man's back with his cane and demanding that he set a brisker pace; this behavior confirmed Téoline's suspicions that it was more than time to leave Le Cap. The previous evening there had been yet another interminable assembly. This time it was at the house of Comte de Peynier, the governor. It sickened Téo to see how the *grands blancs* exaggerated the customs and costumes of the French court. The affair had taken on the bizarre air of a carnival. She had therefore been looking forward to a peaceful ride to help her recover from the previous night, but Albert's mood made that impossible.

Once outside Le Cap, the road was little more than a dirt track. It became even narrower when they turned onto one leading through the foothills into the mountains and toward Cambenet. Sugarcane lined either side, blocking the view. As she heard a second carriage approaching, Téo looked out from under her parasol and lifted the protective veil she was wearing to keep off the dust; she was wondering how on earth the two vehicles could pass each other.

Although she could not see who was in it, it was a very elegant equipage with heavy gilded carvings; the driver and postillions were in handsome liveries. For the past mile Albert had been quiet. His face was hidden by his large straw hat and he appeared to be dozing, as the sun was already hot. But, feeling the carriage slow down, he was quickly up on his feet, loudly demanding to know the cause.

As soon as he saw the other carriage, de Beben appeared to know to whom it belonged. His face turned a bright purple and he tore the whip from Davide's hand. Screaming and searing with rage, he whipped their horses to a frenzy and drove straight ahead, ignoring both Téo's and Davide's pleas to give way.

Hearing the shouts and the relentless thudding of hooves, the horses in the other carriage took fright and reared up on their hind legs. Téoline glimpsed the terrified face of the driver as he tried desperately to control his team. Because the road had been rutted by heavy rains and was now baked hard by the sun, the carriage was thrown off balance. As the front wheels of the two vehicles touched, the other toppled over on its side amidst the sugarcane. Without pausing to look at the damage, de Beben drove straight on.

"Albert," Téoline cried, "for the love of God stop and see what has happened to them."

Her husband's eyes were wild as he whipped the horses on. "Scum!" he cried. "That woman is scum!"

Téo looked back in time to see a disheveled figure scrambling to her feet. Picking up her parasol from the roadway, Babette stood there brandishing it at them and screaming abuse. Her face and her fine silks were covered with a thick layer of white dust. Even though they were separated by a hundred yards, Téo knew the woman's eyes were full of hate.

De Beben was aware that he had angered his wife and wisely settled back to continue his sleep. Although the rest of the journey was uneventful, Téoline was unable to relax. She sat upright and tense on the edge of the seat, not wishing to be near the monstrous man she had married. What kind of a man was he? She now understood why Louise had been afraid for her.

They crested one of the low foothills and drove along beside a wide stream running down the center of a green and fertile valley. Sugarcane gave way to other crops; bananas, coffee, and other forms of vegetation covered the vales and hills up into the mountains beyond. Gradually the valley opened out into a broad savannah. In the distance Téoline saw a small collection of huts; as they drew near them a group of women washing on stones in the stream paused and looked at them with dark, wondering eyes. Téo was glad that a veil covered her face; she found their stares disconcerting. Nearer the huts there was a small area of cultivated land being tended by old men and children too young to work in the fields.

In answer to her question, Davide told her the slave quarters were always built downwind of the house because the stench became overpowering in the heat. Téo was already aware of what he meant. She had difficulty not to be overcome by nausea. The huts were in a better state than many she had seen en route, but they were sadly overcrowded. There was no attempt at proper sanitation, and pigs, chickens, goats, and a donkey or two shared a small space; dozens of babies were in a huge pen where an old woman looked after them.

"I hope you will not be too disappointed with Cambenet, my dear," Albert ventured as they drew near a stone mill. He knew she had not approved of his previous behavior and he was doing what he could to get back into her good books. "You see how fortunate we are to have this stream so near. It drives the mill wheel; water is carried by aqueducts to irrigate the lower fields."

Téoline was very interested, but she refused to discuss its advantages with him. She was in no mood to give in easily. Albert went on:

"When my sister was alive, she took great pride in Cambenet, but I'm afraid I've neglected it since then. However, I'm sure that under your excellent management it will soon return to its former glory."

De Beben's tone was increasingly conciliatory, but Téo still refused to unbend. She was wondering what lay ahead. Joseph

101

and Sonata, along with other household slaves, had traveled overnight to prepare the house for them. Téo was not so concerned about what conditions might be at the house as she was at the sight of so many black faces. They no longer scared her as they had done at first; she had become too attached to Sonata for that. But again it came home to her that she was a white woman in a black world.

They rounded the mill and came to a small wooden bridge, which spanned the stream. Davide brought the carriage to a halt to allow a small party of blacks to come across. Téoline stifled a gasp as she saw that their necks were encased in iron collars; they dragged along limbs heavy with chains. There was a stocky little white man driving them, and when he looked up and saw the carriage he lashed out at their backs with a thick snakeskin whip. "No!" Téoline screamed at his vicious attack.

Not wishing to upset his wife any further, de Beben was quick to react. "That's enough, Lortie! Send them on their way. I wish to speak with you." The man bowed obsequiously and turned to say something to the tall black who had been taking the brunt of the punishment. Then the sad little procession continued on its way and Lortie came forward, curling the whip about his arm.

"Téoline, my dear, may I present Lucien Lortie. He is the manager of Cambenet."

The man's sallow face broke into an ingratiating smile. Taking off a battered straw hat, he bowed and murmured, "Enchanted, madame." His greasy brown hair was tied back into an untidy queue, but matted wisps of it stuck to the grime and sweat on his face. He wore a filthy shirt; his *culottes* were stained and his shoes and wrinkled stockings were caked with mud.

Téo was revolted by him. This was not the shabbiness of poverty but of deliberate neglect. How could the slaves be well cared for if the overseer showed so little self-respect?

Slowly, Téo lifted her veil and stared at him. Lortie did have the grace to look embarrassed. He twisted his hat in his hands and said awkwardly, "I didn't know for sure when you'd be coming, madame. Else I'd have been at pains to receive you properly."

"I'm sincerely pleased to hear that the reception we did receive was not one we should normally see," Téoline said coldly, staring him straight in the eyes. He looked nonplussed and did not appear to know what she meant.

"I am referring to those wretched men whom you were treating like pigs. If you value my esteem, don't ever let me see you raise a whip to a man in chains again." She drew down her veil over her face and turned away. De Beben quickly gave Davide the order to drive on.

"I'll see you at the house after supper tonight," he called back to Lortie. "I wish to inspect the books."

"Can that man even write his name?" Téoline made no attempt to hide her disgust.

"Just about, my dear. I forgive much because he has served me for many years. Cambenet is one of the more prosperous plantations in the northern province."

"Then of course it is expedient that he should stay, regardless of how he treats the slaves!" Téo replied. It distressed her to realize that her sarcasm was lost on de Beben.

The house now lay directly ahead of them at the end of what had once been a gravel drive. The large garden was surrounded by the rubble of a gray stone wall; at the entrance a pair of ornamental iron gates hung from broken hinges. The building itself was of Spanish design, the main living quarters being on the upper floor and fronted by a balcony which ran past them on either side. The flagstone courtyard was overgrown with weeds. In the center of this a headless statue guarded a fountain dried to a blackish green. A stone colonnade of arches led to the kitchens and servants' quarters on the ground floor. It was obvious that this had once been a lovely house, but now the pink paint peeled from the plaster walls and the iron balustrade on the wide staircase that led up to the main doors was rusty from lack of care. It was a sorry picture of decaying grandeur, and Téoline felt only despair as she surveyed it.

"My God!" she said as Davide helped her alight from the carriage. "Thank Heaven my father cannot see this, or he would think you were a pauper, Albert." For once even de Beben was thoroughly ashamed.

"I'm sorry you find it in such a sorry state of neglect. I fear it is even worse than I anticipated," her husband apologized.

"With such a creature as Lortie in charge, surely you're not surprised?"

"As I told you, since my sister died it has lacked a woman's touch."

"It lacks a touch of any kind. At least the walls are still standing. For that I give praise."

"I'll speak to Lortie and have him attend to it immediately, my dear."

"Thank you, I would prefer that he not do so, Albert. Let Lortie keep to the plantation. I'll be mistress in my own house. I do not want him near me or my servants. Is that understood?" Téoline was far too tired and distracted to dissemble and she did not hesitate to declare war on the loutish manager.

"As you wish, madame." Her husband was in no mood to argue, as he had just been told by Joseph that conditions were even worse inside. Lortie had been living there during de Beben's absence abroad, along with his woman and a brood of brats. "My purse is at your disposal as always."

"Thank you, m'sieur! I shall not fail to mention your generosity when next I write to France." Téoline had already found that the mention of her family was the key to keep Albert de Beben in line.

Samson was there, organizing everything and strutting around like a pompous little cockerel. As he led her to the far wing of the house and her apartment, he went to great lengths to explain that it was the very one Mademoiselle Émilie de Beben had used when he came to Cambenet as a small boy. Téoline felt he probably thought she should feel honored to be permitted to walk on such hallowed ground.

While Sonata prepared a bath for her, Téoline explored the layout of her rooms. There was a large salon with several groupings of chairs, a settee, and several small tables. Beyond this there was a boudoir with a splendid view of the mountains and the sea; the last room was a bedroom with a small dressing room to one side. As she had expected, all the furniture tended to be heavy and old-fashioned. Téo inspected the large four-poster bed with its heavy drapes. There was a strange, musty smell that seemed to emanate from the fabric; she called to Sonata to take them down. It was then the maid pointed out that the legs of the bed were standing in pots containing a murky liquid.

"What's that?" Téo asked, wrinkling her nose.

"That is a poison Joseph mixes to keep the insects away from the beds," Sonata explained. Téoline shuddered and wondered if she would ever feel at home on this strange island. At one moment it seemed like a paradise, at others it was a veritable hell.

Téo went back into the boudoir and walked out onto the balcony, which was at the back of the house. She noticed that a flight of steps led to the end of the garden, which was a tangled mass of vines, weeds, and broken statuary. It was all surrounded by a crumbling wall, and beyond that loomed the jungle. She stood there looking up at the purple mountains rising on the other side of a small bay. They were majestic and beautiful, but today, as she often did at other times, Téoline felt there was something sinister about them. "Is there no escape from the mountains?" she asked Sonata, who had come to say the bath was ready.

The girl laughed then said with a sigh, "We have a saying in Creole . . . *'Deye mon ge mon!'* Beyond the mountains there are always more mountains again! Father François says that is the way it is with life."

"The holy father is a very wise man." Téo had gone out of her way to meet him and thank him for what he was doing for the slaves. She would have liked to know him better, but they attended the great cathedral in the center of the town. In any case, she reflected, her devotions were taking up less and less of her time.

Téoline breathed a sigh of relief as the laces of her corset were released; soon she would have to stop wearing one. Robillard had warned her against it, but all women did their best to conceal the ugly fact they were with child for as long as it was remotely possible. In Téoline's case it was merely habit; as each day went by she became more and more enthralled at the thought of having her baby. She would never feel alone again. He would be hers for ever and ever. As she sank down into the cool water and enjoyed the feel of it on her aching back, she pondered on a name for him. It irked her that he would have to take that of de Beben. If she'd had her way, he would have been a de Pavigné. She tried never to think of Cameron, but now he sprang to mind. He would never know he had a son. Téo wondered how he would feel about it if he did. Ah, well, he had made his choice and the loss was his. Téoline had firmly resolved that she would never admit her son's true parentage to any man.

She slipped into a loose negligée while Sonata went in to turn down the bed. Suddenly she heard the girl give a startled cry. Hurrying from the dressing room, Téo found her backing away from the bed, her eyes wide with fright.

"What is it, Sonata? What's the matter?" The slave pointed to a small object half-hidden by the curtains around the bed. Téoline hurried across and, picking it up, started to examine it. It was nothing but a dried gourd. She shifted the contents through the fingers of one hand. There was a collection of herbs, some maize, a few coins, and some strange little amulets. By then Sonata had recovered her sense. Rushing across the room, she snatched it from Téo's hand and, running out onto the balcony, threw it toward the jungle beyond. Then she crossed herself and muttered a prayer. Instinctively Téo found herself following suit, although she hadn't the slightest idea why she was doing it.

"Sonata! Tell me what this is all about!" she said sharply, seeing the girl was on the verge of tears.

"It is the *maldioque!*" Sonata whispered fearfully, and crossed herself again.

"*Maldioque?*"

"The evil eye! Babette has it, and I saw her look at you that night you first came to Le Cap. She had someone put the *ouanga* here . . . it's all her doing. She has always wished ill upon this house but now it is too late. The *ouanga* cannot take effect, for you are already with child." There was an hysterical note of triumph in Sonata's voice.

For a moment Téoline caught her breath and put an arm across the baby in her womb. Then, recovering her senses, she said angrily, "That's nonsense. As Christians we cannot believe in such things."

"I don't believe them, madame," Sonata replied, then promptly contradicted herself by saying, "But I know the power of the *ouanga.*"

"And what is it supposed to do?" Téo felt compelled to ask. She was fascinated despite her feeling that it was all nonsense.

"Placed in a bedchamber, it will prevent conception. But it is too late for that; you already have life in your womb." She turned and looked at Téoline. Her large dark eyes were filled with terror.

Téo sensed an evil presence and she started to sway. Sonata rushed to catch her and helped her to the bed. Then she took a leather thong from around her own neck and gently placed it around Téoline's. A small wooden carving dangled from it.

"Wear this," Sonata said. "Wear it always on your person. It is a *garde*. While you have it your baby will come to no harm."

"But why should she wish me harm? And why does the master hate her so?" Briefly she told Sonata what had occurred that day.

"Many years ago he wronged her. Now his guilt comes back to haunt him."

"Wronged her? What do you mean?"

Sonata hesitated and went to the outer door of the apartment

106

to make sure no one was listening before she replied. "It happened many years ago, before I was born. The old slave who looked after me as a child told me and swore me to secrecy. Although some of the others must know, they would not speak of it. It might cost them their lives. Babette was a slave at Cambenet when *le maître* took her for his mistress. After that, Mademoiselle Émilie hated the girl, especially when she found that Babette was to have a child. She ordered Babette to be whipped, hoping the baby would die. But it didn't, and the baby, a boy, was born before its time. Babette was never allowed to see it. She was told it was already dead, but everyone knew that was a lie. After that Mademoiselle de Beben went away to France and it was said she took the boy with her. *Le maître* must have felt guilty even then, because, while his sister was away, he gave Babette her freedom but turned her out without a penny to her name."

"But isn't she a very wealthy woman now?"

"That's because she owns most of the bordellos in Le Cap. I can remember her coming to the house one day to beg *le maître* to tell her what happened to her son. She said since she had money she wanted to look after him. Monsieur was furious. He drove her away and threatened to have her whipped if she ever came near him again."

"If that is the case, she wouldn't risk coming to Cambenet. Who would she get to help her? Who do you think put the *ouanga* in the bedroom today?"

"Who else but Samson!" Sonata's words struck home like a knife.

"But he is my husband's steward. Monsieur appears to trust him implicitly."

"*Le maître* had a very strong attachment for the dwarf at one time, when the mulatto was a little boy. But time changes things, and now he does not pet him so much. He bought the dwarf's affections, but the bond is not as strong as it was. Samson has discovered a stronger bond."

Téoline looked at her, puzzled by all Sonata had said. "Do you speak of a bond of blood? I don't understand."

"Only one bond of blood is closer than that of a mother for her son." The girl paused and looked towards the door, as though she feared Samson might appear by magic. "That is the bond a sister can have for her brother."

The words made Téo catch her breath. "You mean Babette and Samson . . .?"

Sonata nodded. "They had the same mother."

Chapter Twelve

Téoline did her best not to dwell upon the fact of Samson and Babette's relationship to one another or the discovery of the *ouanga*, but sometimes, late at night, she would lie awake wondering what it all meant. During the day, however, she threw herself into the task of renovating Cambenet. Once she had got over her initial shock and disappointment, she saw the possibilities, and she fell in love with the place.

"Albert, Sonata tells me Benjamin is an excellent carpenter. I should like to have him as one of the household servants. He can restore the furniture and do many of the alterations I wish to have made."

Her tone was deliberately peremptory. Téo was discovering that, like most bullies, when caught off his guard de Beben was nervous. It was certainly true that Benjamin would be useful, but her request was prompted by Sonata's obvious affection for the handsome slave. She was also aware that he seemed to be one of Lortie's main targets for ill treatment.

When de Beben did not respond, she continued. "You told me I might have a free hand. If you allow me, I will make Cambenet the finest plantation house in the province." Téo sensed that her husband was not sympathetic to her request. "I have been writing to my father, and I have told him what a valuable property you have here but that it is sadly in need of repair. People do tend to measure one's success by appearances." As she had judged, de Beben found it difficult to resist the bait she had set.

"You're asking for one of Lortie's ablest men, my dear. Benjamin is brighter than most of the other slaves. They look up to him and he can handle them—"

"Which is why Lortie both uses and abuses him," Téoline broke in.

"Possibly, beloved." Albert was growing weary of her repeated attacks on his manager's treatment of the slaves. "But he will not give Benjamin up very willingly."

"Willing or unwilling, I don't care. I want Benjamin in the house. It is the first time I have asked you to take such a stand, m'sieur. Of course, if it is too much . . . If Lortie takes preference over your wife and the improvement of your estate . . ."

Téo sat down at her little escritoire and picked up a pen. Her sense of timing was perfect.

"Very well, my dear. But you will have to wait until the harvest is in."

For a few weeks, life at Cambenet was comparatively peaceful. The sugarcane was being harvested. This meant every available slave worked from morning till night, as speed was essential if the crop was not to spoil. In spite of the added work the atmosphere was more cheerful than usual. One reason for this was that the manager and his overseers tended to leave the slaves alone providing they got on with their work. They were too busy seeing that the sugar was processed and sent to Le Cap for shipment on time. Another reason was that, traditionally, after the harvest the slaves were allowed a few days for celebration.

Sonata explained to Téo that this was the one time of the year they were free to indulge in their ancient *voudou* rites. With music and dance they would revive customs long buried in their memories and pray to their ancient gods. Téoline was shocked, as the law stipulated that all slaves should be baptized in the Catholic faith, although many owners chose to ignore this. But many slaves, even the devout ones like Sonata, clung to their *loas*.

"They are like the saints," she protested when Téo scolded her. "In many cases they are one and the same. Damballa serves the one supreme God as Erzulie serves the Blessed Virgin . . . And Papa Legba, together with Saint Peter, guards the gates of Paradise . . .!"

Téoline did not approve of such heathen practices, but she said no more. She felt she had no right to approve or disapprove. There were too many times when her own faith seemed to hang on a very slender thread.

The darkness of doubt would come in the evenings. She would sit on the balcony looking out over the bay and watch the fireflies darting amongst the flowers. Slowly, the slaves were beginning to bring order out of chaos, and the garden was once again becoming a delight to behold. It was at such times that Téoline would question her soul, trying to understand the person she had become. Louise would no longer be able to charge that she refused to compromise. Hardly a day passed that she did not use some ploy to get her own way. If necessary she lied to her husband without hesitation; she cheated him out of money if it meant she could get some improvements for the slaves. The only

110

excuse she had was that her motives were pure. But she could not go to confession, nor could she bear to look into herself; her heart was too often filled with an emotion she could only describe as hate.

Yet that was not entirely true. Téo looked forward to the birth of her child more than anything in her life. She already loved it with a passion she had never thought possible. But that love was always overshadowed by her feelings for the man who had fathered her babe. What of Cameron? What part did he play in all this? How could he be responsible for bringing a life into the world, yet turn his back on it? It was a mutual privilege, this gift of life, to be shared mutually by man and wife. At moments like that Téo hated him. Then there were other times when she would wake during the night thinking she felt his touch and longing for the press of his lips, only to find it was a dream. She wanted him so much yet paradoxically hoped she would never see him again.

From time to time Bayon de Libertat would drive over to discuss matters concerning the Colonial Assembly; occasionally his wife would accompany him and she and Téoline would sit and chat about France and other things. Sometimes Bernard Lapointe, de Beben's lawyer, would come out from Le Cap with documents to sign. Téoline would preside over the table and Albert would bask in the glow of compliments about the house.

"I don't like the way the Jacobins are gaining power," de Libertat said one evening. "Then there's Marat and the wretched Cordelier Clubs stirring up the people with their scurrilous pamphlets. I can see more trouble brewing in France."

"Mirabeau can handle it. He'll take care of them," de Beben replied confidently.

"I'm not too sure of that," his guest demurred. "From what I hear, Barnave is gaining more influence at Court. Many do not trust Mirabeau. They say his loyalties are divided. It is said in Le Cap that he has been favoring the mulattoes of late."

"That I do not believe. Do you, my dear?" De Beben looked across at his wife.

"In a recent letter, my father stressed that the Club Massiac is gaining more support," Téoline said, avoiding a direct reply. She had come to like and trust Bayon de Libertat; she thought he was probably right, but she did not dare to side with him. Hélène had mentioned that Monsieur was very worried about Mirabeau and had thrown his lot in with Barnave. "I think there is more danger from the Jacobins. Monsieur Lapointe was saying there are clubs springing up throughout Saint-Domingue," Téo said, hoping to direct their conversation along another path.

"That's true," de Libertat agreed. "They're attracting the *petits blancs* and are particularly active in the south."

Téo was relieved when the two men became caught up in a discussion about conditions in the southern capital of Port-au-Prince. De Beben was particularly worried, as he had another large plantation at Jeremie.

That night Téoline was unable to sleep. What if something should happen to the Comte de Mirabeau? Her hold over her husband rested with the count; her baby's future could depend upon Honoré holding onto power in France.

A few days after de Libertat's visit, Albert made an announcement. "I regret I shall have to leave you for a while, my dear Téoline."

If only he knew how his endearments had come to irritate her. But she smiled happily at his news while trying to sound as though she would miss him.

"Lapointe feels I should visit Jeremie," he continued. "He has just returned from the south and thinks I should see conditions there for myself. Bayon de Libertat has promised to look after things while I am away. You are free to call upon him or Lapointe. I'm leaving Samson behind to oversee the household slaves."

"There is no need for that," Téo replied. "I know them all now. And I have Benjamin, who is proving a tower of strength in many ways. Samson is devoted to *you*, m'sieur."

"I know." Her husband gave a curious smile. "But on this occasion I would prefer that he stay here with you. Your child may very well be born while I'm away. He will be useful to you, I'm sure." He could see that Téoline was far from pleased. "When I return," he said, trying to soften his stand, "I propose we should pay a visit to one of the other islands. The change will do you good. My health is much improved, and we should be able to enjoy the full pleasures of being man and wife, my dear." He patted her hand and Téoline shivered.

Although Téo was certain Samson had been left to spy on her, she said good-bye to her husband with a light heart the day he left for Le Cap. The colony was not very big and Jeremie was not far as the crow flies, but the mountains made an overland route out of the question. He would, therefore, take a brig around the northern tip of the peninsula and down the coast to Port-au-Prince and thence to Jeremie. At best it would take several weeks, and if things were as turbulent as was rumored, he might even be away for a few months.

As the time for the birth of her baby grew closer, Téo began to feel afraid. She was suddenly conscious of a great loneliness. Sonata was her only companion. Madame de Libertat was very kind, but it was not the same as having someone near on whom she could depend. She thought of writing to Peter Robillard and asking him to come to Cambenet. However, she knew of the warning Albert had given him and had no wish to endanger him or his livelihood in any way. And she was well aware that under Samson's ever-watchful eye the letter might not even get through to him.

Matters were not improved when she received a letter from Louise saying that Mirabeau's powers were declining. He had been striving to keep the balance between the people and the Court. He had many enemies in both camps, but probably the greatest was the Queen. Coupled with that, he was sadly in debt, yet he continued to anger his creditors by his extravagant ways. All in all, Louise said, Mirabeau's star was definitely beginning to wane.

The morning after the letter came, Sonata found her mistress's pillow wet with tears. She tried to comfort Téoline, thinking she was merely afraid of the childbirth that was so near. Her sympathy brought Téoline to the brink of tears again. She took Sonata's hands in hers and gazed into her eyes. She was sure she could trust her, but the risk was great.

"There is something more troubling you, madame," the girl said, obeying a sixth sense. "I have suspected it for some time. Will you not share your burden with me? Surely you know I am your friend?" The two girls, being the same age, had grown very close in the recent months.

"Sonata, I cannot keep this to myself any longer. But first I must have your word never to tell a living soul what you are about to hear."

Without being asked, Sonata went to the table by Téo's bed and picked up the Bible that was resting there. "I'll swear," she said, trembling with fear at the solemnity of taking an oath. "I'll swear by Jesus and the holy saints, by Damballa and my *loa*, that I will become a *zombi* before I break my oath." Sonata was too deeply imbued with the traditions of her people to discount the ancient superstitions surrounding them. The idea of

113

becoming a *zombi*, one of the walking dead, was the worst thing she could think of to impress Téoline with her loyalty.

Téoline kissed her maid. Then, haltingly, she told her as much of her story as she felt necessary. She told her that the marriage to de Beben was one of convenience and that the child she was about to have was not his but that he had agreed to act as its father. She made no mention of Cameron nor did she name Mirabeau. The black girl listened with growing concern, although she did not appear surprised.

"I have often thought it strange that *le maître* should have been able to father it," she said when Téo finished her story. "You will not be the first to have an 'outside child'; but I am afraid for it. The master is not a forgiving man nor is he likely to forget. He can be very cruel to women. He has been good to you, but once your child is born he will have a weapon to use against you."

"You are thinking of Babette?"

Sonata nodded. "She is an evil woman, but I don't think she was always that way. Taking her child away and not letting her know whether it was alive or dead was enough to turn her mind."

Her words struck terror in Téoline's heart. They confirmed what she had already sensed. De Beben was merely biding his time. If anything should happen to Mirabeau she would have no further hold over him. She had no fear for herself, but what would happen to her child then?

"Let me fetch Mamaloi. She will be able to tell us what to do."

"Mamaloi? . . . Sonata! You swore . . ." Téoline's agitation brought her to tears.

"You can trust Mamaloi with your life. She is a holy woman. She can converse with the saints. She is also skilled in the use of herbs and remedies, and you need a midwife to look after you. Toussaint learned much of what he knows about herbs from Mamaloi," Sonata said comfortingly.

Téoline was reassured by the mention of Toussaint's name. She had spoken with him several times when he came to visit Cambenet with de Libertat. And it was common knowledge that people of all races would consult him when they were sick.

"If you are sure, then I will trust Mamaloi."

A few nights later, under cover of darkness, Sonata brought the old woman to see Téoline. Making the excuse that her mistress wanted her fortune told, the slave set Benjamin to guard

114

the back stairs leading to the balcony outside Téo's apartment. Both she and Téoline were anxious that Samson should not be aware of Mamaloi's presence.

The old woman sat crosslegged on the floor and listened to Téoline's story. The dark eyes, in a nut-brown face as wrinkled as a walnut shell, were wise and kind, but she kept them closed while Téo was speaking. She made no attempt to speak but merely puffed away on a wooden pipe. When the story was finished, she signalled Téo to lie on the bed. Mamaloi then examined her with gnarled but strangely gentle hands. Téo found her touch reassuring but was disappointed when the old woman spoke in a dialect she couldn't understand.

"Mamaloi says you are well and strong, but the baby will not be here just yet."

"Is there nothing she can do to hasten it?" Téo was anxious for it to happen while de Beben was away.

"She says it would not be right to interfere with the will of God. Life and death are in His hands. They come when He wills, no matter what men do," Sonata said, translating the old woman's words.

"That might be comforting if it were true," Téo said ruefully. "But I have seen babies dying from starvation and known young men who died in their prime."

Mamaloi seemed to sense that Téoline spoke from fear and placed her hands on Téo's head. She murmured soothingly under her breath. Once again Sonata was called upon to translate.

"Mamaloi says that it must have been their time to go, that they had accomplished all the gods asked of them. She says she has heard men and women plead for death to relieve them of their pain, but the gods have not willed it and they have lived." Before Sonata had finished speaking, the old woman had lifted her hands in a silent invocation. Before Téoline was able to ask any more questions, she had disappeared as quickly and silently as she had come, and was already lost in the darkness outside.

"She says you must be at peace for the sake of your child. That you must not be afraid. She will come again when she has news."

"News?" Téoline shook her head in puzzlement. She was somewhat baffled by the evening's events, but she had to admit she was feeling wonderfully calm. She had the curious sensation that she was suspended far above all the cares that had been plaguing her.

"Yes, news. Mamaloi has ways of knowing things without being told in words."

Téoline was scared but at the same time strangely elated. She was conscious she had been in the presence of a power she did not understand, yet she was unafraid. From the first, before Téoline had told her story, Mamaloi had seemed to know what she was about to say. Voltaire had been right when he said, "Men use words to disguise their thoughts." It crossed Téo's mind that perhaps these primitive people had powers civilized men had long forgotten or dismissed too lightly because they could not be explained.

Her days were peaceful until Joseph returned from Le Cap. He brought a letter from Albert saying he was about to leave for the north, and if the weather was fair he should be home in a week or so. The news sent Téo into fresh agonies of despair. Sonata did her best to comfort her mistress, saying they should not worry until they heard from Mamaloi. That evening, without warning, the old woman appeared.

"Erzulie told me to come," was her only response to Sonata's questioning.

Téoline told her of de Beben's letter. Mamaloi listened patiently. Her face was expressionless as she continued to suck on her pipe. Then she closed her eyes and began to rock to and fro to the rhythm of an incantation she chanted softly to herself, still sitting crosslegged on the floor.

The night was humid and the air dense with the sickly smell of sugar; the heavy silence was broken only by the monotonous croaking of frogs. Téoline shivered as an icy draft suddenly blew through the room. Almost instantly Mamaloi opened her eyes and spoke.

"You have no reason to fear. The master will not be coming yet, in spite of what he has said."

A few days later Joseph brought another letter from de Beben which had been dispatched only a few hours after the previous one. It said that rioting had broken out amongst the *petits blancs* in Port-au-Prince. The manager of the Jeremie plantation had been killed, and it was therefore necessary for him to remain until he could find a replacement.

Two weeks later the baby was born. The morning had been bright and clear, but by midday, when Téoline felt the first pain, the mountains were capped by storm clouds. Then in the late afternoon the rains came; the thunder echoed through the foothills and lightning ripped the sky, orchestrating her cries.

Benjamin had gone with Joseph to Le Cap for supplies, and

Téo could not bear to let Sonata go from her side. She paced up and down her apartment or clung to the bedpost, begging whatever spirits were guarding her to come to her aid. When they became too severe she cursed all mankind—especially André Cameron.

It seemed at times as though the pressure would force her downwards through the floor. Finally Sonata persuaded her to lie down and gave her a kerchief to stifle her screams.

All this time the storm roared and crashed through the mountains like a raging fiend. Mamaloi's cabin was several miles away on the fringe of the Bréda plantation; the route through dense jungle was hazardous at the best of times. Téoline was sure that the old woman would not be able to get to her.

Téoline pressed her face into the pillow and tore the handkerchief to ribbons between her teeth. Never in her wildest dreams had she considered that the few hours spent in a man's arms could result in this unending torment. She knew that love would make such agony worthwhile and she was obsessed by the notion that Cameron had rejected her. She vowed in that moment that if her child were all right she would not share it with any man. Since she had been forced to bear the pain alone, then the child would remain hers alone.

Sonata bathed her head with a damp cloth and tried to calm the distaught girl. "Mamaloi will come," she promised through her own tears.

"She can't . . . she doesn't even know . . ." Téo gasped, and screamed again. "Oh, God, let me die . . .!" She clutched Sonata and muttered accusingly, "She is a servant of Satan and you are her slave . . . This is my punishment. I've been wicked and consorted with the spirits of darkness . . .!" She tried to struggle to her feet. She would run out into the storm and let her agony become a part of it. But the effort was too much and she fell back and lay quite still on the bed.

It was only then the two girls became aware of a soft incantation coming from the dark recess in a corner of the room. "Mamaloi!" Téo shrieked. Be she the servant of God or the devil, Mamaloi had come. "Mamaloi . . . For the love of God . . .!"

The old woman got up and shuffled over to the bed. She took a small vial from the pocket of her voluminous striped skirt. Raising Téo's head, she poured a little of the bittersweet potion between her lips and murmured something in her strange dialect.

"What did she say?" Téo demanded of Sonata. She was over-come with panic as she thought she might have been poisoned.

"She says that it is only through pain we learn the value of life . . . ."

Sonata's voice seemed to be coming from somewhere out in space. Téoline drifted away until suddenly she was rent from head to toe by a seething agony. She was convinced that these convulsions were the onset of death, but it was life that came. In a room where there had only been three of them before, there was now a fourth. Téoline had forgotten the pain by the time Mamaloi laid the baby in her arms. All she could think of now was her son.

Within a very few days Téoline was herself again, though a little paler and certainly much thinner. Her strength returned quickly and she was able to sit out and nurse her child. She gloried in his growth and prayed fervently that de Beben would not return until she had had time to plan a future for herself and her baby. She resolutely refused to regard the child as Cameron's.

Mamaloi came frequently to visit them and see how the baby was thriving. It was strange that, although they could not converse, a deep affinity quickly developed between Téoline and the old woman. She was not altogether surprised, therefore, when Mamaloi warned her to be prepared for de Beben's arrival. She was sure he was on his way home although there had been no letter warning of his departure from the south.

But Téo was totally unprepared when, one night a few weeks after Jean-Philippe's birth, Mamaloi arrived suddenly and said she must take the child away. Téoline was nearly demented, but the old woman was insistent and Sonata said she sensed a warning in Mamaloi's words. In the end Téo reluctantly agreed to let her take the baby.

It was as well she did. When she looked out across the savannah the following afternoon she saw a carriage approaching; she immediately recognized the massive figure of Davide on the box. But her heart almost stopped when she realized that Samson was sitting next to him.

Téoline felt her blood chill. The dwarf had made no mention of his master's return, yet he had known when to go and meet him at Le Cap. Obviously Albert had deliberately refrained from letting her know the date of his arrival. There could be no good reason for his having done so.

118

Chapter Thirteen

De Beben greeted his wife cordially, but there was a chill in the atmosphere. He said he was pleased to hear she had been safely delivered of a son, but he did not ask how or where the baby was. It was obvious that Samson must have already told him all there was to know. Neither Téoline nor Sonata had given any hint that Mamaloi had taken Jean-Philippe, but it was more than possible he knew that too. He had his own loyal network of spies. Fortunately Albert had met Bayon de Libertat at the docks and had invited him to stop on his way back to Bréda to take supper with them, so a lengthy conversation was out of the question.

De Libertat was solicitous over Téo's health. He said how pleased his wife would be to hear the news of the baby's birth. He congratulated de Beben on having a son and heir, but the master of Cambenet chose to ignore it. Instead he plunged into a heated discussion of colonial affairs. Things had not gone well in the south. The *grands blancs* were fighting with the *petits blancs*, and both factions were at war with the mulattoes.

"I tell you, the entire colony is on the brink of civil strife unless the governor takes a strong stand," de Beben snorted. He had been drinking heavily throughout the meal and was flushed with wine. "These damned coloreds must be put in their place. And any white found consorting with them . . . like that scoundrel Robillard . . . should be shipped off to France to stand trial."

Quickly and very unwisely, Téoline rushed to remonstrate with him. "From the little I know of him, I would say Pierre Robillard is a moderating influence. He tries—"

"To fool the husbands while he pleasures their wives," de Beben cut in. "He and Mirabeau would make a pair, when it comes to women and their love for the *gens de couleur!*" He glowered at Téoline and the cruel glint in his eyes made her heart quicken.

De Libertat did not understand what was going on, but he couldn't fail to notice the antagonism between de Beben and his wife. "What did you think of the slave market today?" he said. He hoped a change of subject might help to clear the air. "I didn't care much for that big fellow Boukmann when they put him on the block. I understand he led a slave revolt in Jamaica."

"That's why they shipped him out. Now we have to put up with him. Whoever bought him had better keep him under control. He led a bunch of Maroons and knows how to organize the slaves," de Beben replied. Then he turned his attention towards Téoline again. He gave a sickly grin, but there was no humor in his eyes.

"That reminds me, my dear, I have bought you a gift." Téoline recognized the hint of irony in his tone and dreaded what he would say next. "I bought you a young mulatto girl of twelve or so. She's to be your personal maid. She'll arrive in a day or so, but your friend Robillard has to examine her first." He waited for her to reply, and Téo hesitated, sensing a trap.

"That is thoughtful of you, m'sieur," she replied at last, trying to smile as she spoke. "No doubt Sonata will be glad of some help."

"That is not my intent. Élie will take the place of Sonata." His words caught Téo by surprise. She had not been expecting him to attack in such a way.

"But why? I am very pleased with her."

"Possibly. But I am not. Samson tells me that she is rarely without a book in her hands and that she is teaching Benjamin and some of the other slaves to read and write."

"At my behest," Téoline said sharply, but her husband had turned to de Libertat.

"You see how the infection spreads?"

"I can see no great harm in that," de Libertat replied quietly. "As you know, Toussaint has the run of my library. He has taught himself both Latin and Greek, yet no one doubts that he remains faithful to me. I fail to see why knowledge and loyalty should not go hand in hand."

"You cannot tell what fires smolder under his black skin," de Beben snapped as he poured himself another glass of wine. "No, in this matter, I have no intention of being crossed." He turned to his wife again. "Sonata has until the next slave market to school this girl in your ways. Then both she and Benjamin will be sold."

Téoline struggled hard to prevent him from seeing how much his words had shattered her. She glanced across at Samson, who was standing at his master's side, and saw his sly grin. What lies had he been telling to suit his own ends? And what part did his sister Babette have in all this? Pleading a headache, she excused herself and left the two men to talk. Returning to her own apartment, she found Sonata in a flood of tears. Benjamin had been among the slaves waiting upon table and had already told her the news. Téoline sought ways of comforting her, but there was nothing she could say.

While Sonata helped her to prepare for bed, Téo racked her brains for a solution. If she were still alone, she would have been prepared to stand her ground and fight to keep the two slaves. But she had her son to think of, and that made her own position tenuous. Sonata was busy brushing Téo's hair when they heard de Libertat ride away. A moment later there was a loud knocking at the outer door of the apartment, and before Sonata could answer it, de Beben burst in.

He was wild with drink and his normally well-groomed hair was in a state of disarray. His forced entry had caused him to lose his balance and he almost fell; Sonata just managed to rescue the bottle of wine he carried in his hand.

"Get out," he said, pushing the slave to one side. He swayed unevenly across the floor and stopped at the boudoir door. Téoline was still sitting in front of her dressing table, too startled to move.

De Beben paused and looked at her. She was wearing a pale blue negligée and the candlelight fell on the soft gold tresses of her hair. The sight of her sent a renewed surge of rage through his body; he could not bear the thought of his own impotence.

"So, madame, my moment has arrived . . . ? By God, I've waited long enough." His words were slurred, but there was no mistaking his intentions. His very look violated her.

"You're drunk! I'll talk with you in the morning, Albert." Téoline got up and began to edge away.

"I'm not interested in talk, madame. You can save that for Robillard and his colored friends. I want back what Mirabeau stole from me." Lurching forward, he grabbed her arm and twisted it behind her back. "And don't think the de Pavigné name will save you now . . . . My money can always silence them."

Téoline drew in her breath and struggled to break his grasp. As drunk as he was, she was no match for him. In his day de Beben had been a powerful man, and now he had the strength of madness to aid him. Dragging her across the room, he flung her down on the bed, and when she tried to rise, he slapped her face repeatedly.

"You cheated me," he shouted. The pungent odor of wine

made her gasp for air. "And now you're going to pay. By the time I've finished with you, you'll not be fit for any man. Not even that whore Babette will give you a bed!" His hold relaxed as he fumbled with his clothes. Making a supreme effort, Téoline drew back her leg and kicked him in the groin. He crumpled with the pain, and she raced into the boudoir, where Sonata stood trembling with fear.

"For the love of God, fetch Benjamin!" Téo cried. "Tell him my husband's mad and I'm in danger of my life."

A moment later de Beben's hands closed about her throat. "Oh, no, my dear Téoline, you'll not die yet." He shook her as a dog might shake a rat. "Later, maybe, when I've finished with you!"

He dragged her back into the bedroom and ripped away the frail fabric of her gown. Téoline fought like a wild animal. But he was excited by her very screams. He delighted in cruelty. The candlelight blurred into a mist and Téoline knew that in the end he would win.

Suddenly the weight of his body was lifted from her and she heard it crash to the floor. She struggled to sit up and clutched the sheet about her nakedness. Benjamin, his ebony body gleaming in the light from Sonata's candle, was crouched over de Beben's prone form.

"Is he dead?" Téoline whispered, hoping the answer would be "Yes."

"I'm not sure, mistress." Benjamin looked up with terror in his eyes. "I pulled him from you. He struggled and, in falling, hit his head." Sonata knelt down and put an ear to de Beben's chest.

"He lives. . . . Oh, sweet Jesus, he lives . . .! It were better he were dead!" Sonata broke into uncontrollable sobs and flung her arms about Benjamin, who stood there trembling.

"My God! It is merciful you came." Téoline wrapped the sheet about her and came across to the little group. "Without doubt he would have killed me in the end."

But for the moment the two slaves were lost in their own fear. Benjamin bent down to lift the weeping Sonata. He folded her in his arms protectively.

Téoline was terrified but knew she had to recover her wits. "We cannot leave him there. We had better get a doctor." Her thoughts turned to Robillard. If he would come, not only could he attend to Albert, but he would offer her some protection from a repeat attack. "I'll send Davide to Le Cap." She started toward the outer room, but Sonata held her back.

"For the love of Heaven, mistress," she pleaded. "Help Benjamin. What he has done for you this night will mean his certain death." The shock of her words caused Téoline to freeze. She turned to look at Benjamin, an expression of amazement on her face.

"What do you mean? Benjamin was only protecting me. I shall say my husband had one of his seizures. No one will be surprised; many people out here know he is subject to these attacks."

Sonata flung out her hands in a desperate appeal. "That will not be enough. He will be hanged for raising his hand to a white man. When the master recovers he will order him to be put to death . . .!"

"He can't do that!" But as she spoke the words, Téoline knew de Beben could and would. "There would have to be a trial. I will demand that. Benjamin can tell them what took place and I will give witness that it was for my protection."

"You don't understand, madame!" There was a hint of fury behind the slave's words. "As a woman, you will not be allowed to appear. And a colored man, whether he is black or brown, is not permitted to give evidence against a white. A simple death is all he can hope for!" The passion behind Sonata's words shocked Téoline into silence. It was some time before she could collect her thoughts, but at last her mind began to clear.

"Then Benjamin must get away!" While she was speaking she went to her little escritoire and took a bag of coins from the drawer and handed them to the slave. "Have you somewhere you could go?"

"If once I can get to the mountains, I shall be safe. There are several bands of Maroons up there." Téoline knew of these bands, made up of escaped slaves, who roamed the mountainsides. "All I need is a few hours start before they send the dogs after me."

"Go across the border into Santo Domingo," Sonata said.

"No. I want to remain near you. If you are sold I will find you," Benjamin kissed her neck tenderly.

"Go," Téoline commanded. "Sonata and I will see that you have all the time you need. Never fear, I will find some way of looking after her. If it seems best, I'll see that she too escapes." She turned her head away as the two lovers embraced.

"I will come back one day," she heard Benjamin say.

"Yes, one day I'll see that you come back," Téo broke in. "But now you must go. My husband may soon recover consciousness, and I would not want your death on my hands."

123

Benjamin started towards the doors leading onto the balcony. Then he turned and came back to where Téoline stood with her arm about Sonata. Taking Téoline's hand in his, he raised it to his lips, then bowed. A second later he had disappeared into the jungle.

Téoline looked down at the wretched creature at her feet. She thought, not for the first time, how little outward appearances counted against the measure of a man's soul. As soon as Sonata returned from the balcony, where she had been watching Benjamin's departure, they dragged de Beben over to the bed. He was beginning to show signs of life and they were afraid he would call out, but fortunately the wine had taken hold of him. As soon as he felt the soft bed under him he relaxed and made little further attempt to move.

"Undress him to his shirt," Téoline instructed Sonata. "I will go and dress. Everything has to appear normal." She inspected her face in the mirror. It was puffy from the repeated blows, but there were no bruises that some powder and rouge would not disguise. "When I am ready, I will give Davide a note to take to Dr. Robillard." Sonata looked up with a question in her eyes. "It's all right; I shall make no mention of Benjamin in this."

"But surely the master saw him when they were struggling?"

"My husband was crazed with drink. It will be some time before he recovers sufficiently to say what happened." De Beben groaned and started to move his arms on the coverlet. "Quick, help me to tie him to the bed." Téo was not prepared to take the chance of his recovering too soon. Once he was secure she inspected the cut on his head and found it was little more than a skin wound; his thick hair had protected him.

"Now remember, when Samson or any of the others ask, you were asleep on the truckle bed in the dressing room as usual. Nobody saw you bring Benjamin here, did they?" Sonata shook her head. Téo did not doubt it was the truth. For several months now she had known that once she was in bed, Sonata stole off down the back stairs to the little storage room where Benjamin slept. If anyone had noticed her, they would have thought she was going to see her lover.

"I shall say I was finishing a letter before retiring . . . And that my husband was preparing for bed." Téo paused while she concocted the rest of her story. "He had been drinking heavily . . . anyone can tell that from his breath . . . I heard him fall . . ."

"What if anyone heard your screams, madame?"

124

"I doubt it or they would have been here by now. But if they should mention it, I screamed when I rushed in and found him on the floor. We've tied him thus to prevent him injuring himself any further. That will be my story, Sonata. Please remember in case anyone questions you."

Téoline gave a slight smile as she recognized the irony of the situation. "You realize that because I am white there is no one in this house other than my husband who dare challenge me, and no one else would be allowed to give evidence in court. They will find that the pendulum of the law can swing both ways."

Peter Robillard arrived at Cambenet just as the dawn was breaking. He looked at Téoline anxiously. Although she had been at pains to dress carefully, his trained eye noticed the puffiness of her cheeks. He also saw that beneath her calm exterior she was deeply agitated.

"I have been worried about you, madame. I would have called when I came out to Bréda, but . . ."

"I know. It is just as well you didn't. I don't know what might have happened. I fear Albert's mind has become deranged."

"He wasn't far from the edge before. That's what made me fear for your safety. But what of your child? Was your confinement difficult?"

Téoline assured him all was well, but he was not entirely convinced. However, his first task was to examine de Beben.

"It is little more than a drunken stupor. But of course, in his condition it takes more of a toll than it would in a normal man. He'll have a sore head for a few days," Robillard said when he came out of the bedroom.

"Does that mean he'll be about again before very long?" Téo asked, her eyes filling with tears. Her fears, the lack of sleep, and the prospect of having to face de Beben again brought her to the brink of collapse.

"What is the matter, madame?" Robillard took her by the hand and led her to a chair. He sat down opposite her and looked into her eyes. "Don't you think it is time you told me why you are so afraid? It's no good denying it. Don't forget, I know his condition. I also know the reputation he has. He is a cruel man." It comforted Téo to feel that the doctor understood, but she was still afraid to speak. She was not sure what his reaction might be if she were to tell him the truth about Jean-Philippe. She need not have worried, for his next words dispelled her doubts.

125

"I know the child is not his. I've known that from the very first it was impossible." Téoline lowered her eyes and turned away.

"Téoline!" He startled her by using her first name. "I can't help you if you are not honest with me. You do believe I am your friend, don't you? I've been so since that first day at Le Cap."

"I know," she said. "But I've been afraid, for your sake, to involve you in my life. Afraid I might endanger you or your wife."

"Let me be the judge of that. To have visited you in direct defiance of your husband's wishes would have been foolish. But I come now as his physician, and, within limits, there are certain things I can do for his welfare . . . such as ordering his return to Le Cap."

"Would that be possible?"

"I'd highly recommend it. I would be better able to attend him there. What is more, I can keep an eye on you."

"I cannot come," Téoline was adamant.

"You must. Are you thinking of your child?"

Once again Téoline told her story and what had occurred since she had come to Cambenet. She explained how Mamaloi had taken the baby for its safety, and her fears regarding Samson and Babette. She made no mention of Cameron, and Robillard did not press her to reply when he asked who was the father of her child.

"You can't stay here. I've never trusted that dwarf, and if, as you suspect, he incited your husband to behave like this, it would not be safe for you to stay out here alone. I have to go to Bréda to see Madame de Libertat. I'll ask Toussaint to deliver a message to Mamaloi. I know the old woman; I only wish I understood her powers of healing. I'm sure your son will be safe with her, and for the moment it is certainly better for him to be out of the way."

Téoline knew he was right, and it comforted her to hear him speak so well of Mamaloi. She gave instructions to Samson and Sonata to pack the necessary things, while Robillard gave Albert a mild sedative.

She gave instructions for a wagon to be prepared to take her husband to Cap Français. Samson was obviously put out that he was not included in the plans, but he was in no position to protest. However, he requested that he be allowed to ride in the wagon beside the truckle bed they had set for his master; Téo agreed to this. She rode on horseback beside the doctor while

Sonata and Joseph followed in the carriage with Davide up in front.

"He'll sleep for several hours," Robillard said once they'd got Albert bedded down in his apartment at Le Cap. "I shall let it be thought that his condition may be infectious. That will keep visitors away and gossips quiet. It's known he has just returned from the south, and they're prepared to believe the people there are capable of anything."

Within a few days of their return, Albert was almost himself again although the doctor kept him under sedation to a certain extent, saying that rest was essential. Téoline had pleaded with Robillard for as much time as possible. She had to find some means to protect Sonata from her husband's wrath; she was determined not to lose the girl. Also, it was evident that as soon as de Beben was in full possession of his faculties he would have Benjamin posted as an escaped slave with a price on his head.

While Téoline was seeking a solution to these problems she cried herself to sleep at night, sick with worry about her son. Robillard had spoken to Toussaint, but there had been no word from Mamaloi. Sonata had friends among the slaves at Cambenet who promised to send word if they had news of either Mamaloi or Benjamin. In the meantime Samson seemed to be everywhere, watching them with shifty eyes. Both Téo and Sonata were hesitant to speak, sensing his presence at all times.

"I can't keep him in bed much longer," Robillard said toward the end of the week. "He is growing stronger by the hour, and, as you know, he is already suspicious of me. If there were another doctor available, I'm sure he would order me from the house. He was asking to see you, but I told him you were indisposed."

"Did he believe that?"

"I don't know, but I did my best to scare him. I said you must have had a fall, as you were badly bruised. He knows that to be the truth. I think he will be a little more cautious about his treatment of you now that you're in Le Cap; it is more in the public eye, and he does value the opinion of others."

"Sonata tells me he has instructed Samson to see Lapointe. He wants notices posted throughout the province offering a reward for Benjamin."

"I know, but I didn't want to add to your cares. He was also inquiring about the little mulatto girl he bought. I told him she had to remain in quarantine for a few more days. Then he asked Samson when the next slave auction was."

127

Téoline had been arranging some roses in a bowl. Looking down, she discovered that unthinkingly, she had plucked the petals from a bloom. It lay fragmented on the floor, and as she stooped to gather up the shreds, she thought how symbolic of her life it was.

Joseph arrived back from a visit to Cambenet, bringing news of Mamaloi. It took Sonata some time to find the courage to break it to Téoline. The old woman's body had been found beaten to death near her cabin at Bréda.

"And my baby . . . What of Jean-Philippe . . .?" Téoline sobbed.

Sonata shook her head. "There was no sign of him, madame. Joseph was afraid to ask. Like us, he knows what evil forces are at work and he was afraid to call attention to the child. At least we know he was not killed with Mamaloi."

Téoline sent for Robillard and implored his aid. "I must go to Bréda," she said.

"No! That is the last thing to do. It would not be safe for you or your son. You may be followed, and I cannot protect you from here. Believe me, Téoline, I will do all I can. But in the meantime, try not to show your grief. De Beben is mad and takes a sadistic pleasure in your fear. When I come to see him later this afternoon, I think you should accompany me."

"Do I have to? I don't ever want to see him again."

"I know, but we must play for time. You needn't stay long, but you must appear."

Later that afternoon Téo heard angry voices coming from the direction of de Beben's apartment. Thinking it strange that the doctor had not informed her of his arrival, she went along to see if it was indeed Robillard. She went into the small anteroom, hoping to hear more. She had no intention of going into the bedchamber without Robillard at her side. She heard Albert's voice, high-pitched and angry. "Get out!" he was screaming. "Get out! You are never to come here again . . . do you understand?" She stepped back into the shadows as the door to the bedroom opened and closed again.

"My God!" she gasped, staggering from the shock.

"Téoline! Mademoiselle de Pavigné!" A pair of strong arms steadied her, and she looked up into the face of Stefan Cambenet.

"You see, my *loa* did not lie that day; our destiny had to be fulfilled." He took her hand and pressed it to his lips. Time and place dissolved for Téoline. She was once again in Paris, in her sister's salon. A tear escaped from under her dark lashes, and he gently brushed it away with the tips of his fingers.

"My poor child . . . Has life been so cruel?" The tenderness in his voice was more than Téo could bear. He brought back memories of a time when she had felt secure. She swayed toward him and he gathered her in his arms. Before either of them realized what was happening, their lips met. Stefan pressed his mouth against hers with a passion she had no desire to resist. Locked in this embrace, they failed to hear the door to Albert's bedchamber open behind them.

"Damnation!" De Beben's voice tore through the apartment like a thunderclap. They sprang apart. De Beben in his nightshirt was a grotesque figure; he was trembling with a rage that almost choked his speech.

"M'sieur . . .!" Cambenet started to explain. "Mademoiselle Téoline . . . your wife . . . We met long ago in Paris."

"And now you're here to continue your amorous affair!" De Beben was bellowing and his face was purple with rage.

"No, Albert! That is a lie!" De Beben was beyond listening to anyone.

"How many others have you had, you whore? Was it Mirabeau or this bastard that fathered your brat? . . . But you'll learn, I promise you . . . Did you think I'd let it live to take my place . . .?" He had been leaning heavily upon a stick, which he raised over his head. He stumbled toward her, ready to strike, the light of madness gleaming in his eyes. Cambenet was too quick for him; grasping the old man's arm, he forced him to his knees. Albert de Beben let out a cry and clutched his chest. A moment later he lay dead in Cambenet's arms.

The door from the passage was flung open and Samson rushed in, with Robillard hard on his heels. "My husband . . .?" Téoline whispered, kneeling beside the body on the floor. Samson knelt down on the opposite side and put his head against de Beben's chest.

"He's dead!" he said with a malicious smile on his face as he looked across at Téoline.

"I'd be the the best one to judge that," Robillard said, pushing the dwarf away. He made a brief examination before turning to Téoline. The dazed girl had retreated and was in a corner, leaning against Cambenet. "Yes, he's dead, Téoline," he said, without attempting a show of regret.

"What did I tell you?" Samson turned to Lapointe, the lawyer, who had followed Robillard into the room.

"This is most distressing, madame." The lawyer took out a red bandanna handkerchief and mopped his face. He was a large, flabby man, given to pomposity, but in this instance he was acutely embarrassed as he looked at Téoline. "I had no idea Monsieur was so sick. Samson came to me with a message. He said Monsieur wished to alter his will and . . ."

"Yes?" Robillard said impatiently when Lapointe failed to continue.

"I'm afraid the mulatto slave laid some very grave charges . . . very grave indeed. . . ."

"Well, what were they? Out with it, man!" This time it was Cambenet's voice that was raised.

"I'm not acquainted with this gentleman," the lawyer said coolly to Téoline. "I think this matter should be spoken of in private, madame. It is a family affair"—he scowled at Cambenet —"not something to be discussed with strangers."

"Then I'll save any further embarrassment," Stefan replied. "I'm de Beben's son, albeit born on the outside, and though for many years did not know who my parents were." He took Téoline's hand between his own. "It was only when I began to make inquiries as to where you'd gone that I was able to pick up the threads that led me home and to you, dear Téoline."

His words had left the other three men stunned. Lapointe was the first to speak. "Then you are Stefan Cambenet? I've known you by name for many years. Albert de Beben paid you to stay away. He never intended you to know your true identity."

"Cambenet . . .?" A strange change had come over the dwarf, and he backed off into a corner; his look of assurance had vanished.

Robillard had been watching all the actors in this drama, but he was more concerned for Téoline. "These charges Samson made? Since Cambenet appears indeed to be a member of the family, there is no reason you should keep Madame in suspense."

"I don't think it is necessary to worry about that just now," Samson said as he moved for the door.

"Most certainly we should," Lapointe said, attempting to take charge. "In light of all this, his charges may be graver than I thought." The mulatto dwarf looked most uncomfortable. "Is it possible at this point to say what Albert de Beben died from, Dr. Robillard?"

"He was a very sick old man. It appears that his heart gave out. I cannot say for sure until I have conducted an autopsy. But have you any cause for doubt?"

Lapointe shuffled his feet uneasily and stared at the ground. "I can only repeat what this slave told me. He mentioned something about a poison in his master's bed."

"That's absurd!" Robillard's response was gruff. "But we'll put this rumor to rest at once." Grabbing Samson by the shoulder, he propelled him forward into the bedroom. "Show us," he said tersely. "Show us what you found."

A quite remarkable change had come over Samson. All signs of aggression had gone and he cringed away. "I was afraid, madame! Afraid for both you and the master." He looked across at Téoline, who was leaning heavily upon Stefan Cambenet's arm. "One can never be certain of the slaves."

"Stop this sniveling," Cambenet said angrily. "Show us what you found and put Madame out of her misery." He patted Téo's hand reassuringly; that gesture was not lost on the dwarf.

"I found these . . .!" Samson reached under the pillow and brought out a bundle of yellowing herbs. "These . . ." he said in his high-pitched voice. "These have the power to kill a man, but first they destroy his senses, as I believed they were doing in my master's case."

"Then why didn't you remove them?" the doctor asked coldly. "This is all absurd. You know as well as I that he was already half crazed by his disease. Let me look at those." He snatched the bundle from the dwarf's hand. Holding them to his nose, he sniffed. "These have no more potency than a bundle of weeds. His whole story is a fabrication to embarrass Madame de Beben."

"That is not true, m'sieur," Samson spluttered. "I am her most devoted slave. But there are others . . . Sonata . . . She has good reason to wish Monsieur dead."

Téoline gave a slight moan and collapsed at his words. Cambenet caught her in his arms. Murmuring words of comfort in her ear, he carried her out of the room. "I'll see that you hang for this," he shouted as he passed the dwarf. "I'll see you hang!"

Chapter Fourteen

For the next day or so, Stefan Cambenet scarcely left Téoline's side. Peter Robillard was quite relieved to find her alone when he came to deliver the results of the autopsy. He inquired where Cambenet was, and Téo told him he had gone to make the necessary arrangements for his father's funeral.

"You may set your mind at rest about one thing, Téoline. Your husband died from natural causes. I've issued a public statement to that effect."

"Then Sonata is safe?"

"Yes. Although I daresay people will still gossip, human nature being what it is." Robillard shrugged. He didn't want to add to Téoline's burdens by telling her the gossips were already at work about her and Cambenet.

"I can't believe what is happening to me, Pierre." She had reached the stage of numbness. The events of the past few days kept passing in front of her like pictures; she could no longer be moved by them. "Have you had any news of Jean-Philippe?"

"None, I'm afraid. I sent a message to Toussaint. He will be driving Monsieur de Libertat and his wife to the funeral. I shall make a point of seeing him then. In the meantime, I've been busy with this autopsy. If it is any help at all, I don't think you'll have further cause to worry about Samson."

His news was comforting, but Téoline was surprised to hear him speak well of the dwarf.

"I was somewhat surprised myself when he came to see me last night," the doctor continued. "He was in an abysmal state and as anxious as anyone to know the findings of my examination of de Beben's body. He seemed genuinely relieved when I told him I did not suspect foul play. He's a wretched fellow, but in this instance, after listening to what he had to say, I must admit I almost felt sorry for him."

"How could you, Pierre? He was responsible for Mamaloi's death and every horrible thing that has happened to me."

"I'm not absolving him entirely, but he took color from his master. De Beben had used him in many abominable ways since he was a small boy; he can hardly be blamed for having learned his lessons rather too well. But it's true that you reap what you

132

sow, which happened in de Beben's case. Samson's loyalties became divided, and he was ready to sacrifice his master for his sister Babette in the end."

Téoline remained cold. She could find no pity or compassion in her heart for the dwarf.

"He is an evil man."

"You must remember history, Téoline." Robillard passed a weary hand across his brow and tried patiently to explain a situation he knew only too well. "For centuries these people have had to live by their wits. They couldn't afford our standards of morality. The law offers no protection or redress to slaves, and when they're hurt it's only natural they should want revenge."

His last words touched a nerve. In spite of her antagonism towards Samson, her honesty forced her to say, "That is a fault that white men share, as I know to my cost." She was thinking of both Cameron and Albert.

"I don't expect you to excuse him. I'm only saying this so you will understand. Samson was responsible for much of your unhappiness but not for Mamaloi's death. Oh, he wanted you and your son out of the way, he has confessed as much."

Téoline was standing near the door leading into the garden at one end of the salon; at those words she turned and looked at him in surprise.

"Yes, he admitted it because he wants to make his peace with you. He doesn't want any harm to come to Stefan Cambenet. Perhaps you hadn't realized that Cambenet is Babette's son?" It was obvious from Téoline's expression that such a thought had not occurred to her. "It is the usual custom here to name a bastard after the estate on which he was born. It wasn't until he heard his name that Samson knew who Stefan was. For years Babette had planned to be revenged—what better way than to see her son inherit Cambenet, by fair means or foul?"

"Then they had every reason to want my son dead."

"Possibly, but the fact remains that he is not responsible for what happened to Mamaloi. Nor does he know what has happened to Jean-Philippe. De Beben must have been too nervous to enlist his slave's help in this business; he probably judged it too great a risk. He didn't want a scandal attached to himself or anyone on his estate when it became known a grandchild of the Duc de Pavigné was missing."

"Then who . . .?" Téoline could hardly trust her own ears. This was obviously the truth, but it all sounded so bizarre.

"Samson couldn't say. He only knows your husband spoke to

133

one of the overseers on the Turpin plantation. He says they have some bad people there."

"I still do not see that Samson has any right to talk about the evil deeds of others." Some feeling was creeping back into her veins; in spite of her harsh words she did not feel quite so bitter towards the dwarf.

"I have worked for many years among these people," said Robillard, "and I honestly believe that he is telling the truth when he says he had nothing to do with Mamaloi or your son. He does admit he wanted to poison his master's mind against you."

"If he hated me so much, what accounts for his change of heart?"

"When he planted the herbs he meant to discredit you; he accused Sonata as an afterthought when he discovered who Cambenet was and saw that he was deeply attached to you." Téo raised her eyebrows, not sure what point the doctor was making. "He now believes Cambenet to be your lover, the father of your child. He knows his master was impotent."

"I see. That's why you think I am safe now. If Stefan himself can't have Cambenet, it will at least go to his son. Is that what you think, Pierre?" Téo had moved across to the mantelshelf and was watching Robillard's reaction in the mirror. She could see that he was trying to compose himself.

"I don't know, Téoline. He appears to be devoted to you. I've no way of telling how you feel toward him. I have asked you before, but you are not disposed to name the father of your child."

"I will never do that. No man shall ever have the right to lay claim to him. But I *will* say it was not Stefan Cambenet." An expression of relief came over the doctor's face.

"If that's the case, Téoline, you will not think it remiss of me if I beg you not to do as you plan. Sonata tells me it is your intention to ask Cambenet to stand beside you at your husband's grave."

"I mean to, but I'm surprised at Sonata telling tales to you. I thought she was one person here I could trust."

"She is. She is devoted to you, which is why she came to me. She knows I have every reason to be sympathetic to the mulattoes' cause. She also knows the consequences if you chose to defy both society and the law, and she is afraid."

Téoline shrugged and tapped her foot angrily. The doctor went on insistently.

"Don't you realize what it will mean? You are likely to be ostracized at the very least. And if anyone should protest, Cambenet could be forcibly ejected from the church or, at best, compelled to take his place at the back with Marie and the other coloreds."

"That is where you always stand."

"Marie is my wife. When I have a choice, I will not go where she cannot be received."

"It is the house of God. *He* is the host. These petty creatures have no right to deny any man access to his creator, and if they question me I shall tell them so. De Beben was Stefan's father, whether or not he chose to acknowledge it. That is something he will have to answer for. I have made my choice. Stefan Cambenet will stand beside me, come what may." A shaft of sunlight fell across the room, touching the slender figure in her black silk gown.

Despite the sophistication of her words and her dress, Robillard could only think how young and frail she was. He went across the room and took her hands in his. He looked down into her eyes for a moment before he spoke. "Téoline, I have said before that I admire your courage, but I beg you not to be deceived by this man. I grant you he is young and charming, but he is a gambler—an adventurer, well versed in the ways of the world. I've seen his kind many times before. I'm sure he is sincere," he added quickly, as he saw he was not getting through to her. "Nevertheless, I fear his passion will cool. He is a man who does not know what true love is."

"Does any man?" Téoline replied. She was thinking of Andrew Cameron. He had been in her mind so much during the past few hours. In some inexplicable way, he was linked with Stefan Cambenet in her memory.

"Ofttimes more than a woman does," Robillard said rather sadly. "Though I grant you, it sometimes takes them longer to acknowledge it. But there are men—and women, too—who are only capable of loving superficially. They think it's real, but it is like that beautiful butterfly—which lives only for a day."

Téoline watched the beautiful creature, which had flown in through the garden doors, circle the salon and then fly out again. It did not stay long, but while it was there, its magnificent colors lightened the gloom.

"Surely, to love is to love. It cannot be measured . . . One cannot give a little more or a little less?" she asked pathetically.

"It all depends what you mean when you say the word. The value you set on love is the measure of your own worth. From what I know of you, I do not think you would speak it lightly. That is why I beg you to be careful of this man."

"I know you are only thinking of my happiness, Pierre. But be at rest; I feel only friendship for Stefan Cambenet, and I refuse to deny my friends. Which brings me to another matter. From this moment both you and Marie are welcome in this house."

Robillard raised her hand to his lips and bowed. "Thank you, Téoline. Just be sure you know where friendship ends and love begins. . . ." He bowed and left Téoline to ponder his last cryptic remark.

She had met Madame Robillard for the first time that morning; she had accompanied the doctor to offer her condolences. Téoline had been impressed. She was very beautiful, with a creamy magnolia skin; dark curls clustered around her delicate face. There was certainly no reason to doubt, either by her manners or appearance, that she was anything but a Parisian fashion plate. It was easy to see where all Robillard's money went. It was only in the depths of Marie's large, lustrous eyes that Téo glimpsed something that made her feel ill-at-ease. Nevertheless, she told herself, it was as much for the sake of Robillard and Marie that she was choosing to make a stand over Stefan Cambenet.

It appeared that the entire population of Le Cap was determined to be present at the requiem for Albert de Beben. Rumor was rife regarding the handsome young Creole who had suddenly appeared in their midst. Few knew his true identity, but it was already being said he was Madame de Beben's lover.

The square around the church was packed with those unable to find room inside. Soldiers from the garrison had to clear a path for the cortège to pass. Téoline followed in a carriage with Stefan Cambenet at her side; she was nervous and tense, thankful her face was covered by a heavy veil. Her eyes, although red-rimmed from two sleepless nights, were dry of tears. Her honesty would not permit her to weep for Albert de Beben.

Her hand tightened on Cambenet's arm as they entered the gray stone cathedral behind Albert's casket. This was the moment of truth, but no one challenged the right of a de Pavigné to do as she pleased. An undercurrent of excitement ran through the congregation as Téoline and Cambenet walked down the center aisle. Téoline was conscious of a faint buzz of conversation as wives questioned their spouses; they were curious to know the name of the man at her side. There were some who scowled and turned away. Robillard had been right. Téoline knew that she had taken the first steps along a very lonely road.

She knelt and begged forgiveness for her sins and prayed that Albert might be forgiven his in time. She pleaded with God for the safety of her son. It was only when the choir started the opening bars of the De Profundis that she broke down. "Out of the depths we cry unto Thee," the familiar cry, was not one of personal despair—it echoed the agony of all mankind. Téoline could no longer hold back her tears. She endured the service as though it were a distant dream. Finally, Albert de Beben was laid to rest in the elaborate family mausoleum up on the hillside overlooking Le Cap.

As they entered the carriage to return to the house in the square, Téoline almost collapsed with relief that the day was almost over. Stefan held her hand throughout the journey back to the house. No matter what people might say or think, she would always be eternally grateful to him; his strength had been hers when she most needed it.

As soon as she entered the house, Sonata drew her to one side and said Toussaint was waiting in the garden and wished to speak with her privately. Leaving Stefan to mingle with the few mourners who had accompanied them home, Téoline made her way through the shrubbery. She found Toussaint sitting beneath one of the palm trees. As soon as he saw her he got up and bowed, then drew her into the shade so they could not be seen by anyone watching from the house.

"Madame de Beben, I have a message which I could not give to Dr. Robillard. Mamaloi has sworn me to secrecy."

"Mamaloi . . .? Mamaloi is dead!" For a moment she thought he had not heard the news.

"Yes, madame. I wept for the physical loss of my friend, but her spirit is with me still, as it will always be with you. Mamaloi told me that, when she knew she was about to die."

"Mamaloi knew she was to die?"

"Yes. She didn't know by what means, but that did not concern her. She said she was ready for the final journey; she had spent her life traveling between this world and the next. It simply meant that this time the gate would be closed and she would not enter in the same guise. But the love she gave to us cannot die. It is like a thread woven into our lives."

Téoline looked into the large dark eyes and knew what Bayon de Libertat had meant when he said Toussaint seemed to have

137

the wisdom of the ages. She was almost afraid to ask the question so near to her heart. There was no need to put it into words, for Toussaint already knew.

"Your son is safe, madame. My wife has him in her care."

Téoline clasped his hands and kissed them. Both she and Toussaint cried, and their joy and grief became a shared communion. Finally he said, "Would you like me to bring him here or will you go to Cambenet?"

"I think to Cambenet. I'd like to have him to myself for a time. And I think I am more likely to find the spirit of Mamaloi there."

They set a time and a day; then Toussaint was gone. Téoline looked up at the mountains ablaze with the glory of the setting sun. For her, they seemed to herald the dawn of a new day. A new cycle had just begun; the pattern in the kaleidoscope had changed.

All that now remained to be done was to settle the details of Albert's will. The Duc de Pavigné had seen to it that a new one was drawn before his daughter's marriage, and that was the one Lapointe read the following day. Much to the lawyer's chagrin, Téoline insisted that both the doctor and Stefan Cambenet should be present. She felt in need of their support. Apart from a few minor bequests, Téoline was the chief beneficiary. The only other sum of any account was left to the Church with the dictum that regular Masses should be said for the repose of his soul.

"My father obviously intended to insure his place among the saints," Cambenet remarked cynically.

Bernard Lapointe responded with a scowl. He did not approve of the mulatto. Cambenet made him feel inferior. The lawyer's dislike was also heightened by a rumor that Vincent Ogé had escaped from France. The Club Massiac had tried unsuccessfully to stop him, but he was on his way to the colony.

"I wish you to draw up the necessary papers granting the slave Benjamin his freedom, m'sieur," said Téo. "You may do the same for Samson. I do not wish that man to set foot in my house again."

"Madame, do you think that is wise . . .?" Lapointe started to protest. It made him shudder to think of yet more coloreds having the freedom to make trouble.

"I don't wish any argument, m'sieur. I'm contemplating freeing all my slaves in time. Now tell me, what is happening with regard to Monsieur Cambenet?"

"Cambenet has been taken care of. He has a regular allowance, and a previous agreement still stands, providing he doesn't remain in Saint-Domingue." He turned to regard Stefan coldly. "I'd advise you to book your passage back to France immediately."

Téoline saw Stefan's angry reaction to Lapointe's insolence. She placed her hand on his arm and got up from her chair, signaling that the meeting was now over. "That will be remedied, Monsieur Lapointe."

"It cannot be, madame. The money was set aside many years ago and the contract remains inviolate." The lawyer's beady eyes glinted triumphantly.

"Then I shall make another one. What I have is more than sufficient for my needs. But I shall speak to you of that another time." Her first concern was to separate the two men before fresh tensions arose.

Later that day she spoke to Stefan about freeing the slaves.

"Good God, Téoline! Don't you understand that's impossible!" She was startled by the fierceness of his tone. He began to laugh, but his dark eyes did not conceal their contempt. "Your motives are admirable, but can you imagine what chaos there would be? They are illiterate. They have no means of earning a living other than in the house or fields. It would be a crime against humanity to let them loose."

"I believe it a crime against humanity to make them stay," Téoline replied. She wished he had not said that; it spoiled her day and made her furious with him. Yet when she spoke to Toussaint later that week, he said much the same thing, though in a different way.

"No, Madame de Beben, the crime is against the slaves. The men who took away their liberty must now accept the responsibility of caring for them until they have been taught to fend for themselves again. Everything has to be paid for in some way, including tyranny."

Toussaint often came to Cambenet with his master. De Libertat had volunteered to look after affairs at the plantation until such time as Téoline could make other arrangements. She had wanted to dismiss Lortie immediately, but neither de Libertat nor Cambenet would hear of it, and Peter Robillard also told her it was probably unwise.

"The man is doing an excellent job, and the money is rolling in, little one," Robillard said. "It is more expedient to let him stay, at least for a time." In the end Téoline agreed; however, she gave strict instructions as to the treatment of the slaves. The others seemed to think her concern was that of a soft-hearted creature, heartbroken by the cruelty she saw: only Toussaint understood her true concerns. To see a man broken in mind and spirit, lacking any self-respect, debased the entire human race; Téo felt that she was less of a person because of it.

She suggested to Robillard that it would be only fair to sign over the estate in Jeremie to Stefan Cambenet, but he had begged her to wait. Reluctantly, Téo came to think he might be right. Stefan was her constant companion and she was beginning to rely heavily upon him for advice, but there were certain things about him that troubled her.

"Stefan, were you telling the truth when you said you followed me to Saint-Domingue?" Her question caught him off guard and a crimson flush spread over his olive skin. In spite of her disappointment, Téoline smiled. It was impossible to be angry with him. He was so full of laughter, and he made her laugh more than she had done since she was a child.

"What is truth?" he said with a shrug. "If I'd known you were here, nothing would have stopped me from coming to you. Isn't that sufficient?" Stefan plucked a blossom from a magnolia and tucked it in her hair. "If only you knew how much I desire you . . . I have wanted you since that first day we met in Paris." He whispered the words in her ear, and the warmth of his breath on her cheek made Téo's blood race in her veins, reminding her that she was young and that passion was far from dead.

"Stefan, you are utterly incorrigible," she said, smiling up at him. "When we first met I would have been tempted to believe you, but I have grown up since then and have discovered how easily men lie when they speak of love. I am quite sure I'm not the only woman to whom you've said those words."

Stefan gave a sheepish grin and had the grace to blush. "That is possible . . . but they have never meant the same." There was something in his tone that made Téoline glance up quickly. As their eyes met, there was a moment's silence that said more than words. When he spoke again his tone was lighter but there was an underlying tension in his manner. "I can wait. I am a gambler; I have learned to hold back and bluff until the cards begin to fall my way. But . . . " He paused and put his hands on her shoulders and gazed down into her eyes. "One day I will be in a position to come and lay my hand and my heart at your feet, and you will not refuse me."

140

Téoline felt herself trembling. He was so young and vibrant and she was only human. It would be so easy to respond to his passion in that moment. "Now that you have told me that, I shall never know whether to believe you or call your bluff." She laughed lightly, but there was an edge to her words.

"One day I will prove the truth of what I say." Stefan relaxed his hold on her and sat down on the edge of the fountain. He drew her down beside him and, raising her hand to his lips, kissed her fingertips one by one.

A pale gold moon shone down through the giant palm trees. It was a perfect night; the whole sky looked like one enormous sapphire encrusted with a million diamonds. The air was perfumed, sensuous, and intoxicating. In the distance Téo could hear the gentle, lazy sound of the waves lapping the shore, and from the house the slow, soft strains of the piano, which she was teaching Sonata to play.

Quickly she snatched her hand away and, getting up, moved a short distance into the shadows. "Tell me, Stefan, what was the real reason you came to Saint-Domingue?" He shrugged and threw a small pebble into the pond as a brightly colored fish jumped for an insect on the surface. Instinctively, Téo knew he was keeping something from her. "Has it anything to do with the mulattoes and Vincent Ogé?"

Stefan swung round quickly and looked at her. His handsome face had suddenly clouded and there was fury in the depths of his dark eyes. "Yes!" He came across and, taking her hands in his, clasped her against his chest so that she felt his heart beat. "Tonight, more than ever before, I am conscious that the color of my skin does not make me any less of a man. I cannot . . . I will not go on living in a twilight world. I have to help the mulattoes gain their civil rights. I will not be told what I may do or where I may live. De Beben had no right to try and force me to stay in France."

"I would happily have changed places with you," Téo said softly, trying to cool his anger. "I was made to come out here when I would rather have remained in Paris." The memory of it brought tears to her eyes.

Releasing his hold, Stefan gently brushed them away and drew her arm through his as they strolled beneath the trees. "It is perhaps as well you came away when you did, Téoline. The people in the streets have come to realize their strength, and their expectations are rising daily. In the present climate I fear that before long heads will begin to roll under Dr. Guillotine's new knife."

Téo gave a slight shudder at his words. In this instance she knew only too well that Stefan spoke the truth. "What do you intend to do? I will willingly help your cause as long as it will not lead to further bloodshed."

"Don't worry your pretty head over that, Téo," he rejoined brightly. "You will discover that I am a complete coward when it comes to risking my life." He grinned down at her mischievously. "I would much prefer to stay here with you." Then, becoming serious again, he said, "We need money. There is nothing you cannot do if you have sufficient money. There are whites in the Colonial Assembly who would more than willingly support our cause if they could hear the clink of gold."

"Then you shall have all it is in my power to give. If that is the game you are going to play, I will be more than happy to provide the stake."

Stefan stopped and looked at her. "Do you realize what it will mean if we are successful?" he said quite seriously. "One day I shall come to you as a free man and ask you to be my wife!"

"When that day comes, I will have known you longer and be better prepared to answer."

"I will not be refused. No other man shall ever call you his wife while I am alive." There was a passionate intensity to his words that made Téoline catch her breath. It was fortunate that at that moment Jean-Philippe started to wail, reminding her that he was due to be fed.

"I have to go," she said.

Stefan raised her hand to his lips before allowing her to slip away from him. "I must bow to the demands of your son . . . but to no other man. Remember, one day you will be mine. Until then I am prepared to wait."

"And gamble that the cards will fall your way?"

"I have never played for higher stakes."

Téoline broke away and ran into the house. She ran upstairs to her boudoir and, settling down in the fan-shaped rattan chair, took the baby from Sonata.

She cradled her son's small round head in her arm and allowed his soft wet mouth to find her breast. As always, a wonderful feeling of peace pervaded her. She sighed softly as she gently smoothed away a strand of fine gold hair from Philippe's brow and smiled as he frowned at the interruption. His delicate little hands clutched at the lace on the bodice of her gown and she had a job disentangling them. Once again she was lost in wonder as she gazed down at the small creature in her arms. He was so perfect, and she didn't have to question her love for him or share his with anyone. In that moment she knew Jean-Philippe was all she wanted, all she needed; there would never be another man in her life. Yet as he wrinkled his brow impatiently, she could see traces of his father in the tiny features. Try as she might, Téoline knew that from now on, Andrew Cameron would be something more than a bittersweet memory in her life.

Chapter Fifteen

"You're a slut! And you'll remain one until the day you die!" Cameron laughed down at the naked body sprawled across the bed he had just left. The tinge of disgust behind his words was directed against himself; in any case, it would have been lost on the whore. He'd picked her up on the dockside at Martinique. But he couldn't blame her for being what she was; he could find no such excuse for himself.

"Whatever you say, *mon colonel*. I am happy just so long as you pay me and give me a drink from time to time." The girl giggled coarsely and reached for the bottle of wine on the table by the bed. Insults were as much part of the game as the love her clients professed when they were in their cups. At least this one didn't add blows to his jibes. Nor, in fact, had he said he loved her; he was a strange one, but she'd had much worse. It was a pity he wasn't going to let her stay aboard after the ship reached Jamaica.

"No, you've had more than enough of that for this time of the morning," Cameron said, snatching the bottle away and taking it over to his desk with him.

"Not just a little one?" Though she pouted her rouged lips and provocatively rolled her eyes, she could see he was not impressed. From the start it had been strictly business. She was sure she had seen him before, but over the years, in her line of work, she'd been with so many men.

She trailed after him, dragging a sheet but making no real attempt to hide her nakedness. "Just a little one . . .?" She made a playful grab for the bottle but he pushed her away angrily. "You're cruel! You won't let Nina stay with you . . . You won't let her have a drink . . .!" She began to giggle hysterically. Cameron knew the next ploy would be a flood of tears.

"Go and get dressed," he snapped. He swore this would be the last time; each of these women sickened him more than the last. If only he weren't so lonely. He only wanted their company for a few hours, but they always expected the other thing. He went through the motions, but all the fun had gone out of it. He didn't know when it had happened . . . . Maybe he was just getting old. Things had never been quite the same since he had

144

gone back to Paris. People said you should never go back to old haunts. He finished dressing himself, then sat down at his desk to study some papers. Nina was fiddling with her stays.

"Why won't you take me to Boston?" she said sulkily.

"Because I'm not going there. I'm leaving the *Seaspray* at Saint-Domingue, and my captain doesn't want extraneous women aboard. As I told you when you came aboard in Martinique, you can either go ashore at Le Cap or Jamaica, the choice is yours."

"But I want to get to Halifax."

"Now, don't start that again. You'll have to find another ship. Jamaica is a British colony; you'll find it easy enough to get to Nova Scotia from there. Anyway, why this interest in Halifax?"

"I'm tired of the heat and the flies in these stinking islands."

"Up there, you'll have the snow."

"And the money. A girl I met in Saint Lucia told me business is good. She'd been with a real prince."

"That must have been Prince Billy." Cameron had to laugh. "I doubt if there's a whore in Christendom that hasn't had that dubious honor. But you should do well in Halifax, it's a naval base."

"I'm not interested in sailors anymore. It's time I bettered myself. I'd like another gentleman like you." Nina had sidled across to him. Now she gave him a playful nudge in the ribs. Her stale smell disgusted him.

"Well, I suppose there's always John Wentworth. I believe he's a sport. He must be, since he entertained Prince Billy while His Royal Highness was having an affair with his wife. Now go and put on your drawers." Nina turned away. She could see she was getting nowhere with him.

"I suppose you have a woman in Saint-Domingue?"

"It's none of your damned business, but I haven't. I don't trail my heart from place to place. I like to cut all the strings before moving on." Cameron got up from his chair and straightened his cravat before picking up his linen coat. He was going up on deck to get some air. He thanked Heaven that they would soon be entering the harbor at Le Cap and he'd be free of this wretched creature once and for all.

"Like all men, you are heartless. You never think of the women you leave behind." Nina had finished pulling on her drawers and was searching for her skirt under the bed.

Cameron didn't reply. He was thinking how wrong she was,

remembering how often, in the night's long watches, he was haunted by the vision of a young girl with sea-blue eyes and golden hair.

"Anyway, why are you going to Saint-Domingue? I thought you finished your business there last night?"

"What do you mean by that?" Cameron spun round and eyed her suspiciously.

Nina stood up and shook out the tattered skirt. Cameron noted again that the silk was of a rare quality. He could see that even under the dirt, and he doubted that it had been originally intended for her.

"I don't spend all my time in bed." Nina tossed her head. "Leastways, not when I'm alone." If she played her cards right, what she had seen the previous night might be good for a gold piece or two. "After you left me, I went up on deck."

"I told you to stay in the cabin!" Nina merely shrugged. "And . . . ?" Cameron waited angrily for her to go on. "Well . . . what am I supposed to make of that?"

"Well, I saw . . . I saw we was anchored in a small cove." She glared back at him defiantly. She wasn't going to let him intimidate her. "I saw you take those two men ashore. Them two passengers what have been locked in their cabin since we left Martinique."

Cameron gave a grunt of dismissal and turned to the mirror to inspect his hair. He thought he'd have it cut short in the British style when he went back home to Boston. "You were having a nightmare, girl. They were members of the crew going for water."

"And you went to hold their hands, I suppose! What would they be doing going for water in the dead of night, with Le Cap less than an hour away? Slut I may be . . . fool I'm not!"

Cameron laughed to hide his annoyance. It wouldn't do to let her know she'd seen more than was good for either of them. "Here," he said, taking a gold louis from his pocket. "Is this enough to make you forget?"

"Another might do the trick." She grabbed the coins and thrust them into the top of her chemise. "And I can do with a new bonnet."

"Yes," he said, looking at the battered straw with its mangy ostrich plumes. "Very well." He added another two louis to the ones he had already given her and heard them chink as she slid them down inside her gown. It was spattered with grease and wine, but its line reminded him of the ivory silk Téoline de Pavigné had worn that first evening they met. And the bonnet was not unlike the one she had been wearing in the afternoon at her sister's salon. He cursed himself for a fool because he continued to dream of her. Never before had he been plagued by such a memory.

"Now, if you know what's good for you, you'll forget what you saw." He went out and closed the door. He was glad to see her back. He gave instructions to the captain to make sure she left the ship in Spanish Town, then turned his attention to his charts. A few miles away, another of his vessels was heading towards Saint-Domingue. Whether it unloaded its cargo of guns in Le Cap for the use of the garrison or took them to an illicit rendezvous in the cove he'd visited last night would all depend on Stefan Cambenet.

Last night, before he left the ship, Ogé had promised him payment in full before delivery. Cameron was sufficiently in sympathy with Ogé's cause to give him passage in one of his ships, but his sympathies did not allow him to extend credit for the arms. If the revolt failed, he'd never get his money at all. But Ogé had seemed quite certain Cambenet would have it; apparently he'd found himself a white mistress with plenty of money. Cameron picked up his wide straw hat and checked his watch. The ship was docking. He'd just be in time to catch Cambenet at the Coq d'Or.

Téoline heard the sound of horses' hooves on the gravel drive. "See who that is, Élie?" The little coffee-skinned mulatto put down the bundle of clean baby clothes she was carrying and rushed across to the window to oblige.

"It's M'sieur Cambenet, *maîtresse*."

"Who's with him? I heard two horses."

"Yes, mistress. But I don't know the other man."

"Are you sure it's not Dr. Robillard?" Téo asked a little impatiently. She hadn't expected Stefan to come that day, and everything was in a mess. She hadn't troubled to dress and at the moment she was busy feeding her son. Téo wiped the stickiness from his mouth and moved deftly out of the way. Jean-Philippe had been happily squelching a banana through his pudgy hands and he suddenly made a grab for her robe.

"Come, Philippe, we must go and take a look at this stranger." She swung her son up into her arms and went across to the window. She was too late; Stefan and his guest were already out of sight.

147

Within seconds she heard his voice calling her name. How like Stefan to arrive without any warning—but she was always pleased when he came. He had filled a tremendous gap in her life, and Téo had almost made up her mind to marry him as soon as the law would allow. She gave a hasty glance in the mirror. She certainly wasn't looking her best, but Stefan would understand, and he was always pleased to see Jean-Philippe. She hurried down the corridor to greet him. The baby in her arms was happily matting her hair with his sticky hands.

"Téoline, I thought you wouldn't mind. I've brought an old friend to see you. There was no way to let you know, and he must sail again on tomorrow's tide."

"Madame de Beben . . . Téoline . . .!"

The sound made her falter, and Stefan rushed forward to take Philippe from her arms.

"André . . ." she whispered.

Cameron bowed and raised her hand to his lips. His eyes never once left her face.

"I'm pleased to find you so well . . .!" The words faded on his tongue. They were totally inadequate; she was quite radiant.

Téoline snatched back her hand, afraid he would notice how she was trembling. She searched her mind desperately for something sensible to say. "Paris . . ." she said at last. "Paris is such a long way away . . ."

"In time and space," Cameron replied. "Yet at this moment I could believe it was only yesterday."

For a moment the present seemed to dissolve into the past. Then a squeal of delight from the baby brought them both back to reality. Cameron looked at the boy gurgling and struggling in Cambenet's arms, and the expression in his eyes made Téoline catch her breath.

"My son," she said. A wave of panic swept over her and she rushed across to Stefan and snatched the baby away. "Thank you, I'll take him to Élie. It's time he was in bed."

"May I see him?" Cameron barred her way. "What is his name?"

"Philippe! Jean-Philippe. It was my brother's name."

"He does not appear to have anything of de Beben in him." Cameron tickled the baby under his chin.

Téoline sensed the intensity of his scrutiny, but his eyes were hidden by his heavy lashes. She was reminded how she had compared the two men that day in her sister's salon. Against Stefan he was certainly not a handsome man, but he was fascinating, and she could feel his magnetism engaging her senses again.

"He is a de Pavigné," she said defiantly.

"Naturally, on his mother's side, but he must have something of his father in him?" Téoline could not trust herself to reply. She could read the real question all too clearly in his eyes. "I was surprised when Monsieur Cambenet told me of your husband's death . . . and of the birth of your son." Again she felt the underlying meaning of his words.

"No doubt you had quite forgotten the name after all this time." Téo made an attempt at casualness.

"Me . . .? Forget a de Pavigné! You do me an injustice, Téoline, if you think I forget as easily as that."

Stefan interrupted them just then. "Téo, let me return Philippe to his room. I have brought a new toy for him. No doubt, after all this time, you have many things to talk of with Colonel Cameron?"

Téoline noticed Cameron's jaw tighten; it was obvious that he resented Cambenet.

"Thank you, Stefan," she said, handing the baby back to him. It would be better if both of them were out of the way. "Tell Sonata I shall be along presently to say good night to Philippe and dress for supper."

For a few seconds there was silence as Cameron watched them go.

"It's fortunate Stefan Cambenet is so fond of your son," he said, and there was a definite edge to his voice.

"Why shouldn't he be? He is, himself, de Beben's son."

"But not Jean-Philippe . . . . You'll never make me believe de Beben fathered him." His eyes dared her to lie.

"Who else should be his father other than the man who married me?" Téo's heart was racing but she strove to keep the tremor from her voice. It was impossible for her in her present state to know which was the greater fear: that Cameron should lay claim to her son or that she would once again fall under his spell.

"Téoline!" Cameron placed his hands on her shoulders and his strong fingers bit down into her soft flesh. "Anyone but a fool would know he's not de Beben's child. And, judging by his age and the date of your marriage . . . Could it be . . . Is it possible? For God's sake, tell me. I must know!"

Angrily, she wrenched herself out of his grasp. She must not let him feel her trembling or know how deep was her concern. "Jean-Philippe is my son. That is all you're entitled to know, André . . . and all you will ever learn from me. I will never share him with another man."

"Not even Cambenet?" Cameron flashed back angrily.

"Stefan is my friend—"

"More than your friend, the gossip goes!"

"Let the gossips say what they will. My conscience is my own. Now, if you'll excuse me, I must go."

She started toward the corridor leading to her own apartment. But before she had gone more than a step, Cameron was in front of her again. His gray eyes were troubled as he sought to find some means of reaching her. Not for many years had he been in such a position, where he felt the need to beg. He had forgotten how—and the means he used to delay her only added fuel to the flames.

"That is not all the gossips say. This man Cambenet, do you know what he's about? . . . You little fool, don't you know he's fleecing you to finance the mulattoes' cause? Why do you suppose I met him today?"

Only his last question surprised Téoline, but she quickly turned away and looked up at the mountains turning to shadows in the dusk.

"I am well aware what Stefan is doing. It was my wish to help the mulattoes."

"To incite a revolution. I remember you telling me that you were not a revolutionary."

"I can remember telling you many things in Paris. I was very young and innocent. But as you know," she said slowly, "things changed." The bitter memory of that night when she had told him of her love and been rejected suddenly gave her strength.

Cameron heard the resolution in her voice and realized he was not going to win this fight. "Is this to be your revenge, Téoline?" There was a note of pleading in his voice. She was beautiful in her fury; her eyes the gray-green of a storm-racked sea.

But Téoline's agony came from a burning desire to feel his arms about her once again. Another moment and she would have gone to him, but then she saw Stefan coming towards them.

"Forgive me, André, but I have to dress. I'm sure you and Stefan have many things to discuss." She smiled brightly at Cambenet, who blew her a kiss. Then, gathering up the flowing silk of her robe, she fled.

Sonata sensed there was something out of the ordinary about their guest. She had never seen her mistress in such a state before. She used all her skills when dressing Téo's hair, but Téo kept pinning and repinning it, fiercely examining herself in the mirror.

Cameron thought Téoline had never looked lovelier than when she took her place at the head of the table. She was wearing a gown of soft ivory silk, and he wondered whether she had chosen it purposely. Motherhood had brought her figure to full fruition, and the delicate oval face was beginning to show a new maturity, which suited her. Cambenet was effusive in his compliments—and kept appealing to Cameron to confirm them for him.

"Isn't she beautiful, Colonel? Have you ever seen such grace?" Cameron wanted to kill him. He wasn't sure Cambenet didn't do it deliberately to tantalize him. Téoline had regained her composure and was the very essence of dignity. It was impossible to tell the depth of her regard for Stefan Cambenet, but there was obviously a bond between them. Cameron cursed himself again for being such a fool. But he was not beaten yet. He wanted Téoline and his son, and he would come back for them.

"Have you heard anything of Julien?" Téoline asked, feeling that subject was safe. "I have been worried about him. I have heard nothing, but that is like Julien, I'm afraid."

"I've not been to England for some time. The last time I saw him he was well." Cameron did not add that the Comte de Chantal was engaged in raising a regiment, with the intention of aiding the colonists who favored the royalist cause against the growing number of revolutionaries. Perhaps that would be the way back to Téoline's heart; he would make a point of contacting Chantal. He promised he would do that before he said good-bye.

"It is unfortunate that I have to leave Le Cap so soon. But I have urgent business to attend to for Cambenet." He gave Téoline a warning glance as he stooped to kiss her hand. Then he looked across at Stefan and glowered. "But I shall be back before too long, you may rest assured."

Téoline was thankful to see him go. The evening had been a strain, and she had been afraid she would not be able to keep up her pose. In addition to her own emotional confusion, another matter troubled her as well. She waited until Cameron had reached the courtyard and was busy mounting his horse before drawing Stefan into the shadows on the veranda.

"What is it?" he whispered, sliding his arm about her waist.

"Something is troubling you. Tell me, is it Cameron? There is something about him that disturbs you. Perhaps I should not have brought him here . . ." He babbled on in his usual charming way. He held her hand to his lips and interspersed each statement with a kiss on her fingertips.

"No, Stefan," she lied, and tried to laugh it off. "Why should I be worried by him? But I am concerned. It was obvious from your conversation tonight that you have plans I do not fully understand. The money I have given you . . . It was to help win support in the Assembly . . . for bribes . . . nothing more?"

"When have I ever lied to you, my love?"

"Frequently," she said, and tweaked his ear. "You find it hard to know what is the truth."

"Don't we all?" he said gaily. "But over this, my dear, you will have to trust me. You know how much it means that we should win our rights. . . . I want you for my wife, Téoline. About that I will never lie!"

Téoline's heart told her he spoke the truth. She watched the two men ride off into the night and wondered which of them carried her future happiness.

She had often wondered how she would feel if she were ever to meet Cameron again; she had never dreamt she would find it so disturbing. Téo returned to her apartment and stood looking down at the sleeping figure of her son. Now, more than ever, she could see the strong likeness he bore to Cameron; only a fool would deny it. Fiercely she gathered Philippe into her arms, ignoring his sleepy protests. She had to hold him close to her heart. She had to reassure herself that he belonged to her. Yet even as she did so, she felt a certain pride that his father was Andrew Cameron.

For several weeks Téoline neither saw nor heard anything of Stefan Cambenet. All she had to go on was the gossip brought back by slaves taking produce to the docks. Eventually she sent a message to Robillard by Sonata. She knew he would tell her the truth. He sent back word that rumors were buzzing through the air with the speed of fever flies, and often their reports were as deadly. It was said the mulattoes, under Ogé, were massing for attack on Le Cap.

Sonata added that tensions were running very high and that the mulattoes left in the capital went in fear of their lives. Robillard made no mention of that, but Téo guessed he was worried about Marie. Still more days went past, and the lack of news was becoming more than Téo could stand.

"I am going to Le Cap to see for myself, Sonata. Take good care of Philippe if my return should be delayed."

"Madame, I beg you not to leave Cambenet!" Sonata had just come in from the garden, where she had been talking to one of Lortie's men. "A few days ago General Cambefort marched against Ogé with the artillery from the garrison and fifteen hundred men!"

There was no mistaking the fear and pleading in the slave's dark eyes. Téoline did not need to be told that Ogé's cause was lost. What could a few hundred mulattoes hope to do against such odds?

"I have to go," was all she said. Even in the heat of the day it felt as though she had iced water in her veins, but Téo knew she had to go; she had to find out for herself what had become of them.

Taking Davide with her for company, she left for Le Cap in the early hours of the following morning. They rode on horseback because it was both quicker and, under the circumstances, safer that way. The day was breaking as they entered the city streets, and Téo was surprised to find them already thronged with people in a holiday mood. Their numbers were so great she had difficulty in getting through; several times Davide dismounted to make a passage for her. The stench and the din brought back terrifying memories of the Paris mob, and she thanked God that the doctor lived in the nearest outskirts of the town.

"*Mon Dieu!* You should not have come today, Téoline." Peter Robillard, his face ash-gray, drew her inside and closed the door. "I would have come to you, but I dare not leave Marie. The people are crazed with fear; several harmless mulattoes have been murdered in the past few hours."

"Stefan? Have you word of Stefan?" Téo pleaded, following him into their main salon.

The house was small and unimposing, but normally quite neat; however, today it was in a terrible state. Marie sat on the settee, her eyes red from weeping and her face chalk-white.

"The servants have left. They were too afraid to stay. So many threats have been made against Marie's life." A terrible cry rent the air and a roar went up from the crowd outside. Robillard hurried across and gathered his wife in his arms in an attempt to quiet her fears. "They've taken Ogé and Chavanne. They're breaking them on the wheel before they're hanged!" Téoline collapsed into a chair and covered her ears as another roar was heard. "Listen to them!" Robillard muttered angrily. "They've smelt blood."

"Surely they don't have to torture them. Few animals torture their prey." Téoline was fighting back tears.

"You forget, these men are civilized. They regard it as a sport."

"Stefan! For God's sake, Pierre, tell me that he's safe."

"I've had no news that he is among those taken. Some of them managed to escape to Santo Domingo. For your sake, I hope he's one of them." He was sorry for Téoline but angry with the mulattoes who had brought down such terror on the innocent heads of those like Marie.

There was a lull in the noise outside, and he took advantage of it to fetch some wine. "You must go back to Cambenet, as soon as you've had this. Your relationship with Stefan has long been suspect, and it would not be wise for you to be seen in Le Cap today. I wish I could see you safely back, but I must protect Marie."

"You must bring her to Cambenet. I will see that she is safe, I promise you, Pierre." Even in her own terror, Téoline's heart went out to him.

"I shall be forever in your debt."

"It is the least I can do for my friends. I will go back in case Stefan tries to get news to me. Bring your wife as soon as you think it safe to leave."

"I will wait until the streets have cleared—probably around dusk. And in the meantime I will do my best to get news of Cambenet." He saw her to the door and kissed her hand. "Take care, my friend. I know you have courage, but don't do anything impulsive. You must think of Jean-Philippe."

With the ever faithful Davide riding behind to guard her back, Téoline headed back towards the mountains and Cambenet. For several miles, or so it seemed, she could still hear the shrieks of the crowd ringing in her ears. Poor Ogé and Chavanne, they did not deserve such a fate; at least they should have been allowed to die with dignity. Halfway along their route they passed Lortie, who was going the other way. He doffed his hat, but it was the merest courtesy, as he made no attempt to slacken speed. The sight of the man always made Téoline feel ill-at-ease; under the present circumstances it made her press her horse harder. She wanted to get home to Cambenet; she was overcome by a sudden urgency. She breathed a sigh of relief as they slowed down to cross the wooden bridge beside the mill.

Her dress was soaked from riding through the burning heat of the late afternoon sun. She dismounted and paused as she felt a cool refreshing breeze on her skin. Then she heard Sonata calling to her from the balcony.

Looking up, Téo knew instantly that something was wrong. "Is it Philippe?" The girl put a finger to her lips to silence further questions. Without another word, Téoline ran to the back stairs leading from the garden to her bedroom. Sonata was waiting for her and pointing towards the little dressing room.

"My God!" Téo fell to her knees beside the truckle bed kept for her slave. Stefan lay motionless and his shirt was spattered with blood. For a moment Téo thought he was dead.

"I've dressed his wounds," Sonata said as Téo lifted the edges of the bandages about his head and around his leg. "They are not severe, but he is exhausted and has lost a lot of blood."

"How long has he been here?"

"Just after you left—before daybreak. He wants to leave again as soon as it is dusk." They had been whispering, but their voices made him stir, and he murmured Téoline's name.

"Did anyone see him come?" Sonata shook her head.

"I doubt it. Everyone was asleep or about their work. He would have had enough sense to avoid Lortie's guards."

"I pray you're right," Téoline whispered, and soothed his head. "He's burning with a fever. Fetch fresh water and some brandy. I'll stay with him. Tell Élie I am indisposed and that she must watch over Philippe tonight." As soon as Sonata left, Téoline bent down and kissed Stefan on the cheek. He opened his eyes and smiled at her.

"My love . . . My dearest love . . ." He struggled to rise, but she pushed him back against the pillows.

"Hush," she whispered. "You must save your strength."

Sonata returned with the water and spirits. Gently Téo raised his head and cradled it against her breast as she poured a trickle of brandy down his throat. Slowly the color began to return to his face and he seemed more conscious of where he was. He held her hand to his lips and murmured again, "My love . . . my own dear love . . ." Then he slept. Téo left his side only to change her gown. She prayed harder than she had ever prayed in her life before.

The shadows were already deepening by the time he awoke, but the rest and brandy had done their work. "I must go," he said after he had kissed Téo again. "I should not have come . . . but I had to see you once more."

155

"You're not leaving here. You will remain at Cambenet. This is my property . . . no one will dare touch you here!"

Stefan raised her hand and kissed her fingers. "In their present mood, they'll not listen to anyone. If you try to defend me, it will bring down their wrath on your own head."

"I don't care! I'll not give you up, Stefan," Téo said belligerently.

"I know that, *ma chérie*. That is why I shall go. You must think of yourself and Philippe. I shall be safe once I can get into the mountains."

"Then let me come with you. I'll send Élie and the baby to Madame de Libertat." She had left his side, and for the moment was staring up into the purple shadows of the mountains.

"You can't, Téoline. Your heart would be divided. I will be safer alone. But I will come back, believe me. . . . Have I ever lied?"

He made an attempt to laugh, but she sensed he was near to tears. Téo did not hear him move until he stumbled and almost fell. Turning, she ran to him and they clung together while Stefan rained kisses upon her hands and face.

"Believe me, Téo, this is the only way. You stay—and help my people if you can."

Téo knew it was useless to argue. She had already discovered how stubborn he could be. She broke away and went to her dressing-table, taking a small pistol from one of the drawers.

"Take this, you may have need of it!"

The words had scarcely left her lips when they heard a commotion in the courtyard below. Téo hurried to the window as Peter Robillard ran up the stairs to her balcony.

"Quick," he said, his face deathly white in the moonlight. "Help me hide Marie. There is a detachment from the garrison on the road hard behind us. If they are searching for somebody, I dare not let them find her here. It is for your sake as much as hers," he added breathlessly.

"This way!" Téoline grasped Marie by the hand and hurried her into the dressing room. Robillard was about to follow them but was stopped short by the sight of Stefan Cambenet.

"My God! . . . What has happened to you, man?"

"There is no time for that! See to it that Marie and Stefan stay in there, and leave the rest to me," Téo cried as she raced back to close the shutters and lock the outer door of her apartment. Already she could hear the horses' hooves thudding on the dry road; the men were riding at full gallop.

"They're coming for me!" Stefan's dark skin had grown quite pale. "I must go. I'll never let them take me alive!"

"There is no time! Trust me!" Téo implored. She could hear Sonata arguing with them outside the door. She recognized Lortie's voice. Now she knew what mission had taken him to Le Cap. Anger welled up inside her. She signaled to Stefan to hide. "Tell them I have the doctor with me . . . that I cannot see anyone tonight, Sonata!" But her voice was drowned by the hammering and shouting outside the door.

"Madame de Beben, this is Captain Legrand. I must speak with you. We have good reason to believe that the mulatto Cambenet is hiding here!"

Before Téoline could reply, Stefan had reached her side. She was about to speak again, but he silenced her with a kiss as an ax started to splinter the door.

"You are heartless, madame," Stefan's voice rang out. "You have betrayed me for another man!"

Before Téo could stop him, his strong fingers closed over the pistol she was still holding. She felt the trigger move, but the shot was almost drowned by the crash as the door gave way. Téoline was conscious of a warm trickle of blood on her bare flesh. The captain raced across and snatched the pistol, still smoking, from her hand.

"I'm sorry we did not arrive in time to spare you this, madame. But it was courageous of you to kill the cur!"

Stefan was slowly sinking to his knees, his arms still clasped about Téoline's skirts. Grabbing him roughly by the shoulder, the officer shook him free. He crumpled to the floor, his brown eyes beginning to glaze.

Téoline opened her mouth in an attempt to speak, but no words came. She held out her arms to Robillard, who was standing in front of the dressing-room door. It was a gesture of speechless despair. As her lips managed to form the word "Pierre," she sank toward the floor.

In a moment he was by her side, his strong arm about her shoulders. She clung to him, too stunned to know all that was going on. Robillard stroked her hair gently and tried to soothe her with murmured words.

Legrand, who had been kneeling by Stefan's side, got up and gave him a knowing wink. "It's very fortunate Madame had a change of heart in time, m'sieur," he muttered under his breath.

Téoline did not hear. She was watching the soldiers drag Stefan's body away.

Chapter Sixteen

Téoline curled her toes under in the soft white sand as the cool water lapped gently around her ankles. Some distance away, along the beach, Philippe was practicing his first tottering steps. Already he was showing his independence. She watched as he pulled his hand away from Élie's and tried to beat her away with his small fist. If Sonata had not been holding him by his other hand, he would have tumbled, but he would not have cried, except in rage. Her son did not lack courage even at such an early age. Téoline sighed as she thought how much he was going to need it and vowed that at any cost she would never break his spirit, although she was beginning to realize that if he was to become his own man she, in turn, would have to relinquish her hold on him.

Téo wondered if it was her destiny to lose the men she loved. It was a thought frequently in her mind these days, possibly because each day her son forced her to recall something of her father or her brother Julien, as well as Cameron. There was no escaping the past, try as she may. Having come to recognize how much her child meant to her, she found herself thinking more kindly of her own parents. She wondered what her mother would have been like had she known her. Perhaps more significantly, Téo wondered about the man her father might have been had his wife lived. She knew now something of the agony he must have suffered losing the woman he loved; there was no reason to think the loss would be any less painful for a man. She sighed regretfully. If she had shown her affection for him a little more, instead of always fighting him, things might have been different. Why does one always come to realize these things when it is too late to remedy them?

She looked up as she heard an angry squeal of protest from Philippe. He was standing with his two sturdy little legs apart, firmly planted in the sand and refusing to change his chosen course toward the sea. She smiled as she recalled how Cameron often stood with his feet apart, glowering into the distance. What a future for her son, the de Pavigné pride and Cameron's dogged determination to have his own way. Was it possible that, like her father, André used his pride as a shield against the vulnerability of his own heart? Possibly she would never know, for he had not returned and, now that Stefan was dead, there was no reason why he should.

As she leaned back against an outcrop of rocks, her gaze rested on the vast empty horizon. Téo was certain that if she were to reach it, she would find that it dropped away into nothingness. These days she deliberately lived in a world where there was nothing beyond the immediate present. The past was too painful to recall and the future only presented a dark, endless tunnel. Sleep did not come easily, and when it did she almost dreaded it. She would dream and, waking, think Stefan's death had been a part of it. She would call his name to reassure herself, anxious to tell him how frightening it had been. Then she would remember the bitter truth: the dream was the fact, the fantasy was the reality. She had to bear the unbearable, and there was no escape.

She lived from hour to hour, from day to day, trying to think only of what had to be done at that moment. Trying to ignore the awful black void that surrounded her life, Téo concentrated all her hopes and dreams on Philippe. He was all she had, her only reason for living; for herself, life was at an end.

Today was the first time in several months that she had left the house and gardens of Cambenet. She had finally agreed to accompany the girls and Philippe down to the little cove, after Sonata told her how the boy loved to splash around in the sea. She smiled as she thought how soon he had tired of that. Philippe had a restless energy that she recognized as coming from Cameron. It was impossible to eradicate all traces of his father even had she wanted to, and Téo was not at all sure how she felt about that. She was no longer sure how she felt about anything. She had loved both Stefan and Cameron in different ways; all she was sure of now was that she never wanted to love a man again.

The splinters of pain that were lodged in her mind were becoming too acute for her sanity. She felt in the pocket of her gown. She must concentrate on a matter at hand, so she took out the letter she had just received from her sister Louise and read it again. So Mirabeau was dead . . . poor Mirabeau! They said he was a man whose dreams were beyond his reach.

Madame Duval went on to say that she feared what would happen next. While Mirabeau was alive he had managed to keep things in check. But now, with the economy in a terrible state and prices rising by the hour, the different factions were fighting bitterly among themselves. The only thing on which they seemed to agree was their mistrust of the King and Queen and the people that surrounded them. Lafayette and others felt it would be best to go to war with another power in order to unite France in a common goal. Louise went on to say how much better it was that Téo and her son were out of it. If only she knew, Téo sighed; things were no better in Saint-Domingue.

Marie Robillard had stayed with her for several weeks after Stefan's death. But now the feelings against the mulattoes had begun to subside, and she had been able to return to Le Cap. Téo had not been sorry to see her go. She was pleasant enough, but an empty-headed little thing who could talk of little else but fashions and the gossip of the day. Although she wondered what Robillard saw in Marie, she admired his loyalty. Marie's presence had not eased Téo's loneliness—on the contrary, it seemed to deepen it. The only person who understood her was Toussaint.

Téoline had told him the true facts surrounding Stefan's death. Apart from the Robillards, he was the only one who knew what had really taken place that night. The officer at the inquiry had said how Téoline had very bravely, and at the risk of her own life, killed this man who had sought vengeance against her. Legrand did not say directly that it was because Robillard had supplanted him in her affections, but the implication was there. The doctor had insisted that she let it stay that way, and Marie didn't seem to care. As for the general populace, they, as always, believed what they wanted to.

It was Toussaint who had finally begun to prize open the hard shell in which Téoline had encased her emotions. "Life is a continuous thread," he told her. "It is the melody of God which runs through all living things. Birth and death are merely a pause for the rhythm to change, as it does with the seasons, or with the tides. The movement never ceases, but we perceive it differently. Your friend Stefan remains in a state of being. If you deny he exists, and remain frozen in your grief, you are denying him the right to go on living. You must acknowledge his life force, or his spirit will never find peace."

Téoline thought of Toussaint's words as she kicked some loose pebbles into the oncoming waves. She watched as the white foam eddied about her feet before being drawn back into the main current to form another wave. Life had to go on; there had to be another wave, another dawn—perhaps even in the heavens when a star died another was born. Téoline went in search of the others, and together they returned to the plantation. She felt an upsurge of energy. She knew that she must do something, she could no longer allow herself to drift.

She was thinking of this as she scanned the newspapers Louise had sent from Paris. It was criminal how they distorted the facts. Marat's writing was particularly inflammatory, and she recalled how Charlotte Corday had railed against the wretch, saying that one day he would pay for his sins. Thinking of Charlotte and the convent at Caen, she was reminded of her own love of words. She thought of a motto that the Mother Abbess had instilled in them: "The pen is mightier than the sword." Téo suddenly realized that she had a weapon that would help her accomplish her aims: words. If Marat could use them to incite the Paris mobs, why couldn't she use them to make the colonists see sense? Perhaps her writing could bind them together. Eager to set to work, she discussed her ideas with Toussaint and later with Peter Robillard. Before long a series of broadsides began to appear on the streets of Le Cap. The doctor had insisted she use a pseudonym. At first Téoline had refused, saying she was not ashamed to put her name to her words; however, she had given in for Philippe's sake. It wasn't long before she had to admit Pierre had been right.

She tried to be fair—to give all sides of the arguments. But try as she might, it seemed a hopeless task. It distressed her to learn that people see only what they want to see and hear what they want to hear. Tempers became inflamed and there were calls for the writer's blood. The only bright spark in all of it was that no one, for one minute, thought the author might be a woman.

A few weeks after she started her crusade, Téo was playing with Philippe on the lawn at Cambenet when Bayon de Libertat and Toussaint arrived. Bayon had been to a meeting of the Colonial Assembly that afternoon, and it was obvious from his manner that things had not gone well. Téoline was concerned. She had become deeply attached to both the de Libertats. Since Albert's death, Bayon had seen to the details of running the plantation, and she felt indebted to him.

"It is hopeless," he remarked to Téoline. They were sitting in rattan chairs on the lawn, and Toussaint was talking to Philippe. "I despair of them ever seeing sense. The majority in the Assembly are demanding that Governor Blanchelande ignore this new directive from France granting the mulattoes full civil rights. They even threaten to secede from France and hoist the British flag over the colony."

"Oh, my God! Has it come to that?"

"I'm afraid so. They appear to have a certain support among the people. The streets of Le Cap are at this moment littered with tricolor cockades. The French Assembly were angered by Ogé's cruel death and passed this decree in haste; they are determined to see that it is enforced. The Jacobins are sending commissioners determined to make the *grands blancs* obey. I've no doubt that when they arrive the radicals amongst us will feel they have support, and then the fun will start."

"Is there nothing to be done? You know you can count on me if there is any way I can help," Téo said, pouring out some lime-water into the glasses set before her.

"I know, Téoline. And I think it only fair to say that I have guessed at the part you have been playing." A slow smile played about Bayon's lips, and he raised his glass to her. "I know you too well not to recognize some of the opinions which have been voiced in the broadsides of late."

Téo was about to deny it, then she shrugged. "Have others guessed?"

"I don't think so. They are not as familiar as I am with the way you think. But I must warn you to be careful—feelings are running high. I had not intended to mention it, but Blanchelande has asked me to locate someone with a powerful pen who could sway the slaves."

Téoline raised her eyebrows quizzically. "Few of them can read. He must expect a miracle overnight."

"He wants a miracle! He and Procurator Gros between them have conceived a complex plan which, in my opinion, is doomed to failure from the start, but"—he shrugged—"they are set on it. My main concern is that they want Toussaint to be a part of it. I am worried for his sake."

"Have you spoken to him?"

"I made Gros do it for himself. Toussaint!" he called to his slave. "Come and tell Madame de Beben the proposal that was made to you this afternoon."

Toussaint put down the ball he had been tossing for Philippe and came across the lawn. "They want me to stage a revolt of the slaves, madame."

"They what? . . ." Téoline thought her ears were playing tricks.

"They want me to choose slaves that I can control. The procurator will supply us with food and arms, and I am to take them into the mountains and wait."

"And wait for what?"

"The white colonists will be frightened when they hear the slaves are in revolt. They will give in to the governor and obey the French decree. It will unite the whites and the mulattoes against the blacks, forcing them to realize they cannot control a slave uprising without the support of the army."

Téoline had never seen him so distressed. "And when all this has come to pass, what then? What happens to the slaves?"

"Toussaint will bring them down from the mountains, hand back the arms, and return the slaves to their masters," Bayon de Libertat replied.

"*Mon Dieu!*" Téoline had to laugh. "Forgive me . . . but only a man could have dreamed up such a scheme. Do they really expect that men who have been in bondage for years will play out this charade as they have planned?" she said on a more serious note. "And what if any of them are caught? Will Blanchelande intercede for them, or stand by while they are hanged?"

"I thought of that, but the governor assures me he will sign passes guaranteeing their safety in such an event."

"And what do the slaves get, apart from this piece of paper?" Téoline gave a snort of disgust.

"Toussaint and the other leaders will be granted their freedom. The others, when—and if—they return, will be given an additional free day every week. And the whip will be abolished."

"Does the governor think he can guarantee that, when he can't even get the colonists to obey a government decree?" Téo said scathingly. She certainly knew Lortie would not obey such an order.

"The governor has given his word," Toussaint said, but he deliberately made no attempt to look Téoline in the eyes.

Téoline looked across at de Libertat, but neither of them spoke. To say what was in their minds would be to betray the value the blacks put upon the word of a white man. In Bayon's case it was self-preservation and loyalty to his own kind; for Téoline it was nothing but shame.

"Do you think such a plan could succeed, Toussaint?" she asked after a few moments.

"I don't know, madame" he said hesitantly. "But if it would save further bloodshed, perhaps I should try." He turned and set his eyes upon the mountains.

163

"But you are not at all sure it would, are you?"

Slowly he turned back and their eyes met. "No, madame. I fear my action could light the underbrush which would set the forest aflame. And—" He stopped short and looked uneasily from one to the other. His master gave him an unusual degree of liberty, but he was wise enough to know there were limits even with a man he looked upon as his friend.

Téo understood his hesitation and sighed. "And you cannot be sure how much weight you can put on what was said. The trap of words!" Téo gave Toussaint a smile and he knew she had read his thoughts.

De Libertat got up from his chair, his face flushed with embarrassment. He was a fair-minded man, but he found himself caught in the midst of a situation which he could neither approve nor deny. "I must be going, my wife is expecting me. Toussaint, will you see to the horses?" he said, dismissing his slave.

"Bayon, you're not going to agree to Toussaint being a part of this, surely?"

"I'm not sure I can refuse. There is a fine distinction between an order and a request, when it comes from those in power."

"And what was the part you proposed I should play in this?" The sharpness of Téoline's tone already expressed what her answer was likely to be.

Bayon looked around to make sure Toussaint was out of hearing. "The procurator sensed Toussaint had doubts about the safety of the slaves if they were to take part in all this. He feels they would be happier if they felt the directive came from the King himself."

"That is another joke. Poor Louis is nothing but a powerless puppet locked up in the Tuileries."

"But few out here realize that. Certainly not the slaves. Gros intends to have some special copies of the Paris newspapers printed with an article purporting to express the wishes of the King in this. It will back the governor's statement about the concessions to be made to the slaves who take part in it."

"And you want me to write . . . this article . . .?" Téo said contemptuously.

"Your words have the skill to move men's hearts."

Lightning flashed in Téo's eyes and she clenched her fists. "I find it insulting that you should think I would be party to such deceit," she blazed. "You know as well as I that neither the governor nor Gros cares a fig for the slaves. They are merely using them for their own ends."

Bayon put his hand on her arm in an effort to calm her. "Téoline," he pleaded. "You cannot be more grievously ashamed than I, but what alternative is there? We must grasp at any straw that may prevent outright war. Believe me, my dear, there are many times in life when all we can do is follow the course of expediency. I surely do not have to tell *that* to *you*."

Within hours of their visit, Téoline would have reason to remember Bayon de Libertat's last words. It was a hot August night and Téo was sitting by the window of her boudoir. She was endeavoring to embroider a blue silk jacket for Philippe, but the guttering candle was blown out by a sudden gust of wind. Téo set the work aside with a gesture of impatience. She would have to send Élie for fresh candles, but at the moment she didn't want to disturb the girl; Sonata was busy giving her a reading lesson in the salon.

For some time Téoline had been planning to build a school on the plantation. With this in mind, she went out onto the balcony to survey the landscape. She thought that possibly the best site would be beyond the back wall of the garden. At the moment that area was nothing but jungle, but she planned to give orders for Lortie to have it cleared. He had been slightly more cooperative since Stefan's death. She had charged him with betraying Cambenet, but he had denied it, and she had no proof. She had wanted to get rid of him, but again Lapointe and the others had recommended she keep him. It was more expedient, they said.

The moon was a golden orb in the sky, but its light cast strange shadows from the trees and shrubs she had had planted in the garden. She stood drinking in the silence; only the buzz of the myriad insects and the frogs croaking in the mud by the bridge broke the stillness. But suddenly her instinct told her she was not alone. Téo drew back into the deeper shadows and waited. Before long, whoever or whatever it was would have to make a move. Her pulse was racing and she felt her throat go dry.

Lortie always had guards patrolling the house at night, but they made no attempt to hide their presence and two of them had recently passed the gate in the back wall; she'd seen the glint of their weapons in the moonlight. Téo's thoughts flew to the small boy asleep in his cot near her bed. She must be prepared to protect him; there was no one else on whom she could depend. Cautiously she edged her way back into the boudoir, being careful not to disturb Élie and Sonata. There was no point in scaring them unnecessarily. She took a pistol out of her dressing-table drawer. It was not the one Stefan had used, for she could not bear to look at it again after his death. Peter Robillard had bought her another to replace it. Cocking it ready for use, Téoline held a trembling finger on the trigger and stole back onto the balcony again. A tall, dark figure was edging his way quietly up the stairs.

Her first instinct was to scream. But she was learning to control such womanly frailties. If the man were not alone, a sudden noise could bring others to his aid. Rarely a day passed without reports of plantations being attacked by gangs of Maroons; several plantation owners had been murdered in their beds.

"Stay where you are," she hissed between clenched teeth.

There was a second's silence before a deep voice whispered, "Is that you, *maîtresse?*"

She thought she recognized the voice. Taking a chance, she moved into the moonlight but kept her pistol trained upon the stairs. She heard a sigh of relief as the man stood to his full height. There was no mistaking him now—it was indeed Benjamin.

"For the love of God, how you frightened me!" Téoline's voice quivered as she relaxed her hold on the pistol and let her arm fall to her side.

"I am sorry, mistress, but I had to come." She could see him quite clearly now. He was much thinner and his clothes were no more than tattered rags. But there was a new dignity in the way he carried his head.

"I'm glad you did. You want to see Sonata . . . I'll call her. She is quite well. We have so often spoken of you and wished you would return. My husband is dead, Benjamin. You are free. I'll give you the papers proving it."

"Thank you, *maîtresse!*" His dark eyes shone. "But it is to you I must speak first." He leaned against the side of the house and put his hand to his head. Téoline guessed he was weak from lack of food.

"I'm sure whatever you have to say can wait until you have rested." She went back into the boudoir, signaling Benjamin to follow. She called Sonata to look after him, then went in to pack Élie off to bed, leaving the lovers alone. She could imagine what this reunion would mean to them.

After Benjamin had eaten, Téoline sat down to hear what he had to say. "I've come to warn you, mistress."

Téo reminded him he was no longer a slave and told him from

henceforth to call her "madame." She gave him the official documents, and he kissed her hand. Though he was clearly grateful, it was easy to see that his mind was on other things.

"There will be bad trouble soon, madame. There is a new restlessness among the slaves. They see their masters fighting among themselves and they feel the time is ripe for them to rise. The sailors at the docks tell them to strike for their liberty. Soon there will be no way to hold them back."

"Does François Toussaint know of this?" Téoline was in a difficult position. There was no way for her to know if Benjamin had heard of the procurator's planned uprising or if this was something entirely new.

"No, mistress—madame," he corrected himself. "This is Boukmann. He has been planning it for some time. The entire Turpin plantation is behind him, and many groups of Maroons will join him. I fear others will not be far behind. Boukmann is an evil man. He will not spare anyone, not even his black brothers, if they dare to cross him. I wanted to make sure that you and Sonata were safe. It would be better if you went to Le Cap."

"Toussaint must hear of this. He may be able to stem the tide. You must go to him in the morning and tell him I sent you. He will understand. But first you must get a few hours' sleep. Sonata will find you a bed and you can leave at daybreak. I shall have a letter for you to take to Monsieur de Libertat." She watched them go out, hand in hand, knowing they would share a bed that night and trying not to envy them. Once again she was engulfed by a great loneliness.

When they had gone, she went over to her desk and took up her pen. A planned uprising would be better than the carnage Boukmann would let loose upon the land. Using all her skills, Téo wrote her article, making it simple and to the point. When she had finished she picked up the little silver shaker and sanded it. She read over how the King had said he would personally guarantee the slaves the rights and privileges as promised. She was tempted to sign it "Hypocrite" because she knew that once the danger was past, the men in power would not be bound by promises.

The following day was hot and humid. A storm was threatening and the evening brought no cooling breeze. The mountains were black and ominous; their peaks were hidden in the clouds. By nightfall there came the unmistakable throbbing of the drums, calling to the slaves from miles around. Téo was becoming used to them. She knew they were summoning worshippers to take part in a *vaudou* ceremony up in the hills. She stood by the window, watching the flares snaking their way up through the jungle, and caught her breath as she saw the direction in which they were headed. They were going towards the Turpin plantation.

She summoned Sonata and they made their plans, but by morning it was already too late to risk leaving for Le Cap. Toussaint arrived with instructions from de Libertat to take her to Bréda. She left on horseback, with Sonata, Élie, and Philippe and a few belongings in a carriage. She could not know, but it was the last time she would see Cambenet.

Hell had broken its bounds and the northern peninsula went up in flames. Each day brought fresh terrors. Boukmann put men, women, and children to the sword. Afterwards she learned that Davide and others among her slaves had done their best to save Cambenet, but it had been useless. Lortie was murdered by his own men. Toussaint rallied his supporters and they managed to keep Bréda safe for a while. But eventually he said he could no longer guarantee their safety and he escorted the de Libertat family and Téoline with the others to Le Cap. He said he was taking his family to Santo Domingo, and Téo wondered if she would ever see him again.

Le Cap was protected by the garrison and a ring of barricades. It disgusted Téoline that even with all the carnage going on out on the plains, the average citizen remained immune to the chaos; life went on much the same as it had done before. They still held their balls and their assemblies and said it would not be long before the rebels were caught and hanged. They ignored the fact that the divisions in their ranks were becoming deeper day by day. Eventually some of the *grands blancs* began to realize their predicament. They swallowed their pride and sent for Téoline, using Robillard as their emissary.

"The mulattoes have been gathering their forces in the west," Robillard said. "They have the backing of a royalist army of émigrés. The colonists feel it is time to join forces with them to quell the white revolutionaries in our midst."

"It is a pity they were not so inclined two years ago. We might have been spared this present bloodshed." Téoline tossed her head. "But why are you telling me this, Pierre?" She knew from the doctor's manner that there was something more on his mind.

168

They were sitting in the *grand salon* of the house in Le Cap. The doors leading into the garden were open and the sunlight sparkled on the waters of the fountain. One could almost be misled into thinking everything was at peace.

"After all that has happened, there is a great deal of mistrust on both sides. The members of the Assembly feel they need someone to speak for them . . . someone the mulattoes will trust."

"You're not suggesting they will listen to me, after what happened to Stefan?"

"In their hearts there are very few who don't know the truth behind Stefan's death. Certainly the mulattoes do; I can vouch for that. Like you, they didn't challenge the official report because it was more convenient to believe it."

"You mean it was more expedient at the time?"

"Yes, you could say that. It was better to let things rest. It would only have led to more deaths. Like it or not, Téoline," he said gently, "there are times when you have to compromise."

"I know, Pierre." She smiled. "I'm slowly learning that." She was relieved to think that most people knew the truth. She had felt it was a mark of her own weakness that she had not been strong enough to stand up and tell the real facts. "Even so, the mulattoes will not listen. It will not mitigate the responsibility the *grands blancs* have for Ogé's brutal death."

"They want you to speak for them. Tell the *gens de couleur* it was a regrettable mistake and that they wish to make amends. The whites now understand the full contents of the civil-rights decree, and they will accept it." Robillard gave a sheepish grin.

"Until such time as it suits them to renege!" Téo snapped. "But what makes them think my word on this will carry any weight?"

Robillard's eyes lit up with mischievous delight and he had a job to keep from laughing outright. "Because you have the ear of the leader of the Royalist Army." Téoline regarded him blankly. "But Pierre, I do not even know who is in command. Please stop this nonsense!" She was bewildered to see him smile.

"My dear Téoline, the army is under the command of Comte Julien de Chantal!"

"Julien! Here in Saint-Domingue?" Téoline shot up out of her chair, unable to suppress her joy. All thought of Robillard's reason for coming fled from her mind. To see Julien again after all these years, just when she was feeling she had lost all purpose in life, was almost more than she could bear.

Before the doctor left, she had penned a hasty note to Julien and sealed it with the de Pavigné crest. If fortune smiled, her brother would be here within a week. She scarcely waited for Robillard to be on his way before running upstairs to break the news to Philippe. He turned his large gray eyes upon her with a wondering stare, then dropped his heavy lids and smiled.

There were times when she could hardly bear to look at the child, so poignant was his resemblance to his father. It was a crime, she thought in exasperation, that he should be so like Andrew Cameron.

Chapter Seventeen

"Do you remember Colonel Cameron?" Julien said as he released Téoline from his arms. She had been far too ecstatic at the sight of her brother after so many years to pay any heed to the tall figure who had followed him into the salon.

"Am I likely to forget?" Téo offered Cameron her hand. She was bubbling with happiness, and for one moment she almost forgot herself and embraced their guest. Cameron realized this and grinned. Fortunately, brother and sister had so much to say that there was little time to stand on ceremony.

"My God! You have changed, Téo. Let me look at you," he said as he twirled her about the room. "Why, you are almost a woman, instead of a scrawny girl," he said, viewing her with obvious admiration. "Tell me, is it men or money? You see, André, she has grown up at last."

Téoline pulled a face of mock indignation, and, picking up a cushion, heaved it at Julien. For a few precious seconds they were boy and girl again. Téo pursed her lips and moved around her brother. She shook her head with apparent disapproval, but really it was to hide her grin.

"And you are still a popinjay . . . although I will admit that uniform gives you a certain *je ne sais quoi*." She knew he was waiting for a word of approval, but she wished to tease him a bit longer. "Perhaps you will not make a bad soldier after all. You know, André, there was a time when I feared that with Julien in the army we should be in even more danger than with him out!"

"Thank you, dear sister." Julien laughed as he came smartly to attention.

They both dissolved into a gale of giggles and embraced again. There was a delicious gaiety about Chantal. For the first time Téo recognized that Stefan had shared the same quality; it was the very essence of Paris, and she delighted in it.

"Enough of this!" Julien said at last. "André tells me I have a nephew. Let me see the latest member of the de Pavigné family."

Téoline rang for Sonata and told her to fetch Philippe.

Cameron had been standing quietly throughout all this banter, observing the two at play. Responding to Julien's last re-

mark, he said drily, "He is a de Beben . . . or so I'm led to believe."

Julien looked up sharply, but, seeing the twinkle in
Cameron's eyes, answered in what he took to be the same vein.
"It is as well you are our friend, André, or I should be forced to
defend my sister's honor for a remark like that." He laughed.
"But if you would know the truth, I'd be more than happy to
know the boy has no de Beben blood in him."

Cameron smiled as if joining in the joke. Téoline looked at
the two men and turned away. A sudden chill had cooled her
joy.

At that moment, Sonata entered the room with the boy.

"But he is big!" Julien cried as he tossed his delighted nephew
into the air. "We'll soon be able to make a soldier out of him!"
Philippe chortled and began to play with the medals on his un-
cle's chest.

"He's growing into a fine lad, Téoline. You have every reason
to be proud of him," said Cameron, who had quietly come
across the salon and was standing at her side.

"Will you take supper with us, André?" Her tone was icily
polite and almost demanded that he should refuse the invitation.

"No, thank you, Téoline. I think that tonight you should be
alone with Julien. I know you have many experiences you will
wish to share. But never fear, I shall return tomorrow. Unlike
the last time, I have no plans to leave Saint-Domingue just yet."
He smiled down at her, and once again she felt herself
trembling.

Courtesy demanded she should respond. "You will be welcome here, André."

"I hope that will always be the case." He raised her hand to
his lips. "I have brought some toys and trinkets for you and the
boy. Until tomorrow, then." Before she could protest, he was
gone.

In spite of all that was happening outside Le Cap, the next
few weeks were happier for Téoline than any she had had since
Stefan's death. Julien moved into the gray stone house and
made it ring with laughter. Like Stefan, he had a rich enjoy-
ment of life. The only real matters of importance to him were
the cut of his clothes and his losses at the gaming tables.

At first Téoline was quite happy to finance these foibles.
Julien was pleasant company and, like Stefan, he made her see
the funny side of things. But slowly she came to realize that
there was a startling difference between the two men. For all his

172

gaiety and wit, Stefan had a passionate commitment to certain things, as he had proved by his death. Whereas Julien didn't seem to care a fig for anything. He viewed the battles going on between the different factions as though they were a game. When Téo challenged him, he shrugged.

"Let them get on with it, Téo. Don't trouble your pretty head. Just let them get on with it!"

"But Julien, you don't seem to realize the carnage that is going on out there on the plains. This isn't just another uprising, no matter what people may say. This is a revolution, and in the end the blacks will win because they outnumber us. If Toussaint were in command, I believe I would stand up and cheer, for he has more wisdom and compassion in one of his fingers than all the Assembly put together. But it isn't Toussaint. Boukmann and his kind are ravaging the land, and it will be fit for nothing when they are done."

Julien was playing with Philippe. They had a model of a sailing ship that Cameron had brought along that day. Téo realized her brother wasn't paying attention to a word she said.

"Julien, I cannot afford to keep paying your bills like this. Don't you understand, apart from the violence and the human misery . . ." She paused, knowing there was just one thing to command Julien's attention. "The plantations are not producing anything. Jeremie has been laid waste and Cambenet is in ruins. My money will not last forever, and I must think of Philippe."

"Oh, if that's what is troubling you, I'll speak to Cameron. He'll tell you how to invest what's left. He's making a mint of money now that France has declared war on England. He'll probably let you buy into his line, if you ask him nicely." He got up and brushed off his coat. "Incidentally, Téo, I wish you would be a little warmer towards him. He's a very useful friend . . . and he rather fancies you, I think."

He pecked his sister on the cheek and waltzed out of the room. For a moment Téo could not trust herself to speak. Then she rushed after him and called out as he was going up the stairs.

"If you so much as dare to breath a word of this to André Cameron, I'll never let you in this house again."

"Oh, dear! That sounds very ominous. I trust that whatever Julien is likely to tell me against your will, the crime will remain his and not be held against me."

Téoline stood quite still with her back to Cameron, wishing the floor would open wide and swallow her.

"I'm sorry, André," she said, when she felt calm enough to face him. "Obviously you were not meant to hear that."

Joseph had just opened the front door to him. Cameron came into the vestibule and took her arm.

"I understand," he said, leading her into the salon. "But I would not be human if I weren't curious. I'll make a bargain with you, Téoline. I'll forget it ever happened if you in turn will tell me what I shouldn't know." His gray eyes glistened with mischief.

Téoline was too embarrassed to be angry. "There would be no point in what I said to Julien if I were to do that." She smiled.

"True." Cameron grinned. "But it was worth a try. At least I've made you smile at me, which is more than you've done for weeks."

After that it was very difficult for her to be on her dignity with him, and they began to converse as friends. Cameron was a regular visitor to the house. He came almost every day with gifts for her and Jean-Philippe. It distressed her to see that the boy was growing very fond of him.

"Have you no business to attend to in the States . . . or some other place . . .?" Teo asked with a little shrug.

She had tried to make the question sound casual, but she was torn between wishing he would go and longing for him to stay. For herself, she loved to hear him speak her name and yearned to feel his touch. He, however, had been very circumspect and never attempted to do more than raise her hand to his lips when they met. It had reached the stage where she was beginning to hate him for what he did not do. On the other hand, she was often angry with him for the proprietary way in which he spoke to Philippe, as if he knew the boy were his. Téoline knew there was no way she could win.

"That sounds as though I may have outstayed my welcome, Téoline."

They were alone. Philippe was in bed and Julien was out, as usual. His favorite haunts were the gambling dens or bordellos down near the docks. Cameron had stayed to supper with them both, but had not attempted to go when Julien left.

"I merely thought that with all your business ventures . . ." As her words trailed off, she attempted to start over. "Undoubtedly, with this war, you are engaged in shipping armaments . . ." She was fishing for words that would make good her argument. "You must be busy . . . there is always a good trade in slaves . . ."

Cameron's eyes were like two pieces of flint. "Do you think so little of me that you believe I would deal in human flesh?"

"I don't know how you feel about men," she said pointedly.

"But you think you know how I feel about women?"

"I don't think—I know about that!" The words were out, and she would have given the world to take them back.

Cameron had been standing watching her for some time. She was sitting in the candlelight sewing. It had amused him to see the way her needle flashed in and out of the embroidery frame. Even his untutored eye could see that the pattern was suffering from her attack. At her last words, he could take no more. Striding across the room, he snatched the frame from her hand and threw it to one side. Then, reaching down, he drew her up into his arms.

"Téoline," he murmured, softly fondling the curls about her ear. "Why are you trying to hate me so?"

"Hate you? André, don't be absurd!" She tried to pull away, but his arms pinioned her like a bird.

"There was a night when you welcomed my love."

"That is a night I wish to forget."

"All of it? There are some things that happened, I too wish to forget . . . But not this . . . ." He kissed her forehead and his hand caressed the white column of her neck. Then, tightening his grasp, he held her face close to his and his lips reached her mouth in one long passionate kiss. She beat her fists against his chest, but the magic was already at work. Cameron held her closer, knowing that in the end she wouldn't—she couldn't—refuse his love.

"We are both older and wiser. . . . You are a woman now, Téoline." He buried his face in her hair and the sweet perfume of her warm body intoxicated his senses and quickened his desire. "Why not let us try again . . .?"

It had been so long since she had felt the touch of love, she had neither the will nor the strength to refuse. Cameron felt her body yield to his as her hand stole up and her fingers caressed his neck. He swept her up like a piece of thistledown and carried her upstairs.

"I'm afraid I shall have to leave Saint-Domingue in a day or so." It was several weeks later. Cameron lay back against the pillow watching the first shaft of sunlight filter through the shutters and to illuminate the drowsy head at rest upon his shoulder. With one hand he gently traced the high cheekbones and the firm line of her jaw. "You may rest assured, I'll not be away longer than necessary." He leaned forward and kissed her ear.

Téoline stirred. "Must you go so soon?" she said sleepily. She knew he would have to go one day, but she had dismissed the idea from her mind. The last few weeks had been idyllic; she had refused to give the outside world a thought.

"I'd hoped to delay my departure a little longer, but I had a letter from Hamilton again yesterday. Alex is anxious that this new venture of his will succeed, and I long ago promised him my support."

"Oh, let him get on with it. What can you do anyway?"

"Put pressure on several people who do business with me, among other things. America needs a national bank, Téoline. It affects our credit internationally, and it will help to tidy up the economic mess at home."

"Money and power . . . is that all you ever think about?" Téo yawned and stretched contentedly. Her beauty made her words lose their sting.

"Surely you know better than that, Téo." He kissed her again and she tweaked his nose.

"I still say Jefferson is the better man."

"Only because you like what he writes. He's a dreamer. Alex is the practical man we need. You can't build a nation on dreams."

"That's where you're wrong, André. If I had my way, we would all live in a world of dreams . . . and they would all come true."

"If you have money," he said cynically. "But when I'm in Boston, I will buy you a dream. I've seen the very thing."

Téoline's curiosity impelled her to pay attention to this. She opened her eyes and stared up into his. "Let's see," she began. "I'll never need another gown, with all that silk you brought me from the Orient . . . and I don't need jewels . . . I've enough of those to sink the proverbial ship . . . What could it be?"

Cameron laughed and, swinging his legs off the bed, began to dress. "A woman never has too many jewels. But that's not what I mean." He paused and waited until he had reached his shirt, knowing she was bursting to hear what he had in mind.

"André, stop teasing me!" Téo sat up in bed and pretended to be cross with him.

"I'm going to buy you a house." He paused for his words to take affect.

"A house . . . What would I want with a house? I have one here in Saint-Domingue!"

"But you can't stay here when you're my wife. I'd never get any business done if I were forever in Le Cap." He grinned.

"Your wife? But this is the first mention you have made of this." Téoline scrambled out of bed and pulled on a negligé the color of her eyes.

"Now that I've found you, surely you didn't think I would just go and leave you behind?" Cameron cursed his cravat and tugged the thing from his neck.

"You did once!" Téoline said quietly. She did not know how she felt about this sudden turn of events. He had made no mention of marriage until now.

"That was a long time ago. And I thought that was all behind us. I have so many plans for us, Téoline." He was busy brushing his hair, and his enthusiasm was carrying him away. "Philippe will go to Harvard. I think we'll make a lawyer out of him . . . that's if he doesn't come into the business with me. I have a powerful friend in Hamilton. He could well end up in the government . . . I wonder if he should be Secretary of State . . . Perhaps he should have the Treasury . . . ?"

"Oh, money . . . I should make it the Treasury . . . It's money that counts, isn't it?" Téoline was more angry with herself than she was with him. She knew she would regret what she was doing, but his complacent attitude angered her.

Unfortunately, Cameron was too happy to pay much attention to her at that moment. His head was full of dreams. "While I'm there, I'll start proceedings to have his name legally changed to Cameron."

"Philippe is *my son!*" Téo's voice was as hard as stone, but still Cameron did not perceive what he was doing to her.

"Of course he is . . . and mine. You don't think I haven't known from the very first? Now he's even beginning to look like a Cameron." He chuckled. "We both know de Beben could never have fathered him. It takes a man to produce a boy like Philippe."

"So you say. I suppose I had no part in it!" Téo was seething by this time.

Cameron had finished dressing and turned to pick up his hat. It was then that he saw her face, her eyes like a stormy sea. "Why, Téoline, what's the matter? You didn't think you had fooled me for one minute about Philippe . . . ?"

For some insane reason Téoline wanted to hit him. "You take

177

too much for granted, André," was all she said. But it was enough. She had made her point.

"What do you mean, Téoline?" Cursing as he stumbled over a stool, Cameron strode round the bed and shook her by the shoulders. "Téoline, tell me what you mean."

"I have told you again . . . and again. Philippe is my son. I'll not share him with any man."

"But I am his father . . . not *any man* . . .!"

"So you say."

"I know it. Who else could it be?" Cameron was on the defensive, and Téo was glad. This was one thing he couldn't buy. "It must have happened in Paris . . . And you were too young . . . I know you had not been with any other man."

"Have you forgotten that afternoon in my sister's salon? You hardly took your eyes off me."

"I know. I wanted you then, as I still want you now, Téoline."

"No, André. You want my son. But I'll not give him up to you or anyone. You obviously did not notice the man who was kissing my hand that day, or you would have recognized Stefan Cambenet!" She tossed her head defiantly.

"Are you telling me Philippe is Stefan Cambenet's son?" Cameron's face was grim, and his gray eyes had turned to granite.

"I'm saying he could be, and that is all you'll ever know, André."

Without another word, Cameron turned away from her. Picking up his hat and cane, he stormed out of the door. The moment he had gone, Téoline collapsed on the bed and sobbed at her own willfulness. His pride and her anger had destroyed the world that love had created for them.

Chapter Eighteen

"That is the position, Citizeness. All the monies are in from the sale of the last crops from Jeremie and Cambenet, and you can discount any further income from them. There is nothing further I can suggest, unless you are prepared to sell the house in Le Cap." Lapointe closed the ledger with a snap. He didn't have time to waste; Sonothax, the new commissioner, was waiting to speak to him. He was an important man. He had the ear of Robespierre and the Committee for Public Safety in France. "Perhaps you should consider doing that. It is a charming property, and, if you wish, I will use my influence to bring it to the attention of Citizen Sonothax. It would do very nicely for him." The lawyer sat back with a fatuous smile on his flabby face.

"Thank you, M'sieur—"

"Citizen!" Lapointe corrected her. All titles had been abolished by the Committee. Citizens were not even allowed to use the prefix "de" before their names. Now all men were truly equal, and he was every bit as good as any de Pavigné. It was a pity this was not Paris. By now the former Mademoiselle de Pavigné would probably have lost her head like the rest of her kind.

"Thank you, Citizen Lapointe. I will give the matter some thought. But my son and I, along with our servants, need somewhere to live." Téo got up from her chair in front of the lawyer's desk and went towards the door.

"You're fortunate to still have servants. All my slaves have run away." Lapointe leaned back in his chair, leaving her to open the door of his office by herself.

Her hand on the doorknob, Téoline looked back at Lapointe in disgust. "Mine were never slaves—at least I never regarded them as such. They have chosen to remain with me for the most part. Good day, *m'sieur!*" Téoline made a point of using the old title. It was one of the few weapons she had left. She swept out with as much dignity as she could muster, slamming the door behind her.

There was no chair waiting for her. She had spared Davide and Joseph the task of carrying her that day. They, along with Sonata and Élie and one or two of the older slaves, were all the servants she had left, in spite of what she had said to Lapointe. Consequently she tried to spare them extra work when she could.

As she walked home up the narrow, steep streets of Le Cap, Téoline pondered what to do next. Affairs in the colony had rapidly gone from bad to worse. Le Cap was in a desperate state of siege. If it hadn't been a port, the plight of the people would have been pitiful; as it was, food and the money to buy it were both scarce. Viewing only the surface, a visitor might not have realized that. The *grands blancs* and the officers at the garrison still kept up a social whirl, spending what money they had as though there were no tomorrow.

The Colonial Assembly had been unable to reach any lasting agreement with the mulattoes. As for Julien, he seemed to have completely forgotten why he had ever come to Le Cap in the first place. He spent his days in bed and his nights carousing. The *petits blancs*, like Lapointe, had thrown in their lot with the new commissioners sent by Robespierre.

In Paris the Jacobins had their way; Louis had been sent to the guillotine and everyone knew it was only a matter of time before Marie Antoinette followed him. That day Téo had received a rare letter from Charlotte Corday which had been written many months before. She said, "There is a reign of terror here, and the streets run with blood. The revolution has become a cause in itself and feeds on its own blood." Every week, those with any pretension to nobility were packed into tumbrils and taken to the guillotine. Hundreds were dying all over France. Téo did not dare to think about her own family.

That night she had to attend a reception for Commissioner Sonothax. It would not be politic to refuse; he wielded too much power. Citizeness Beben was a particular favorite of his because she was a friend of Toussaint, and the revolution was pinning its hopes on the ex-slave.

Toussaint had returned from Santo Domingo and was endeavoring to bring about some sort of order among the slaves on the plantations. Although food was short in Le Cap, the situation was much worse outside. No crops had been planted, and what might have been harvested had long ago been burned. Starvation was beginning to take its toll, and many of the blacks were now prepared to listen to him. He promised them their freedom if they would return to work voluntarily.

Sonata had some mysterious means of getting through the barricades. She steadfastly refused to leave Téo but she paid regular visits to Benjamin, who was trying to bring life back to the scorched earth around Cambenet. She told Téo he had even made a start on rebuilding part of the house. But Téoline knew it would be many years before there was enough food to feed the workers, let alone market a crop.

Téoline tried to look as though she was enjoying herself as Sonothax offered her his arm. Whatever Lapointe might think about equality, the commissioner had his own ideas on the subject. Though he preached the gospel of the Jacobins, he strutted beside her powdered and peruked, as colorful as a parrot.

"Well, that rascal Blanchelande has arrived back in France and will no doubt reap his just desserts," he remarked as they went into supper.

Poor Blanchelande! Téo suppressed a sigh; it would not be smart to let Sonothax know her true feelings. The ex-governor would more than likely lose his head. He had only tried to do his best for the colony, foolish as his plans had been.

"We are expecting our new governor to arrive before long," said the commissioner, smiling across at her over the supper table with his small hard eyes. Téo shivered as she recalled the touch of his damp and clammy hands. "You've no doubt heard it is to be General Galbaud, Citizeness?"

"That rumor has reached my ear," Téo replied. She was thankful that her neighbor asked Sonothax a question at that point, as she had no wish to discuss her feelings about Galbaud. She could only wonder what they were thinking about in sending a man like the general. They blamed Blanchelande for the dissent in the colony; what could they expect from this next governor? Galbaud had property on the island and would therefore need slaves to work his plantation. It would be in his interest to keep the status quo as desired by the *grands blancs*. Whatever he might have persuaded the Jacobins to believe, Téoline doubted that he was a revolutionary at heart. Once he was away from their influence, with an army at his command . . . Téo's heart sank. She could see nothing but more trouble ahead.

As soon after dinner as it was possible, Téo made the excuse that she was fatigued and felt slightly feverish. The fever season was at hand, so Sonothax was quite prepared to believe her and murmured his sympathies. She had no desire to stay; assemblies had long since lost any appeal for her. Most of her friends had already left Le Cap. Toussaint had managed to salvage sufficient money from the Bréda estates to give to Bayon de Libertat, so that he and his family could leave for the States. If only she had gone with Andrew Cameron.

Téoline had regretted their quarrel so many times. A day did not go by in which she did not replay the terrible scene of their parting. She knew now beyond any doubt that she loved him and would do so to the end of her life. But beyond that, her pride and stupidity had cost her son his chance of future happiness. Already she could see signs that Philippe needed a father's hand. He had inherited the virtues and vanities of both the Camerons and the de Pavignés, and he needed both parents to help him control them. But it was too late. She had no idea where André was, and if she found him he would be unlikely to believe her if she admitted the truth about his son. He might believe her, she mused, but certainly he would never forgive her, so there was no happiness in it either way.

If only she had someone to turn to, someone with whom she could discuss her troubling problems. Julien was quite hopeless; he cared little that she was going deep into debt. Peter Robillard was the only other person she would trust . . . and that was another problem for Téoline.

The fighting meant that the doctor's services were in constant demand; on top of that, he had his regular patients and an increasing number of fever victims. He had little time to be with Marie or see his friends. Téo had to admit there was some excuse for Marie finding other companionship, but she wished her choice hadn't fallen upon Julien. Robillard never gave any sign that he knew what was going on, but it was common gossip among people in Le Cap. The two were often seen together at the less salubrious assemblies in the city. Téo had tried to speak to Julien about it, but as usual he had only laughed and said they were just friends. Téoline had believed him because she wanted to.

She gave orders to be taken straight home and settled back against the cushions of her sedan chair. The cobbles in the square gleamed after a recent storm. Téo leaned forward and slid the window down to let in some of the cool night air. For the moment the rain had washed away the pervading stench of garbage from the gutters. She took a deep breath and caught the heady perfume of myriad flowers; satin-petaled camellias shone like marble in the moonlight, while fragile orchids hid beneath their slender fronds and the fragrance of oleander mingled with the scent of roses.

Téoline's heart skipped a beat as they passed a cassia tree and she saw it was in bloom. Unlike most of the trees in Saint-Domingue, the cassia was not an evergreen. At certain seasons its gray-white bark would peel away from the trunk, leaving it stark and dead. Then suddenly, overnight, it would blossom in a shower of yellow flowers, giving death the lie. Téo knew the blossoms would fade almost as quickly as they came, but they were beautiful while they were there. She looked upon the tree as a symbol of both hope and despair.

Sonata met her in the vestibule, and whispered that Dr. Robillard had been waiting for her for some time. Leaving her cloak, Téo went into the salon. Robillard was sprawled out in a chair with his eyes closed. She realized how much he had aged since the day they first met, when she arrived in Le Cap. At first she thought he was asleep, but he opened his eyes as she entered the room.

"I'm sorry to trouble you at this time of night, Téoline," he said, getting to his feet. "But as you know, of late I've had little time to plan my life." He swayed slightly and had to support himself by clasping the back of his chair.

"My poor Pierre," she murmured. "You look utterly exhausted. I don't suppose you have eaten all day. Let me have a tray made up for you," she said, ringing for Sonata.

"No, Téoline, don't trouble her. I just want to have a word with you." He put his hand to his head, and Téoline thought he was about to collapse. She hastened to pour Robillard a drink, though it had just occurred to her that perhaps he was already a bit drunk.

"I don't know if I should," he said, though he took the proffered glass and gulped the wine. "I think I've had too much already."

Téoline had refilled his glass before she realized that what he said was true. Never, in the years she had known him, had she seen the doctor the worse for drink. When Sonata entered the room, Téoline disregarded Robillard's protests and told Sonata to bring some cold meat and cheese for her guest.

"Sit down, Pierre. You will feel better when you've had some food."

Flopping down in a chair, he took her hand in his and looked up into her face. "You're looking tired yourself, Téoline. I'm a brute coming here like this and burdening you with my cares." He struggled to his feet again and put his arm about her shoulders. "Tell me . . . love of my life . . . tell me what is wrong." He gazed at her through bleary eyes, as though he were looking through a fog. "You know I've always loved you, Téoline . . . always . . . through all these years . . ."

"Sit down, Pierre; you're drunk. Don't say things you will regret."

"Why should I regret loving you?" He swayed and she had to support him. "Don't you love me . . . ?"

"As you love me, and that is as a friend. Your heart belongs to Marie . . ."

"And yours . . . Oh, yes . . . I know to whom your heart belongs. . . . It belongs to Andrew Cameron. . . . You can't fool me. . . . You fooled Stefan Cambenet . . . I know your secret . . . I know who fathered Philippe . . ." He started to giggle like a small boy consumed with delight at his discovery.

"Sit down, Pierre. You disgust me, and you're making a fool of yourself." Téoline's anger was triggered more by fear of what the doctor might say next than by the fact that he was drunk. It is hard to forget things that have been said aloud, and she knew him well enough to know he would regret his behavior once his senses returned. she didn't want anything to come about that might harm their friendship irreparably. "You're to have something to eat. Then you are to go home. Marie will be wondering what has become of you."

At her words, Robillard started to weep. They were the lacrimose tears of a drunk. "You're wrong," he sobbed collapsing into a chair. "Marie has gone."

"Gone?"

"Yes, with Julien. . . ." Speaking the thoughts that were uppermost in his mind seemed to have a sobering effect. He sat up and stared ahead, making a valiant effort to regain control of himself.

"No!" Téoline's hand stifled her cry of surprise. "That can't be true . . . Julien is here. I saw him myself only a few hours ago!"

Robillard shook his head. "They sailed on the evening tide." It was Téoline's turn to reach out for support. Robillard stood up and took her hand. His speech was still slurred but his senses were returning. "I'm sorry, Téoline. So sorry that I had to be the one to break the news. But you're not to blame . . . neither is Julien. He's young . . . little more than half her age. He's not the first, you know . . . There have always been other men. If it hadn't been Julien, it would have been someone else."

Téoline stared at him in utter disbelief. "I tell you, he is here," she said firmly. "His things are still upstairs in his rooms."

184

Without another word, she fled out of the salon and up the stairs to what had once been Albert's apartments. It only required a glance to confirm what Robillard had said. The Comte de Chantal had gone. Téo ran through the apartment, looking in the armoires and checking the drawers, but there was nothing left to show Julien had ever been there.

Téoline ran past Robillard, who had followed her upstairs. She dashed along the gallery to her own rooms, hoping to find an explanation there.

The letter was propped against the mirror over the mantelshelf. Furiously she snatched it down and broke open the seal with the de Pavigné crest. *"My dear Téoline,"* it read. *"Forgive my not waiting to make my farewell personally, but I must catch the tide. The situation here is hopeless and I find the arguments tedious in the extreme. I have been offered a commission in the British army, and it would be foolish of me to refuse. God willing, we shall meet again before too long. Good luck, little one. Your loving brother, Julien."*

Téoline crumpled the letter in her hand and instinctively looked across at the escritoire. It did not take a second to see that the lock had been forced. She hurried across and looked in the secret cupboard where she hid her jewels, but she already knew they would be gone. Julien had taken everything except the portrait of Mirabeau and the ring bearing the de Pavigné crest. It was fortunate she had been to the assembly that evening; she was still wearing her diamonds, but they were all she had left. In rage and misery, she drummed her knuckles on the desk until they cracked and bled.

"I'm so sorry, Téoline . . . ." Robillard came across and took her hands to prevent her doing further injury to herself.

"Damn you," she said. "And damn all men . . .!" Blinded by her tears, she turned and ran from him.

1793

Chapter Nineteen

There was a sharp tap on the door of the cabin, and Téoline hurried across to open it. It was almost certain to be the young lieutenant, Michael Dryden, whom the captain had detailed to look after her. But Jean-Philippe was still asleep in his bunk and she didn't want him to wake up just yet. She opened the door a little way and put a finger to her lips. The young man gave an understanding smile and whispered his request.

"Captain Ferris presents his compliments, ma'am. We shall be docking in Halifax within the hour, and he would like to see you before you leave. He asks you go to his cabin as soon as you find it convenient. Shall I wait and escort you there?" His tone was full of enthusiasm and there was frank admiration in his blue eyes. For the past few weeks it had been his main duty to attend Madame, and he was her most devoted slave. He might only be eighteen years of age, but he was the envy of every man aboard H.M.S. *Prometheus*, of that he was sure.

"Thank you, Lieutenant Dryden, but I think I can find my way."

"Very well, ma'am!" A flush spread over his fair skin and disappeared into the brown curls that stuck out in an unruly crop under his tricorne hat. Téoline de Pavigné only had to look at him and he blushed a bright red. "But if there is anything I can do . . . anything at all . . . please be sure to mention it. You know you can call on me at any time of the day—" He broke off. He had been about to say "day or night," then realized she might think he was trying to take advantage of her predicament.

"Thank you, m'sieur. You have already proved that in giving up your cabin to me and my son."

"Please don't give that another thought. But if you're sure there is nothing more I can do, I'll away and get a seaman to fetch your luggage and stow it aboard the dory. We're bound for the Bedford Basin, but Captain Ferris says I'm to escort you ashore in Halifax and see you settled."

"That is most thoughtful of the captain. As to my luggage, I have only the one small bundle I brought on board with me. That is the one consolation that comes with only having the clothes you stand up in, it takes so little time to pack." Téoline smiled a little ruefully.

With all the gallantry at his command, Michael Dryden rushed to her aid. "Never fear, ma'am. That will be my first job to hand. I'll have you and your Master Philippe kitted out in no time at all. I have plenty of connections in Halifax." He beamed down at her, came smartly to attention, saluted, and went whistling happily on his way.

Téoline caught sight of a redcoat in the distance and hastily closed the cabin door. It was more than likely Colonel Leadbetter, and she had no desire to encounter him. She would never forget the humiliating way he had treated her the first night aboard. But that was not to be wondered at. Every detail of that wretched night was burned into her memory along with the sight of Le Cap in flames.

General Galbaud had arrived in the north while Sonothax was in the southern province. And, as Téoline had expected, he immediately threw off all pretense of supporting the revolution. He sided with the wealthy white colonists and, supported by his officers, he attacked the dissidents within Cap Français itself. The Jacobins, aided by most of the enlisted men in the garrison, defended themselves, and fighting broke out in the streets of Le Cap. Toussaint had established a headquarters at Bréda, and Sonothax returned there. Against their commander's advice, the commissioner ordered the blacks to attack the city. He hoped this move would restore order. But Toussaint had known it would be difficult to control the ex-slaves once they had broken through the barricades. They were too intent on paying off old scores. Within hours the entire city went up in flames.

All Téoline could think of was getting Philippe away. She told Sonata to take Élie and the others to Benjamin at Cambenet. They would be protected by the color of their skins, but she had little hope for herself and her child. She fled through the streets to the docks with Philippe in her arms; behind her the roar of the fire grew closer by the second. The air was black with smoke and the acrid smell of burning sugarcane. The narrow streets were jammed with people trying to flee. At last they understood that the danger was at hand, but for most of them the awareness had come too late. Téo was reminded of the Paris mob as she pushed and pummeled her way through the throng. Desperation gave her a wild strength. She had to think of Philippe; she couldn't afford to feel sympathy for those that fell by the way.

She had managed to bribe the Spanish captain of a vessel flying a French flag to take her aboard. Téo had no idea where he was bound, all that mattered was that he was ready to put to sea. The following day they spied the *Prometheus*. The Spaniard quickly ran up an American flag, but the British ship of the line had been tracking them for some time. They merely had to fire a shot across the bows and the small schooner surrendered. A prize crew was put on board and the crew informed they were prisoners of war. If any of them attempted to put up any resistance they were clapped into irons. As the only woman among them, Téoline was taken aboard the H.M.S. *Prometheus* to see the captain. She recalled that interview, several weeks ago, as she made her way along the companionway this morning.

It had been Colonel Guy Leadbetter, whose regiment was being taken to Halifax, who had started the investigation that day. "You say your name is Téoline de Pavigné and this is your son Philip?" He was a tall, big-boned man, with sandy-colored hair and heavy brows that shaded watery blue eyes. His face was squarish and its only distinguishing feature was a long pointed nose. He got up from behind the captain's desk where he had been sitting and circled around Téoline and Philippe as if they were slaves on the auction block. At any moment she thought he would come and inspect her teeth.

"What were you doing on a French ship sporting an American flag?"

"My only concern was to get my son away from Saint-Domingue. I did not look at the color of the flag, m'sieur."

"Colonel!" he said irritably. They had been up all night keeping their sights on this vessel, and a poor prize it had turned out to be. "Lieutenant Colonel Guy Leadbetter. You understand your country and England are at war, and that makes you my prisoner?"

"*Oui, m'sieur* . . . Colonel."

"That's better. And mind you only speak English while you're aboard—you know the language, don't you?" He rounded on her suspiciously. When he had heard her speaking to the men helping her aboard, she appeared to have a good command of it. Now she was tending to lapse into her native tongue. Obviously the woman was devious—undoubtedly a spy.

Téoline nodded to show she would comply. She was feeling utterly exhausted by all she had been through in the past twenty-four hours; moreover, she was afraid of saying the wrong thing. She clutched her son's hand and waited for the colonel to speak again.

"Have you papers to prove what you say?"

Téo shook her head but took from her finger the ring with the de Pavigné crest. Leadbetter twirled it around, then threw it on the desk. "That doesn't prove a thing. You could have stolen it."

"I'm not a thief, m'sieur!" Téo responded indignantly.

"That remains to be seen. Why were you so anxious to leave Saint-Domingue?"

"Le Cap was going up in flames around us. We were running for our lives, Colonel Leadbetter." Téo's resistance was beginning to stiffen. There was a limit to how much more she could take.

"A pretty story to cover your lack of identification. Now there is only your word for it."

He put his big, hard hand under her chin and, lifting it up, stared down into her face. She was a pretty woman under the dirt and grime. Just the sort the French would choose to spy for them. Leadbetter was a soldier through and through. He would see his men flogged to death or a spy hanged without turning a hair. But there was nothing in campaign rules that said he couldn't have some fun with her first.

"I'm not a liar or a thief, m'sieur. Certainly not when my son's life might be at stake."

"Hmm . . . well . . . that remains to be seen. We may be able to find a way you could convince me." His hand slid down her neck and rested on her shoulder.

Téoline tried not to let him feel her cringe at his touch. She was relieved that the captain of the ship came in at that moment.

"I'm sorry to keep you waiting, madame. I had to make arrangements for a prize crew. I am James Ferris captain of His Majesty's frigate *Prometheus*." He bowed and offered his hand.

Téoline smiled gratefully, and when she took his hand he led her to a chair next to his desk. He ignored Leadbetter completely, and Téoline sensed there wasn't a great deal of love lost between the two men.

"What is this?" He picked up Téo's heavy gold ring from his desk. "Ah, I recognize your family crest, Madame de Pavigné."

"There's no proof the ring is hers," Leadbetter broke in.

"Colonel Leadbetter, have you ever met the Duc de Pavigné or any members of his family?" The captain's voice was icy. He had no time for this upstart army man who had been a pest ever since he came aboard. A pompous oaf if ever the captain had seen one.

"No, I can't say I have, Ferris."

189

"Well, I have. As a young man I spent many months in France. My aunt was married to a Frenchman of noble birth and I had the privilege of meeting the late Duc and Duchesse de Pavigné. There is no mistaking this lady's birth."

Téoline was too overjoyed to take in the full import of the captain's words. Without thinking, she said happily, "That is most fortunate, Captain Ferris. But my father is not dead . . .?" The words died on her tongue as she saw the expression on the captain's face.

"I'm sorry, madame. I presumed you would have heard." He leaned across and poured a glass of wine from the decanter on the desk. Handing it to Téoline, he said gently, "Drink this!"

Téoline was too shattered to refuse. The tears were already burning her lids. A very frightened little boy was clinging to her skirts, and she knew she must not cry.

"I'm afraid your father's name was on a recent list of victims who have been guillotined. It happened some months ago, but the news has only just come to hand. I should have known that you were unlikely to have received it in Saint-Domingue. Forgive me, madame. I cannot forgive myself for the cruel way in which I imparted the news."

"You could not know, m'sieur. I think, in a way, I have been expecting it. My father was a proud man . . ."

"And I've no doubt he died a brave one." He could see that Téoline was shattered and thought the best way to help her regain her composure was to talk of other things. There would be time for her to grieve later.

"Now, as to you and your son, madame. The French schooner is in a shocking state and will be lucky to make any port. I have directed she be taken to Jamaica. For ourselves, the *Prometheus* is headed towards Halifax, Nova Scotia. There are a number of French émigrés there, including Monsieur Danesville, the former governor of the French islands of Saint-Pierre and Miquelon. He is in actual fact a prisoner of war, but we do not treat him as such. He is a charming gentleman, and the lieutenant governor has set him up in Brook House and given him a pension for the duration of the war. I say this because I think you and your son would be better off in Halifax. "However, if you insist, I will make arrangements to put you ashore anywhere you choose. But there will be more trouble in these islands before long. If you will permit me to advise you, I think you would be safer in the north." He smiled at Téoline and waited patiently while she made up her mind.

"I have nowhere to go, m'sieur. I have little money and no friends, so I am touched by your interest and sympathy. If you are willing to take us there, my son and I will be happy to come with you to Halifax."

"A very wise decision. I will speak to the governor myself and see that some provision is made to accommodate you. We have many of your countrymen at home, in England, as you no doubt know. This revolution is a tragic business and has divided your own countrymen."

"There are also many spies in Halifax," Leadbetter cut in waspishly. He had grown tired of the way the captain was getting along with the French woman. He was also a little embarrassed to find that Téoline was who she had claimed to be. "You need to be very careful, madame, that you don't become entangled with them."

"There's little fear of that." Captain Ferris scowled. "Madame de Pavigné has little cause to love the Jacobins. Now, madame, I'll put you in the charge of a young lieutenant of mine. Michael Dryden is a charming boy—a little green in many ways, but as honest and upright as they come. I know you'll be safe in his care." His face was stern as he looked across the cabin at Leadbetter. He had no illusions about the army and he disliked Leadbetter more than most of its officers.

Téoline had thanked him and welcomed the attentions of Lieutenant Dryden. He had a frank, open face and was plainly proud of the honor the captain had bestowed on him. He had gone out of his way to make their journey as pleasant as possible, although, as he was at pains to explain, the *Prometheus* was a man-of-war and lacked many facilities. Young Philippe had adored him as he might an elder brother who took him around and showed him all the nooks and crannies. Fortunately, Philippe had thoroughly enjoyed himself, once he got over his initial fears of the night they left Le Cap. The seamen took him to their hearts, and Téoline had scarcely seen him throughout the voyage. She was wondering how he was going to react when he found it was coming to an end.

"Well, Madame de Pavigné, your journey is at an end. I have instructed Lieutenant Dryden what to do to see you settled. You have no cause to concern yourself—I will personally see that he is reimbursed. But I've no doubt that in time the British government will make provision for you until such time as you are in funds again."

"That is most generous, Captain Ferris, but I have no idea

191

when that will be. François Toussaint promised that if he could ever restore order in Saint-Domingue, he would see that I drew a reasonable revenue from my estates. I have every reason to believe he will keep his word if that should ever come about."

The captain smiled. "This former slave must be a remarkable man for you to have such faith in him."

"Oh, he is, believe me. He is *un homme d'une grande ouverture d'esprit* . . . How should I say . . . ?"

"A very open-minded man, I think you mean. Is that why he has added L'Ouverture to his name? Everyone in the West Indies now speaks of him as Toussaint L'Ouverture."

Téoline smiled a little ruefully; it was the trap of words again, and it made Toussaint appear immodest. "I don't think he uses it in that sense. From all he has said to me in the past, I believe he uses it in the sense of an opening . . . a span . . . the archway through which he can lead his people into the world of the white man."

"I see. I'm rather sorry you told me that," Ferris replied quietly. "It is not easy to look on such a man as an enemy, but I'm afraid that is how we must regard him. Technically, you see, his loyalties are to France."

His words brought home to Téoline the dire predicament she was in. England was at war with France; therefore, in a sense, she was going into enemy territory. She would be accepted because they thought of her as a royalist émigré, but her sympathies had never been entirely with the Court and the excesses of Versailles. Yet she hated Robespierre and the Jacobins for what they had done to her father and to France . . . and, not least, poor Hélène. The captain had shown her the list, and beneath the Duc de Pavigné's name came that of Hélène Beaulieu. Téoline felt that her world and all she had ever loved was growing smaller by the hour. She was without a family, without a country, and without friends . . . there was only Philippe.

"You can see the Citadel on top that hill!" Michael Dryden pointed enthusiastically towards the shore. Téo strained her eyes to try and catch a glimpse of Halifax through the early morning mist. "My father holds it to be the finest harbor in the world—barring our home port, of course." It was obvious from the lieutenant's tone the elder Dryden was the authority on such things. "He was here with James Cook in '59."

"Then I'm sure I shall find it more than adequate." A smile twitched at the corners of Téo's lips. The boy was doing his very best to make her feel at home, but with all the coltish clumsiness of youth. He had just told her she would be safe there from the scurvy French. Then, blushing bright scarlet, he had tried to redeem himself, swearing he meant no offense. But nothing he could say could lighten her heart as she viewed the rocky shoreline and the dark tree-covered hills. She had grown accustomed to the warmth and brilliance of Saint-Domingue, and Nova Scotia presented a forbidding aspect in contrast to that memory.

They were in the dory, making for the harbor while the *Prometheus* went on to her moorings in the Bedford Basin. "Can you hear the bell from Saint Paul's church?" Michael grinned. "That should make you feel at home, madame. It has a French ring to it. When our General Ogilvie captured the governor of Saint-Pierre, he also brought home the bell."

"I see." Téoline laughed. "So once again you British have robbed Saint Peter to pay Saint Paul eh?"

"You know, you have a remarkable knowledge of many things, ma'am." The boy looked at her adoringly.

"Perhaps that is because I seem to have lived many lives." She sighed.

"Come, ma'am, I doubt you are that much older than me," he responded gallantly.

"It has nothing to do with age, m'sieur. It is a matter of events in time." She smiled. He obviously didn't understand. Téo thought she must be growing old if she could find the simplistic judgments of youth amusing.

Dryden had the seamen tie up the dory in a small cove just off the harbor. "This will give us easy access to the Great Pontac Hotel. I propose you lodge there until we can find a more suitable dwelling for you and Philippe," he said, lifting the small boy ashore.

Téoline nodded her agreement. She could do little else, the setting was so strange. She had thought Le Cap a busy port, but the number of masts in this harbor made it quite a forest. The wharves alongside the docks were a hive of industry. But beyond that bustle, the town itself appeared no more than a small collection of wooden buildings overshadowed by the fort on top of Citadel Hill.

Dryden led them to a three-story wooden structure, which he explained was on the corner of Duke Street. He thought it was as well if Téo started to learn her way around. Téoline paused on the steps of the wide veranda and looked about her.

"Don't they ever build with stone?" she asked innocently.

She had heard remarkable tales of the grand buildings in London, and she was a little surprised to find that such an important place as Halifax was little more than a group of huts in a wilderness of trees.

"It is the best inn in town," Dryden said apologetically. "You will be much safer here than at the Tavern of the Split Crow on the waterfront."

"Oh, no! I am not complaining. It is just that I am a little . . . how you say?" Téo shrugged. The words escaped her, for, if the truth were known, she was appalled by what she saw.

"Shocked?" Dryden supplied the missing term. "I can understand. It hits all the ladies like that at first. They come out from England expecting to find Hyde Park and Bond Street waiting for them, and find this . . .! But you will like it better when you come to know the people. You will also find that the merchants can offer you a wide variety of goods."

Michael Dryden was as good as his word, for, having seen her safely esconced in a suite of two rooms on the second floor, he went in search of dressmakers and milliners. He told them to supply Madame with anything she wanted and send the accounts to him. Téoline had to suppress a smile as she saw the knowing looks they gave him, and even he had the grace to blush.

By the time he returned later that afternoon to take her for a drive around the town, Téoline was refurbished with a wardrobe that might not entirely have suited a princess, but one she found entirely adequate. At Michael's suggestion she visited a Mistress Fraser who might have rooms to rent. She was an Arcadian by birth and so could speak French fluently, which pleased Philippe, who had scarcely mastered his native tongue as yet.

At first the woman appeared a trifle dour. She complained that she had difficulty getting her money from some of the French émigrés and prisoners of war. "And a dreadful mess they make with bits of bone and shells."

Téoline raised her eyebrows and looked at Dryden for an explanation.

"Many of these refugees augment their income by making trinkets—snuffboxes, toys, and such—out of bones and shells, ma'am."

"I doubt I would be very good at that, but I can try." Téoline sighed. Both she and Philippe would have to learn a whole new way of life.

"There'll be no need. I would not hear of you doing such a thing," Dryden said indignantly. He set down enough to cover a year's rent, and it was agreed before they left that Téoline should have the upper floor of the house.

Only one incident really marred that day for Téoline. When Michael Dryden led her in to supper that evening at the Great Pontac, the dining room was full of officers and their ladies, both from the ships in the harbor and the garrison. They were very courteous when the young lieutenant introduced Téoline, although the men chaffed him unmercifully behind her back. Only Guy Leadbetter added a sour note.

"I shall present my compliments, ma'am, once you have settled in. No doubt by then you'll be pleased to have the company of a man instead of a young whippersnapper from the nursery."

"Thank you, Colonel." Téoline bowed. "But I am more than content to be in the company of this gentleman," she said icily, and slipped her arm through Dryden's.

As might be expected, Michael turned bright red and didn't know how to hide his embarrassment.

"I should have called him out for that," he said when they had taken their seats. "I suppose you think me a coward. But Leadbetter is the finest swordsman in Halifax."

"I think you would have been very foolish to do anything other than ignore him. You are a gentleman, Michael, and he is a wretched creature not fit to brush your boots."

Téoline tried to soothe his pride by letting the people around think she was flirting with him outrageously. He was grateful, and his standing improved among both the ladies and gentlemen in Halifax that night.

Chapter Twenty

The summer faded into fall, and that season's beauty helped to heal Téo's spirits. She had wept hours over her father's death and that of the gentle Hélène. For all her father's faults she knew there was a bond of love between them. It was a sad time for Téoline. On top of her own woes came the news that Charlotte Corday had been executed for the stabbing of Marat. Téoline prayed for the repose of her soul and in a strange way envied her childhood friend. Charlotte had remained true to the principles they had espoused as pupils at the Abbaye-aux-Dames, while she had merely learned to compromise.

Captain Ferris had kept his word. Sir John Wentworth had awarded her a small pension, but, as he had explained, there were so many émigrés that funds were in short supply. Téoline was grateful for that money, but it was not sufficient to cover her expenses; Philippe was a growing boy with many needs. But somehow she managed that first winter by selling off the remaining pieces of her jewelry one by one.

The winter itself was another thing. Philippe adored the snow and was not bothered by the cold, but there were many times when Téo longed for the tropical warmth of Saint-Domingue. She hated to venture out into the cold and kept very much to herself in those days. Sir John and Lady Frances frequently invited her to the glittering assemblies they held at Government House, but Téo always made the excuse that she couldn't leave Philippe. He was still prone to nightmares since his frightful experience at Le Cap. Although their landlady was very kind and had grown fond of the boy, Téoline had no wish to impose on her, and she could afford no other servant.

Because of the war, both Michael Dryden and the dreadful Colonel Leadbetter were away. His Royal Highness, Prince Edward, was engaged in a campaign in the West Indies which included a landing in Saint-Domingue by the British, so the garrison and naval strength of Halifax were depleted to support the Prince. It was rumored that when it was over His Royal Highness would be coming there as Commander-in-Chief. Téoline tried to push the war from her thoughts. Her loyalties were too divided. She found it impossible to hate these people, who had given her sanctuary, but she knew she would always remain a Frenchwoman at heart.

The town of Halifax was growing rapidly and prospering from the war. Apart from the social elite, which included members of the governing class sent from England and naval and army personnel, every week saw an increase in the merchant class, intent on profiting from the increasing trade. Among these there was also a growing group of British immigrants. They left their homes to escape dire poverty and industrial unrest. Among them was a group known as the English Jacobins. Inspired by the revolution in France, they were intent on causing trouble in the colony. It was already hard for the original settlers to make a living from the barren land. They looked to the sea for the major harvest, but fishing took its toll of men, and now they had to contend with the increasing demand for experienced seamen. Every day men were being hauled away from their families by the notorious press gangs to serve in the navy. In this atmosphere an increasing resentment began to grow against the French. Under the pressure of war, people no longer cared whether their guests were genuine royalists or revolutionaries in disguise. They treated all with open hostility. This was another reason why Téoline chose to keep to herself, but it made for a very lonely life. Sometimes Téo looked back on her early life with disbelief, wondering if it had all been a dream. Had she worn beautiful gowns and turned men's heads when she walked into the room? Had she really had a beautiful boudoir and spent her days in luxurious surroundings? That time was so remote to Téo as to make her feel ancient. It was beginning to seem as though she had always lived this solitary life, struggling to stretch her meager funds, worrying about her beloved child and his future.

She could not keep her thoughts from turning to Andrew Cameron and what he had offered her, as she carefully picked her way up the steep streets, slippery with the melting snows of early spring. She had been to the Split Crow tavern on the waterfront to speak with the captain of an American vessel she had been told was leaving soon for the West Indies. She had written to Toussaint, Sonata, and Robillard to let them know where she was. There was no way of knowing if they were safe or that they would ever receive her letters; she could only hope. The captain had said he would do his best to get the letters to Saint-Domingue, and Téo had paid him well for his pains. She had to trust that he was an honest man.

She was so deep in thought that she didn't notice she had already turned into Grafton Street. This was an area Michael Dryden had warned her to avoid. Along with Barrack Street, it was a noted place for pimps and prostitutes. It was also a favorite haunt of the press gangs. She thought this was what was happening when a loud scream interrupted her reverie; it was probably some poor soul having to watch while her man was carted away. Then, as Téo's mind surfaced and she became conscious of where she was, she realized that the screams were coming from a small group a few yards ahead along the road.

She hurried closer and saw a huge black man holding a small girl by the arms. Another figure, a fiend in gaudy finery, her face painted and rouged like a devil's mask, was belaboring the child's back with a wooden stick. Téoline's first instinct was to run. Of late she had not been so quick to become embroiled in other people's arguments. Her courage was not what it used to be. But the girl could not have been more than twelve, and her cries were pitiful, so Téo braced herself and went to her defense.

"Stop that!" she commanded, with some of the fire she thought she had lost. "Let that child be, or I shall call the press gang to do their work. They could use a strong man like you in His Majesty's fleet."

Her unexpected assault took all of them by surprise. The man looked up, startled, and loosened his grip, allowing the little girl to escape. She ran and hid trembling behind Téoline's skirt. Before the surprised woman could recover, Téo had relieved her of the stick. Then she rounded on the man again.

"You had better go. I passed a gang only moments away. If you stay, I'll not hesitate to send them after you—I'll pay them if necessary!"

The black man did not wait to see if she meant what she said, but ran up a nearby alley and disappeared from view.

Téoline put her arm about the girl and drew her into the voluminous folds of her cloak. The wind was bitter and the half-naked child was blue with cold. The woman let out a shriek of rage at losing her prey and rounded on Téoline, prepared to continue the fight. The hood of Téoline's cloak had fallen back to reveal her face, and as the woman saw her, the cry quickly faded into a muttered oath. For a few seconds the two women stared at each other, scarcely able to believe their eyes. It was Téo who recovered first, and she said one word.

"Nina!"

"Mademoiselle de Pavigné . . . I mean Madame de

Beben . . .!" Without realizing what she was doing, the former maid instinctively started to curtsy. Then she stopped, stood up, and threw back her head defiantly. "Fancy meeting you here, of all places," she said with deliberate familiarity. "Have you come looking for work? From the look of things, life doesn't appear to have treated you too well." She cast a practiced eye over Téoline's simple gown and lack of jewelry.

"Compared to you, Nina, I would say I have done well. I have sufficient for my needs. At least I still claim some dignity." Téo made no attempt to hide her disgust at what Nina had so obviously become.

"You can forget your airs, madame. I'm no one's servant now. I own this place." Nina jerked her head to indicate a shabby wooden shack. It bore a painted sign which said it was a dancehall, but it was plainly a brothel.

"You bought it with the money and jewels you stole from me, no doubt?"

For the first time Nina's gaze faltered and she shifted her feet uneasily. "That was a long time ago. I thought you'd have forgotten that."

"I haven't, and neither has the law. Sir John Wentworth is a friend of mine. I'll away this minute and swear out a warrant for your arrest."

Téo could see that even under the thick layer of paint, Nina's face had grown pale. In her mind's eye, the former maid could see herself hanging from the gibbet on Gallows Hill. She had no way of knowing how much influence Téo could command in Halifax, but she remembered the power of the de Pavignés.

"No, madame, you wouldn't do that to me . . . You were always kind . . . " She flung herself down in the slush at Téo's feet and made a grab for the cloak.

"Get up!" Téo brushed her away with a gesture of contempt. "At least as my maid you had some pride. Now you are less than the vermin in the gutter." Téoline reached for the hand of the child at her side. "Tell me," she said, pushing her forward slightly, "who is this?"

"She's naught but a young trollop I bought from a sailor passing through. I did 'em both a good turn, if you ask me. I took her off his hands. And she has her bed and board regular with me."

"You mean she has to share her bed with every villian you choose, and if she doesn't oblige, she has your board across her back."

199

"My girls pleasure some of the best gentlemen in Halifax," Nina retorted indignantly.

"Nonsense. I'm taking this child home with me. And rest assured, from now on I shall be watching this place. If you take my advice you will think seriously of leaving Halifax. For, by God, I swear I'll lay charges against you if ever I hear of you again." She glowered at Nina, who quickly stepped back to let her pass. Wrapping her cloak about the little girl and holding her close to her side, Téoline hurried away.

"She's a bad 'un, ma'am. She'll not forgive you for what you've done this day," the child whispered, clinging desperately to Téo's hand.

"What is your name?"

"Kiltie, ma'am. I can't remember another. Me mother and father, along with me brother, died of fever on the way out. That's when the sailor took charge of me."

"Well, Kiltie, that's all changed. You can stay with me if you like. I can't pay you anything, but you'll have a bed and your keep. You can be my maid and help look after my little boy."

The child put her head against Téo's hand. Her face was wet with tears, but her eyes were shining happily. Téoline smiled wistfully. She had noticed a lilt in the girl's speech that reminded her of Andrew Cameron.

By the time May came, the winter storms had given way to spring gales. The snow and ice that had made the streets about the Citadel into toboggan slides had disappeared and there was a hint of warmth in the sun.

Téoline twirled about in front of a pier glass admiring her new velvet gown. It had been clever of Michael Dryden to bring a shade that matched her eyes. The dress had been a gift to celebrate his promotion to the captaincy of a small craft. He was very young for such an honor, but he had acquitted himself gallantly in a recent battle with the French.

Kiltie was delightedly admiring her mistress, taking a moment out from her struggle with Philippe, who was protesting mightily about wearing his new shoes. Téoline set her new bonnet at a jaunty angle and settled the plumes. She had sat up most of the night completing it, but the results more than repaid her efforts.

"Come here and let me look at you, Kiltie. That old dress of mine that you have cut down suits you perfectly. You're beginning to sew very well, my dear. If only you were as diligent with your lessons . . . But never mind. Today is a holiday." Téo pulled out the frill around the girl's white mob cap. "I wish I could afford you some lace to trim it with," she sighed.

"I'm not grumbling, ma'am. I've more now than I've ever had. That's what I told 'em in the market when—!" She broke off and a bright flush covered her young face.

"What were they saying? That you were a fool to work for nothing but your keep?"

"I told 'em it was no business of theirs. That I'd work for whom I pleased. I said I'd rather be the maid of Madame de Pavigné than King George himself."

"Thank you, my sweet. But you had better not tell the Prince, should you meet him today." Since leaving Saint-Domingue, Téoline had chosen to be known by her family name; she had no wish to be reminded of de Beben in any way. Mistress Fraser called up the stairs to say the carriage was waiting. Very thoughtfully, Michael Dryden had provided it so that Téo could take Philippe and Kiltie to see Prince Edward arrive from Martinique.

The streets of Halifax were packed with people in a holiday mood. They were celebrating not only the arrival of the new Commander-in-Chief but the onset of spring. Téoline stopped the carriage and bought Philippe a paper favor to wave while the orange sellers and peddlers clustered around trying to sell their wares. Eventually the carriage was able to get through the throng, and Téoline stepped out to greet the Prince, with Philippe at her side and Kiltie bringing up the rear.

He was a tall, commanding figure resplendent in full military uniform; the white plumes in his hat rustled in the sharp spring breeze. As he walked towards them along the carpet that had been spread from the slip to Government House, Téoline could see why he had the reputation for being a stern man. He was a very strict disciplinarian who had his men flogged for the slightest mishap, although his soldiers were among the first to say he was just. The Wentworths, who were noted for enjoying a very full social life, were looking forward to his arrival, as he was known to be a charming and attentive host.

Téoline had attended an "at home" at Government House recently, when plans for the Prince's reception were being made. Something had occurred then to make her anticipate this day with great enthusiasm.

"We are going to let him have 'Friar Lawrence's Cell,' our country cottage near Bedford Basin," Lady Frances had told

Téoline. "You see, my dear, he must have somewhere for this French lady of his to live. I'm just wondering what Madame Saint-Laurent will be like—I hear she's quite charming, but one can never tell. Of course there will be many here who won't approve of their arrangement, but they can hardly expect the son of the King of England to marry a commoner, can they?" her ladyship chattered. Téoline was left wondering if whether the Prince's mistress could be the Julie Saint-Laurent she had known in Paris.

The Prince paused in his passage to allow Sir John to present some of the local dignitaries. Téoline was not included in these, but the Prince, although faithful to his Julie, had never been able to pass by a pretty face. He stopped and the lieutenant governor introduced them.

"De Pavigné?" He rolled the name on his tongue. "I am delighted, madame," he said, bowing over her hand, "as I know my friend Madame Saint-Laurent will be. I believe . . . in fact I'm sure . . . I have heard her mention Téoline de Pavigné. We shall expect you to be a frequent visitor once we have settled in."

His Royal Highness continued on down the line, leaving Téoline overcome with joy. At last she would have one of her own kind, someone who in a small way shared her background. She was so entranced that she found herself smiling at the passing honor guard. This was most unfortunate, as Colonel Leadbetter was among them and he went out of his way to salute her. Her thoughts were so taken up by this surprising turn of events that she ignored Philippe when he tugged at her sleeve as they got back into the carriage. "What is it, little one," she said plaintively as he tugged again and again.

"Mama . . . Mama . . . That man . . . Why does he keep staring at me?" The urgent note in his small voice brought her back to earth.

"Where, Philippe?" Her eyes scanned the crowd.

"It's that ugly little fellow over there," Kiltie said. But as the man saw her pointing at him, he turned and scurried off into the crowd. "I know where I've seen him afore. Leastways I think it was him. He was one of them what asked me if I liked working for you, ma'am. And how much was I paid."

Téoline searched the faces in the crowds milling around, but there was no one that she recognized. It troubled her a little, but she put it out of her mind. Michael Dryden had asked her to accompany him to the reception that evening, and she had so

202

much to do in preparation for that event that she gave it no more thought.

However, later that night she did mention it to Michael Dryden. "Halifax is riddled with agents of the French," he said. "They come over the border from the States and it's difficult to keep track of them. But don't trouble your head. His Royal Highness has already put plans in hand for strengthening the defenses. He's having a new fort built to replace the old one on Citadel Hill."

"Don't tell me more, Michael. Now that you are a captain, you must be discreet." She laughed and put a finger across his lips.

"I don't know much more than that myself. And the fort is there for everyone to see. Besides, I would trust you with my life, Téoline." He was holding her in his arms as they danced and his eyes were shining with pride. His experience in the recent campaign, coupled with his promotion, had added a new manliness to his attitude toward her. Suddenly he said with some of his old impetuous enthusiasm, "Téoline, will you marry me?"

"Michael, that is no way to propose," Téo laughingly scolded. "A woman needs proper notice of these things."

"Have I offended you?" he asked as his face turned bright red.

"Of course not!" Téoline led him off the floor to sit in a small alcove where they could speak privately. "I am deeply honored that you should ask me to be your wife, but I would prefer to remain your friend. I am more grateful to you than you will ever know, but that is not enough to make us happy as man and wife." She saw a look of relief come into his eyes and knew there was more behind this than first seemed. "But why did you ask me tonight? We have never spoken of this before."

"Because I don't like the way some people speak of you. Do you know it is said that you are my mistress?"

"And you find that shocking?"

"No," he said a little sheepishly. "It makes me quite proud. There are at least a dozen fellows I know who would give a limb for that privilege. It's just that . . . well, I was thinking of your good name, Téoline."

"What is it your Master Shakespeare says? 'What's in a name . . .?'" Téo smiled. "I would rather let them say what they will than have anything break this bond we have, Michael."

"I know what you mean. I don't really feel ready for the responsibilities of a married man and my pay leaves much to be desired. I wouldn't worry about the others, but I dislike the attitude of that cad Leadbetter. Be careful of him, Téoline, he is very ambitious and very dangerous."

But both of them forgot their worries as they drove home from Government House. There was still a hint of frost in the air and the stars shimmered in the clear night sky. Téoline chattered happily about the magnificent decorations at the official residence and the Wentworths' beautiful furniture.

"Yes," Michael replied with a grin. "There is a lot of grumbling about that. There'll be even more now that the Prince has ordered so much to be brought out from England. The stuff is packed into men-o'-war and takes up room that should be used for armaments. A lot of these people don't seem to realize that we have a full-scale war on our hands."

Téoline sighed to herself. She seemed to hear echoes of the society at Saint-Domingue.

From the moment Julie Saint-Laurent arrived in Halifax, Téoline's life was changed. Like Téo, Julie was lonely. Her position was a difficult one. The Prince was devoted to his mistress, but there were many places she could not be received. She turned gratefully to Téoline, knowing she would understand. The royal residence in Halifax and, later, the house the Prince built to replace the cottage at Bedford Basin became Téo's second home. Téoline was delighted as her life took on new meaning again, but she failed to realize that with the expenses such high living incurred, she was slowly getting deeper and deeper into debt.

She arrived home from a visit to Julie one day to find Kiltie waiting for her at the door. Her young face was as white as the apron she was crumpling in her hand. "It's 'im, ma'am," she said, jerking her head in a birdlike fashion towards the stairs. "You know the one I mean . . . the one what was watching us the day the Prince came."

Téoline felt her throat go dry and she ran past Kiltie and up the stairs.

Though the man had his back to her, there was something familiar about him. When he turned round, she stared at him, unable to believe her eyes. She had never seen him without a white wig before, but there was no mistaking the face—it was her father's steward, Le Beau.

"Good day, citizeness! How pleasant to meet you again after

204

all these years." The small eyes narrowed as he spoke, as he tried to smile.

"Why, Le Beau, what are you doing here? Have you brought news from France?" Téoline longed to hear that her sister Louise was still alive. He might even have news of Julien.

"Indeed I do. . . . Well, that is, in a kind of way." Without waiting for her offer, he took a seat, stretched out his spindly legs, and proceeded to take a pinch of snuff.

"Please don't play with me, m'sieur!"

"*Citizen* Le Beau, if you don't mind, Citizeness Beben—or, as you prefer it, Pavigné." His studied insolence did not escape Téoline.

"Le Beau," she said impatiently, "tell me if you have news of my family. Is my sister, Madame Duval, all right?"

"If you mean by that does she still have her head, the last I heard she was all right. That of course could change."

"What does that mean?" Téo noted his game of cat and mouse.

"It means, citizeness, that the revolution needs your help. I was told you knew Sir John and Lady Wentworth, but now I find you have even more influential friends."

"Who told you this? How did you know where I was?"

"Oh, my men and I have been watching you for some time. But it was a mutual friend I met in Boston a little while ago who told me you were here."

Téoline's thoughts immediately flew to Andrew Cameron, but she just as quickly dismissed the idea. He would have no truck with a man like Le Beau.

"I see you are puzzled, citizeness. You do not appear to have a good memory where your old friends are concerned."

"I have few friends, and none in Boston that I know of."

"It was here that you met. I happened to run into her in Boston because you had been unkind enough to threaten her if she stayed in Halifax." Now it was clear.

"Nina!" Téo spat the name as if its very sound was distasteful.

Le Beau smiled and inclined his head.

"I might have guessed. Scum gravitates to the gutters. But now that you are here, say what you want and go." Téoline's eyes flashed angrily. It took her all her will not to heave something at the wretched little man.

"Oh, please, let us remain friends. It will make for pleasantness in our future dealings."

"I shall leave orders that you are never to be admitted again."

Le Beau tutted disapprovingly. "I wouldn't do that. It would be most unwise if you wish to see your sister alive. I suggest you listen to what I have to say. I am a very nervous man, and my present calling makes me even more so."

The gloves were off at last. Now Téoline knew he was playing some evil game with very high stakes. "I prefer to stand. But say what you have to quickly and then go." She pointed to the door.

"Very well." Le Beau sighed like a man constantly doing his best but always being misunderstood. "I have been pleased to note how attached you are to Madame Saint-Laurent . . . indeed, even to the Prince himself. Being a loyal Frenchwoman, no doubt you are prepared to put that friendship to use."

"I don't know what you are hinting." Téoline felt her cheeks begin to burn.

"I think you do. In fact, I'm sure you do . . . you were never a fool. You are in a perfect position to find out all we need to know about the new defenses. We know about the fort and the new signaling system, but we need details . . . and you must get them for us." The menace in his tone was unmistakable.

"And what if I won't? These people have taken me in and given me shelter, when I needed it. I will not betray them even for my sister's life. And I have only your word she would be safe."

"I had thought you might say that. Your father died with the same disdainful pride in his eyes. I was there when they beheaded him, and he cursed me with his dying breath."

"Thank God for that." Téoline faced him, anger in her eyes.

But he had another card to play. "I can only hope, for his sake, that your son Philippe has inherited some of your courage. He may well need it in the days ahead."

Téoline had to stifle a cry. "You couldn't . . . you wouldn't . . . Philippe . . ." She ran to the window and saw that he was playing in the garden with Kiltie.

"He is quite safe . . . for the moment, citizeness . . . but I cannot guarantee he will always stay that way. Fouché is a hard taskmaster, and if he should give the orders . . ." He shrugged. "Then we should have to obey. But I'm sure it will not come to that. There is no immediate hurry for your reply." He picked up his hat and, bowing, went to the door. "But think on it, citizeness, before I have cause to call on you again."

Chapter Twenty-one

Téoline's life took on a nightmarish quality; she was afraid to let Philippe out of her sight for even a moment. If she did, she always made sure Kiltie was with him. She longed to leave, but had no idea where she could go. At least in Halifax they had some money to live on, although she was getting still deeper into debt. Coupled with that, people's attitude towards the émigrés was changing as rumors spread that the French navy was planning an attack on the port. In view of this, she was afraid to take even Michael Dryden into her confidence. The slightest suspicion of intrigue with the enemy could ruin his career. Having no other comfort, Téoline increasingly turned to drink.

"I hate to say this, Téoline, but don't you think you've had more than enough?" Michael Dryden said one day when he saw her refilling her glass. It was the third or fourth time she had done so in less than an hour, he was sure.

"Yes, I suppose I have." Téo pushed the glass away. She got up and went across to the window. Her brain was tired and fuzzy and she found it restful to look out upon the sea.

Dryden watched her anxiously. He had been away at sea for some weeks and was shocked to see such a change in her. "There is something troubling you. Won't you tell me what it is? Is it money, Téoline? If it is, please let me help. I'm being given command of the *Prometheus* and it will mean an increase in my pay."

"That's wonderful," she replied, thankful to have an opportunity to change the subject. "Does that mean you won't have to hunt down Yankee merchantmen anymore?" She knew that was a duty he hated.

"I hope so. But I'm praying that if my present mission is successful we may see an end to that bothersome business entirely. It is futile in the extreme and has helped to bring the States and England to the brink of war."

Dryden had explained the problem to her before. The British seamen were deserting in numbers because pay and conditions were better on the Yankee ships. In the present state of emergency the British navy could not afford to see them go, and had taken to stopping and searching the American ships in an attempt to get their men back.

"How do you tell whether a fellow's English or American? It's easy enough to forge papers, and I'm damned if I can tell from their accents. The trouble is we speak a common tongue for the most part." He laughed ruefully.

"What is this you are doing that you hope will ease the situation . . . or shouldn't I ask?"

"I see no harm in telling you. Hamilton is concerned with getting the States on its feet economically. He rightly judges the British navy to be a bigger threat to his shipping than that of the French. He sent John Jay to England to negotiate a treaty."

"And this will insure American neutrality, you think?"

"It is to be hoped so. We have enough trouble on our hands as it is. But to make doubly sure, Hamilton's sending an unofficial deputy to discuss the question with the Commander-in-Chief and Sir John. It is my task to meet him and escort him during his stay in Halifax." He took an envelope bearing the royal crest out of his pocket. "It is one of the reasons I am here today. The Prince is giving a ball out at Bedford Lodge."

"Have the renovations been completed, then?" Téoline knew that Julie and the Prince had almost rebuilt the place. Madame had gone to great lengths to describe how the Prince was having a rotunda built. There was to be a heart-shaped pond, and all the paths were being laid out to spell JULIE.

"Enough for them to entertain. I know several of our battleships have been unloading furniture for them at the docks. Will you let me have the pleasure of escorting you again?" He handed her the elaborate invitation. "Madame Saint-Laurent expressed the hope that you would be there. She was saying she has seen little of you lately."

"I know. I'm afraid I have had other things on my mind." She made a determined effort to sound casual about the whole thing. If the truth were known, she was terrified of going anywhere near the Prince or Julie, lest she should hear anything of interest to Le Beau and his friends. Téoline was working on the assumption that she couldn't tell what she didn't know.

"But you will come with me?" Dryden said eagerly. "See, I knew you wouldn't let me give you the money for a new dress, so I have bought you this length of chambray. I'm told it is the latest thing." He handed her a package of lightweight fabric with a fine blue thread running through it.

"Michael, you are very naughty, but you have exquisite taste. One day you will make some girl a perfect husband."

"If I do, she will have you to thank." He blushed.

After Dryden left, Téoline went to see her dressmaker. She hoped she could persuade the woman to extend her credit for a few weeks more. The only thing she had left of any value was the portrait of Mirabeau in its diamond frame; she planned to sell that to pay more pressing bills. The dressmaker surprised her. Instead of haggling as she usually did, she proved most affable and promised to give Madame de Pavigné's order top priority. She recommended that Madame should have the fabric made up in the new simple lines being favored in Paris. When it was time for her to leave, Téoline knew she should mention something about the bill.

"That is no longer a problem, madame. Your gentleman friend has paid all you owe," the woman said.

"My gentleman friend? . . . Captain Dryden, you mean?"

"No, I don't believe that was his name. One moment, I have the receipt here. He expressly asked me to give it you." The dressmaker ruffled amongst some papers on a desk. "You are very fortunate to have more than one patron, madame . . . Ah, here it is. The account was paid in full by a Monsieur Le Beau."

Téoline never knew how she got out of that shop or how she got home. When she did arrive back at Mistress Fraser's there was another shock waiting for her. Kiltie handed her a note.

"It was him," she said. "You know the one I mean. He gave it to Philippe."

"But I told you he was never to be left alone. Not for a minute." Téoline felt herself become weak. If Le Beau had been able to get that close to her son, she could not bear to think what he might do.

"I didn't, ma'am. Honest!" Kiltie's eyes filled with tears. I took him and young Samuel Cunard down to the beach to watch the ships. You know how young Samuel likes them. I was sitting on some rocks not a yard away from them the whole time. It beats me how I never saw him. But there it was, young Philippe came running over to me with this in 'is hand."

The girl was so upset that Téo hadn't the heart to scold her anymore. Instead she hurriedly tore open the note. It read: *"As you can see, citizeness, you cannot protect your son all the time. If you are concerned for his future safety, it would be as well if you were to meet me at six o'clock this evening at the tavern known as the Split Crow."* There was no signature, but Téoline knew only too well who it was from. Her hands were trembling as she poured herself a glass of wine.

* * *

The landlord stopped in his task of polishing a pewter tankard with a filthy cloth and nodded towards the stairs. "He's waiting for you. First room at the top of the stairs," he said with a wink before Téo had time to tell him why she had come. The place was crowded with seamen and the air heavy with smoke and the stench of ale. Téoline pulled the hood of her cape closer about her face and hurried along a narrow passage and up the stairs. The door was slightly ajar and she peeped inside before entering.

"Come in, my dear. I've been waiting for you." The door slammed shut behind her and she turned to find herself staring up into the face of Guy Leadbetter.

"Why, Madame de Pavigné, this is a pleasant surprise!" It was obvious he had been expecting a woman, for he was dressed in nothing but his breeches and a shirt. "But since you are here, I shall be more than happy to make the best of it." He pulled at the ribbons of her cloak, and when they wouldn't give, he tore it off impatiently. His long broad face was flushed with drink and his watery eyes glinted at her through a haze.

"I'm sorry, Colonel Leadbetter. There has been some mistake." Téoline backed away. "I was expecting to meet someone else."

"Young Dryden, no doubt. Well, he'll be unlucky, my dear. It's my turn now." He grabbed her round the waist and, holding her close, pressed his mouth down over hers until she could have cried with the pain. "I've waited a long time for this, Téoline."

"Let me go!" she said, stamping hard on his bare feet.

"Oh, no, my pretty." He grabbed her wrist and pulled her back into his arms. "You'll not escape me this time. And don't play hard to get. There's only one type of woman who comes to the Split Crow and they come here for one thing . . . and that, my dear, is what you're going to get." She struggled against his hot wet kisses as his fingers tore at the fastenings of her gown. "If you want to play rough, my dear, I'm always willing to oblige." Leadbetter grabbed at the bodice and ripped it, leaving her naked to the waist. "Now that's better, isn't it."

He began to fondle her breasts while dragging her towards a bed on the other side of the room. At that moment there was a sharp tap at the door, and he pushed her into a chair. "Stay there, I'll be back!" he said as he went across to open it. He stuck his head outside and Téo heard a woman's voice.

"No!" the colonel replied angrily. "Get out! I've no use for you today." Téoline lost no time in retrieving her cloak. She didn't know how she was going to do it, but she was determined to make her escape. Much as she hated to be seen in her present state, it would be better than being raped by this wretch. She ran over to the door where Leadbetter and his unwanted visitor were still arguing. Before the colonel could stop her, she had pushed it open wide. There was a moment's silence as she found herself looking into Nina's raddled face. The heavy makeup creased as her former maid cackled with delight.

"Why, Madame de Pavigné, you'll never know what pleasure it gives me to find you in this place."

"Whore!" Téoline spat. "Let me pass!"

"Not on your life! You can have her, colonel, with my compliments!" Nina's laugh was cruel. It was plain to see that Téoline was Leadbetter's unwilling guest.

Fear had begun to clear Téoline's mind from the haze the wine had left. In this she had the advantage over the other two. "I suppose Le Beau put you both up to this?" she said. "But why does he want me, when he can get all the information he wants from the colonel here?"

Her words found their mark and caught Leadbetter off his guard. "What does she mean?" he said to Nina.

"Le Beau has no part of this," said Nina, starting to back away from the door.

"Liar!" Téo screamed and, grabbing her, pushed her to one side so she could escape. "Tell your master—there is his spy, if he doesn't know it already. And as for you, Colonel, you may rest assured His Royal Highness will hear of this."

Her accusations had shattered both of them. Téoline did not wait for more, but fled down the stairs and out through the door. A group of sailors laughed derisively and she suddenly realized how she must look. Her gown was in rags beneath her cloak and she clutched at it to hide her nakedness. Hailing a passing sedan chair at the corner of Salter Street, she sank back into its depths, thankful that it was dusk and people were unable to see her face.

Her mind was in a whirl as she relived what had just passed. Leadbetter was no fool. When he recovered from his surprise, he would certainly question Nina further, of that Téo was sure. What if her wild guess had been correct and he was in fact tied in with Le Beau? Either way, her position was now extremely precarious. Her immediate thought was to go and tell Julie, throwing herself on the mercy of the Prince. But on second thought she realized it could not be as easy as that. It would be only her word against Leadbetter's that she was not involved with Le Beau. The colonel would do anything to save his reputation with his Commander-in-Chief, and of course he might have more to hide than his attack upon her. But most important, there was the safety of her son.

By the time she got home, Philippe was in bed. She sent Kiltie down to talk to Mistress Fraser, feeling that she had to be alone. She had to resolve the dreadful situation she was in. She changed into a house gown but left her hair hanging loose about her face. She looked at her reflection in the mirror and shivered at the sight. Her face was thin and drained of all color. There were deep shadows under her eyes. But Téo was past caring; she only wished to pour another glass of wine and let the drink take its effect.

Outside, a fiery sunset streaked the sky out over the sea. Another time she would have thought it beautiful, but tonight it conjured images of blood and flames. She sat by the window watching it and quietly sobbing to herself, far too preoccupied to hear the repeated knocking on the apartment door.

"In the name of Heaven!" She came to her senses with a jerk. "Just a moment," she called, as she glanced into the mirror and tried to powder away her tears. "One moment!" she called out again as she hurried to unlock the door. Whoever it was did not intend to wait patiently. She only hoped it wasn't Le Beau. After a struggle, the lock finally gave to the key and she opened it slightly to look outside.

"André!" Téoline swayed forward, and Cameron just managed to catch her in his arms. "André!" All the years of loneliness and agony were in that one word. Keeping his arm about her, Cameron drew her back into the room and closed the door.

"Let me look at you," he said. But the glimpse he had caught of her pale face in the flickering candlelight had caused him to catch his breath.

"You haven't changed." Téo put a hand up and touched his hair. "Except that you've had this cut. . . ."

"And there is a fair sprinkling of gray, if you look close enough." It hurt him that he could not say the same for Téo. She was still beautiful, but the ravages of all that she had gone through had left their mark. The sight disturbed him more than he could ever have dreamed it would. He was suddenly aware that time and his dreams were slipping by.

"I had to come to Nova Scotia on business. When I heard you

212

were here, I couldn't leave without seeing you again." He held her hand to his lips and kissed it again and again.

"What brought you here? . . . Of course you came to see your father . . .?"

"No, my father died last year." He was reminded again how foolish it was to wait. He had waited too long to make his peace with the elder Cameron and it was something he would regret for the rest of his life. "I came on a mission for Hamilton."

"Then you are his emissary? Was it Michael Dryden who told you where I was?"

"Yes, but you mustn't blame him for that. If he hadn't, I would have wrung his neck. When he mentioned your name, my world was suddenly alive again." His tone conveyed a depth of feeling that was as much a surprise to him as it was to Téoline. She drew him over to a chair and poured some wine. "The captain holds you in great esteem. Without realizing it he was constantly mentioning you . . . and Philippe," he added with a slow sad smile.

"Philippe regards him as an elder brother. Michael is one of the dearest friends I have ever had. I owe him more kindness than I can ever repay." She looked up and saw the expression on Cameron's face. "No, I'm not his mistress, André."

"I rather gathered that from various things he said. But I would not have blamed him had it been the other way."

Téo found it a bitter compliment because she was well aware how she looked, but Cameron was sincere, she felt sure of that. For a time they sat in silence, neither of them knowing quite what to say. Now that the first thrill of reunion had passed, they were both remembering old scars and wondering if the years had healed them. Téoline had long ago regretted her part in their quarrel and she wondered if his pride would allow him to forget how deeply she had wounded him. She only had one card to play, and it was one she had vowed never to use.

"André, would you like to see your son?"

Cameron stood up and, putting both his hands on her shoulders, looked into her eyes as if trying to reach her very soul. But at such a moment there were no words to express what he felt. He bent his head and his lips sought her mouth. His kiss told her all she needed to know.

"Come," she said, leading him by the hand. "He is asleep in the other room."

Cameron stood looking down at the bed where the small boy lay curled up fast asleep. Had he seen him before Téoline spoke, there would have been no need for words. The fair curls had darkened to a chestnut hue, and the lids drooping over the gray eyes gave evidence of the Cameron blood.

"Thank you," he said, gently stroking his son's head. "You know, this is the greatest gift a woman can ever give to a man." He squared his shoulders and suddenly he looked quite young again. He turned to her and laughingly said, "Now, Téoline, I'll ask you once again . . . and for the last time, because I will not accept your refusal. Will you marry me?"

"Yes, André."

"Even if it means living in Boston?"

"That never really worried me!"

"Then why in Heaven's name did you refuse? Why have we wasted all these years?"

"It wasn't that. I was a fool. I was so afraid you meant to take Philippe away from me and bend him to your ways." She laughed softly. "Now I'm not afraid for him. He has inherited the Cameron's willfulness, and I know you have met your match. Lead him and he'll come—force him and he'll go the other way."

"Then he's my son all right; there's no doubt of that."

"No doubt," Téoline replied. "And I renounce my right to him." The tears brimmed into her eyes as she spoke.

Cameron could not read what was in her heart, and mistakenly thought her remark was directed against him. "I never wanted to take him from you, Téoline. You will always be an inseparable part of him. Whenever I look at Philippe I shall see you, and I wouldn't have it any other way." He drew her close and together they stood looking down at their son.

That night Cameron's love washed away the brutal memory of Leadbetter's attempted rape. Téoline awoke the next morning with an easier heart. At least now she was sure Philippe would be safe. About herself she was not so sure.

A fresh surge of fear came over her when Kiltie came in with some coffee the following morning. Cameron had left early, as he had an appointment with Prince Edward and Sir John Wentworth. He had cautioned Téoline not to set foot outside until he returned. "I'm not going to risk losing you a third time," he said. "In fact, I'm seriously considering buying a ball and chain." Laughingly, Téo had settled back against the pillows and watched the sea birds swooping and whirling in the summer sky outside the window. For the first time in a long while the plaintive note had gone from their cry.

"Ma'am . . . Ma'am . . . What do you think . . .?" Kiltie barely knocked. She set down the tray of coffee beside Téo's bed and nearly sent the lot on to the floor.

"How do I know what to think until you tell me what all this excitement is about?"

"It was 'er, ma'am. I saw 'er with my own eyes when I went to the market to fetch the milk. They was just fishing 'er out of the 'arbor with a long hook!"

Instinctively Téoline knew who Kiltie was speaking of, but her lips framed the word. "Nina?"

"Yes, ma'am," the girl chattered on. "They thought she'd been drowned, but as soon as they got her up onto the quay, everyone could see the cord about her throat. It serves 'er right, but it was 'orrible . . . really 'orrible. And that's not all. The town's fair bristling with redcoats. Goin' from 'ouse to 'ouse along the waterfront."

"What are they looking for?" Téoline was almost afraid to ask.

"I don't rightly know. I asked one of them and he told me not to be nosy. His mate said they were looking for spies. I thought I heard one of them ask if anybody 'ad seen a fellow called Lee Bow. Shall I go back out and see if I can find out some more?"

"No, thank you, Kiltie. I want you to stay and look after Philippe. I have to go out to fetch my gown for the ball tonight." Téoline scrambled out of bed and flung on her clothes. She had to go and find out for herself.

It was just as Kiltie had said. Wherever she went, she came across groups of redcoats questioning passersby or going from place to place around the waterfront. Téo hurried down the steep streets, past the crowded wharves to the outskirts of the town. She had no knowledge where she was going or how far she went. Eventually she stumbled into the shade of a willow and sank down upon the grass amidst a carpet of moss speckled with wild white strawberry blooms. Reaching into the small bag hanging from her wrist, she brought out a small flask. The contents were warm and did little to quench her thirst, but they helped to deaden the terror that gripped her heart.

It was obvious Leadbetter had taken her accusations to heart. Whether he had started this hue and cry out of revenge or genuine concern was impossible for her to know. Whoever killed Nina and whatever the colonel's part in the matter, Téoline recognized that her own future was extremely precarious. Whatever she did now would embarrass the Prince and Julie. The

Commander-in-Chief could not afford to ignore this new spy scare, and, pleasant as he was, he was a stickler for duty. He would insist on a full inquiry. A new thought entered her mind just then. How would all this affect Andrew Cameron? With tensions running high between England and the States, there would be many prepared to say he had a part in all this. It was some time before she had the courage to go home. She sincerely hoped that if they were going to search Mistress Fraser's house, they would have done it while she was away. It would save her giving the lie to any questions regarding Le Beau.

Chapter Twenty-two

Téoline finished tying a narrow red ribbon about her throat and stood back to judge the effect in the mirror. It had become a custom for émigrés who had lost friends and relatives to the guillotine to wear such ribbons at assemblies as a sign of protest. In Téo's case it was more because she had no jewels. Her gown's straight, simple line and low bodice had come into fashion under the new French regime, which was called the Directory. Having finally rid themselves of the Jacobins and sickened by the stench of blood, the French were trying to return to some semblance of normality, and there was a renewed interest in dress. Some of the women in Paris were actually wearing their lightweight gowns with nothing underneath, Téo had been told; nudity was all the rage, but she felt she had gone quite far enough.

"The other ladies with their petticoats and powder are going to be mad when they see you, ma'am," little Kiltie said with pride. She was thrilled that she had been allowed to help Téo arrange her curls on top of her head in the Grecian style.

"I wonder . . . ?" Téoline was thinking along the same lines as Kiltie, but for other reasons. The last thing she wanted was to attract too much attention to herself. All afternoon she had played with the idea of not going to the reception, but in the end she decided it would cause more of a furor if she refused. Leadbetter hadn't mentioned her name or she would certainly have had some word from Julie. He was plainly playing a waiting game. It could well serve his purpose not to appear at the last minute. . . . And of course both André and Michael would be distressed.

"I wonder if it is not too revealing?" Téo was wishing she had chosen something that would cause less comment, although the effect was all she could desire. A skillful use of cosmetics had helped her recapture some of her former allure. She was anxious to see André's reaction. Picking up a tiny lace kerchief, Téo tucked it in the bodice of her gown.

There was a loud guffaw from the doorway, and she turned to find Cameron had been watching her. "What's the matter, Téo? Don't tell me your courage is failing you!" He came toward her, thinking how enchanting she looked but with a grow-

217

ing awareness that she had changed a great deal as a result of her suffering and deprivation. "Never mind, I think this may solve the problem." He removed the red ribbon about her throat and the lace from between her breasts. The delicate perfume of her powder had been released by the warmth of her flesh. Cameron held it to his lips before sliding it into his pocket.

"I'll exchange your kerchief for these." He took out a magnificent rope of pearls and fastened them about her neck. "I was fortunate to happen on these. There was an auction at which they were selling off some of the prizes captured by a privateer. It wouldn't do for the future wife of Andrew Cameron to look so bare—except when she's alone with him." He stooped and kissed her shoulder.

Téoline nestled her head against his chest so that he couldn't see her face. "I shall always think of you when I wear these, André"

"There will be plenty more, but I hope there will be other things you will prefer to remember me by." He grinned at her mischievously, reminding her of the way their son liked to tease.

"Come, we shall be late. Michael will wonder what has become of us." She picked up a muslin scarf and arranged it about her hair.

The road out to Bedford Lodge took them through the woods. It was a clear night and the stars were high in the sky. The branches of the trees, trembling in a slight breeze, patterned the golden orb of the moon in filigree. Their carriage swung into impressive gates, set in a low wooden fence and looking completely out of character, but Téoline was gazing at the hundreds of tiny lanterns swinging from the branches of the hemlock trees. The soft strains of an orchestra playing in the rotunda drifted over to them and mingled with the perfume of the flowers. Whatever happened after tonight, Téo thought, she would always remember this moment. She was looking her loveliest, and much of it was due to having the man she loved at her side.

His Royal Highness was a most generous host; the tables were laden with food and wines. Neither he nor his mistress were fond of large gatherings, and by midnight they made their excuses and retired to the privacy of their own suite. The younger officers were dancing, while the others had drifted off to join gambling tables that had been set up under the trees and in alcoves around the lawns. Téoline had been in great demand as a partner, and both Andrew and Michael Dryden had long ago excused themselves. Cameron said he was too old for so much exercise and Dryden said he must stay with his guest. Téoline laughed, knowing it was merely an excuse. Cameron had gambling in his blood, and Michael wasn't averse to a game of faro. Later, when some of the younger crowd started dancing a Scottish reel, Téoline also excused herself and went in search of the two men.

She found them in a bower hidden behind some flowering shrubs. Cameron was in a high good humor having won. Michael and some of the younger men did not look so happy. She watched them anxiously, knowing many of them were more than likely chancing all they possessed on the turn of a card. Often, in the morning light, a gambler would find the results too grim and end it all by putting a bullet through his head.

All the players had been drinking heavily, and now and again tempers flared. This was not helped by the sarcastic comments from many of the ladies watching them. It was intended as a game, but the tension was mounting by the minute. Finally, Peter Bowen, a young naval lieutenant and a friend of Dryden's, had enough sense to throw in his hand. Téoline whispered to Michael that he should follow suit, but he was not persuaded. When she looked up, she saw that Guy Leadbetter had taken Bowen's seat. She looked across at Andrew to avoid the colonel's eyes, but she felt conscious that Leadbetter was staring at her.

Leadbetter took his time settling himself into his seat. He sprawled back in his chair, stretching out his long legs and making it difficult for those who had been standing watching the game. He appeared to be making a deliberate effort to disrupt the play.

"Are we going to play, or has this turned into a one-man military display?" Cameron said impatiently, pushing a deck of cards across the table.

Leadbetter gave a drunken laugh. "You're quite right, my friend . . . We're wasting valuable time. But may I suggest we use another pack . . ." He fumbled in the jacket of his scarlet uniform. "I have a very amusing little pack here. It's French. I found it on a French spy we just captured who went by the name of Le Beau."

Everyone clustered round the table, anxious to see his prize. They were all aware of the hunt that had been going on. Téo bit her lip and tried to control an insane desire to run. "Of course these will be of great interest to Madame de Pavigné. No doubt she has played with them, or similar ones, many times." Téoline

219

knew what was behind his remark, but it was lost on the others, who thought the colonel was referring to her French origins.

"You see, here we have the queens. . . ." Leadbetter laid them out on the table for all to see. "This is *Egalité*, the queen of clubs . . . and diamonds is *Fraternité* . . . and here we have *Liberté*, the queen of spades . . ." He paused and gave a little laugh, which sent a shiver down Téo's spine. "And last, my friends, we have the one and only Téoline de Pavigné—the queen of hearts!" Some of the men started to applaud, but Leadbetter cut them short by saying harshly, "Now, gentlemen, all we have to do is play, and so find the traitor in their midst!"

There was a sharp intake of breath by a number of women standing close to her. The men murmured under their breath and fidgeted nervously. Téoline gripped the back of a chair to prevent herself from swaying as she felt the intensity of the eyes focused on her. She started to move away, but the stress was too great and she stumbled into Cameron's arms.

"Confound you, Leadbetter!" Michael Dryden was on his feet. His kick overturned the table and sent cards and coins scattering on the grass. "You have insulted Madame de Pavigné, and I demand satisfaction in her name."

"You stupid young pup!" Leadbetter was on his knees scrambling for his stake. "You've quite spoiled my game."

Dryden turned as red as the colonel's jacket and, lifting his foot a second time, he sent Leadbetter sprawling on the grass. A nervous titter of laughter went through the crowd. Téoline leant back against Cameron's shoulder and closed her eyes.

"Behind the rotunda at dawn," Leadbetter shouted as he scrambled to his feet. "I'll teach you some manners yet, you whelp!"

"André, for the love of God stop them. Michael does not stand a chance. . . !"

"There's nothing I can do, Téoline. Dryden's honor is at stake, as well as yours."

"He cannot win . . . but if he should, his career will be finished. Prince Edward has forbidden dueling. He will be furious if it should come to his ears." As proof of what she had just said, the crowd had suddenly melted away. Only a small group of Leadbetter's friends and young Bowen were left, along with Cameron and Dryden.

"Go and wait in the carriage. I will meet you by the gate when it is over. In another fifteen minutes we will see the dawn." Cameron looked at his watch and then up at the sky, where already light was showing. He gave Téo's arm a gentle squeeze and turned her toward the lodge. "We'll be your seconds, Dryden." Then, turning to Leadbetter he said, "As you know, it is your right to choose the weapons!"

"I'll take small swords." Leadbetter's lips curled in a cruel smile.

"You would," Cameron muttered under his breath as he gave a formal bow of acknowledgment. Anyone with a knowledge of weapons knew that, given the colonel's height and weight against Dryden's youthful frame, small swords would prove a great advantage to him.

Téoline went across to Michael Dryden and took his face between her hands. She kissed him gently. "God go with you, my friend. You know you have my love and prayers."

He kissed her hand and held it to his heart. Then he saluted smartly and followed the others up the hill.

Téoline raced back to the house and ordered the carriage to wait for them near the gate. Drawing her cloak about her, she retraced her steps towards the rotunda. She dreaded what she might see, but she couldn't bear to wait and wonder. Michael was such a boy. She was always imagining what Philippe would be like at his age. Surely it was not his destiny to die so young? Memories of Stefan Cambenet came back to her and she relived the terrible circumstances surrounding his death. Was it her fate that men loving her should die?

The small building with its domed roof was surrounded by a colonnade. In the harsh early light the pillars cast deep shadows along the walls. Keeping well within them, Téoline crept forward, making sure she was not seen. She could already hear the clash of steel on steel and knew a sudden sound might put Michael off his guard. She could almost feel the thud of their feet upon the hard ground.

As the duelists came into her view, she took cover behind some shrubs. Even to inexperienced eyes there was no doubt that Leadbetter was the practiced swordsman. Téo held her breath as she saw him lunge at Dryden's chest, but the captain parried and forced the other's point to pass under his arm. It missed his body by an inch. Michael quickly riposted, but the colonel was already on his guard. He laughed as he circled Michael's blade with his own and continued the movement to thrust his weapon along the length of Dryden's steel.

Michael stepped back and almost stumbled as he hastily attempted to deflect Leadbetter's blade. The colonel came on relentlessly and then, with a sudden disengage, flicked Dryden's sword with his point. The speed and vigor of his attack had left the captain's chest exposed. With a swift lunge, Leadbetter drove his sword between Michael's ribs. The boy gave a groan, staggered forward, and fell to the ground.

"A doctor! . . . Fetch the doctor!" Cameron had already rushed over and was kneeling by Dryden's side. In seconds he was joined by Téoline. The colonel drew his sword out of the inert body at his feet and wiped the blade on a handkerchief he pulled from his sleeve. Without another glance at the group, he walked away to where his seconds were conferring under some trees. Bowen had been speaking to them and was now hurrying back.

"Where's the accursed doctor, man?" Cameron raged.

"There is none." Bowen's young face was snow-white and his eyes wide with terror at what he had just seen. "Leadbetter's seconds said they would bring one. Then they became scared the Prince would get to hear about the fight and thought it better no one else should know."

"Aren't they aware that to duel without a doctor present makes it murder, by law?" Cameron lifted Dryden up and carried him into the rotunda. He laid him gently on the floor. Téoline took off her cloak and, folding it up, put it beneath his head. Michael opened his eyes and looked up into her face.

"I had to do it for you, Téoli—" The words faded on his lips. Téoline let out a sob and looked across at Cameron.

Cameron stood up and started to peel off his coat. There was no mistaking the fury in his gray eyes. "No . . . André . . .!" Téo put out her hand, but he swept it to one side. Striding out on to the hill beside the rotunda she heard him shout.

"Leadbetter!" His voice was full of rage. "Come back here. Do you hear me, sir? I'm calling you out!"

The colonel turned and reluctantly retraced his steps until he was facing Cameron. "I have no quarrel with you, sir!"

"Yes, you have," Cameron replied, picking up Dryden's sword from the grass and flexing the blade. "You have killed a boy young enough to be your son and insulted the lady who is to be my wife. On guard!"

It was Leadbetter's turn to be nonplussed. He did not like fighting against unknown odds and had no way of assessing Cameron's skill with a sword. He circled nervously round his opponent before making an opening thrust. Cameron riposted with such speed it almost caught him off guard. He stepped back out of range. As an experienced swordsman, he was quick to appreciate that the man now facing him posed a more serious threat than the young naval officer he had so easily dispatched.

Nerving himself for the fray, he plunged into the attack and reengaged his sword with Cameron's. They indulged in a few feints and rapid disengagements while they took each other's measure.

Becoming more sure of his ground, Cameron lunged. The colonel parried, but Cameron dipped his blade and, with a slight movement of his fingers, continued his onward thrust. Leadbetter circled his opponent's weapon and slid forward along the blade.

"Et lah!" he shouted triumphantly. He was beginning to enjoy the fight. This Yankee was a worthy opponent and he would enjoy cutting him down—especially as he could see Téoline watching them. The colonel pressed his advantage home with a series of rapid thrusts. Cameron calmly retreated until he was ready to stand his ground again.

The colonel was a showy fencer and expended far more energy than was necessary. Panting from his exertions, he began to slow in his attacks. It was this moment Cameron had waited for. With a sudden burst of fury he advanced, destroying Leadbetter's timing. Punching Leadbetter's sword to one side, Cameron struck home and his blade penetrated the colonel's shoulder.

The pain galvanized Leadbetter into action and he came back, whipping his sword in and out like a snake. Cameron stepped back to regain his balance, but the early morning dew had dampened the grass and his foot slipped. Téoline screamed as he fell to one knee. Leadbetter sprang forward to deliver the *coup de grace*. She covered her eyes, able to bear no more. But Cameron was not finished yet. He deftly rolled to one side and came to his feet as Leadbetter gathered momentum for a final attack. As Cameron drove his sword upward, his opponent ran into it. The blade went through Leadbetter's ribs and pierced his heart. He let out a gurgled scream and dropped to his knees. For a brief second he stared at Cameron, then fell forward on his face.

Cameron covered his eyes with his hand. "God forgive me," he said, and turned to Téoline, who had run to his side. Already they could hear voices coming from the direction of the house.

"André, you must not be a part of this. It will ruin all you are trying to do for Hamilton." They had reached the rotunda, where Bowen knelt mourning over his friend.

223

"I'd like to get him away from here," Bowen said, looking up at them pathetically. "The last man killed in a duel His Royal Highness ordered to be buried where he fell, in unhallowed ground. If I can get him back to the *Prometheus*, we'll bury him at sea."

Cameron finished putting on his coat. Now he stooped down and pulled Dryden's body up on to his shoulders. "You take the carriage and go home Téoline. I'll find a horse and follow you." He signaled to Bowen to lead the way and within seconds the little group was hidden from sight among the trees.

Téoline gave orders for the carriage to make all speed. She was now certain of what she had to do. She could not allow the evil influences that were clouding her life to fall on the two people she loved most. As soon as she reached the apartment, she bundled some clothing into a valise and penned a note to Cameron. As briefly as she could, Téo told him about Le Beau and how she feared for Philippe's safety. She did not mention that she was afraid Cameron might be considered guilty by association. If she were gone, whatever Le Beau might say was unlikely to reflect on André, but if she stayed it might ruin him. She asked him to take care of Kiltie. She said she gave him their son to guard forevermore. Finally, she begged Andrew Cameron to forgive her but never to forget what their love had been.

She went into the bedroom and kissed Philippe, thinking her heart would break. He was asleep and did not feel the tears she shed as she knelt and prayed beside his bed. Then, racing down the stairs, she hailed a chair and ordered the men to take her to the docks. With any luck she would find a ship that would take her somewhere . . . anywhere . . . before Cameron returned.

1802

Chapter Twenty-three

"Julien says Napoleon means to become Emperor of France. I don't think so, do you, André? He told me he believed in the revolution . . . ." Téoline's voice quavered and her words ended in a sigh. "Of course, people change . . . I've changed, haven't I, André? You don't have to lie. I could see it in your eyes that night in Halifax."

There was a long pause before she spoke again.

"Poor Josephine, she'll never be Empress if Bonaparte divorces her. She's so kind. Did I tell you how much she helped me when I eventually got back to Paris . . .? She's a Creole, you know . . . ."

"Téoline, I want you to drink this. It may help you to sleep." Robillard gathered her thin figure into his arms and held the small gourd containing the potion to her pale lips. He could see Téo growing weaker before his eyes. If she could get some rest, there was still be a chance she might survive.

The yellow plague had left her weeks ago, but she hadn't recovered her strength. Sonata was sure Téoline had lost all will to live. "She's just waiting out her time until God lets her die," the ex-slave had said, as she sat patiently by her mistress's side day after day.

If they only had somewhere else to take her, away from this wretched shack. The doctor and Sonata had brought her to this disused fisherman's hovel to get her away from Le Cap. It was the best they could do. Her house was in ruins, like most of the city. And if it had become known she had the fever, she'd have been sent to the plague house to die. People were so scared of the disease they often didn't wait to make sure the victim was dead before burying him. At least she had been spared that, but the heat and the flies in the small cabin made her life unbearable. Robillard settled her back on the straw that served as pillow and mattress on the wooden bench near the window.

He walked over to the door and surveyed the beach. Sonata should be returning soon, and he would have to go back to his patients in Le Cap. Robillard took out a handkerchief and mopped the sweat from his brow. As he did so, he wrinkled his nose in disgust. In spite of bathing himself thoroughly before coming out to see Téo, the stench of the plague was still in his nostrils and on his clothes.

What a fool Bonaparte had been. Why couldn't he have left things as they were instead of sending his brother-in-law out with an army from France? Neither Leclerc nor his men were used to the heat, and then yellow fever had hit. Fifty thousand were dead in a year, including Leclerc. It would have been so much better to have left it to Toussaint. He was making an excellent job of restoring the colony. He had freed the slaves and they had gone back to work. Though he had appointed himself governor, he had been willing to acknowledge a loyalty to France. But he kept the money raised from the crops to help the colony; that was the rub. Napoleon needed Saint-Domingue's wealth to finance his grandiose plan of conquering Europe. He sent Leclerc with a show of friendship, but privately he referred to Toussaint as "that gilded African." It was rumored he intended to bring back slavery. Was it to be wondered at that the blacks chose to fight?

"It was Josephine who first introduced me to Barras . . ." Téo started to sob wildly. Robillard returned to her side. In the past few weeks he had heard these words repeatedly, and he knew she would shortly become terribly distressed. He took a damp rag and laid it on her forehead, praying the drug he had given her would soon take effect.

"I didn't want to become his mistress . . . nor Talleyrand's . . . You do believe that, don't you, André? I've only ever loved you in that way. Hélène was right . . . the gutters of Paris are an unfriendly place. Barras offered me food and a bed. And once you become a courtesan, there's no turning back." Téo struggled to sit up and the doctor had difficulty calming her down.

"André, promise me you'll never tell Philippe . . .? I couldn't bear him to think ill of me . . . He's young . . . He won't understand."

Robillard wiped away the tears that were coursing down her cheeks. When Sonata came back, he would get her to bathe Téoline, in the hope of reducing this secondary fever. He picked up a fan of plaited palms and stirred the air around her face. At least the air was a little purer out here.

Le Cap reeked of plague. The death toll had been so great there were few people left now to bury the dead; bodies were left rotting in the sun for days. The fighting had died out in the city itself, but it was still continuing out on the plains. The smoke from burning coffee and sugarcane drifted across Le Cap, holding in the stench. The only respite was when the rains came, and they brought their own evils.

Robillard sat down on one of the wooden barrels that served as chairs and stroked Téoline's hand, hoping his touch might help to soothe her dreams. In spite of the fever she was quite beautiful again. Her skin was free of the artificial aids she had been using. The harsh dye had faded from her hair, and though it was a shade paler than it had been in her youth, it still glistened like gold in sunlight. He recalled how shocked he had been the day she came ashore with Pauline Leclerc. She had been overdressed in some of the exaggerated fashions of the time, which had made her look quite old. He hadn't recognized her at first glance. She was so unlike the girl he had first met some ten years before when she arrived with Albert de Beben. Téo had called his name and he had recognized the voice.

"Pierre, don't you remember me?" He had been as upset as she was, because the memory of Téoline de Pavigné was firmly imprinted on his mind. She was the daughter he might have had —the woman he wished his wife had been. Téoline would always hold a special place in his heart.

Téoline had been so pleased to see him again, but not more so than he was to see her. "I had not hoped to find you here after all this time. I thought you would have left Saint-Domingue years ago," she had said.

"I am waiting," Robillard had replied. "If Marie should ever want to return, it is here she will look to find me."

Téoline could have wept at that moment. He looked an old man before his time. She thought again how strange love was; it seemed to be beyond human control. Knowing her faults, Robillard still loved Marie, as she had discovered she loved her father in the end. She thought of Julien and Stefan Cambenet, both of whom had brought her grief, yet she loved them as she would always love André. Once brought to life by whatever magic lit its flame, love burned throughout eternity and beyond —if that were possible.

"Marie left Julien a long time ago," Téo had said apologetically. She would always feel guilty about the part her brother had played in breaking up the marriage. She also thought Robillard should be prepared for the new Duc de Pavigné who would be arriving in Saint-Domingue. Napoleon had restored the titles of the old aristocracy and welcomed back the émigrés; Julien had accepted a commission in the French army even though it meant coming back to Le Cap.

"I'm not surprised," Robillard replied. "I knew she would. But I shall wait. I can't forget Marie any more than you can forget Andrew Cameron."

If only he could find Cameron. Robillard got up and walked to the door of the hut. He had written so many letters in the past few months and sent them to every port at which Cameron's vessels might call. But he couldn't be sure they would reach their destination or if Cameron would even trouble to reply. Surely the man loved her . . . or had his only desire been to gain possession of his son? Téoline had said only that she had left Philippe with his father in Halifax many years ago. After that she appeared to have wandered from the States to England, then to France, and finally back to Saint-Domingue. It would have been difficult, Robillard had to admit, but surely Cameron could have found her if he had really tried.

He walked down onto the beach a little way and looked toward Le Cap. Sonata should be back from the market before too long. Not that there was much left to buy. There were no crops left to trade and little money, so few ships troubled to call at Cap Français anymore, having found more profitable ports of call. He hoped that today Sonata would have had some success in getting food. A lot would depend on whether she had been able to find a market for Téo's pearls.

Téoline had clung to them as her only link with Cameron. She admitted that she had often been forced to pawn them, but as soon as she was in funds again they were always the first things she retrieved. Robillard had tried to dissuade her from selling them, but to no avail. It had been in one of her more lucid moments, and Téo had told him she wanted to make provision for Sonata. "Life has been so cruel to her," she had said. "Benjamin killed and now her children dead of the plague."

The doctor left the beach and went back to check on Téoline. The sight of her lying there made his throat go dry. There was a strange beauty that often came when death was near. He had seen it many times. Even very old people seemed to regain something of their youth. If was as if the cares and troubles they had lived through fell away and they were young again. So it was with Téoline. For all her thirty years, she looked now as she had at sixteen. Robillard prayed that she might live, but if that could not be, then he prayed that her soul should find peace. She had lived so many lives and seen such tragedy, it was not surprising if her courage had failed her at last. He had done what he could, and now he could only remind himself that while there was life there was still hope.

He looked up as Sonata came in. The lined face under her prematurely gray hair was troubled, and she shook her head dejectedly. "I couldn't find anyone who would buy these." She handed him the pearls. "You had better take charge of them, m'sieur. Those that had the money said they couldn't eat beads." Robillard took them from her and slipped them in his pocket.

"There is a vessel due to dock later this afternoon. I'll go and meet it. There may be a passenger aboard who will buy them. In the meantime, have you any food at all? She should have some nourishment. I'm afraid she's fast losing what little strength she has." Sonata produced two small fishes from a basket and said she would make some broth.

"I'll leave you, then," Robillard said. "There are some patients I have to attend. All being well, I'll return this evening. Keep her as cool as you can. And if she rambles, try and humor her. She's living between so many worlds it's difficult for us to make sense of what she says." He sighed. "If only she had some reason to live."

Sonata's dark eyes filled with tears. "I can understand," she said. "Her spirit is lonely for her son. When a child you have carried for so long under your heart dies, part of you dies with him. I know that only too well."

Robillard put his hand on her shoulder in a gesture of sympathy. "I know, but we mustn't encourage her to think that way. Philippe isn't dead . . . as far as we know."

"For her he is . . . along with her man. It makes the world an empty place." She followed the doctor to the doorway and watched as he went down the beach.

Téoline heard their voices through a haze of half-forgotten memories. "Is that you, Julien?" She struggled to sit up and clutched at the thin threads of reality. "No, of course Julien is dead. I remember now; I placed an orange between his folded hands before we buried him. That was to show he was the last de Pavigné. . . . the last of a line. . . . Should I have claimed the title for Jean-Philippe, do you think?" She fell back on the bed murmuring to herself. "It doesn't matter. He is a Cameron now. Titles, like medals and uniforms, don't make the man." She drifted off into a timeless, spaceless world of her own. How ironic that Julien had to come back to Saint-Domingue to die of plague . . . Poor Julien . . . He was always so unreliable . . . And he didn't even die a soldier's death. At least Stefan had died trying to achieve his goal . . . but Julien had just drifted through life at other people's expense. She was so sorry. "I do hope Philippe doesn't take after him, André?" Then the pattern in the kaleidoscope changed.

Téoline opened her eyes and watched the white sails of a ship disappearing over the horizon. That would be the frigate taking General Leclerc's body home to France. . . . Or was she back in Halifax watching Michael Dryden sail away in the *Prometheus*? She could see Sonata outside on the beach struggling to light a fire under the old cooking pot.

She managed to prop herself up on one arm so that she could keep the ship in sight a few moments longer. Then she fell back, exhausted by the effort, but not before she had caught sight of the yellow blossoms on the cassia tree outside.

Téo had thought it was only yesterday that she had said goodbye to Pauline Leclerc. She had watched while Pauline cut off her curls and laid them in the coffin with her husband's body. "I'll never forgive my brother for sending us to this hellhole," she had said. But Téoline had known she would. No one could be angry with Napoleon for very long.

It must have been longer ago. Téo remembered how dead the cassia had looked that day. Maybe it was last week . . . or last month . . . Perhaps it was another tree, in another place.

Yes, Pauline would forgive her brother, for she loved him as Téo loved Julien. Besides, Napoleon had a way with women. Hadn't he persuaded *her* to return to Saint-Domingue?

"Toussaint has written that you should return and claim your estates. I ask you to go as a service to France. It is imperative that Toussaint take more account of France, as these blacks are far too independent. Tell him I will let him remain as governor. Go to him, Téoline! Give him my assurances that we mean well." It was the trap of words again. Téoline had been foolish enough to believe him when all the time he had been giving secret instructions to Leclerc.

She had sat next to Toussaint that night at the banquet given in his honor. He had trusted her and come only at her instigation. What a Judas affair that had been! Leclerc had stood up and read a letter from his brother-in-law.

"Tell them," Napoleon had said. "Tell them that there are no more slaves in Saint-Domingue and Guadaloupe. All are free there; all will remain free."

How they had fêted Toussaint that night, calling him the savior of his people. Then, after the meal was finished, after they had all sat round the same table breaking bread together, Leclerc had called his men. Before anyone could stop them, they had Toussaint bound and gagged. He was carried out and put aboard a frigate that was waiting in the harbor. No one had time to protest. He was on his way to his death in France, before they had even had time to catch their breath. Was it any wonder the country had been plunged into war again!

Did anything ever really end, or were people and events just like the pieces of glass revolving in an ever-changing series of patterns? Always different, yet somehow always the same. Did it matter whether it was Stefan or Julien, Michael, or even Albert de Beben who died? Perhaps they were all part of one man and the love or hate she had felt for them depended on the pattern at the time. Perhaps her love for everyman was embodied in Andrew Cameron. She hoped the pattern would not be repeated after death. If God had any pity, it would be finished. She would never again have to bow to expediency. She would never again betray or be betrayed by words spoken without meaning or with meanings she did not understand. Téoline lay back on the straw pillow and slept.

"Robillard!"

The doctor stared up at the man standing at the head of the gangplank.

"Don't say you've forgotten me? Although I'll admit a lot of water has flowed under the bridges of Paris since we last met."

Robillard shaded his eyes from the glare of the setting sun. "Cameron?" He went forward to take the proffered hand. "Now I do believe in miracles. Thank God you've come!"

"Then I'm not too late?"

"No. But I must warn you, unless there is another miracle I'm afraid it will not be long."

"I came as soon as I received your letter. It had been waiting for three months in New York."

"I hoped that was the only reason for the delay."

"Why did you think? Did Téoline think I wouldn't come?" Cameron said sharply. "My God, doesn't she know how I have been searching for her all these years!"

"How could she know? She does not even know I sent for you. She would never have agreed to it."

"Is that how little regard she has for me?" Cameron took off his straw hat and mopped his brow. Robillard noticed that his curly hair was now iron-gray. It was obvious from his attire that he was still a wealthy man, but the old arrogance was missing. It was almost as if he had been beaten by life, and that was the last thing Téoline needed just now.

"It was because she held you in such deep regard that she ran away from you in Halifax. She was willing to sacrifice her own happiness for yours and Philippe's."

"Didn't she know that she was the entire measure of my happiness? That without her my life ceased to have any value for me?"

"Perhaps you failed to convince her of that. . . . Perhaps you did not even realize that yourself at the time." Robillard led him to a carriage drawn by an old horse, little more than skin and bone. "I'm afraid this is the best we have to offer you in Le Cap. It is a wonder this creature hasn't been eaten for food."

Cameron stood for a moment and looked at the devastation of the city that had once been hailed as the Paris of the New World. "My God," he said. "How has anyone managed to survive in all this?"

"The human will can overcome almost anything providing that there is the will to live. And that is what I'm afraid is missing with Téoline!"

"Then it is my will against hers. She must not die! I will not let her die!" Some of his old fire was returning. He squared his shoulders as if ready to take on the whole world. "I shall take her away from all this. She shall have everything money can buy."

"I'm afraid that is not enough. Téoline is beyond the help of material things."

"Then what do you suggest?" Cameron turned on the doctor aggressively, as though Robillard were somehow denying him his right to Téoline.

"I don't know. I wish I could help you. I have done all that is in my power. Now it is up to you. Only you know how strong the bond is between you and Téoline," Robillard said sadly. Throughout all his years as a doctor he had never been able to fathom the alchemy that transmuted love to hate or death to life, yet he had seen it happen many times just by a spoken word or the touch of a hand.

Cameron remained silent after that. For the first time in his life he felt desperately afraid. This was a fight he had to win, yet he came to it unarmed. He thought back to that night in Paris when Téoline had said she loved him and he had said it was desire. He had made love to her many times since then, but he had never questioned what it was he felt for her, other than desire. Now he realized that what he had been feeling was a great need —a great longing, which transcended physical love yet at the same time was a part of it.

"I must warn you, Cameron, she is very much ashamed of some of the things she did . . . the way she had to live. I think she feels she has nothing worth giving to you now. That was why she wouldn't hear of my trying to get in touch with you."

Cameron turned away and looked out over the sea. He didn't want Robillard to see the tears in his eyes. "She gave me all I needed years ago. I was too insensitive at the time to know the value of what she was offering me. Words are very inadequate, aren't they, at a time like this." He spoke brusquely. He was terrified lest the doctor should see how deeply moved he was. It was then he recognized for the first time his greatest flaw: He had never really let people see how he felt about them. He had lost Téoline once because he had appeared arrogant instead of loving. And the second time, in Halifax, he had made love to her and said he intended to marry her, but he had not made her feel she was so secure in his heart that she was sure he would rather die than lose her.

"Would you like me to come in with you?" Robillard asked. They had left the carriage at the end of the dirt road leading from Le Cap and were walking towards the shack along the beach.

"No!" Cameron took off his hat and tossed it on the sands. The movement made Sonata look up from the cooking pot. Her face lit up with pleasure when she saw who it was. Cameron put a finger to his lips to stop her speaking, but touched her arm gently as he passed and whispered, "Pray for me."

He stopped at the open door and looked up towards the purple mountains in the distance; they seemed to give him the strength he needed. He broke a spray of blossom from the cassia tree. Then, stooping down, he went inside.

It took a moment or two for his eyes to adjust to the dim light inside the cabin. A shaft of late sunlight filtered through the leaves of the palm trees and fell across the pale, thin figure lying on the straw. She was even more beautiful than he remembered her. But there was an ethereal quality about her that turned his blood to ice. She stirred in her sleep and gave a sigh that seemed to echo the same longing in his heart.

He picked his way softly over the dirt floor. He had no knowledge of what he would do or say. He reached her side and, bending down, gently kissed her cheek and laid the sprig of yellow cassia in her hand.

"André," she murmured in her sleep. He took her hand and lifted it to his lips. "André . . . !" She opened her eyes, but it was obvious her thoughts were far away. "Is it really you or just another dream? . . . Don't leave . . . let me come with you . . . !" She stretched out her hand as though to follow a dream way out in space. For one terrible moment Cameron thought he had lost her.

Gathering her in his arms, he sat down on the edge of the rough wooden bed. He sensed she was beyond anything he could say. He held her close and, with a strength born of despair, willed her to live. His lips sought hers and he tried to infuse her with his own energy . . . his own life force. Her lips were cold against his mouth. He kissed her again, a long, slow, passionate kiss; he was trying to make it speak for him. He had to convey all that was in his heart. Slowly, very slowly, Cameron began to feel her lips warm against his mouth.

Téoline opened her eyes. "A dream . . . This is another dream, isn't it, André?"

"No, Téoline, I am here . . . I am flesh and blood. But I want to live only if you are by my side . . . you are my life." He saw the recognition in her smile. "Téoline, live for me, I need you and so does Philippe."

She lifted her hand and touched his face. Cameron took it and held it against his lips. It no longer mattered how he appeared or what he thought. He was lost in his love for Téoline. They sat there for a time in a silent communion. Eventually Cameron was able to put into words what he had at last discovered about himself and life.

"I have learned at last that we are given form and substance by those who love us and those whom we love. Without them, we cannot recognize ourselves or know our worth in the world."

Téoline nestled against his shoulder and fingered the yellow blossoms of the cassia tree. She looked up into his eyes and whispered, "All else faileth, only love endures . . . !"

From <u>New York Times</u>
bestselling author

Patricia Hagan

**Three magnificent novels that rip across the
tumultuous landscapes of the Civil War—and the
embattled terrains of the heart, as they depict the
romance between Kitty Wright and Travis Coltrane.**

LOVE AND WAR   80044/$3.50

Lovely, golden-haired Kitty Wright, abducted from her
plantation home by a band of rebel deserters must
fight for her life—and for the freedom to choose the
man she will love: Nathan Collins, the Rebel; or Travis
Coltrane, the Yankee who makes her wild with fury
one moment and delirious with passion the next.

THE RAGING HEARTS   80085/$3.50

As the Civil War draws to a close, Kitty Wright's
ancestral home stands abandoned and ruined, and two
men who ravaged her heritage prepare to turn their
hunger to her beauty. But Kitty will surrender to no
man until a special one from her past returns—Travis
Coltrane, a victorious soldier who knows that a man's
greatest field of honor is a woman's heart!

LOVE AND GLORY   79665/$3.50

After the War has ended, Kitty Wright and Travis
Coltrane are married and farming the North Carolina
land which was her inheritance. But quiet Southern
life makes Travis long for adventure. While Travis is
away in Haiti, Kitty is kidnapped by an old enemy. When
Travis returns home and finds Kitty gone, he realizes
how vital she is to him. And when they are miraculously
reunited, their love is sealed forever.

Available wherever paperbacks are sold, or directly from the
publisher. Include 50¢ per copy for postage and handling;
allow 6-8 weeks for delivery. Avon Books, Mail Order Dept.,
224 West 57th St., N.Y., N.Y. 10019.

Hagan 3-82